THE NAZI'S SON

A Joe Johnson Thriller

ANDREW TURPIN

The Write
Direction
Publishing

First published in the U.K. in 2019 by The Write Direction Publishing, St. Albans, U.K.

Copyright © 2019 Andrew Turpin
All rights reserved.
Print edition — The Nazi's Son
ISBN: 978-1-78875-012-7

<<<<>>>>

❀ Created with Vellum

WELCOME TO THE JOE JOHNSON SERIES!

Thank you for purchasing **The Nazi's Son** — I hope you enjoy it!

This is the fifth in the series of thrillers I am writing that feature Joe Johnson, a US-based independent war crimes investigator. He previously worked for the CIA and for the Office of Special Investigations — a section of the Department of Justice responsible for tracking down Nazi war criminals hiding in the States.

The other books in the series about his various war crimes investigations are all for sale on Amazon. In order, they are:

Prequel: *The Afghan*
1. *The Last Nazi*
2. *The Old Bridge*
3. *Bandit Country*
4. *Stalin's Final Sting*
5. *The Nazi's Son*
6. *The Black Sea*

If you enjoy this book, I would like to keep in touch. This is not always easy, as I usually only publish a couple of books a year and there are many authors and books out there. So the best way is for you to be on my Readers Group email list. I can then send you updates on the next book, plus occasional special offers.

If you would like to join my Readers Group and receive the email updates, I will send you, **FREE** of charge, the ebook version of another Joe Johnson thriller, **The Afghan**, which is a prequel to the series and normally sells at $2.99/£2.99 (paperback $11.99/£9.99).

The Afghan is set in 1988 when Johnson was still a CIA

officer. Most of the action takes place in Afghanistan and Washington, DC.

To sign up for the Readers Group and get your free copy of **The Afghan**, go to the following web page:

https://bookhip.com/RJGFPAW

If you only like paperbacks, you can still just sign up for the email list at the above link to get news of my books and forthcoming new releases. A paperback version of **The Afghan** and all my books is for sale at my website, where you will find large discounts on bundles of my books. I can currently ship to the US and UK:

https://www.andrewturpin.com/shop/

Or if you live outside the US and UK you can buy them at Amazon.

Andrew Turpin, St. Albans, UK.

DEDICATION

This book is dedicated to my parents, Gerald and Jean Turpin, who are getting to grips with technology and enjoying my books in Kindle format at the ages of ninety-four and eighty-nine respectively.

"We know that this mad dog of the Middle East [Muammar Gaddafi] has a goal of a world revolution, Muslim fundamentalist revolution, which is targeted on many of his own Arab compatriots. And where we figure in that, I don't know. Maybe we're just the enemy because—it's a little like climbing Mount Everest—because we're here. But there's no question but that he has singled us out more and more for attack."

US President Ronald Reagan speaking at a news conference on 9 April, 1986, four days after the bomb attack on the La Belle Discotheque in West Berlin and six days before retaliatory air strikes were launched against Libya.

PROLOGUE

Saturday, April 5, 1986
West Berlin

The KGB officer pulled out a half-empty pack of his favorite Belomorkanal cigarettes from his jacket pocket and put one in his mouth. He offered one to his colleague, who was standing on the darkened balcony beside him. She accepted. He lit both using a cheap red plastic lighter, cupping his hands around it to prevent the breeze from extinguishing the flame.

He shivered as he took a deep drag on the cigarette, which glowed bright. The nicotine hit felt good. They were standing on the sixth story of an apartment building overlooking Hauptstrasse, the main street running through the Friedenau district of West Berlin. Across the street, high up on the soaring brick tower of the town hall, a giant illuminated clock read quarter to two in the morning.

The two Russians smoked in silence for a few minutes.

"*Skoro sluchitsya*," the woman eventually said in her native language. It's coming soon.

The man nodded. "*Oni uzhe opozdali*." They're already late.

On the sidewalk far below the KGB apartment where they had been staying undercover for the previous few days, a group of West Berlin youngsters staggered along, laughing and drunkenly trying to support each other. He had watched as they emerged from the entrance of a nightclub, more than two hundred meters from their vantage point. A red-and-white sign above the door read La Belle Disco Club.

La Belle was on the ground floor of the four-story art deco–style Roxy Palast building that had originally been a cinema. At this hour it would be packed with hundreds of music and dance lovers writhing to the latest American sounds, some of which were not yet even available in West Berlin's record stores.

A few minutes later, another group emerged from the club, walked along the street, and climbed into a car. From the way they looked and dressed, the KGB officer knew they were United States soldiers. The club, southwest of Berlin's center, was very popular with American servicemen stationed in the city.

On the sidewalk nearby, someone had painted in large white letters the words *Amerikaner Raus!* Americans get out.

One of the city's ubiquitous white police cars, an Opel with its distinctive green doors, Polizei sign on the side, and blue light perched on the roof, crawled along Hauptstrasse.

The man stepped forward and leaned over the iron railing at the edge of the balcony. He scrutinized the street scene below and pointed. "I think that may be them."

Two women, both brunettes with shoulder-length hair, had exited from La Belle and were crossing the street, striding away quickly without looking back. It was a giveaway.

Both were dressed in tight black skirts and leather jackets. They disappeared around the corner and out of view.

"Yes, it was them," the KGB woman said. "A couple of minutes now." She finished her cigarette, stubbed it out on the balcony railing, and tossed the butt out into the gloom, where it floated to the ground. Then she gripped the rail, her knuckles going white as she leaned forward and watched.

The man also finished his cigarette and threw the butt off the balcony.

A group of twentysomethings, laughing and joking, crossed the street below, followed by a couple who were holding hands. Neither the man nor the woman on the balcony spoke as the people below crossed the road, drawing closer to the disco entrance.

A few seconds later, a boom tore through the night air, causing the KGB man to jump involuntarily. Despite the distance, he felt a little of the force of the explosion against his face. The entire ground-floor frontage of the building that housed La Belle disco was blown outward across the street in a storm of glass, steel, concrete, and wood debris.

The group of youngsters vanished behind a cloud of smoke and dust that was propelled outward and upward, hiding much of the building from view, and the sound of people screaming echoed up from the street.

Security and fire alarms triggered by the explosion were ringing, and after a short time, the sound of police sirens could be heard in the distance.

As the dust cloud began to clear, blown by the breeze, the piles of rubble scattered across the street gradually became visible. A man ran over to two girls who were lying spread-eagled on the road amid the debris and knelt next to one of them, placing his hand on her body.

"My God," the woman said. She instinctively stepped back from the balcony's edge into the shadows as two police cars screeched to a halt at the point where the spread of rubble began. She turned to face her colleague. "They did it."

The man pressed his lips together and nodded. He reached out and caressed the nape of the woman's neck. The entire operation had gone completely according to the plan that he had seen in meetings. The Libyans had done a good job: the carnage inside La Belle must have been enormous. "I need to let the boss know," he said.

He walked to the rear of the balcony and through the open door into the dimly lit living room of the apartment. He went into the bedroom and sat on the mattress. The sheets were still all awry from their lovemaking earlier.

The man picked up a secure phone that lay on a table. Next to the phone was a West German passport and papers that identified him as an interior design adviser. He dialed a number.

After the usual three rings, a voice answered in Russian. "*Da?*" Yes?

"FOX is done," the man replied. "FOX is done."

"Understood. Thank you. Please keep me informed about the next one." The line went dead.

PART ONE

CHAPTER ONE

Tuesday, March 4, 2014
Washington, DC

Applause rang around room 603 at American University's College of Law as Joe Johnson wrapped up his lecture on the history of Nazi war crimes prosecutions and the effectiveness over the years of the International Criminal Court in implementing them. He concluded, as he often did, with a few thoughts about the validity of continuing to pursue former SS officers who were now almost all in their nineties.

About 120 students had turned up, which pleased him. Usually his occasional talks for the college's War Crimes Research Office attracted fewer than that. And judging by the reaction, almost all of those attending seemed to agree with his closing comments that there was complete justification for pursuing justice on behalf of the estimated six million Jews who had died at the hands of the Nazis during the Second World War.

Johnson turned off the PowerPoint slide deck that was

being projected from his laptop onto the screen behind him
to illustrate his talk. He slowly gathered up his lecture notes
from the wooden lectern and shook hands with the director
of the WCRO, Sarah Southern, who had been sitting nearby
with her deputy, William Cadman.

"Thank you, Joe," Sarah said, a twinkle in her eye and a
half smile creasing her face. "That was incisive as usual. It
might just get you another invitation sometime."

Sarah's mother, like his mother, Helena, had been a Polish
Jewish concentration camp survivor, and they had developed
a close bond through their shared family histories. Sarah was
passionate about her job, something he greatly respected, and
he always appreciated the guest-lecturer invitations she still
sent him. The WCRO ran a regular program of guest
speakers on a wide variety of topics relating to international
criminal law and human rights.

"Sure," Johnson said. "I'd like to talk about Afghanistan
next time. I was there last year. There's a lot of interesting
issues."

"Afghanistan would be a good idea," Cadman said. "We
haven't done anything much on it for some time."

Johnson always smiled every time he bumped into
Cadman: the academic was almost a spitting image of
Johnson himself. He was of similar age, at fifty-five, of similar
height and build, and even had the same semicircle of short-
cropped graying hair. The only difference was that Cadman
wore a pair of black-rimmed glasses. The two men got on well
—like twin brothers, Sarah often joked.

Sarah indicated with her thumb toward the back of the
room. "There's someone over there who came in to see you
just before the lecture started. I found him a seat at the
back."

Johnson didn't need to be told to whom she was referring.
He glanced in the direction she was pointing. Most of the

students had stood and were filing out of the room, chatting and laughing as they went. In their midst, still sitting in the rear row of seats with his arms folded, looking utterly out of place among a crowd thirty years his junior, was a familiar figure.

He had seen Vic Walter sneak in just before he began his talk. His friend and former CIA colleague had known Johnson was going to be in town for the lecture because they had spoken briefly on the phone the previous week. But he had given no indication that he was going to turn up and listen. Something must be afoot if he had taken time out from his now crazily busy job at the Agency's Langley head-quarters to drive the seven miles to the College of Law.

"I spotted him. I'd better go and have a chat," Johnson said to Sarah. "Thanks again, and let's speak soon."

He picked up his coat, tucked his papers under his arm, and ambled down the aisle between the rows of seats to the rear of the room.

"What the hell are you doing here?" Johnson asked, looking down at Vic, who hadn't moved.

"You need someone to tidy up those slides for you," Vic said in his familiar gravelly voice. "They're high school standard."

"Thanks. Carrie helped me with them, actually," Johnson said. His daughter, aged seventeen, *was* in high school. "I thought she did a good job."

Vic grinned and looked at Johnson over the top of his metal-rimmed glasses. "Ah, sorry. Don't tell her I said that." He stood, tossed his empty plastic takeout coffee cup into a nearby trash can, and shook hands with Johnson.

"You having an easy day today, Vic?"

"Not really. None of my days are easy now. Quite the opposite."

"But you need to talk?"

Vic waved a hand. "I thought it would be good to catch up for a chat while you're in town. Don't see you very often these days. Spur-of-the-moment thing. But let's not talk in here. Outside?"

Johnson suppressed a grin.

Spur-of-the-moment? Bullshit.

But he nodded, put on his coat, and turned to head out of the room, Vic following behind. They moved down the corridor and out through the glass and metal swinging doors that formed the entrance to the College of Law's sprawling brick and stone building at 4801 Massachusetts Avenue NW, about a mile and a half east of the Potomac River.

It was an unseasonably warm March afternoon, and daffodils in a bed around the circular fountain in the plaza were waving in a light breeze. A few students, some of whom had removed their coats, were sitting at outdoor tables on the white concrete surface.

Johnson stopped next to a row of bike racks, to which were chained an assortment of bicycles in varying states of repair. He turned to face his former colleague. He and Vic had worked together for the Agency, mainly in Pakistan and Afghanistan, in the 1980s.

"So, how's the new job going, Vic? You surviving up on that seventh floor, buddy?"

"Not really. I'm still suffering nosebleeds from the height."

Johnson chuckled. His old friend's self-deprecating air was one of his most endearing characteristics.

To many people's surprise at Langley—mostly those who hadn't worked directly with him—Vic had been appointed the previous September as acting director of the CIA's National Clandestine Service, generally known as the Directorate of Operations. Despite being seen by many as something of a fringe candidate, he was then confirmed in the role in December by his boss, Arthur Veltman, the director of

Central Intelligence, confounding the promotion ambitions of two associate deputy directors who had both upset the DCI in the preceding months.

Vic's appointment followed the eventual resignation of the previous director of the NCS, Terry Jenner, in the wake of two successful investigations by Johnson and Vic into one of Jenner's senior lieutenants and close ally, Robert Watson.

Watson was convicted and imprisoned on an assortment of charges, including corruption and illegal profiteering from arms deals over a long period of time while he was a senior CIA employee. Indeed, Watson had been Johnson and Vic's boss as chief of the CIA's Islamabad station in the 1980s and had been largely responsible for having Johnson fired from the service in late 1988.

Given that Johnson was a freelancer, Vic received most of the internal credit for Watson's demise. But the promotion was more a reward for thirty years of service, much of it spent successfully organizing and running operations in the Near East and Asia, particularly Pakistan and Afghanistan, but also from time to time in Eastern Europe and Russia. Vic had previously had a zigzag career, sometimes taking two steps forward and one back, depending on whose star was in the ascendancy at the Agency. But he had survived and had now adapted to his new more demanding role in his usual understated, laconic manner.

"Get through the first year. Then you'll be fine," Johnson said. "Anyway, tell me what's happening. If you've driven here to ask me to do a job, the answer is probably no right now."

Although it had been several months since the last long overseas investigation Johnson had carried out, in Afghanistan, the effects of being in a couple of life-threatening situations had remained with him. During occasional days off at home in Portland, Maine, he had been recently ruminating once again on whether, as a single dad with two teenagers, he should be carrying out such work at all.

Vic averted his gaze. "Why don't we go for a coffee?" he suggested. "It's still chilly out here."

Johnson sighed. "Did you hear what I said?" He scratched his chin.

"Yes, I did."

Johnson glanced across the plaza, past the leafless winter trees, at the streams of traffic running two lanes in each direction up and down Massachusetts Avenue past the university buildings.

"Okay, a quick coffee. Then I'm going back to the airport. My kids are expecting me to take them for pizza tonight."

Vic nodded. "Good." He beckoned Johnson. "This way. My car's out the back."

CHAPTER TWO

Tuesday, March 4, 2014
   Glen Echo, Maryland

Half an hour later, Johnson and Vic were sitting on a pair of wooden chairs nursing cappuccinos in the bar at the Irish Inn at Glen Echo, a stone's throw from the east bank of the Potomac River—the Maryland side. A mile or so away, across the other side of the river in Virginia but hidden from view by a thick expanse of trees, lay the CIA's offices at Langley.

The bar, with its heavy wooden furniture and gourmet menu, was in a low-slung sandstone building with a gray slate roof and a canopied outdoor area. Two flags hung on poles over the entrance—one American, the other Irish.

It had only a smattering of customers, allowing Johnson and Vic to choose a quiet indoor table away from others.

Johnson had been to the Irish Inn several times during his sixteen years in DC as a war crimes investigator with the Office of Special Investigations; it had been given a few makeovers over the years but remained fundamentally unchanged. It had always been one of Vic's regular haunts when he needed a quiet chat with somebody without any danger of surveillance.

By this time, Johnson was braced for the sales pitch that he knew was coming.

But, as usual, Vic first asked about how Johnson's kids, Carrie and Peter, were doing and then gave an update on his own two children, a boy and a girl, who were now in their twenties. Vic lived not too far away, in the DC neighborhood of Palisades.

After ten minutes of chitchat, Johnson glanced at his watch, then leaned forward and propped his elbows on the table. "All right, Vic," he said, "let's cut the crap. I've only got forty minutes before I need to leave for the airport. What is it?"

Vic rubbed his graying temples. "Listen. Normally I wouldn't bother you with this, but since I was promoted I've had more freedom to draw on certain external resources that I might not have had before."

"Like I said, I'm not doing CIA work for you."

"No. War crimes only, I know that," Vic said. "But there's an element of that in an operation we're looking at. You could add some value to it. I think you'd be interested."

"*Add some value to it?*" Johnson muttered. "Is it compulsory to use corporate speak now that you're in the top job?"

"We've got someone incoming in a couple of weeks," Vic said, ignoring Johnson's jibe. "From the other side."

A defector, then. Interesting. "Who? From China? They're the big threat now, aren't they?" Johnson asked. "Or Moscow?"

"Right second time. The Chinese are after our technology and industrial intelligence, true, they want to overtake us. But the Russians matter more politically—they'd still like to destroy us. The guy is SVR. It's a joint operation with the Brits."

The SVR was Russia's foreign intelligence service. It operated in tandem with the Federal Security Service—the FSB—its domestic equivalent. Until 1991 both units were part of the KGB, which after the dissolution of the Soviet Union was split into two separate organizations.

"Why is he important?" Johnson asked. "What's the background?"

Vic hesitated. Clearly, he was about to venture into classified territory, Johnson assumed. It hadn't stopped him before —his friend had trusted him implicitly ever since he had saved Vic's life in a shoot-out while the two of them were on a CIA cross-border operation from their Pakistan base into Afghanistan in 1988.

"It's a bit sensitive," Vic said.

"It always is." Johnson fingered the small nick at the top of his right ear, a legacy of that shoot-out in Jalalabad, when he was clipped by a bullet from a KGB sniper while he and Vic were trying to escape back to Pakistan.

"It's someone who's got a lot of massively useful information. An SVR colonel. Some of it's about current issues, but some is historic too, which is where you come in."

"Why are you bringing him in? If this guy has good access in Moscow, why not leave him in place?"

"He's been in place for a long time, actually," Vic said, lowering his voice even further. "Been very useful to us and to MI6. They've been handling him with plenty of input from us. He notified his handler, Six's head of station in Berlin, that he wanted to come across. We're going to be heavily involved in the operation and the debrief."

Johnson drummed his fingers lightly on the table. "Is he blown?"

"No. But he would be if he gives us what he's got and

stays. They would know exactly where the information came from. It would be a one-way ticket to Butyrka or Lefortovo."

The basement "interview" rooms of Russia's two most notorious prisons remained the usual destination for those who were caught betraying the Motherland, despite all the modernization that had taken place in some other respects across the country. The thugs in the SVR's counterintelligence department, known as Line KR, would ensure that anyone caught spying for the enemy would pay a full price— quite probably the ultimate price.

"So, he's got no choice?" Johnson asked.

"Correct."

"Must be big, then?"

"It is. Or so he tells us. I mean, he's given us only an outline. We'll get the full juice when he's safely over the line." Vic leaned back in his chair and sipped his coffee. "Believe me, I'd prefer to leave him where he is. He's been good."

"So what has he hinted at that's prompted you to come here and talk to me?"

Vic drained his coffee and leaned forward again, his face just a couple of feet from Johnson's. "The current stuff supposedly involves the identity of a mole—a highly placed one—in Western intelligence."

"From which service?" Johnson asked.

"It's either MI6 or—God forbid—the Agency," he murmured. "If it proves to be the Agency, and it's someone in my directorate, I could become the shortest-serving head of the DO in living memory. We've had serious leaks to Moscow, including in the past few weeks alone a lot of naval intelligence relating to US and NATO's planned response to Russia's annexation of the Crimea. There have been other leaks, all involving joint operations with the Brits, which makes it harder to trace the source."

"And the defector somehow knows who this mole is?" Johnson asked.

"Yes. So he says." Vic sat back and folded his arms.

"And the historic material?" Johnson asked.

"It goes back to the '80s. Cold War dirty tricks in Berlin."

Johnson raised his eyebrows. "Stasi or KGB?"

The Stasi was the East German State Security Service during the postwar years when the country was split, responsible for both internal and foreign intelligence and security. It had a massive number of informants across the country, including a network of ordinary citizens who spied on their neighbors and even their own families.

"Apparently both services," Vic said.

"Is that going to be of interest now?"

Vic pursed his lips. "I don't know. It's a long time ago. But . . ." He let his voice trail away.

"But what?"

"It's difficult." Vic hesitated and wiped away a small blob of cappuccino froth from the corner of his mouth with the back of his hand. "It's personal, actually."

"Come on, Vic."

"All right. Do you recall the La Belle disco bombing? Berlin nightclub in the Friedenau area. About 229 people maimed for life or injured, mostly Germans, but many were Americans. Three people died."

Johnson did recall it, at least the broad details. He had spent four years studying for a PhD at Berlin's Freie Universität from 1980-84, but had left the city and was working for the CIA when in April 1986 a bomb planted by Libyan terrorists blew apart the La Belle disco. The media coverage in the States had been massive given that the club was a favorite of US soldiers serving in the divided city.

It had been one of the most symbolic terrorist attacks of the Cold War era in Europe and had come at a time when

Johnson enjoyed visiting discos. He recalled thinking how it would feel if a bomb had gone off at a similar club in Portland.

"Yes, I remember it. Of course I do. But what's the connection that you think might be of interest to me? And why is it personal?"

"Like I said, I've hardly any details yet, but the word is that our man has some information of not just who was behind the bombing but some other deeper stuff, apparently."

"Intriguing. Going higher up the chain of command, you mean? Something criminal that could lead to prosecutions?"

Vic inclined his head. "Can't say exactly. But the guy was working for the KGB in East Berlin at that time and knew the key players both on the Soviet side and on the Stasi side, given that the Stasi were effectively just KGB lackeys."

"But I thought some Libyans were convicted? Gaddafi's crew." Johnson remembered reading reports of the trial that had taken place years later. The Libyan leader, Colonel Muammar Gaddafi, was seen as having ordered the attack for which five people were eventually imprisoned in 2001. As part of an anti-American, anti-Western capitalist agenda, Gaddafi also ordered the bombing of Pan Am Flight 103, a jumbo jet that exploded over Lockerbie, Scotland, in December 1988, killing 270 people. Two decades later, Libya paid compensation to victims for these and other atrocities.

"Yes, they were. But it seems there was more to it than that." Vic stroked his chin. "Exactly what, we will find out, no doubt. But I thought it might conceivably be something you would find interesting. My team and the Brits, the MI6 lot, will be entirely focused on the current issue I've described— the mole—whereas this other historical material, the Cold War criminal element, might be right up your alley. I would really like you to have a go at it."

Johnson screwed up his eyes. "I don't think so, Vic. I'm sure there must be someone in your team who could handle this alongside whatever other material the guy is going to give you. It's not a war crime, is it?"

"I would say it definitely is. A Cold War crime."

A group of middle-aged men in suits, laughing and joking among themselves, walked into the bar and began a raucous discussion about which of the beers available on tap they should opt for. They had probably finished work early and stopped in for refreshments en route home.

Johnson turned his attention back to Vic. "Look, where is this guy going to be debriefed?"

"Berlin, strangely enough. He'll be coming in on a train from Prague, where he's meant to be visiting one of his agents."

Johnson shook his head. Berlin: his old stomping ground during the early 1980s when he spent four years at the Freie Universität studying for a PhD. He'd loved the place and the sinister, mysterious atmosphere that encompassed it at the height of the Cold War.

"You want me to travel to Berlin for this when you've got any number of guys at the CIA station there on the doorstep who could handle it?" Johnson asked.

Vic nodded.

"But why?"

Vic looked down at the floor and then back up at Johnson. "Like I said, it's personal."

"How?"

"There were seventy-nine American soldiers injured in La Belle, and two of the three who died were American. One of the injured lost his right eye and eighty percent of the vision in his left eye, as well as his hearing. A few years later he committed suicide because of severe depression brought on by the long-term effects of the post-traumatic stress disorder he suffered from because of his injuries."

"Go on," Johnson said. He was intrigued now, not least because Vic was visibly struggling to get his words out. "Who was that?"

Vic turned his head and gazed out the window. "My brother."

* * *

Wednesday, March 5, 2014
Portland, Maine

"What's your definition of a traitor then, Dad?" Carrie asked.

Johnson glanced at his daughter, who had a slight grin on her face. She was always asking provocative questions. Now in eleventh grade at high school, it was no wonder she was aiming to be a journalist after college.

"It depends on your point of view," Johnson said. "If you are sitting in Moscow and your man deserts to the US, you would call him a traitor. We might call him a defector. And vice versa if he was an American who left to sell his secrets to Russia. Thankfully we don't have too many of those."

"There are always some, though," Carrie said.

"Yes, unfortunately there are some."

"I'm honestly surprised you haven't been tempted to be a traitor, Dad. We could have had a bigger house, couldn't we? Think of all those rubles. Easy money."

"Are you trying to put your old dad in jail?" Johnson pretended to chase after his daughter, waving his fist. She ran off, laughing, her long dark brown hair trailing in the breeze behind her.

Johnson, Carrie, and his son, Peter, who was in tenth

grade, were walking the family dog, Cocoa, along the three-and-a-half-mile trail that ran around Back Cove, an inlet off Casco Bay on the Atlantic coast. It lay at the end of Parsons Road, where they lived in a two-story cape house with green shutters on all the windows.

Johnson had just broken the news to his two children that he was about to head off overseas on another work trip, this time to Europe. He found himself in that position every so often, and it never got any easier.

"So will you be hunting traitors again on this job?" Carrie asked. She knew that was often his role, although he never gave his children any specifics.

"I can't say exactly," Johnson said. He was unable to give them any details of the operation he was about to embark on, other than to tell them it was important. He couldn't say where, who, why, or how—which were the usual questions from his daughter, not necessarily in that order.

"Will you be back in time for spring break?" Carrie asked.

The high school she and her brother both attended, not far from their house, had its one-week spring break scheduled for mid-April. Carrie was already planning for it.

"Of course. This shouldn't be a long job," Johnson said, although in truth he wasn't quite sure how long it might take.

"At least you won't be missing any of my basketball games," Peter said, running a hand through his short dark hair.

"No, it's good timing from that point of view," Johnson said. Peter, now almost six feet tall and very close to his father's height, had continued to make excellent progress through yet another basketball season during which he had excelled as point guard on his school team. He was without doubt the best passer in the squad, with an average of 8.2 assists per game.

"I hope this job will be safer than that Afghanistan investigation you did last year," Peter said.

"It will be. That was an exception," Johnson said. He had given them only a brief taste of the dangers he had faced in Afghanistan. It was important to let them know what he did for a living so that they didn't think the money appeared from nowhere, but he did try not to worry them more than he had to.

Cocoa suddenly lurched at a man riding a bike along the path toward them and started barking. "No, Cocoa!" Johnson shouted. He pulled the lead sharply to get him back.

"And you'll get some of Aunty Amy's great cooking for a week or two while I'm away—she's miles better than me," Johnson said.

"No, she's not," Carrie said. "I love your roast chicken dish."

Ever since the death of Johnson's wife Kathy in 2005 after a battle with cancer, his sister, Amy Wilde, would move temporarily into his house to look after the kids while he was away on work trips. She and her husband, Don, didn't have their own children, and she relished the opportunity to play mother for a short while. These days, however, given the kids' ages, little supervision was required; Carrie often even did a share of the cooking.

"So, will you be hunting Nazis this time, Dad?" Peter asked.

"No, not this time. No Nazis involved," Johnson said.

"Russians?" Peter asked.

Johnson laughed. "I can't say. I'm not allowed. Nice try, though—you could go through the list of possibilities and work it out if I let you."

"It's called detective work," Peter said, a grin on his face. He had occasionally hinted that he might like to be a police investigator one day.

"Yes, well, maybe I should take you with me after all. I might be doing some of that type of work."

"It's what you're good at, Dad."

Johnson nodded his head and watched the sun glinting off the small waves that rippled across Back Cove. Yes, his son was right. It was what he was good at and what he enjoyed doing. He felt fortunate that he could earn a living that way.

CHAPTER THREE

Friday, March 21, 2014
   Berlin

Johnson peered out of the blackened one-way windows of the fake Deutsche Telekom–branded Mercedes surveillance van down Friedrichstrasse toward the railway station at the far end of the street.

Bahnhof Friedrichstrasse, proclaimed a sign attached to the railway bridge with a glass-sided canopy that formed part of the station and spanned the street ahead of him. A train pulled out of the station, gathering speed as it crossed the rail bridge, high above the heads of the melee of commuters, shoppers, and tourists who were touring the city's key landmarks: the Reichstag, Brandenburg Gate, and Checkpoint Charlie.

A young arty-looking woman with a Canon camera stood on an island in the center of the street that formed a tram and bus stop, busy taking shots of a tram approaching from the north. A group of well-dressed girls brandishing shopping bags rounded the corner past an Opel car showroom and almost collided with a middle-aged man in a tracksuit who was jogging in the opposite direction.

It was the kind of typical Friday afternoon scene to be found in any city center across Europe.

Inside the heavily disguised telecoms engineering van, Johnson sat next to Vic, who was carefully watching a bank of five video monitor screens mounted above a desk that ran along one side of the interior wall. His secure smartphone beeped, and he picked it up to scrutinize the incoming message.

"BLACKBIRD's on the train out of Prague," Vic said. "No sign of any surveillance, he's reporting. Our boys are watching him, and they're confirming he's black."

BLACKBIRD was the code name by which Vic's team now referred to the defector. Vic had disclosed to Johnson that his actual name was Gennady Yezhov, a KGB and SVR operative from St. Petersburg who had worked in a variety of roles across different functions during a twenty-eight-year career.

"Has he got family?" Johnson asked.

"He probably doesn't see much of them, but yes. Wife, Varvara, two children, daughter and son, aged twenty-five and twenty-two. Katya and Timur," Vic said. "They'll be left behind in St. Petersburg, but they'll join him as soon as they can. Moscow might make their life miserable in the meantime, which worries me considerably."

Vic had set up a secure text connection so that he could communicate directly with BLACKBIRD if needed, although such messages would be kept to an absolute minimum and would be brief.

Vic turned to a laptop keyboard, typed in a short message, and pressed send. "Just letting Mark, Langley, and Bernice know he's safely on the train."

Bernice Franklin was the CIA station chief in London, who was a key liaison person for Vauxhall Cross—the London headquarters of the Secret Intelligence Service, the UK's counterpart to the CIA and better known as MI6.

The small MI6 team involved in the operation, which had been kept tight, was led by Mark Nicklin-Donovan, whom Johnson knew because Mark had been the former boss of his British partner in several war crimes investigations over the previous few years: Jayne Robinson.

Nicklin-Donovan had since had a couple of promotions from his previous role as chief of the UK controllerate to his current job as director of operations, effectively deputy chief of the entire MI6 organization.

Also heavily involved was the MI6 head of Berlin station, Rick Jones, a platinum-haired man in his fifties, who had been handling BLACKBIRD and was responsible for liaison with the German team at the BND, Germany's federal intelligence agency. He was now sitting at the rear of the van, perched uncomfortably on a folding stool, peering at his laptop.

BLACKBIRD had completed his scheduled meeting with his agent in Prague over lunch, according to secure text messages he had dispatched during the afternoon. He had then retired to his hotel room for a rest and to change his appearance before beginning a two-hour surveillance detection route around Prague's old town area prior to boarding the train, leaving his suitcase and most of his belongings in his hotel room.

He was now carrying a false passport, had dyed his graying hair black, and was wearing a pair of black-rimmed glasses.

The journey to Berlin was scheduled to take around four and a half hours. Johnson glanced at his watch. BLACKBIRD was now about halfway through the trip, assuming there were no delays, and would be arriving at around quarter past six, just after sunset.

BLACKBIRD's train would arrive at Berlin's futuristic new central railway station, the glass and steel Hauptbahnhof. The defector would then take the S-Bahn local train to Friedrichstrasse station, just under a mile away to the southwest and situated right at the point where the rail line and the street named Friedrichstrasse crossed the River Spree.

He would emerge from the S-Bahn station onto Friedrichstrasse and be picked up by a CIA car disguised as one of Berlin's taxis before being whisked to a safe house near the Botanic Garden where the debriefings would take place. This was deemed a more secure and anonymous location than the CIA station within the huge US embassy building at Pariser Platz, next to the Brandenburg Gate.

BLACKBIRD would then be taken to London, where Nicklin-Donovan and his MI6 team would continue the debriefing process, helped by the CIA station, and would find him a berth under a new identity somewhere well out of the limelight.

Vic folded his arms, stared at the van ceiling for a few seconds, and let out a long sigh. He was looking nervous, as well he might do. The risk of a Russian counterintelligence team tracking BLACKBIRD appeared to have been minimized, thanks to all the precautions that had been taken. But there was a huge amount at stake.

"Don't worry, Vic. It'll be fine," Johnson said.

"It had better be fine," Vic said.

Since their initial conversation in the Irish Inn a couple of weeks earlier, Vic had hinted at some of the damage done by the leaks that had come out of a number of CIA and MI6 joint operations over recent months. Three highly placed Western moles within the SVR—two of them handled by the CIA, one by MI6—had vanished off the radar. Both intelligence agencies were now working under the assumption that many of their operations across Eastern Europe and the Middle East were blown.

After Vic's personal disclosure about his brother Nicholas, Johnson had found it difficult to follow his initial instinct to decline the invitation to get involved in the debriefing process with BLACKBIRD. If it was personal to Vic, then given their close friendship over the years, he felt some obligation to help.

Vic had confided that he couldn't face getting tangled up in a historic investigation that involved his brother but wanted someone he could trust on the case.

The revelation had come as a surprise to Johnson. He vaguely knew about the suicide, of course, and that Nicholas had been injured while on military service in West Germany. But Vic had always appeared unwilling to discuss his brother's death, and Johnson had never liked to press him. In fact, he couldn't remember the last time the two of them had mentioned Nicholas in conversation.

Johnson's resolve to assist had only hardened after a visit the previous afternoon to the site of the La Belle bombing twenty-eight years earlier, the Roxy Palast building at 78-79 Hauptstrasse, about four miles to the southwest of the vehicle in which he was now sitting. Various shops and an organic food market were now occupying the ground floor, making it difficult to imagine the horrors of that night.

Johnson had stood for some time staring at a gray metal plaque that was mounted on the exterior wall of the Roxy Palast building.

"In this building on 5 April 1986 young people were murdered by a criminal bomb attack," it read in German.

Johnson looked around the van. He certainly wasn't the only friend whom Vic had asked for help. On one wall, a monitor screen showed the figure of a man hunched over his laptop, tapping away. This was one of Johnson and Vic's long-term CIA colleagues dating back to their Islamabad days, Neal Scales, who was also in Berlin but working at the Botanic Garden safe house and joining the action by secure video link. As soon as Vic's appointment as head of the Directorate of Operations had been confirmed, almost his first act had been to promote Neal, who was now number three in the department.

The move to promote Neal had upset a few senior members of the Directorate of Operations. They included a small number of station chiefs in major capitals who had spent years jockeying for position to take the number three slot. However, the vast majority of those at Langley held Neal in high esteem, and overall, the promotion was a popular one that had helped cement Vic's power base.

It was highly unusual for so many of the senior leadership team to become actively involved in an operation such as this, but it was in character for Vic, who had always been hands-on. He liked to lead from the front. Quite apart from the personal elements involved, it also reflected the importance to him of ensuring the first major operation of his tenure went well.

Another member of the CIA's Berlin-based operations team, Mary Gassey, was sitting opposite Johnson, in front of five other monitor screens. On one of her screens were twelve thumbnail video images from which she could choose for display at full size on any of the four other monitors.

The CIA's technical team, working with Jones's team at the MI6 Berlin station and Germany's Federal Intelligence Service, the BND, had arranged to draw on the outputs from a series of CCTV security cameras along the route that BLACKBIRD would take upon arrival in Berlin. Most of the cameras belonged to the S-Bahn rail network. Vic and his team in the surveillance van had access to all the video feeds via their monitor screens.

Johnson felt his phone vibrate twice in his pocket as a couple of messages arrived. He fished it out and checked the screen. The first message was from Carrie, asking if he was okay and reassuring him that everything was under control at home.

The second message was from Jayne Robinson, encrypted as was usually the case with messages between them. Jayne had been first on Johnson's list of people to call as soon as he committed himself to the Berlin trip. If there was going to be an investigation, then he would want her to be involved. However, that depended on the information to be obtained from BLACKBIRD, which was still an unknown quantity. Johnson had therefore decided to put Jayne on standby rather than bring her to Berlin for the debriefing.

Any update? Jayne's message read.

Johnson took a breath. He had been thinking about Jayne quite often in recent months. He had known her since 1988, when they had worked together in Pakistan and Afghanistan, helping the Afghan mujahideen in their battles against occupying Russian forces. She was with MI6, he with the CIA. For a short while, they had also been lovers.

They got back together in 2011, albeit only in the work sense, when Jayne, still working for MI6, helped Johnson in his hunt for an old Nazi concentration camp commander. She then left MI6 in 2012 after a twenty-six-year career to go permanently freelance, initially working with Johnson on a war crimes investigation focused on Bosnia and Croatia.

Johnson was halfway through tapping out a quick reply when a sharp sound from the other side of the van interrupted him. Mary slammed her hand down on the narrow desk in front of the monitors and swore.

"Shit, *shit*. These damned feeds are useless."

Johnson looked up to see that two of the four screens had gone black, apart from a series of flickering horizontal white lines moving up and down the screen.

"Which ones are down?" Vic asked, stepping across to take a closer look.

"We've lost the one on the platform at the Hauptbahnhof and also the one outside the Friedrichstrasse station entrance, where BLACKBIRD's going to be picked up," Mary said.

She turned to Jones, who had also stood and was looking at the screens.

"Rick, can you get those frigging tech guys to figure this out? Otherwise we're going to be working in the dark when BLACKBIRD turns up."

As she spoke, the third monitor went black, then the fourth.

"Yes, I'll get them on it right now," Jones said, running a hand through his hair. "How annoying."

Mary threw her head back. "*Annoying?* It's more than annoying. This is a joke. BLACKBIRD's due here in a couple of hours, and we've got no video feeds."

CHAPTER FOUR

Friday, March 21, 2014
  Berlin

To everyone's relief, the CCTV camera feeds were restored twenty minutes before BLACKBIRD's train, operated by České dráhy, the Czech railway company, was due to arrive at Berlin Hauptbahnhof. Johnson noticed, however, that given the tightness of the time frame, it hardly helped to reduce the tension in the van, which had been at fever pitch.

By then, the CIA team had reverted to their backup plan to use a street surveillance team to check that no suspect individuals were present either in the two railway stations through which BLACKBIRD was due to travel or in the street outside the Friedrichstrasse exit.

A squad of eleven innocuous-looking individuals, ranging from a tall hippy guy who appeared to be smoking something dubious to a smart-suited businessman and an old granny carrying shopping bags, were carrying out a continuous sweep of the entire route. Six photographs of bystanders, taken using smartphones, had been dispatched to both Langley and Vauxhall Cross for checking to ensure they were not on any register of suspected hostile operatives; all had come back negative.

Johnson stood and watched in silence as Vic and Neal ran through a final checklist to ensure that everything was in place.

Apart from the surveillance team, other watchers were in place at various fixed points for the entirety of the route that BLACKBIRD would take, including four bogus uniformed inspectors stationed at electronic ticket barriers and two vagrants. He would also be tailed by four of the team.

Jones, as handler, had put on a light disguise and left the surveillance van to wait in the rear of the bogus Berlin taxi, a cream-colored Mercedes complete with advertising slogans for one of the city's hot night spots on the side and a yellow roof sign, which was parked farther north up Friedrichstrasse. The driver confirmed that he was ready to move and collect BLACKBIRD as soon as Neal gave the signal.

The taxi would then be escorted by three plainclothes armed motorcyclists to a lockup garage, large enough for all the vehicles to drive straight into. There BLACKBIRD would be thoroughly searched and checked for bugs or tracking devices.

Once the team was satisfied that he was clean, they would all continue to drive on to the safe house where Neal was based. Vic, Johnson, and the team in the Deutsche Telekom surveillance van would follow behind them at a discreet distance.

With five minutes to go before the train was due to arrive, Vic sent a secure text message to BLACKBIRD's phone. Johnson sat down next to him and watched as he typed.

All clear. Proceed as planned.

A reply came back almost immediately.

Ok.

Vic leaned forward in his seat. "Mary, get me the video feed from the platform. Now, please."

Mary clicked on one of the thumbnails. On the lower right screen, an image immediately appeared from platform eight, one of the tracks deep underground that served long-distance trains. It was constructed of silver steel and gray concrete and illuminated by strings of fluorescent lights overhead, and the only signs of color were the blue numbered signs and train information boards that were suspended above the platform.

"It's the next train in," Mary said.

A few passengers were visible on-screen, presumably waiting to board the train, which according to the board was continuing on to Hamburg.

"That's Eric," Vic said, pointing at a man dressed in jeans and a leather jacket with a small backpack slung over his shoulder. Johnson had been introduced to Eric Tonner, a member of the CIA surveillance team, during briefings the previous day.

No one spoke.

Two minutes later, from behind the escalator that rose from the left side of the platform, three bright headlights appeared, growing rapidly larger on-screen as train number EC-170 from Prague glided into the station. The red engine at the front was followed by a string of cars painted in the white-and-blue branding of České dráhy.

"He's in car E," Mary said. "It should be center of the screen, all being well."

The train came to a halt with a slight squeal of steel on steel, and seconds later, the electronic doors slid open.

Vic and Johnson leaned forward, elbows propped on their knees, cupping their chins in their hands, eyes glued to the screen.

There, just visible on the side of the nearest carriage to the camera, was the letter *E*. First out of the door were two middle-aged businesswomen carrying briefcases, followed by a man in jeans and a denim jacket carrying a large suitcase. Then came a couple of backpackers, and finally there appeared a man in dark trousers, a maroon polo-neck sweater, and a jacket, with slightly untidy black hair and black-rimmed glasses.

"Made it," Vic said.

BLACKBIRD walked along the platform away from the camera toward the escalator, which he ascended until he was out of camera shot.

"Next," Vic said.

Mary clicked on another thumbnail image, which showed BLACKBIRD continuing up another escalator and then along a walkway. She clicked again, and he next appeared on another platform, beneath a vast glass dome that sheltered the entire station complex from the elements.

There he stood near the platform edge, waiting patiently, quietly, and seemingly unworried amid a crowd of Berliners in their dark duffle coats or leather jackets, many wearing woolen beanie hats. Johnson noticed that Eric was visible several yards away in the top corner of the screen, busily tapping on his cell phone.

A couple of seconds later, Mary's phone beeped. She glanced at the incoming message. "BLACKBIRD is clear, Eric's saying. No sign of any tail," she reported.

By now the sun had set, and the light was declining rapidly. An enormous neon advertising slogan that hung beneath the dome, Bombardier: Willkommen in Berlin, was highlighted brightly in the gathering gloom, and the head-lights of an approaching train shone like beacons along the tracks.

"It's the S-Bahn platform," Mary said. "He'll take an S3."

Sure enough, two minutes later, the feed showed a yellow-and-red train pulling into the platform with a digital display on the front that was marked S3 Erkner.

BLACKBIRD boarded the train, which accelerated quickly out of the station.

"One stop to Friedrichstrasse," Mary said. "He'll be there in a couple of minutes."

"Good," Vic said. The van fell silent again as the team waited for the next scene to begin.

It struck Johnson that the sequence playing out in front of him on the video screens resembled one of the Cold War movies he had always enjoyed, not least during his student years in Berlin from 1980 to 1984. Indeed, Friedrichstrasse station was an iconic location at that time, being located in East Berlin but with trains continuing to serve it from West Berlin. As a result, the station itself was a key border crossing point, and various walls and barriers were built inside it to separate the two territories, in effect forming an extension of the Berlin Wall. The border crossing, passport checkpoints, and customs controls had been located at ground level within the complex.

Mary clicked on another thumbnail, this time on the platform at Friedrichstrasse, also covered by an expansive canopy, although less modernist than Hauptbahnhof. A couple of minutes later, the train carrying BLACKBIRD pulled in, and the feed showed him disembarking and walking confidently along the platform and beneath a covered walkway, heading toward the exit and stairs down into Friedrichstrasse, as instructed. There he again disappeared from camera shot.

Mary immediately tapped a message into her phone and dispatched it to Jones in the bogus Berlin taxi, telling him to instruct the driver to start moving to the pickup point where he would collect BLACKBIRD.

There was an instant reply from Jones confirming that the taxi was about to begin its journey.

Mary clicked yet again on one of the thumbnails, and a feed from a camera mounted beneath the rail bridge over Friedrichstrasse appeared. It showed the S-Bahn entrance and exit, sandwiched between a bistro and a clothing shop and looking somewhat dark in the poorly lit area beneath the bridge.

It wasn't so dark that the video couldn't pick up the figure of BLACKBIRD, however. The Russian was clearly visible as he strode out of the station, turning immediately left and heading along Friedrichstrasse in the direction of the surveillance van in which Johnson, Vic, and the team were concealed, about 150 yards away.

Once he had emerged from beneath the gloom of the bridge, another camera showed BLACKBIRD as he crossed the street and its tram tracks, dodging between a couple of slow-moving cars, and headed toward the pickup point just outside a Rossmann drugstore on the corner of Friedrichstrasse and Georgenstrasse. There he paused on the sidewalk and turned to face the oncoming traffic, waiting for his taxi pickup. There was no actual stopping area there, but the plan was for the taxi to halt momentarily, allowing BLACKBIRD to jump into the passenger seat, before the driver accelerated away again.

Johnson glanced at Vic, who was watching BLACKBIRD intently, and then turned back to the screen. A yellow tram sped past in front of the camera, blocking the view of BLACKBIRD for a few seconds. Then he came back into view, standing next to several shoppers and tourists who were waiting for an opportunity to cross the road. Behind him was the brick facade of the Friedrichstrasse station.

"Where's the damned taxi?" Vic asked, his voice raised in pitch. "There's no sign of it."

"Must be coming soon," Mary replied. "Rick confirmed it was on the move."

Right at that moment, BLACKBIRD jerked sharply backward and fell to the ground on his backside, his arms outstretched and flailing, as if he had been punched hard and sent flying. His body twisted as he fell, and the back of his head cracked onto the concrete sidewalk.

In that moment, Johnson caught a glimpse of a splash of red behind him—it took him less than a second to realize that it was BLACKBIRD's flesh and a large portion of his internal organs, propelled out through an exit wound in his back. The Russian lay still on the sidewalk, his head at a terrible sideways angle, as the group of people around him jumped back and away from the stricken man, some of them throwing up their hands, visibly panicked.

Both Vic and Mary jumped to their feet.

"Shit," shouted Vic, stamping his foot on the van floor. "They knew."

CHAPTER FIVE

Friday, March 21, 2014
Berlin

There was no time for recriminations over the death of Colonel Gennady Yezhov, at least, not immediately. That would come later. The first priority was to lay a smoke screen, as thick and fast as possible, and the second to try and work out how and why the meticulously planned operation had gone wrong.

Johnson was surprised that the German media swallowed most of the story that was swiftly peddled by a cooperative senior officer at the Bundespolizei, the federal police, at the request of Rick Jones. The public explanation stated that the man who had been killed on Friedrichstrasse was the victim of a suspected drive-by shooting. It was possibly a business deal that had gone wrong and could have involved drugs, although this was speculation. No identity could be released until the man's relatives had been informed, and that might take some time, they reported.

Thanks to some quick thinking by Eric, who had managed to remove Yezhov's false passport and wallet from his jacket while delivering an utterly pointless and very messy CPR and mouth-to-mouth resuscitation, the ambulance crew and local police officers who quickly arrived on the scene were unable to obtain any identification.

Jones, in the rear of the fake taxi, had arrived at the scene just after Eric. But he said that upon seeing the body he had instructed the driver to continue, not wanting to become entangled in a difficult situation.

The truth, it later emerged, following forensic tests and measurements carried out on the entry and exit wounds, was that Yezhov had been killed by a single 9x39 mm round. The bullet had almost certainly come from a sniper rifle fired from some height.

The best guess was that the weapon was a VSS Vintorez, often used by Russian Spetsnaz forces on clandestine operations because it fired its rounds at subsonic speeds and was therefore far quieter than some of its high-velocity rivals.

Following further investigations, it became clear that the shot had come from a fifth-floor hotel room window about sixty yards farther down the street, not far from the Deutsche Telekom van. From that distance, the killer could hardly fail—the Vintorez could pierce a thin steel plate at five hundred yards.

The room had been booked in the name of a German, Herman Günther, from Düsseldorf. It took very little time to establish that this was a false identity. Needless to say, there was no trace of the occupant by the time the BND and Bundespolizei arrived at the hotel. Further forensic tests found minute traces of gases, propellant, and other gunshot residue on the carpet, thrown off when the round was fired.

"He was a dead man walking from the moment he left Prague," Vic said, sitting in a small meeting room in the

Pariser Platz CIA station later that evening with Johnson and
Neal. "That was planned down to fine margins." He placed his
hands behind his head and rocked back in his seat. "It had
Moscow Center's hallmarks stamped all over it. And I've said
that to Nicklin-Donovan."

Moscow Center was the headquarters of the SVR at
Yasenevo, a dozen miles southwest of the Russian capital.

"Someone leaked it," Johnson said.

"Yes—yet again," Vic said, his face drawn tight. "And I'm
going to find the bastard."

"How many people knew?"

Vic shrugged. "Too many. There are the MI6 London
people on Mark's team, including his head of UK controllerate, Will Payne, and his guys here in Berlin, like Rick. Of
course, there's C, Richard Durman. I have no idea whether
he has privately told Harriet Miller, the foreign secretary. I
suspect so. But either way, too many of the Brits, in my view.
There's all of our team in DC together with Bernice and
Louise, of course, and others in London. Plus the small BND
team, although we hadn't given them much detail about the
importance of what BLACKBIRD was bringing. Only the
logistics."

Louise Bingham was the US ambassador to the United
Kingdom, the latest in a series of increasingly high-flying
appointments that she had been given within the State
Department, where she was widely viewed as a future secretary of state. Many thought she could go even further, given
her well-known close working relationship with the president, who relied on her for guidance in navigating the so-
called special relationship with the UK.

"A lot of people knew, Joe," Vic said. "That's the bottom
line. But they needed to know. We can't restrict
everything."

"Yes, it's difficult," Johnson said. It just wasn't feasible to cut people in important roles out of information flows. That could spell career suicide.

The shooting had given a dangerous new twist to a case that Johnson had assumed would simply be a question of a debrief to assess whether Yezhov's material was worth his involvement. He had hoped it would pan out simply because of the personal link to Vic's brother—anything that might help bring closure to his friend's private grief would be worth doing.

But now the situation was dramatically more complex. The man he was supposed to help debrief was dead, and whatever secrets about the events of 1986 he had held had been blown away by a sniper's round on a busy Berlin street. Johnson found himself feeling somewhat redundant. He supposed he might as well head back to Portland.

"So where are you going to start?" Johnson asked. Vic and his team seemed somewhat shell-shocked at what had happened. "From what you've said, it seems the leaks have come from joint operations with the Brits."

Vic and Neal exchanged glances.

"Yes. All of them. We start in London," Vic said. "That's my gut feeling."

"That sounds logical. I guess I'll book myself on a flight back to Portland, then," Johnson said. "Good luck. I suspect you'll need it."

Vic held up both hands, palms upward. "Whoa. Wait a minute," he said. "I'd like you to come to London with me and join the debriefing with Mark."

"Why?" Johnson asked. "How? This is internal for you now, isn't it? And I told you, I don't want to get tied up in CIA work."

"I know that," Vic said. "But Neal needs to stay here and finish the cleanup operation, and I need someone to support me in the Mark meeting—it's likely to be a tough one. You know all the background, and you were in the van and saw exactly what happened. You can fly home from London when we're done. It won't hold you up for long. Come on, buddy."

Johnson didn't reply immediately. He wasn't surprised at the request. Vic doubtless wanted a close ally with him given the disastrous turn of events with Yezhov. One last briefing. He didn't want to do it, but in truth, it would probably hold him up for no more than a day. He could live with that.

Johnson nodded his head. "All right. I'll do you a favor. You'll owe me a beer, though."

* * *

Friday, March 21, 2014
Tuapse, Russia's Black Sea Coast

Yuri Severinov used his hand to shelter his eyes from the afternoon sunshine that was reflecting off the white concrete quay of the deep-water oil terminal. He was dwarfed by the ocean-going Suezmax oil tanker *Yekaterina Alekseyevna,* named after Catherine the Great, that stood next to the quay, its bow soaring more than forty meters above him.

Yekaterina Alekseyevna was one of the oil tankers from Severinov's own fleet and its cargo of crude oil from Syria was being unloaded for processing at his Krasnodar oil refinery, near to Tuapse on Russia's Black Sea coast. The multibillion-aire oligarch, through his oil company, Besoi Energy, owned and operated the refinery.

He felt his cell phone vibrate in his pocket and removed it to check the incoming message, written in Russian. It was a secure message, for which he needed to use his key.

Operation Redtail has succeeded. I am leaving Moscow soon, will be in contact x

It was the first piece of good news he had received in almost a year.

He read the note twice, and as he did so, he hoped that a little of the tension that had been accumulating over many months would drain from him. Yet it did not. His mood had been so dark and depressed in recent months that even this news seemed to make only a marginal difference.

Severinov turned and strode back along the quay toward the broad gangplank that led up to the deck of the tanker.

For the past ten months, Severinov's fortunes had taken a sharp turn for the worse following Besoi Energy's catastrophic and failed bid for a raft of oil and gas assets being sold by the Afghanistan government.

The bid failure had been directly caused by an investigation carried out by the American war crimes investigator Joe Johnson, a former CIA officer with whom Severinov had a bitter history dating back to the 1980s, when they were intelligence officers on opposite sides of the Afghan conflict. The investigation made public details of Severinov's role in masterminding the destruction of many Afghan villages and towns during the Russian occupation of that country.

The Russian president, Vladimir Putin, had been a longstanding patron of Severinov's, dating back to their shared background in the KGB when they had both worked together in Soviet-controlled East Germany during the Cold War.

But despite that, the president's icy blue eyes had showed no hesitation or emotion when penalizing him heavily for the embarrassing oil and gas bid failure and the revelations. Although celebrated in private circles in Russia, the atrocities associated with the Afghan occupation were not something that Putin wanted to be highlighted publicly. Nothing that allowed the world to criticize the Motherland was acceptable.

To Severinov's greater despair and embarrassment, Johnson's inquiries had also made public his ancestry. Both his father, Sergo, and his half brother were the bastard sons of former Russian leader Josef Stalin by different women: Severinov's grandmother and mother respectively.

Both women had been seduced by Stalin, who cared little about the fact that the latter woman was married to his own son.

Severinov had a deep regard for what Stalin had achieved in Russia and in a blinkered fashion ignored all the killings and human rights abuses. But quite apart from his own desire to keep Stalin's reputation untarnished, the party leadership had forbidden him from disclosing anything that could damage the great leader's reputation. To have it all out in the open had caused massive problems in Moscow.

The consequence was that Putin had effectively confiscated one third of Besoi Energy's stakes in three oil and gas fields in western Siberia—the powerhouse of the business— dealing a major blow to Severinov's cash flow.

And that was the problem: he relied on cash flow from those fields to repay loans obtained from banks to finance other acquisitions, of which there had been many, ranging from oil and gas production in Kazakhstan, a 40 percent stake in a gas pipeline from Turkmenistan to China, the Krasnodar refinery where he was now standing, and gas-fired power generation facilities in Thailand, China, and the Philippines.

As a result, Severinov had turned to other short-term measures to generate additional cash flow alongside his main energy operations. He stuck to what he knew best and what had served him well in the past: arms dealing.

Next to the gangplank leading to the tanker's decks stood four trucks. A gang of dockworkers was busy positioning the trucks and removing tarpaulins that covered their loads so that a crane could lift a series of wooden crates aboard the tanker.

Yekaterina Alekseyevna—a 270-meter-long monster—was scheduled to sail from the Krasnodar refinery the following morning and head through the Bosporus Strait for Syria, where it would be reloaded with more crude oil. But on its journey, it would have another secondary but highly lucrative load on board: an array of antiaircraft and antitank missiles, rocket-propelled grenades and launchers, assault rifles, including a large number of AK-47s, and mortars. The weaponry was being hidden in one of a series of secret storage areas concealed within the stern of the ship.

A large percentage of the weaponry would be sold to Syrian President Bashar al-Assad's government for use in the ongoing battle against rebel forces. Russia had long been a supporter of Assad, and Severinov's ongoing contract was worth about $500 million a year.

But Severinov was potentially doubling his money—and taking a large risk—by also off-loading a significant volume of the arms to the Syrian rebels. These were the opposition forces fighting Assad.

This was a highly lucrative contract but one that he necessarily needed to keep very quiet. If the Russian president got wind of it, the consequences would be doubtless even worse than those incurred from the Afghanistan fiasco. But Severinov felt he had little choice. To repay his bank debt, he needed cash, and the massively depleted returns from his Siberian operations were no longer covering the requirement.

To complicate matters further, the military temperature in the Black Sea had heated up significantly in recent months since the Russian president ordered the annexation of the Crimean Peninsula from the Ukraine. This had been completed in recent weeks, and now there was speculation that international forces, led by the United States, might threaten a military conflagration in the region. There had been news stories speculating that a US aircraft carrier, the

USS *George H. W. Bush*, could enter the Black Sea. If that posed a further threat to Severinov's refinery operations, flows of crude oil, and arms dealing, his entire business could be sunk. He felt highly nervous about the entire situation.

Severinov leaned against the door of his black Mercedes Maybach parked on the quay—it was one of several in his fleet. He gazed out over the waters of the Black Sea southward in the direction of the Turkish coast, a couple of hundred miles away.

Today, under an azure sky, the sea was a deep blue, not black.

But neither the hue of the ocean nor the good news he had received altered Severinov's frame of mind. Redtail was a much-needed victory. But his battle to shake off the mood that had encompassed him had so far been a losing one.

CHAPTER SIX

Saturday, March 22, 2014
London

As soon as she was clear of passport control at terminal four of London's Heathrow Airport, Major General Anastasia Shevchenko of Russia's foreign intelligence service, the SVR, headed straight to a toilet designated for disabled users and locked herself in. There she removed an unused pay-as-you-go SIM card from her purse and inserted it into the cheap burner phone that she was carrying in her hand luggage.

She typed a message into a voice synthesizer app on her main cell phone, then dialed a number from memory on the burner device, and when the call was answered, she pressed the play button on the synthesizer and held it close to the microphone of the burner. The message, in a woman's voice speaking an electronic but fluent form of English, began to play.

"Hello, this is Anna from Private Finance Advice Line," the voice said. "Have you been sold payment protection insurance at any time in the last three years? If so, we might be able to help. We have four simple checks we would like to run through with you."

But the recipient of the heavily coded call replied, "No, thank you, I'm not interested." The call, largely indistinguishable from thousands of uninvited electronic sales calls made to phones everywhere in the world each day, was immediately terminated.

Shevchenko turned off her burner phone and immediately removed the SIM card and battery. She deleted the message from the synthesizer, flushed the toilet, washed her slim hands in the basin, and dried them using the electric drier in the corner. She put the burner phone and battery in her hand luggage and, after quickly brushing her neatly groomed shoulder-length black hair, left the cubicle.

She then wandered around the baggage hall for ten minutes, checking yet again that there was no sign of coverage from British counterintelligence officers. When she was sure she was clean, she threw the SIM card into a bin near to a help desk where she knew there was a blind spot between CCTV surveillance cameras. She continued through customs control toward the exit and the car waiting for her outside the arrivals hall.

It had been a good few days for Shevchenko. Just that morning, she had received two short encrypted emails and a secure text message, all congratulating her on a job well done. None of them mentioned Gennady Yezhov, and there was no reference to the previous day's incident in Berlin. But the fact that not just the SVR director but the Russian president himself—the senders of the emails—had noted the work she had done left her feeling puffed up with pride.

The text message was from someone who was no longer in the SVR but who had a strong interest in Yezhov's demise. He was also someone with whom she had remained extremely close. In fact, he was her occasional lover whenever she was in Moscow on business and had an opportunity. Her husband was rarely at home and her two children, both now in their midtwenties, had moved overseas to work.

There was no doubt in her mind that her handling of her mole in Western intelligence had been flawless over the past few months. She knew she was now in an increasingly strong position to eventually push for the SVR director's role—in charge of Russia's entire foreign intelligence operations—once the current incumbent, Maksim Kruglov, had slipped on a banana skin, as he was bound to do at some point.

Shevchenko, a wiry, attractive woman who looked younger than her fifty-eight years, checked her watch as she climbed into the black Mercedes S-Class with its diplomatic plates. It would now carry her down the M4 from Heathrow to the Russian embassy at Kensington Palace Gardens, next to Hyde Park in central London.

The sunshine made London several degrees warmer than Moscow, from where she had just flown with the Russian airline Aeroflot. It was a nice welcome back.

Shevchenko knew for certain that following the demise of Yezhov, not just the CIA and MI6 but probably all Western intelligence agencies would be on red alert, humming with activity and panic, carrying out witch hunts right, left, and center as they tried to detect the identity of the traitor in their midst.

She conjured up an image of the anthill-like chaos that she was certain was underway at CIA and MI6 stations from Washington to London to Moscow.

As a declared intelligence officer, she had official status in the UK as an SVR employee attached to the embassy, unlike most of her SVR colleagues in London, who were mainly undeclared, working under the cover of other job titles and functions.

However, her official status did mean that she was subject to constant surveillance by MI6 teams. It was difficult to deal with and made any covert meeting hazardous. So, she relied on her skill on the street to combat that because there were times when such meetings were simply necessary.

In an hour or so, after checking in at the *rezidentura*, the SVR's station within the Kensington Palace Gardens building, she would need to start the lengthy surveillance detection route that was necessary prior to her scheduled rendezvous if she was to be sure she was free of the normally ever-present eyes that were on her.

They were good, but she knew she was better.

CHAPTER SEVEN

Sunday, March 23, 2014
London

Johnson and Vic were only ten minutes away from MI6's futuristic-looking headquarters at Vauxhall Cross, on the banks of the Thames in west London, when Vic's secure phone rang. It was Mark Nicklin-Donovan with some terse instructions.

Johnson could hear only one side of the conversation, but it was rapidly evident that the MI6 director of operations wanted them to sit in on a briefing he was about to give on the Yezhov shooting to a small group of senior people from the CIA, US embassy, and MI6 teams.

"He wants me to sit at the table," Vic said when he had finished the call. "I may have to contribute. He wants you to join the meeting given that you saw the whole thing—you can supplement my responses if needed, and he might also want to ask questions about the process involved in dealing with historic crimes. He said you'll have to sit at the back and we can bring you in as needed."

"Suits me," Johnson said.

Half an hour later, the two men were sitting in a secure briefing room on the fifth floor of the SIS building, over-looking the river. Both had already been security vetted and cleared by Vauxhall Cross as soon as the visit to London had been confirmed. In Johnson's case, given that he wasn't a CIA employee, the process had been somewhat more complex but nevertheless went smoothly.

Vic joined five others around an oval maple conference table, with Nicklin-Donovan sitting at the head. Johnson was perched on a chair at the rear of the room next to a drinks cart, his back to the wall.

A tall, unsmiling man with a slight paunch and graying hair combed forward into a fringe, Nicklin-Donovan cut a slightly formal air as he spoke, quite different than Vic's easy manner, Johnson thought. He reminded Johnson of some sort of middle-aged schoolboy, perhaps because of his gray V-neck sweater and white shirt with open collar.

Johnson knew something about the others around the table because Vic had spoken about them at length as the operation had gone on, but he had only met a couple of them previously. To his surprise, they included Richard Durman, the chief of MI6, known universally as C, who in turn reported to Foreign Secretary Harriet Miller. Durman, an urbane man with a neat parting in his brown hair, was clearly taking the issue seriously enough to come in from his country house during the weekend. Johnson had seen his driver drop him off in a silver Porsche 4x4.

There was also Bernice Franklin, whom Johnson knew from his CIA days in the '80s. The two of them had joined the Agency at around the same time, and she had been helpful and encouraging to him in those early days. She had even been among those who had called him after he had run into trouble in Islamabad and asked if there was anything she could do to help.

A slim, athletic woman, Franklin's long dark hair was now showing more than a few flecks of gray but she was clearly still keeping fit: she turned up wearing Lycra cycling gear and a somewhat loud orange bike helmet. Before changing into a business suit, she casually mentioned that she had pedaled to Vauxhall Cross from her home.

She was flanked on one side by Peter Ogrizovic, an assistant to US Ambassador Louise Bingham, and on the other by Will Payne, the head of MI6's UK controllerate, who was rotund, bald, and bespectacled but, somewhat incongruously, was also carrying a cycle helmet.

Johnson was thankful that Payne hadn't opted for the Lycra like Franklin and was instead wearing chinos and a polo shirt. He looked as though he needed the exercise more than she did, Johnson couldn't help noticing.

He's the Fat Controller, Johnson thought, his mind going back to a character in the children's train storybooks he used to read to his kids when they were small. For a few seconds, he had to resist the temptation to laugh.

Nicklin-Donovan started by explaining that Vic and Johnson were there because of their direct involvement in Berlin and then launched into a factual, blow-by-blow account of what had happened, based on the detailed briefings he had received from Vic and others. He used a few PowerPoint slides that showed maps and photographs of the area around Friedrichstrasse station and some video taken from the security cameras, including the footage showing Yezhov's death, to illustrate his points.

"Yezhov was a dead man walking from the moment he got on the train in Prague," Nicklin-Donovan concluded. "It has Moscow Center's hallmarks stamped all over it. We and Vic's team will, of course, be doing our utmost to locate the source of the leak."

Johnson caught Vic's eye. He could see his friend was holding back a smirk at hearing Nicklin-Donovan replay the same language Vic had used in describing the incident.

There followed a barrage of predictable but largely unanswerable, questions from those around the table.

"What is your gut feeling about the source of the leak?" Ogrizovic asked. "And do you think it came from the same source as the other leaks we've seen in recent months?"

Nicklin-Donovan shrugged. "Logic would suggest that, but I've no more certainty than you have."

"How tight were the security processes you have in place with the BND?" asked Franklin. She propped her elbows on the table and cupped her chin in her hands, addressing Nicklin-Donovan directly. Without waiting for an answer, she continued, "I can see that the CIA team has been tight, but you were managing the BND. How much did they know? I'm assuming quite a lot. And how many of them were in the loop?"

Johnson was thankful that Franklin appeared to be supporting her own CIA colleagues, but she was apparently intent on having something of a dig at the British contingent. He had always remembered her as a combative character from his early days in the CIA—she obviously hadn't changed, and he could see that Nicklin-Donovan was fighting to keep his temper in check.

"It was need-to-know with the BND," Nicklin-Donovan said, beads of sweat now decorating his forehead. "Rick Jones was handling that relationship, and he tells me he kept the information strictly compartmentalized. Only the logistics details went to the BND."

"That's a relief, then," Franklin said, a note of sarcasm in her voice. "Who's going to run the inquiry into how this happened?"

"The question of who will run it and what shape it will take is something I'm currently deciding." Now Nicklin-Donovan's voice held a distinctly irritated tone. "It will be low-key and discreet. I will keep you all informed when I have done that, and I don't need to stress, as always, that those details should go no further unless you are instructed otherwise."

Fat chance of that, Johnson thought. *They're all going to have to report back to superiors.*

There were more questions, but Nicklin-Donovan concluded the meeting after an hour. Durman left first, with a curt nod of the head to all around the table, followed by Will Payne, fastening his cycle helmet under his double chin. Then Nicklin-Donovan escorted Franklin and Ogrizovic out of the secure area to the elevators, leaving Johnson and Vic in the meeting room.

A few minutes later he returned. "Get your things," Nicklin-Donovan said. "We're going somewhere else for a further discussion about all this."

"Where?" Vic asked.

"I can't tell you. I'll drive."

CHAPTER EIGHT

Sunday, March 23, 2014
London

Nicklin-Donovan had driven three miles west from Vauxhall Cross before Vic asked the question for a second time.

"Where are we going?" he said.

"Safe house," Nicklin-Donovan said. "A village called Datchet, around twenty miles west of London. We can talk more freely there." He had obviously chosen somewhere that was free of the surveillance and hidden microphones that kept a twenty-four-hour watch on everyone and everything that moved and spoke at Vauxhall Cross.

During a circuitous route to Datchet, Nicklin-Donovan several times doubled back on himself, parked temporarily down side streets, and went through a couple of red lights. Despite his seniority—or possibly because of it—he was clearly still hands-on when it came to surveillance detection precautions.

He finally pronounced that he was satisfied they were

clean and proceeded to the safe house, an anonymous Tudor-style property set back from the street down a short driveway. The village was quaint, well maintained, and clearly well heeled. Its main feature was the River Thames, considerably narrower here than in London, that formed a natural boundary to the west.

The three men crunched their way across the gravel driveway to the rear door of the house, past a hedge that was showing the first green shoots of spring. There Nicklin-Donovan stepped into the shadows of a stone porch and unlocked the door.

He led the way to a kitchen and made coffee for all of them.

"As you can imagine, I'm doing my best to keep the almighty screwup in Berlin beneath the radar," Nicklin-Donovan said as he led the way to a living room. "I could have done without that meeting this morning, but some of the others, unhelpfully including C, were demanding a briefing and an update."

"I bet you are," Vic said. "Must be difficult to stomach for you. Even harder for me. Tell me who *doesn't* know what happened."

"We've so far kept it away from the politicians who make the noise, from the prime minister downward," Nicklin-Donovan said. "And internally I've tried my best to keep it tight, but it is difficult, as you have just seen."

"That's why I brought you two here," Nicklin-Donovan went on. "I wanted to speak to you both about a few different aspects of this whole business." He sat in an armchair, leaving Johnson and Vic to take positions at either end of a long sofa.

Nicklin-Donovan took a sip from his coffee. "Now, first, I just want to say I don't know what your surveillance team was doing on the ground in Berlin and why that sniper wasn't spotted," he said, alternating his gaze between Vic and Johnson, "but I'm sure it will all come out eventually."

"As I am sure will the details of the other busted operations with your people over recent months," Vic said pointedly.

"I'm talking about *this* operation," Nicklin-Donovan said. "The basic surveillance on the ground seemed to be lacking."

"Unfortunately the surveillance team left their sniper detection kit at home," Johnson said. He had always hated playing the blame games that were so much a part of the intelligence agency culture. "Strange as it may seem, nobody assumed the other side was getting a briefing on BLACK-BIRD's movements."

Vic cut him a look. "The ground team handled everything in the immediate vicinity according to plan, but snipers add a different dimension."

Johnson leaned forward, looking at Nicklin-Donovan. "I think it would be more constructive to look forward, not back."

"Yes, but we're going to have to do some looking backward if we're going to move forward, aren't we?" Nicklin-Donovan said. "We're missing a few vital ingredients, all of which were in BLACKBIRD's head."

"By looking backward, you mean an inquiry?" Vic ventured.

Johnson tried to avoid sighing. Of course, Nicklin-Donovan was going to make use of the small amount of ammunition he did have, which was to blame Vic and the Agency for the operation on the ground.

But surely an official inquiry was the last thing the MI6 man would want, given it appeared the much bigger problem —the mole—was buried somewhere underground at his end. He would be the one holding the bag if such details emerged, and he would also be blamed if an inquiry failed to deliver a result. Either way, he lost.

The MI6 chief looked at Johnson, his gaze steady. "What are your plans now?"

"I'll be heading home soon, back to Portland. I don't want to get under your feet. It seems you've both got a lot on your plates."

"Hmm. I know your background, Joe," Nicklin-Donovan said. "And I know your record. Jayne Robinson told me all about you. We keep in touch. And Vic briefed me that you're here because of the historic angle of the information Yezhov was bringing out. It crossed my mind that your curiosity about that might have been deepened by what has happened, not reduced. Is that a fair assumption?"

Johnson sat up. Surely the MI6 chief wasn't suggesting what Johnson thought he was suggesting. The answer was going to be no.

"The situation is now very different," Johnson said. "Yezhov is no longer alive, and with him has gone the information he held, possibly for good."

"But don't you want to consider the possibility that the reason Yezhov is dead is because of the nature of that historic information? Doesn't that pique your interest?"

"I think that's unlikely," Vic interrupted. "Let's be honest. It was almost certainly a self-protective move, given that Yezhov was about to blow the mole's cover. That was the prime reason. It's obvious."

"We don't know that for sure," Nicklin-Donovan said with a faint grin. "It could be either reason. Or maybe both. But my thinking is that if Joe were, hypothetically speaking, of course, to go away and do some private investigative work into why a mole might want to suppress historic information, he would need to find out who that mole is. Or am I barking up the wrong tree?"

Vic paused and sipped his coffee. "Then if he finds out, you could take the credit for unearthing the bastard." A thin grin crossed his mouth. "But if he doesn't?"

"In that case, everyone goes home quietly, and Joe gets on with his next search for a ninety-year-old Nazi commander hiding in Baltimore or somewhere," Nicklin-Donovan said. He inclined his head toward Johnson. "It's somewhat off-piste for me to be suggesting this rather than getting my own teams to investigate, I know. But I need to know what secrets Yezhov had, and I need to know how the operation leaked. I don't want to make such inquiries out on the open prairie, so to speak, and I know you do that kind of thing very well."

"I don't think it's for me," Johnson said. "I think you guys need to deal with this now. Isn't it more about the present than the past? I feel the dead hand of the Russian president—he must have given the green light to what happened in Berlin."

"If I launch an official inquiry, I'll need to ask C to inform the foreign secretary about what happened," Nicklin-Donovan said. "And included in that intel report would be details of the failure of the CIA operation on the ground to bring the defector in safely. She would then most likely feel obliged to brief the rest of the government and perhaps have to make some sort of public statement. You can imagine the media frenzy that would ensue. Alternatively, Joe could just stay for a couple of weeks and see what might emerge from a rather more unofficial inquiry."

Which you could deny was ever taking place, Johnson thought. *Typical bureaucratic ass-covering.*

Johnson glanced at Vic. At the back of his mind there was still the feeling that Vic probably did want him to do this. If he could somehow find out the information Yezhov was intending to pass on, it would represent Vic's last chance to get closure on what had happened to his brother—and so many other victims—in La Belle years ago. And he figured Vic must also be almost as desperate as Nicklin-Donovan to find out who the mole was, if only for the sake of all the joint operations that could be blown in the future if the SVR agent continued to operate unimpaired.

Should I give it a couple of weeks?

"All right," Johnson found himself saying, almost instinctively. "I'll do a couple of weeks, and that's all. If nothing turns up, I'm heading back home. You two can split the cost or agree on whatever suits you both."

Nicklin-Donovan smiled. "Thank you."

"You're going to owe us for this," Vic said.

"I'm sure the tables will be turned at some point," Nicklin-Donovan said. "As you'll doubtless discover in your newly elevated position at Langley."

Johnson folded his arms. "There'll be a few conditions, though."

"What?" Nicklin-Donovan asked.

"First, no hassle from your guys. I don't want to find counterintelligence hounds from your service following me around Western Europe like our family dog, Cocoa, when we're late giving him dinner. Hands off, okay?"

Nicklin-Donovan threw up his hands. "Okay, okay. And the other conditions?"

"I'll need help with this. So second, perhaps you can both ensure I get access to whatever equipment, resources, and information I need. Including phone, email, data monitoring, and so on, as needed, from both the MI6 and CIA sides."

"Not officially, no. Unofficially, yes."

"Thanks. Third, I bring in Jayne Robinson to work with me on this, even if it's only for a short period."

Nicklin-Donovan exhaled a little. "Does that mean doubling my budget?"

Johnson shrugged and spread his hands wide.

"Anything else?"

"Is this investigation being kept solely between us, or will you need to inform others?" Johnson asked. "I would prefer the former."

Nicklin-Donovan hesitated. "So would I, in theory. But we live in the real world. I will probably need to inform a very small circle—that is, the people who were at Vauxhall Cross earlier. If I didn't, and they found out, there would be hell to pay. I'd lose my job."

Johnson glanced at Vic, who shrugged. It wasn't ideal.

"I am having some analysis done on the leaks that have happened over recent months to see if there is a pattern and also whether there is any correlation with known changes in personnel at the *rezidentura* here," Nicklin-Donovan said. "That work should be completed imminently, so I will let you know the outcome."

"That's sensible," Johnson said, turning back to Nicklin-Donovan. "But if we are to get involved in an investigation, there is also the issue of where to start, or rather with whom. Can you give me a clue?"

Nicklin-Donovan stood and walked to the window, looking down the garden toward the River Thames across the other side of the street. He tapped his fingers on the window ledge.

"This might sound like an odd suggestion from me, seeing as I'm second in charge of the service." He turned and leaned back against the window ledge, supporting himself with his hands behind his back. "But this is another reason why I've brought you all the way out here to discuss this. I would like you to start by having a close look at someone in my camp."

"Who?" Johnson asked.

"Our head of Berlin station, Rick Jones. I've been considering putting him under the microscope for some time. Now I've got an excuse."

"There were certain aspects of the operation involving him that I was concerned about," Johnson said. "He seemed a little disengaged, and there was the late arrival of his bogus taxi. That meant BLACKBIRD was standing on the sidewalk for quite some time before he was shot."

"Yes, and why didn't he get the taxi to stop?" Vic asked. "He drove straight past. Then he was more concerned with concocting a story to feed to the German media."

Nicklin-Donovan nodded. "Those are things we need to look at, yes. But there's more to it than that."

"Such as?" Vic asked.

"A few reasons. One is purely administrative in that as head of station, he's frankly been an underperformer who's been struggling somewhat to develop the sources and assets we need. He's got a slight booze problem, apparently, according to my sources. I've been seriously considering removing him from that role—possibly removing him from the service altogether."

"That's a performance issue. You could probably say that about a lot of people," Johnson said. "Anything else?"

"Yes. I've also been told that he might have some sources about whom he's not reporting back to us, which is not just odd for someone in his position, it's dangerous and it's worrying me. Those worries have multiplied massively given what happened to Yezhov."

"You think he might be on someone's payroll," Johnson said. "And if so, might he have knowledge of the historical information Yezhov was going to pass on?"

Nicklin-Donovan shrugged. "Don't know. I'm not ruling anything out. That's why I want to find out more."

CHAPTER NINE

Sunday, March 23, 2014
London

The two boarding passes that Johnson had printed at his hotel sat side by side on Jayne Robinson's dining table.

Jayne emerged from the bathroom at her apartment in Whitechapel, in the east end of London, wearing a bathrobe around her slim frame and with a towel wrapped around her short dark hair.

She had always been naturally attractive, and Johnson couldn't help noticing the glow that she had following her shower. His eyes lingered on her face for a while as she stopped next to the table and glanced down.

"What the hell are these?" she said. "Berlin?"

Johnson had arrived at her second-floor apartment twenty minutes earlier than he had indicated to find Jayne answering the door in her robe, about to take a shower after a gym session. The traffic back into central London from Datchet had been light, and unusually, there had been no holdups. Likewise for the cab journey to Jayne's place from his hotel in west London, near to Vauxhall Cross, where he was staying.

He then had to wait while she disappeared into her bathroom to get ready.

"Yes, Berlin. We're going tomorrow morning. That okay?" Johnson said with a straight face. "Although you don't have to, if you don't want to."

Jayne placed her hands on her hips.

Like a double teapot, Johnson thought.

"Can you just explain what's going on? You've been to see Mark—I thought that was for a final washup over what happened in Berlin?"

Before leaving the German capital, Johnson had texted her briefly to explain he was traveling to London with Vic to see Nicklin-Donovan for a final briefing before heading back home.

"Yes, I thought so too—Vic said it was just going to be a washup. But the conversation took a somewhat different turn," Johnson said. He explained as briefly as possible what had happened in Datchet during the conversation with Jayne's former boss and the details he had been given, along with the background relating to the La Belle bombing and Vic's brother and the suggestion they start by checking out Rick Jones.

"I committed to a couple of weeks of work," Johnson said. "Mark wants an arms-length inquiry, below the radar, into who leaked the operation. He understandably wants to cover his ass."

"Why you, though?" Jayne asked.

"It seems quite possible that one reason the mole wanted Yezhov dead was the historical factor—because of what he was about to tell us about La Belle. Mark asked because of my track record, and I thought it was up my alley. It's potentially an interesting case, and it means a lot to Vic. I did, however, lay down a few conditions before agreeing."

Jayne surveyed him from beneath furrowed brows. "What?"

Johnson gave a faint smile. "One of them was that you came on board with me. Mark agreed."

"For God's sake, Joe. What right have you got to—"

"Sorry, I thought you'd be interested. It's only a short job."

Jayne walked to the end of the living room of her apartment, a modern place within a building on the corner of Portsoken Street and Minories, above a Starbucks coffee shop.

She stood gazing out across her small balcony toward Tower Bridge beyond, her back toward Johnson, who sat on a black leather sofa.

"You said Mark suggested starting with Rick Jones," Jayne said eventually. She turned to face Johnson.

"Yes, that's what he said."

"I worked with him for a while at Vauxhall Cross a few years back. Then he went to Moscow station. He was good out there, made a few recruitments, but got very close to some of his assets in the SVR. Too close, some people thought—he seemed sometimes more concerned about them than about the intel they were delivering. Then he was promoted to head of Berlin station."

"Interesting that you should say that," Johnson said. He gave Jayne more details about the concerns that Nicklin-Donovan had about Jones.

Jayne listened, then frowned. "How do you feel about all this? Are you really interested in pursuing it?" she asked.

"I'm interested in La Belle and what happened there. I told Vic I'd help him with that. If one thing leads to another, I'll go with it for a while. Frankly, I can't see us making any progress in two weeks, though."

"Well, I don't have anything on currently," Jayne said.

"And it sounds interesting. I like Mark—he's a decent guy—although we'll need to be damned careful with Rick. And I've worked in Berlin before, remember. La Belle was still a massive sore, open wound when I was there. So yes, I'll join you if it's going to help."

Indeed, Johnson knew that Jayne had done a stint for MI6 in Berlin starting in 1989, after leaving Afghanistan, spanning the period when the Berlin Wall came down in November that year, during the collapse of communism. That was when she had become fluent in German to add to her other languages, including French, Spanish, and Russian. That was one reason why he thought she might be interested in the operation he was now involved with.

Johnson got up from the sofa, walked over to her, and gave her a hug. It was a spur-of-the-moment thing. Having not been able to do so earlier, on account of her disorientation at his early arrival and desire to get back into the shower, he realized he had subconsciously been looking for an excuse.

"Thank you. That's good to hear," Johnson said. "To be honest, having seen what happened to Yezhov, the Russians worry me."

Jayne, who at about five foot nine was only about four inches shorter than Johnson, extracted herself from the hug. Keeping her hands behind Johnson's neck, she held him at arm's length. "Don't worry. We've got a track record of seeing off the Russians."

CHAPTER TEN

Thursday, March 27, 2014
Berlin

Johnson adjusted his plain black-rimmed reading glasses and pulled down the woolen cap over the short-cropped blond wig he wore. He glanced at Jayne, who suppressed a smile. She too was wearing a light disguise: a shoulder-length brunette wig and stylish designer glasses. Both were wearing smart casual clothes: the type of attire worn every day by thousands of office workers and tourists across Berlin.

They were simple changes, but effective.

"*Sie sind Berliners,*" Vic said. You are Berliners.

Vic, who was fluent in German, had watched with interest as the CIA station's disguise officer quickly changed the appearance of his clients for that morning.

It had been many years since either Johnson or Jayne had run a proper street surveillance operation. They both felt it important to participate in the operation to tail Rick Jones, which meant using the light disguise, but also recognized the need to draft in a small team with current experience and practice who wouldn't be burned by rusty skills if the unexpected happened.

Johnson hoped the surveillance operation would be a good starting point in his investigation.

So after Vic had quietly taken recommendations from Mary Gassey in the CIA's Berlin station, they opted for three retired BND officers who occasionally worked for the Agency —Otto and Maria, who were a couple, and a single woman named Gertrud, all in their sixties—together with another woman in her thirties named Renate who had recently left the BND. The four of them were supervised by a BND surveillance team leader Klaus Ortner.

Johnson immediately dubbed them *die Rentners,* the German word for "pensioners."

To avoid an obtrusive gathering at the CIA station at Pariser Platz, they held a planning meeting instead at a safe house near the Botanic Garden—an anonymous detached two-story property in Limonenstrasse, a quiet cobbled residential street. It was the same place where they had been planning to debrief Yezhov.

There they agreed on a strategy with Ortner, under which the professional surveillance quartet would spearhead the work, while Johnson and Jayne would fit in and play a floating role as instructed.

The three retirees, plus Johnson and Jayne, would be the foot soldiers, while Renate would be on standby in a car if Jones took to a vehicle. The idea was to get some eyeballs on Jones to see if he met with any of his agents and, if appropriate, to put surveillance on the agent afterward.

The logistics were slightly awkward, given that Nicklin-Donovan wanted to keep the operation at arm's length from MI6 and obviously did not want his head of Berlin station to have any idea of what was going on. But eventually, a work-able plan was devised.

For the first two days, nothing happened because Jones had no meetings scheduled and sat at his desk in the MI6 station at the British embassy on Wilhelmstrasse, a modern sandstone building with a slightly garish purple-and-blue structure at the entrance. He hardly ventured out of the embassy, less than two hundred yards from the American embassy, for any unscheduled reason either, apart from a stroll down the road to buy a sandwich and some chocolate.

On the third day, Thursday, Jones's diary was fuller. He had two external meetings in the morning, one with a coun-terpart at the BND, another with a lecturer in German poli-tics from the Humboldt University of Berlin, apparently as part of efforts to broaden his knowledge in that sphere.

After a sandwich lunch, he then set off on foot again. First, he headed south along the broad open expanses of Wilhelm-strasse, then cut into a clothing market and quickly examined some T-shirts and jeans before leaving by another exit. John-son, some ninety yards behind, watched as, on the other side of the street, a nondescript elderly couple, Otto and Maria, followed Jones as he cut left into Französischestrasse beneath a covered ancient stone footbridge connecting two buildings.

It was by now obvious that Jones was undertaking a surveillance detection route. He stopped twice to make calls on his cell phone, each time using them as cover to stop and check his tail. After a couple of zigzag stair-step turns, still heading broadly south, he went into a bank, emerged a few minutes later, and then bought chocolate at a small grocery shop.

The retired but sprightly couple on the other side of the street scrutinized the flowers on display under the cover of a sunshade outside a florist, and another woman with gray hair,

Gertrud, found change for a beggar. Johnson had to admire the former BND officers' skill; Jones had shown no sign of having detected surveillance.

Now the *Rentners'* target was heading south down the cobbled part of Mauerstrasse, to the point where it joined Friedrichstrasse, next to Checkpoint Charlie, the old crossing between East and West Berlin where any non-Germans had to pass through during the Cold War period.

A crowd of tourists was bustling around the old checkpoint, taking selfies and photographs under the white sign: "You Are Now Entering The American Sector," it read. Jones neatly dodged his way through the throng and ducked beneath some scaffolding that ran alongside a building on the right of Friedrichstrasse.

Johnson stuck to the right side of the street, following Jones, while Jayne tucked in behind the elderly couple, who made their way down the left side, past the historic white hut labeled US Army Checkpoint, with its old search lights, American flag, and sandbagged barrier.

Once past the Kochstrasse U-Bahn subway station, the crowds quickly thinned. Jones was moving more quickly now, and after another block he cut left onto Besselstrasse, then right through a park with rows of trees.

The elderly couple was hanging well back now since there was little cover, and Johnson did likewise. He could just about see Jones through the trees as he paused, lit a cigarette, and made another phone call, leaning on a tall gatepost as he did so.

Then he abruptly turned a right corner and vanished from view. By the time Johnson arrived at the corner, the elderly BND couple had also vanished. Jayne caught up with him a few seconds later.

"Where the hell have they gone?" Jayne asked.

Johnson shrugged. But then Gertrud emerged from the

door of a small hotel about fifty yards farther ahead. She walked toward them and signaled that they should return to the park, off the street.

"He is in the hotel," Gertrud said in her fluent English when they were all together in the park. "He is meeting another man. They are sitting in a corner in the bar. It is busy in there. But Otto and Maria are also in the hotel bar. It is fine. Maria will probably get a photo somehow—she is very good at doing that. And then they will follow the man afterward and find out where he lives. If Jones goes with him, they will report back."

Johnson raised his eyebrows. *Get a photo?* Could that pair of pensioners really get away with following an MI6 officer trained in spotting surveillance for over an hour and a couple of miles, then sit near him in a hotel bar and still remain undetected?

"We should go now," Gertrud continued. "We do not want him to see us when he comes out of the hotel. Our job is done. We can make any identification from what Otto and Maria tell us and hopefully from the photo too."

Johnson worried that their target would inevitably realize what was going on—that would be another operation blown. However, he didn't have much of a choice and needed to trust the team. He nodded to Gertrud and then Jayne, and they left the park together.

* * *

Thursday, March 27, 2014
  Berlin

. . .

It was late into the evening by the time the *Rentners* regrouped with Johnson, Jayne, and Vic in a small meeting room at the Limonenstrasse safe house.

Otto and Maria had written a short report, which they had already sent to Johnson, but they talked everyone through the events of the afternoon anyway.

It turned out that Jones and the man he was meeting had stayed in the hotel bar for only a short time before disappearing upstairs, presumably to have a private conversation in one of the hotel rooms without any danger of being overheard. It had not been possible to follow them because the entrances to the hotel's corridors all required passkeys. They also had not been able to obtain a guest list and so didn't know whether the room was booked in Jones's name or the other man's.

"Don't worry," Johnson said. "It would almost certainly be in a false name anyway."

The two men had remained in the room for an hour and a quarter, Otto continued, at which point Jones had reappeared downstairs and immediately left the hotel by himself. Otto had followed Jones, leaving Maria behind, but the MI6 head of station had simply returned to his office. He had taken one of the taxis waiting near the hotel and Otto had managed to follow him in another taxi. Jones was dropped a block away from the British embassy and had walked the rest of the way.

Maria then took up the story. "I waited in the hotel reception area, and about ten minutes later, the man Jones was meeting came down and left the hotel. I followed."

She had tailed him to the Kochstrasse U-Bahn station, near Checkpoint Charlie, where he had taken a U6 train heading south for nine stops to Westphalweg. Then he had jumped on a number 282 bus heading east for a few stops before getting off and finishing his journey on foot. He appeared to be living in a large house on Liviusstrasse. Maria gave Johnson the exact address.

"A house?" Johnson asked. He knew that people in Berlin tended to live in apartments, mostly rented.

"Yes. A two-story house. Chalet style," Maria said. "It must be expensive. I do not know how much—maybe worth a million and a half euros. I do not know if he rents it or owns it, but either way, he must have money."

"Interesting," Johnson said. "You've done a great job. I really don't know how you pull off this kind of operation."

Maria smiled at the compliment. "I just imagine myself invisible. I am not there. I am unimportant. And of course, I use street craft. Years of practice. I changed my appearance twice this afternoon, you know. Once while waiting for the man to come out of the hotel and then again quickly in the U-Bahn. I was three different people."

Johnson nodded. "And did you manage to get a photograph?"

Maria fished out her cell phone and showed Johnson two pictures she had somehow taken: one in the hotel reception area as the man walked out and another on the U-Bahn, showing him sitting in his seat scrutinizing his phone.

The picture showed a man with a full head of crew-cut black hair that was graying around the sides, and he had a slightly dark complexion. He was wearing a black leather jacket, zipped up to the top, and dark slacks.

Johnson studied the photo, then passed the phone to Jayne. "What do you think? Forties? Probably similar age to Jones, I'd say."

Jayne took the phone. She sat up in her seat and frowned, examining the photo closely. "I would say that he's one of those men who look younger than they are. Trendy haircut, but craggy face. I feel like I recognize him somehow, but I'm struggling to think exactly where from."

Johnson glanced at her. She was rarely wrong about people's faces. "Someone from when you worked here?"

"I've a feeling he was someone I tried to recruit, perhaps 1989 or 1990. I think he might have been one of several Stasi agents I was working on and didn't make any progress with."

"*Stasi?*" Johnson asked, surprised.

Jayne nodded. "Maybe." She looked up at Maria and Vic in turn. "Can you send us these photos? We'll run them through our system. And Vic, can we do checks on the address and find out who the owner is?"

Twenty minutes later, the photos had been dispatched to Nicklin-Donovan at Vauxhall Cross and to Langley along with a brief note from Jayne outlining her thoughts about the target's possible background.

The MI6 team was the first to respond. A secure call some time later from Nicklin-Donovan to Vic informed him that facial-recognition analysis of the photograph and cross-checks against written files showed that the man was known to Vauxhall Cross: he had indeed worked for the Stasi during the 1980s.

Vic ended the call and turned to Jayne in mock rebuke. "You should have remembered his name. You contributed to his file in 1989 and 1990. It's still all in the system. You *did* try to recruit him."

Jayne scratched her nose. "His name?"

"Reiner Schwartz."

A flash of recognition crossed Jayne's face. "I remember him now. Yes. He was on my list because he had good access to the Stasi files at their HQ. I made no progress with him, though."

The Stasi was the East German state security service— the secret police—who were notorious for the extensive and repressive nature of their operations during the Cold War and who worked closely with the KGB. Their officers had been major targets for Western intelligence organizations who were trying to infiltrate the Stasi's sprawling East Berlin headquarters at Normannenstrasse, about four and a half miles east of the Pariser Platz embassy.

The last update to Schwartz's file had been two years earlier. It showed that for the past decade he had been a senior employee of the German Ministry of Defense—the Bundesministerium der Verteidigung. He was currently in its directorate for strategy and operations, one of the most critical parts of the organization, often working closely with the minister, the senior civil servant who ran the ministry, and the executive team. He had divorced eight years earlier, had no children, and lived by himself.

The reason for the update to Schwartz's file, written by none other than Rick Jones, was that there was a suspicion he might be working for the SVR. The file note stated that Schwartz frequently traveled to Moscow, Kiev, and St. Petersburg for part of his role in the ministry and was therefore ideally placed to pass on information if he chose to do so or if he had been compromised and subsequently forced into doing so. He also visited other capitals in the former Soviet Union. But there had been no more recent entries in the file, and there was nothing to indicate that the BND had been informed of the suspicions.

Johnson found it astonishing. "Good to know that the German Ministry of Defense is finding space for a former East German Stasi officer. What the hell?"

"Don't be surprised," Vic said. "There's a lot of ex-Stasi employees like him. Actually, there's thousands of former Stasi in the German civil service. Reinvented themselves, and if they'd done wrong, probably argued they were only following state orders."

"But if there have been more recent suspicions about him,

why have there been no updates to his file, I wonder?" Jayne asked.

Johnson shrugged. "Maybe it's because Jones had his own reasons for not doing so. If we can't ask him why—at least not yet—we need to find out via Schwartz."

"Not a problem," Jayne said. "Let's catch him outside the ministry building and ask him."

"Very amusing. I was thinking of other methods."

Johnson must have had a look on his face, because Jayne gave him a stare. "I hope you're not thinking what I suspect you are."

"What would that be?"

Jayne paused. "I don't know. You sometimes go beyond the law when you don't need to. Not his house?"

Johnson shrugged again and folded his arms. "Only for the greater good," he said.

Vic gave a slight grin and looked away. "I'm not hearing this conversation."

"I know you're not. Keep your ears shut, buddy," Johnson said. "And don't say anything to Nicklin-Donovan. But I might need some equipment to help do what you didn't hear. Also for the greater good, if required."

"What? Don't tell me," Vic said. "A Beretta for you and a Walther for your good lady?"

"They would be a start, yes. And a few other items." He began to run through a list.

CHAPTER ELEVEN

Monday, March 31, 2014
Berlin

The white Deutsche Telekom–branded van, complete with plastic tubes, a ladder, and a small satellite dish on the roof, looked no different from any other van belonging to Germany's principal telecoms company as it crawled north-ward along Rixdorfer Strasse, took a right past a Croatian restaurant. and then a sharp left.

It moved along Liviusstrasse and pulled onto the side of the street about halfway along. The two people on the side-walk, a man with a Doberman pinscher on a lead and an elderly woman pushing a shopping cart, took no notice as the driver killed the engine. Such vans were commonplace, and in any case, both people were more focused on staying upright in the face of a fierce March wind that was buffeting them.

But this van was the same vehicle that had been used for the surveillance operation on Gennady Yezhov prior to his assassination.

Johnson, the driver, made a quick call on his cell phone to Vic to confirm his arrival at his destination and, without turning his head, spoke to Jayne, who was ensconced in the rear of the van, out of sight.

"I'll message you when I'm inside and then send an update every five minutes," Johnson said. The plan was for Jayne to remain in the van, concealed from sight but able to keep a watch on the street outside using video cameras concealed in the plastic tubes attached to the roof rack. She could contact Johnson using a secure cell phone at any time.

After a lengthy debate, Jayne had accepted Johnson's argument that entering Schwartz's house was probably the fastest route to obtaining evidence of the kind they needed—and time was short.

Johnson picked up the Beretta M9 that Vic had procured for him from the weapons locker at the Pariser Platz CIA station, along with a Walther for Jayne, and pushed it down into his belt before covering it with his Deutsche Telekom jacket.

The *Rentners* surveillance team, who had been on duty since just after four o'clock that morning, had observed Schwartz leaving the property at about half past seven in his BMW 5 Series sedan, presumably to head into the Ministry of Defense building on Stauffenbergstrasse, about half an hour away.

Johnson put on his pink Deutsche Telekom safety helmet and zipped up his black jacket, climbed out of the van, and picked up a small plastic toolbox from behind his seat. He closed the van door, then made his way up a narrow driveway that ran up the side of the house to a garage at the rear. If challenged, his cover story would be that he had been sent to deal with a broadband failure.

When he drew level with the rear of the house, he turned right through a gap in the fence and along a path that led to the rear door. The layout of the rear garden was exactly as the *Rentners* had described: there was a fence that ran right up the left side of the property along the driveway, which protected Johnson from any observers. However, the right side was open, with just a low hedge and flower beds between Schwartz's property and the one next door. The wind was blowing an array of daffodils almost to the ground and whistling through the hedge.

Johnson needed to work quickly and unobtrusively to ensure that no nosy neighbors called the police.

The *Rentners* had, helpfully, already checked that Schwartz's house had no burglar alarm. It made sense, Johnson reasoned: he wouldn't want the police poking around his property in case of a false alarm while he wasn't there.

The team had also, under cover of darkness, established exactly what type of lock was on the rear door. It was of the modern pin tumbler variety, which for a skilled person was normally pickable using a tension wrench and a set of rakes. Indeed, Johnson often carried a small set in his wallet when working away on jobs, just in case they were needed, as they occasionally were.

However, using such tools was sometimes time-consuming and unpredictable. The previous year, a sympathetic locksmith friend in Portland, who had taught Johnson the finer art of lock picking over the years, had given him a set of eight bump keys of varying shapes and sizes. They were normal keys, but each of the V-shaped gaps between the teeth had been shaved down to the minimum. Johnson also carried a bump hammer, a small black tool with a rubber head attached to a handle by a slightly flexible metal neck.

Most tumbler locks consist of either five or six internal pins of different lengths, each with two parts that rest one on top of the other and with springs at the top to keep them in position. The teeth on a normal key, which are of differing lengths, push all the pins up to the same level—the shear line —at which point the key can be turned.

A small porch over the back door gave Johnson some cover, although he would have liked more. He pulled a pair of thin rubber gloves from his pocket and put them on, then tried three different keys, inserting them into the tumbler lock, until he found one of the correct length that fitted snugly. It was a six-pin lock.

Then he pulled the key out one notch and removed the bump hammer from his pocket. He had practiced the technique at home until he was able to execute it swiftly and with minimum time wasted.

Holding the key in the lock between the thumb and forefinger of his left hand, he rapped the end of the key hard with the bump hammer. The force of the blow, transmitted through the metal of the key teeth and the lower pins—the key pins—that were touching them, caused the upper pins—the driver pins—farthest away from the key to jump upward momentarily before being pushed back down by the springs.

The trick Johnson had been practicing was to apply just the right amount of slight rotational force on the key with his thumb and finger so that when the upper driver pins jumped above the shear line for that fraction of a second, he could get the key to turn in the lock.

As always, it took a few tries. Johnson hit the key five times before, on the sixth attempt, the key turned smoothly in the lock. He pulled the handle down, and the door swung open.

Johnson pocketed the key, stepped inside, and closed the door but left it unlocked. He found himself in a long open-plan room that contained a kitchen, a dining area, and, at the far end, a sofa and two armchairs. A set of double doors, secured by locks similar to the one he had just picked, led out onto some wooden decking that was shielded from the street by a wooden fence.

He knew he had limited time. There was no way of knowing when Schwartz might return or if any other visitor might come to the house.

Johnson glanced at his watch. Just over five minutes had gone since he had left the van. He sent a message to Jayne.

In.

The question was, where did Schwartz keep his documents, his computers, and other potentially helpful items? Moving carefully but as quickly as he could, Johnson decided to explore the floor he was on before heading upstairs. Apart from the large open-plan family room, there was a separate TV room with its window blinds pulled down that had a giant flat screen on the wall and an extensive speaker system. There was also a utility room and a further reception room lined with bookcases, three armchairs, and a well-stocked liquor cabinet.

Finally, at the end of a hallway, Johnson found a small office. On the desk was a large monitor screen, a keyboard, and a mouse, but no computer was connected. Presumably Schwartz used them with a laptop that he had taken with him. There were two filing cabinets, a low cupboard that stood against a wall with a coffee machine and two cups resting on top, and two shelves that ran along the length of the right-hand wall containing books, stationery, and an assortment of power, USB, and other cables. A broadband router, its LED lights winking, stood on the desktop.

Johnson felt as if he were on a fishing trip. He had no clue what he might find, although his hope was that there would be something that might give clues about Schwartz's extracurricular activities: documents, communications gear, anything that might hint at surveillance or covert data transfers. He wasn't holding out much hope.

He sent another update to Jayne: *Still searching.*

Ten minutes later, Johnson had been through every folder in the filing cabinets and the few papers he found in the other cupboard. There was nothing of interest.

He sighed a little and unzipped his jacket. It was warm in the house, and he knew this could be a long search. He then began going through the other downstairs rooms, but after another quarter of an hour and three more updates to Jayne, he had still found nothing.

Johnson slowly ascended the bare wooden stairs to the upper floor, his rubber shoes squeaking a little on the polished surface. There he found four bedrooms, but only the largest was being used. Schwartz obviously led a solitary existence.

The master bedroom had wooden flooring with a couple of rugs, an en suite bathroom, a large fitted wardrobe, and three freestanding chests of drawers. The duvet was carelessly pushed to one side where Schwartz had clearly gotten out of bed in a hurry, but the room was otherwise spotlessly tidy.

Johnson went through the drawers first, but there was only a selection of underwear, handkerchiefs, and socks. He slid open the doors of the fitted wardrobes, which contained suits, shirts, and ties as well as casual clothing, ranging from jeans to T-shirts and sweat tops, and checked through the cabinets in the en suite before returning to the bedroom. There was nothing.

He sank to his haunches next to the fitted wardrobe and fingered the old wound at the top of his right ear, trying to think through his next move.

His options in terms of searching the obvious hiding places seemed to be shrinking rapidly. He had been hoping not to have to do a more extensive search, but that was rapidly becoming the likely scenario.

As he crouched, a floorboard beneath his feet gave a slight

creak. It was scarcely audible, despite the silence in the house. He lifted his foot, and the board squeaked fractionally again as it moved. Again he put his weight down, and the board moved marginally beneath him. Upon closer examination, Johnson could see that the floorboard, about nine inches wide, ran from beneath the bed to the wall at the back of the fitted wardrobe.

It was strange that the board was not 100 percent secure. There was a tiny gap, maybe just a millimeter or two, between it and the one next to it, whereas the other boards looked watertight. Johnson got down on his knees and traced the crack to the back of the wardrobe, illuminating it with the flashlight on his iPhone, which he propped against the baseboard at the back of the wardrobe.

This might be worth a closer look, he thought.

He took out a penknife and, using the smallest blade, worked it carefully into the gap between the boards. Pressing on one side for leverage, he slowly started to ease the board upward.

Johnson was concerned that the penknife blade would snap, but moments later, he had raised the board sufficiently to get a finger underneath, creating a gap of an inch or so. He put the penknife down and shone the light into the gap.

There, lying on a board in the cavity, was a round disc-shaped object made of brushed steel. There was a small button on one side, a red LED light, which was turned off, and a USB socket.

Johnson was immediately certain what this was. He had seen a similar device at Vic's house in DC only a few months earlier. The two men had discussed espionage technologies that the CIA was deploying in the field in certain sensitive territories, including Moscow, where it needed to collect data from agents in the field who were often employees of rival intelligence agencies.

It was an SRAC device, used for short-range data transfers.

He lifted the board enough to get his hand beneath, removed the SRAC device, and took several photographs of it from different angles with his phone. He momentarily contemplated switching it on but decided against it.

He was about to replace the device in the cavity when he noticed there were also three identical micro SD high-speed memory cards lying in the space. He took one of them out: it was a 32 GB SanDisk card. Should he take one? Should he take all of them? He decided against it but took photographs of the cards as well.

Was all this the gear that Schwartz had been using to communicate with Jones and pass on the information to Moscow Center? Had this been the route via which Yezhov's identity and plans had been leaked, leading to the assassination on Friedrichstrasse? It seemed highly possible.

The equipment itself was evidence enough of wrongdoing, in Johnson's view. It would certainly be sufficient to warrant the German police raiding the property and holding the owner on suspicion of espionage against the state. He sent all the photographs to Jayne and Vic using a secure message with an accompanying short note.

Interesting.

Now it was time to get out. He replaced all the items beneath the floorboard, lowered it carefully back into place, and ensured it was fitting as snugly as when he started.

Then Johnson retraced his steps out of the bedroom, across the landing, and down the stairs. His shoes again squeaked a little on the wooden stair boards.

He got to the bottom and was about to head for the door to the large open-plan room and the exit when a gruff voice came from the doorway ahead of him.

"*Was zur Hölle machen Sie hier?*" What the hell are you doing here?

Johnson jumped as if he had been electrocuted, his guts flipping over inside him, as he looked up to find a middle-aged man with a dark crew cut pointing a pistol straight at him.

CHAPTER TWELVE

Monday, March 31, 2014
Berlin

"Hold on," Johnson said in German, raising his hands slowly above his head. "I can explain—"

"Don't explain," Schwartz interrupted. "I can see that gun in your belt under your jacket. Just very slowly nudge it out so it falls on the floor, then kick it over to me. Don't pull it out by the grip. If you try anything, you will get a bullet through the head."

Johnson paused for a second, then complied with the instruction, using his fingers to ease his Beretta out from beneath the belt. It eventually fell onto the floorboards with a heavy clunk. Johnson pushed it with his foot so it slid across the boards toward Schwartz.

How the hell had Schwartz gotten back into the house without Jayne, outside in the van, seeing him?

Shit.

Had he shot her?

He must have—she had a clear view right up and down the street in both directions from her monitor screens in the van. What else would have prevented her from alerting Johnson? Schwartz's pistol had a long suppressor attached, which would explain why Johnson had heard nothing.

Shit, shit, shit.

The German slowly crouched, his eyes still fixed on Johnson and his pistol pointing, and picked up the Beretta with his left hand. He placed the weapon in his left jacket pocket and stood.

"I think I can also see the shape of a wallet in your front trouser pocket," Schwartz said. "Throw it on the floor, and your phone, and kick them here also."

Johnson slowly repeated the exercise with the wallet and phone, which Schwartz picked up.

"How did you know I was here, anyway?" Johnson asked.

"Underfloor movement sensor, you fool. It's linked to my phone. Now shut up. Keep your hands up high. Just move that way," Schwartz said, gesturing with his gun along the hallway toward the doorway to the TV room.

Johnson moved slowly along the corridor and into the TV room. Schwartz instructed him to sit on a wooden chair that stood against the wall, which he did, his mind now moving fast.

There had to be a way out of this.

Schwartz stood facing Johnson, his back to the door, the gun, which Johnson could see was a Heckler & Koch, still pointing at his head. He opened the wallet with his other hand and glanced at the credit cards and Johnson's driver's license inside.

"Joe Johnson. You are American," Schwartz said, switching to English as he closed the wallet. "Who the hell are you, and what are you doing here? Explain."

Johnson decided his best approach was to lay his cards on the table.

"I am a private investigator specializing in war crimes, but I also look at other situations as well, and here I'm working alongside the CIA and the British Secret Intelligence Service. The reason I'm here is because I'm investigating espionage activity against various countries, including Germany, the United States, and the United Kingdom. We have reason to believe that—"

"So you think it's okay to just break into someone's house? No search warrant, I am sure."

Johnson shook his head and paused for a moment. "No. I mean, we could call in the police if you prefer, but I don't think you would like us to go down that route."

"You are completely wrong. I have no connection to any espionage activity. You are mad. I have a senior job at the Ministry of Defense, and you have no right to be here."

Johnson decided to take a chance. "It seems odd that a senior Ministry of Defense employee has been developing contacts with intelligence agency officers, holding covert meetings with them in hotel rooms, and transferring data using short-range high-speed comms equipment."

Now feeling a little calmer, Johnson continued. "Perhaps you would like to tell me a little more about your career in the Stasi and your long-standing links to the SVR as well as to Western intelligence agencies. Why exactly would you have those connections on both sides?"

He surveyed Schwartz's face closely. He had been almost entirely inscrutable, but Johnson was sure he saw a flicker, a slight twitch, across the German's face when he mentioned the SVR.

"You are talking *Scheiße*. Absolute shit. There's no proof of anything," Schwartz said. "I never worked for the Stasi, and I have never had any links to intelligence officers or the SVR. Where the hell did that all come from?"

"We already have plenty of proof. And it would be easy enough to get more and then take action that would put you inside Stammheim for life," Johnson said, referring to one of Germany's most famous high-security prisons, situated on a sprawling site near Stuttgart.

"I could shoot you dead right now and end this crap."

"Go ahead. But it wouldn't end this crap, as you put it. The evidence is already with intelligence agencies. They have proof that you've been using illegal comms gear, keeping it in this house together with files saved on memory cards. You've been stealing secrets from the highest level of government, then passing them to the Russians for whom you've been working since the 1980s, haven't you? So killing me won't change a thing. Except then you'd be facing murder charges as well as espionage."

Johnson had no idea whether the bit about stealing secrets and the SVR was actually true, but he felt he had to take a gamble to pave the way for his next move, which had just come to him.

"But if you cooperate with me, I might find a way to cooperate with you," Johnson said.

Schwartz rolled his eyes. "I find this unbelievable. You are bullshitting me."

"No, we are not bullshitting you," came a woman's voice in German from the hallway. "Drop that gun now; otherwise I'll blow off the back of your head. *Now! Drop it!*"

Johnson craned his neck and caught a glimpse of Jayne, standing behind Schwartz wearing her pink Deutsche Telekom helmet and black jacket and pointing her Walther at him.

Schwartz rotated his head—he could presumably see

Jayne out of the corner of his eye. For a few seconds he said and did nothing, visibly calculating his options.

There came a deafening gunshot that echoed round the room, and a large chunk of plaster fell from the ceiling above Schwartz's head, narrowly missing him and causing a cloud of dust to spurt outward from where Jayne's round had blasted a hole in the white-painted surface.

"Drop it," Jayne repeated.

Schwartz let the H&K fall to the floor.

"Thank you. Now put your hands above your head, and kick that gun to me."

Schwartz paused for a second, but when Jayne wiggled the barrel of her gun, he raised his hands and kicked the gun to her. Johnson then walked to Schwartz and retrieved his Beretta, phone, and wallet from his pockets. As he did so, Schwartz spat in his face.

Johnson stood back and eyed the German, then wiped the spittle from his cheeks and nose. "You might just regret doing that," he said, lowering his tone a fraction.

Schwartz was staring at Jayne. "I remember you, you *bitch*," he said eventually. "Nineteen eighty-six, wasn't it?"

"Eighty-nine, I think. Good to know your memory remains almost intact," Jayne said in a level tone. "Maybe you'll be more helpful to us now than you were then."

In response, Schwartz spat again, this time in Jayne's direction, but the blob of spittle missed her.

Ten minutes later, while Jayne pointed her Walther at Schwartz's head, Johnson had lashed the German to the same wooden chair on which he had made Johnson sit, using some thin cord taken from a cupboard in the utility room.

It turned out that Jayne, in line with their preplanning, had acted after Johnson failed to give his five-minute update twice. She told Johnson that she had seen no one enter the property but assumed that something had to be wrong. So she had made her way to the rear door, which Johnson had left unlocked. Once inside, she heard Schwartz and Johnson talking and realized what had happened. Schwartz had apparently entered the property via the double doors that led off the large open-plan room to the wooden decking—one of the doors was still slightly ajar. He must have returned to the house via a neighbor's back garden, Jayne surmised. He had most likely not seen the telecoms van standing in the road or had not realized its significance.

Johnson went to the utility room, shut the door, and made a call to Vic to outline what had happened and what he was thinking of doing.

There was a short silence at the other end of the line as Vic digested Johnson's suggestion.

"Obviously, if our friends at the BND find out about this, all hell will break loose," Vic said. "They are our biggest allies in Europe, apart from Six."

"I know. But do we just let him go, then? Or would you like me to inform the BND and get them to take over seeing as it's on their territory? That should really speed things up for us."

"No, we both know we can't let him go. I'm just pointing out what you doubtless already know. There's a risk."

"I'll take that as a yes, then," Johnson said. "Will keep you updated. In the meantime, I need someone to come pronto and collect three flash drives and what I assume is an SRAC device for analysis and to extract whatever's on them. I as a private investigator don't happen to have the necessary skills or equipment to do that, unfortunately."

Johnson took the snort from Vic as confirmation that his request was going to be granted. They agreed that the SRAC and flash drives should be collected by Neal, who was still in Berlin.

Johnson's next call was to Nicklin-Donovan in London.

His reaction was guarded but also amounted to a tacit go-ahead. He made clear it was up to Johnson to get on with the job the best way he could.

"I just need to be able to say it's not my operation," Nicklin-Donovan said.

"I know," Johnson said. "But let's keep this real. You're up to your neck in it. It's your Berlin head of station's activities we're trying to get to the bottom of."

There was a long pause at the other end of the line. "Yes, yes," Nicklin-Donovan said eventually. "But just remember that if things go sideways, you're both out of there, and the investigation is finished, as far as I'm concerned. I'll help wherever I can—beneath the counter."

Johnson then returned to the TV room and stood in front of Schwartz. "Now it's your turn to talk. I'll give you two options. The first is we call your Ministry of Defense and inform them about the comms equipment I found in your bedroom and the flash drives and your covert meetings and turn you over to German criminal investigators. Or you could help us, in which case we might find a window of time during which you can clear up your affairs here in Germany and disappear off to wherever you want to go. It must be obvious that either way, your career at the ministry is finished. If you want to keep some sort of freedom, help us."

Johnson felt something gnawing at the inside of his stomach as he spoke. It went utterly against the grain for him to allow someone who appeared to have committed treason to have an option to walk away, but he felt the chances of getting the information he needed were otherwise minimal.

And he needed that information.

The alternative was to involve getting the German police and prosecutors involved, and that would almost certainly become a massively drawn-out, complex legal and judicial process during which Schwartz would inevitably say little of help.

In that scenario, the chances were almost zero of finding out immediately whether Jones really was the mole at the heart of Western intelligence. And even if there was a possibility of getting the information further down the line, it might take so long that more critical secrets might be leaked in the meantime, causing all kinds of other damage.

Moreover, and just as important from Johnson's point of view, it would also mean losing any chance of finding out the information that Yezhov had been carrying about the La Belle bombing twenty-eight years earlier. Schwartz was their only lead at the moment.

But Schwartz shook his head at Johnson's offer. "Go screw yourself," he said.

CHAPTER THIRTEEN

Thursday, April 3, 2014
  Berlin

Once it became clear that Schwartz was not going to cooperate, the CIA team eventually had little choice but to transfer him to the Limonenstrasse safe house. He wasn't falling for the bluff of calling the German authorities, and the risks attached to keeping him at his home were too great. There was no way of knowing what visitors, private or from the ministry—or worse, the SVR—might turn up at any point.

At the safe house, one of Johnson's concerns was that they were forcibly detaining a German national in a country where they had no jurisdiction. They were all effectively committing kidnap. He knew it was extremely unlikely that Schwartz would later go to the German police, but nevertheless, it was an issue.

He took Vic and Neal to one side. "I know this is about the greater good, but we could all end up in a German prison here."

Vic averted his gaze. "What's the alternative? I don't want to do it. I'd rather keep my team as much at arm's length as I can. It's your investigation. But . . ." His voice trailed off.

"But it's partly about your brother, so you'll do it."

Vic shrugged. "Yes. We're going to have to be flexible in our approach, and let's be honest, this guy is the only lead."

"I agree," Neal said. "When we eventually let him go, he's not going to complain to the police, is he? He's guilty of treason up to his neck."

Johnson paced slowly to a two-way mirror that allowed a view into the room next door, where Schwartz was sitting, guarded by two armed CIA officers, his wrists and ankles bound with black plastic flex-cuffs.

"I'll do the questioning, then, with Jayne," Johnson said. He turned to look at Vic. "Your guys can take charge of the physical stuff. I don't want any of your specials, though. No pharma treatment, mind drugs, waterboarding, electrics on his testicles. You know what I'm saying?"

Vic frowned. "Agreed. This guy isn't Spetsnaz or SEAL material—he may crack."

For the next three days they kept Schwartz in a bare room with light-proofed windows—a makeshift interrogation suite —so that he would not know the time of day. He remained strapped to a chair, apart from toilet breaks, was given water but no food apart from an occasional banana, and they used a shift system and an electronic device to keep him awake while continuing their questioning. The unit, which had pads attached to his chest, gave him a mild electric shock if he fell asleep and emitted a series of raucous squawks.

Johnson just had to hope it worked. Enforcing sleepless-ness and hunger was one thing. Breaking fingers and water-boarding were quite another.

Nevertheless, they needed answers somehow if they were to move forward in any direction. Johnson had it in the forefront of his mind that it wasn't just about Vic's brother and what happened at La Belle. It was about pinpointing a mole working at the highest levels of Western intelligence whose ongoing leaks were likely to put at risk the lives of many good men and women—CIA and MI6 agents working in sensitive positions in hostile environments.

In the meantime, the CIA station's data analysis experts went to work on the three micro SD cards and the SRAC device.

It turned out that the flash memory on the SRAC had been wiped clean, but it was very similar to a couple of other devices that had been captured from Russian agents over the past few years, including one in Washington, DC, and another in Helsinki. The unit was capable of receiving and transmitting data at very high speeds and operated on a high-capacity, long-life lithium battery.

Two of the SD cards were empty, but the third contained four files, all encrypted, the keys for which proved resistant to the efforts of the local CIA team.

Eventually, Jayne contacted a long-standing friend, Alice Hocking, at GCHQ, the UK's Government Communication Headquarters, based at Cheltenham, with whom she had liaised regularly during her years at MI6. Alice, in turn, pressed someone in GCHQ's Edgehill data decryption program team to try and unlock the documents.

At the same time, Johnson and Vic had a meeting with Gareth Power, head of the Special Collection Service at Pariser Platz. The SCS was the highly classified joint unit set up by the CIA and the National Security Agency, the US government agency focused on collating so-called signals intelligence, with communications at its core, particularly in monitoring of phone, email, and internet traffic.

The SCS's Berlin unit had been monitoring Yezhov's

communications traffic round the clock from the day he indicated he was going to defect. Johnson requested that they
revisit the captured material, with a special focus on calls,
emails, and messages sent to Yezhov's wife, Varvara, and their
two children. Johnson knew from long experience of dealing
with defectors that scraps of crucial evidence could often be
found in communications to and from families.

Perhaps there might also be copies of documents hidden
at his family home. Unlikely, but possible.

Power promised to carry out a full audit and report back
as quickly as possible.

On Thursday morning, Johnson tried once again to
persuade Schwartz to talk, reiterating that he had no intention of turning him over to the German authorities. Schwartz
was now in a zombielike state from hunger and lack of sleep
and struggled to keep his body upright in the chair.

This time, rather than make vague references to meetings
that he knew Schwartz had conducted with intelligence officers, he decided to be a little more specific. He referred to
sources inside the British embassy building whom he believed
Schwartz had recruited, specifically an MI6 officer. It was as
far as Johnson felt he could go without compromising Jones.

Somewhat to Johnson's surprise, after several days of
refusing to communicate, Schwartz finally began to talk.

"You have talked about the Stasi and the SVR," Schwartz
said in a whisper, his voice bubbling through spittle that had
collected around his mouth and over his chin. A thick layer of
stubble covered his face.

"Yes," Johnson said. He had mentioned them several
times, although in general terms.

"I was in the Stasi, correct. And I have had links with the
SVR for some time."

Schwartz appeared to have raised the white flag.

"When were you in the Stasi?" Johnson asked. He wanted to verify what he had been given from the MI6 files.

"Until 1991. Until then I always worked for them."

"In Berlin?"

"Yes, at the Normannenstrasse headquarters."

Johnson made a mental note to return to the topic of the Stasi in the '80s later in the interrogation. Maybe Schwartz knew of people or operations that might help unearth the information that Yezhov had intended to bring about La Belle—although he didn't want to refer directly to Yezhov. That was far too sensitive.

For now, though, the more urgent task was to establish Schwartz's part in current espionage activities.

"So you have been passing the SVR information from your employer, yes?"

"I have done some of that, and I have also acted as a *Vermittler*, how do you say, a 'go-between,' for some information from other sources."

"Go on," Johnson said, leaning back in his chair, his mind now whirring. "What other sources?"

Despite the bindings that held his arms fast to the side of the chair in which he was sitting, Schwartz's body slumped down as far as it could go and his chin fell to his chest.

Johnson jumped to his feet. Had the German suffered a heart attack or stroke?

But after a few seconds, the German's head lifted a little. "The information, the documents, came from other intelligence agencies, from government sources, from highly placed civil servants. But not people whom I meet, or handle, or people I know. I am just a go-between, like I said. I do not even know what is in the files I pass on. They are all encrypted."

"Right. So you receive this information and you pass it on

to Moscow Center?" Johnson asked. "How do you receive it and pass it on?"

Schwartz gave a slight shake of the head. "I do not know who provides it. I receive it either on an SD card from a courier, at a dead drop site in Berlin, or electronically, using a receiver. I travel frequently to Moscow and St. Petersburg for business, and I pass the drives on to an SVR person at that time."

"How often?"

Schwartz shrugged. He paused, seemingly trying to catch his breath before replying. "Every two, three, maybe four weeks. It depends."

"When was the last time?"

Schwartz's head rolled backward, and another dribble made its way down his chin. "It was about two weeks ago."

"Before March 21?" Johnson asked. That had been the date of Yezhov's assassination.

"I think March 18."

Johnson nodded. That most likely explained how details of the Yezhov operation had been transmitted to Moscow Center. The plan had only been finalized in the few days prior to that.

"When are you expected to receive the next lot of files, and when are you expected to travel again?" Johnson asked.

Schwartz shook his head. "There is nothing planned."

"How do you get communications from your handlers?"

"We use a secure message service on my phone."

"Show me the messages."

Johnson picked up Schwartz's cell phone from the table. The CIA team had previously scoured the phone, which required Schwartz's thumbprint to gain access, but had found only personal messages, contacts, and documents.

Johnson stepped over to Schwartz, grabbed his right

thumb, and pressed it to the button at the bottom of the screen. Schwartz directed him to a messaging facility that was concealed deep within one of the social media apps that were loaded onto the device. It required an additional six-digit password to gain access.

Johnson tut-tutted internally at the CIA team's failure to spot the facility as he scrolled down the list of messages. All were extremely brief and mainly consisted of dates, times, and locations using GPS coordinates. The last message received was dated March 17.

Thank you. Received safely. Will advise next delivery when ready, it said in German.

"These are all from your handler, are they?" Johnson asked.

"Yes."

"What is his name?"

"I only know him by a code name—VIPER."

"Are you sure there is nothing scheduled? No deliveries, no meetings?" Johnson's immediate concern was that Schwartz's handler would realize from a missed appointment or delivery or a failure to respond to a message, that he had been blown.

Schwartz screwed up his face but shook his head. "Nothing."

"Do you have to check in to tell them you are alive and available or something?"

Schwartz nodded.

"When is the next check-in?" Johnson asked.

"What day is it today? I've lost track."

Johnson wasn't surprised. "It's Thursday. The third."

"It's today, then."

This time Johnson battled to avoid rolling his eyes. "What is the message you need to send?"

"Just three words: *alles ist gut*. Everything is fine."

Johnson had little choice but to trust that the information was accurate. He had no way of verifying it, but his instinct was that Schwartz was telling the truth.

"We are going to send that message now," he said. "If I find out you are lying, you'll regret it. Tell me what to do."

Reluctantly, Schwartz directed Johnson on how to compose and send the message.

"Thank you," Johnson said after he had pressed the send button. He stroked his chin. "Maybe the files, the information, you receive come from an agent in MI6?" He continued, "Perhaps one who is based here in Berlin? Maybe he gives you SD cards, or you pick up his short-range transmissions using that receiver of yours?"

"I swear. I do not have contact with any agents inside MI6 giving me information," Schwartz croaked.

Johnson leaned forward. "You are not telling me the truth. I know you had a secret meeting in a hotel room only a few days ago with an MI6 officer who works here in Berlin."

"That is true that I had a meeting, but it is not what you think."

Schwartz was in such a state by this stage that he could hardly speak. From his long experience of interviewing and interrogating suspects, Johnson was convinced that finally, some truth was emerging, although it would all require thorough checking to corroborate the facts.

He turned to Vic, who was standing behind him. "Let's give him some food. He's starting to cooperate. Maybe something to eat will encourage him further."

Johnson turned back to Schwartz. "In that case, please do tell me what I should really think, then."

"The truth is not that he was passing information to me or that I was recruiting him," Schwartz said, his voice now scarcely audible. "No. Actually, he was trying to recruit me. He has been trying for a long time."

"What was your reply?"

"I said no."

"So where do your files and your SD cards that you pass to Moscow come from originally?" Johnson asked.

"I understand from London."

CHAPTER FOURTEEN

Thursday, April 3, 2014
Berlin

A few hours after Schwartz's disclosure in the interview room, the Edgehill team at GCHQ returned the documents to Jayne, via Alice, on the SD card by secure transfer. Thankfully all had been unlocked.

It quickly became evident that the documents were copies of internal CIA and MI6 material that had already been circulated to a number of people, including Vic and Nicklin-Donovan. They related to two joint intelligence-gathering operations being run by the CIA and MI6: one in Turkey, the other in Ukraine. Both were concerned with a series of complex moves to counter Russian operations designed to unmask British- and American-run assets in the respective governments of those two countries.

If the plans were now in the hands of Moscow Center—which Johnson and Vic assumed had to be the case—then all of those operations were effectively blown.

Vic and Johnson went for a walk in the Botanic Garden, with its sprawling array of winding paths, to discuss the findings in a location where there was no danger of being overheard and no listening devices would be present. After checking carefully for any sign of surveillance, they sat on a bench.

Vic took out his phone and checked his emails. He bent over the screen, concentrating on the contents of one of them, then turned to Johnson.

"I've just been sent a precise list of CIA and MI6 people with clearances to access those documents that Schwartz had," Vic said. "There are, unfortunately, quite a few people in those specific security compartments in both services."

"Including Rick Jones?"

"Here's the interesting thing, Doc. The answer to that is no. He's not on the list for any of those documents. Nobody in Berlin is. They're all in London apart from a few in the local stations in Kiev, Ankara, and Istanbul."

Vic had christened Johnson with the nickname Doc during their stint together in Pakistan and Afghanistan after learning that he had spent four years in the early 1980s, prior to joining the CIA, doing a PhD on the economics of the Third Reich at the Freie Universität in Berlin.

After a pause, Vic continued. "So unless someone else in London has passed them to Jones, which I believe is not the case, he is not the source of the leak that went to Schwartz."

Johnson exhaled. The GCHQ findings and the list that Vic had received completely corroborated what Schwartz had eventually told him and which Johnson now believed to be the truth.

He stood. "We're going to need a lot more information from Schwartz about his London connections, and I need to grill him about the '80s too. We can't afford to let him go, but . . ."

"But what?" Vic asked.

Johnson shook his head. "I'm worried this could cause a diplomatic firestorm. The Germans, from Angela Merkel downward, would go berserk if they knew we were holding him, no matter what this guy has done or whatever information he's telling us—*they* would expect to be handling it, not us. It's been four days."

"You're right." Vic threw up his hands. "But what other options do we have? Anyway, given he's been committing high treason, he's not exactly going to complain to the police, is he? And as you've said, his job at the ministry is over."

Johnson inclined his head in acknowledgment. "But I'm also worried about the SVR. I know we've sent that *alles ist gut* message, but it's still possible it could be a coded alert to indicate he was under duress rather than a reassurance."

"Possible. But I doubt it. Let's get back there and get on with the questioning."

When they walked into the safe house in Limonenstrasse after a forty-five-minute circuitous route to ensure they were not being followed, Schwartz was asleep on a long brown leather sofa, an empty plate of what had been spaghetti Bolognese lying on the floor next to him. He was guarded at gunpoint by one of the CIA security staff.

"Wake him up," Vic said.

"He's only just gone to sleep," the guard said.

"Just wake him. Do it."

The guard pulled Schwartz upright but he immediately fell back down again, still unconscious. The guard slapped his face. Eventually, his eyes remained open, albeit unfocused, and he hauled himself up to a sitting position.

Vic ordered the guard to leave, then poured a strong black coffee from a flask on a table and instructed Schwartz to drink it. The German left it untouched.

Johnson sat with Jayne and Vic opposite Schwartz on the other sofa.

"Thank you for the information you have given us so far," Johnson began. "It has been very helpful."

"I will kill you bastards when I'm out of here," Schwartz said, his eyes glazed from the lack of sleep. "Don't thank me."

"I'm sure you will. But there are a few other questions I have."

"Go screw yourself." Schwartz slumped back into the cushions.

Johnson stood and did a lap of the sofa, then stood in front of Schwartz, his hands on his hips. "Listen, we can put you back on the same diet as you were on previously and tie you back to the chair until you talk again, if you prefer. Just let me know."

The German remained silent, which Johnson took as a sign of surrender. He sat down again.

"We need to know more about the London connection," Johnson said. "Now drink that coffee."

Schwartz reluctantly drank the coffee and sat there, a sullen expression on his face.

"The SD cards that I pass on to Moscow come from a courier who travels from London to Berlin," Schwartz said eventually. "The courier deposits them with VIPER, who lives here, and then I collect them and take them to Moscow."

"Where do you collect them from VIPER? At his house?"

"No, at a safe house." Schwartz gave an address in the Kreuzberg area of Berlin.

"How do you know about the courier?" Johnson asked.

"I bumped into him once, by accident. We both arrived at VIPER's safe house at the same time. There had been some mix-up, a mistake, with the meeting times. We spoke briefly."

"Where does the courier collect his SD cards from—do

you know?"

This time there was a long silence. Schwartz's eyes appeared unfocused, and Johnson wondered if he was about to fall asleep again.

"Schwartz," Johnson said in a sharp tone.

The German blinked slowly and shook his head, as if to refocus. "I do know. There is a dead drop in London. I know because I had to collect a drive from there once, six months ago. There was a problem with the courier. It was urgent, so I traveled there instead."

Johnson leaned forward. Now he was getting somewhere.

"Where is the dead drop? Is it an apartment? Do you know who deposits the items there?"

"It is not an apartment."

"What then? A hole in a wall somewhere?"

"A motorbike."

"A *motorbike?*"

"Yes."

"How does that work, then?" Johnson said.

"When needed, it is left locked up near St. Paul's Cathedral. I was given a code to undo the lock on the pannier bag. One of those fixed fiberglass panniers. The SD card was inside."

Very clever, Johnson thought. A flexible, mobile drop site that could be loaded elsewhere, then left along with lots of other motorbikes in a busy, fairly secure location, arousing zero suspicion.

"Where exactly is the motorbike left?" Johnson asked.

"It's in a bay on the corner of Bread Street and Cannon Street, a short distance from the cathedral."

"Do you know the license plate number for the bike?" Johnson asked.

Schwartz closed his eyes. "I did know. I can't remember all of it. It had a number *11* in it, followed by three letters,

PXX. I know that bit. There were also two letters at the start, but I can't recall them."

"All right, that might do," Johnson said. He had enough information for now on the mole, but there still remained the question of Schwartz's past with the Stasi in the '80s and whether he could shed any light on what information Yezhov might have been intending to pass on regarding La Belle.

"Do the words *La Belle* mean anything to you?" Johnson asked.

Schwartz shrugged. "If you are talking about the disco bomb, yes, I know of what happened. It was a long time ago."

"Apparently there is information relating to that bomb attack that has not been disclosed previously. An informer was intending to give us that information but has been unable to do so."

"Gennady Yezhov, you mean?"

Johnson could not help recoiling a little. How the hell did Schwartz know about Yezhov?

"Don't worry, I know what happened to him a couple of weeks ago," Schwartz said. "I keep my ears open. I knew Yezhov from the 1980s. He was KGB in Berlin when I was in the Stasi."

Johnson lifted his eyebrows. "In that case, you might be more use than I thought you would be. What I would like to know is whether there is anyone who might have some insight as to what Yezhov was going to tell us about La Belle. Who knew about it?"

Schwartz gave a short, low-pitched laugh. "Everyone knew a little about it. Not many knew much."

"Explain."

"There were rumors."

"What rumors?" Johnson asked.

"About who was behind it."

"The Libyans were convicted in court."

Schwartz laughed again. "Yes, they were convicted. The question is whether others should have been too."

"Such as?"

"I don't know. I was at the fringe of it all. But maybe certain Soviet and East German intelligence people."

Johnson consciously suppressed his instinct to jerk upward. Instead he calmly leaned forward. This was obviously significant, but was Schwartz telling the truth?

"Well, who?" Johnson asked. "If you're saying that, you must have someone in mind."

"I don't know. I just heard that a few individuals in the KGB and Stasi people knew more about La Belle than has come out."

Johnson could feel his adrenaline start to pump again.

"Well, is there anyone who might be able to tell me more?" Johnson asked.

And if you say "I don't know" one more time, I'll punch you.

Schwartz shrugged. "Have you spoken to Yezhov's wife, Varvara?"

Johnson, Vic, and Jayne had discussed at some length about trying to talk to Yezhov's wife. But she lived in St. Petersburg, and the logistics of getting into Russia were complex: it would have to be done under a false identity. It was also far too risky to call her, as her lines would inevitably be all monitored by the FSB's communications experts at the Lubyanka.

"Should we meet with her?" Johnson asked.

"I think you should," Schwartz replied. "She was also KGB at that time. That's how she and Gennady met. They operated together in Berlin—they were a work team, and they were lovers."

A KGB work team, and lovers. Even as Schwartz spoke, an idea came to Johnson as to how he could sneak into St. Petersburg undercover to find Varvara Yezhova.

PART TWO

CHAPTER FIFTEEN

Thursday, April 3, 2014
London

"Hello, this is Anna from Private Finance Advice Line," the electronic voice coming from the synthesizer said. "Have you been sold payment protection insurance at any time in the last three years? If so, we might be able to help. We have four simple checks we would like to run through with you."

As usual, there was a quick response. "No, thank you, I'm not interested." The line went dead.

Anastasia Shevchenko turned off her burner phone and took out the SIM card and battery. The SIM was consigned to a bin hanging beneath a lamp post near the Baker Street underground station on Marylebone Road, just after she had turned a corner and was confident she was not being observed.

Her coded message had confirmed the previously arranged meeting—for April 3 at four o'clock—with her agent ANTELOPE.

Now Shevchenko needed to make her way to the SVR safe house, an apartment in the St. John's Wood area of London.

ANTELOPE was the crown jewel in the network of agents whom Shevchenko had recruited in various foreign capitals over several years. The agent, an international operator with years of experience, had only been on board for a few months but had already provided a wealth of extremely high-quality intelligence that had enabled the SVR to put an end to various damaging operations run against Moscow by the CIA and MI6.

ANTELOPE had also rooted out a number of SVR traitors who had betrayed the Motherland in return for large sums of money, of which Colonel Gennady Yezhov was the latest.

Despite the glow of achievement that she currently carried inside her, however, Shevchenko knew that she was taking a lot of risk in continuing to meet and handle ANTE-LOPE in person: it had to end soon. Yezhov's attempted defection had been a close call, a wake-up alarm—if he hadn't been shot in Berlin, she and her agent would have been blown.

As with all the other agents Shevchenko had recruited inside Western intelligence, she could not continue the meetings herself indefinitely. She had therefore arranged with her colleagues in Directorate S at Moscow Center to be substituted by an "illegal"—a civilian who was not operating under diplomatic cover and who never went near the Russian embassy. Most illegals were expatriate Russians operating under false passports and doing ordinary day jobs such as IT contractors, filing clerks, and even lecturers.

The illegal in this case would be Natalia Espinosa, a raven-haired single mother of two. She was the same person who was currently collecting Shevchenko's own dispatches of leaked documents and placing them in a dead drop near St. Paul's Cathedral for a courier to collect and ferry to Moscow, usually via Berlin.

Shevchenko had never met Natalia and normally left Directorate S to pass on messages, but she had seen her file. She held Spanish and Russian passports, thanks to having a father from Barcelona and a mother from Moscow, where she had grown up. The Spanish passport enabled Espinosa to enter and live in the UK quite freely, and she had worked in London for the previous two decades as a freelance language teacher.

The illegals were tasked with collecting information from agents either via occasional personal meetings or more normally by using short-range agent communications units, or SRACs. This technology enabled encrypted data to be transmitted wirelessly over short distances in very short concentrated bursts between small, portable individual devices, making it difficult to intercept. Sometimes the receiving device would be permanently buried in a secure location so files could be uploaded and downloaded by means of simply passing near to the unit on foot or in a slow-moving vehicle. The information would then be dispatched onward to Moscow either electronically or more likely on micro SD memory cards that were transported using old-fashioned couriers.

Shevchenko had already ordered the necessary SRAC kit from Moscow Center for ANTELOPE to use.

Once Natalia was in place and operating as intended, Shevchenko would head back to Moscow. Indeed, she had notified the Russian ambassador in London of her intentions to move back in eleven days' time, on April 14.

She expected that ANTELOPE would then be able to continue operating completely undetected for years to come, doing indescribable damage to Russia's rival intelligence operations globally.

Shevchenko set off on her surveillance detection route. She was certain that there would be coverage of some kind. It was rare for them to leave her alone. But she mostly managed to find a way to see them off, and if she didn't, she just aborted and tried again the next day.

Mostly she went on foot and used underground trains and the ubiquitous red buses that went everywhere in the capital, but sometimes she used her car, a black BMW 5 Series sedan, that she kept parked near her apartment in Dorset Square, close to Marylebone station.

Today her route took her into the Baker Street underground, where she rode two stops southbound down the Bakerloo line to Oxford Circus, walked around the labyrinth of tunnels and corridors for twenty minutes, then swapped lines and went straight back north again, returning to Baker Street.

One of Shevchenko's greatest assets was a more or less photographic memory for faces. Coupled with a ratlike sense for danger, it was something that had gotten her out of trouble on many occasions during her career.

Now there were a couple of faces she thought she'd seen at Baker Street previously: a middle-aged man carrying an umbrella and a girl in her late twenties wearing a denim jacket, seemingly engrossed in a book. So she repeated the same exercise, this time heading north two stops to Edgware Road, where she again changed lines and went back the way she had come. This time, she got off one stop down the line, exiting the car just before the doors closed, and waited for the next train before continuing back to Baker Street.

Now there were no repeating faces, nobody behaving remotely surreptitiously, turning to avert their faces or swiftly entering stairwells or ducking down corridors. Nobody who she would have bracketed as possible MI6 surveillance candidates. But she needed to do much more to be certain. She exited Baker Street station, walked past Madame Tussauds, and turned left into Regent's Park.

The open acres of the park, with its array of avenues, pathways, and sports fields, would flush out any observers, and she took a long, long walk right up past London Zoo, pausing to sit on a bench, drink a coffee at a café, and watch a game of soccer. Eventually, she began to loop back westward, making her way toward her destination.

She hailed a taxi and got the driver to drop her at the northwestern corner of the park. There she entered an apartment block with eight floors, slipping in as a resident came out of the security door. She bypassed the elevators and began climbing up the stairwell, pausing for a minute or two at each landing. This was her final check. If nobody came running up the stairwell after her now, she was clear.

Shevchenko could not afford to make a mistake. But by the fifth floor, she was finally satisfied that all was well.

Carefully, she put on a woolen hat and a pair of nonprescription glasses, turned her double-sided jacket inside out, making it look blue instead of beige, and descended to ground level. She exited the building and continued on a zigzag route that took her to the apartment building where ANTELOPE should be waiting.

She just hoped that ANTELOPE had taken just as much care with surveillance detection precautions as she had.

CHAPTER SIXTEEN

Thursday, April 3, 2014
London

When Shevchenko finally arrived, ANTELOPE was sitting in an armchair in the apartment on the seventh floor of a modern nine-story building on St. John's Wood Road, overlooking Lord's Cricket Ground. The SVR had acquired the apartment on a long lease through an anonymous front company, and it was the location where Shevchenko most often met her agent.

Shevchenko did not understand cricket but had been to a couple of games at Lord's in an attempt to find out more and to give her something to discuss with her British contacts, particularly the male ones, who seemed to think of little else, especially in summer. She had done the same with football and baseball when she had been based in the *rezidentura* in Washington, DC, and had been to see a few of the Washington Redskins and Washington Nationals games. Conversations about sports were definitely an icebreaker in diplomatic circles.

Today, as was normally the case, it was just the two of them at the safe house, which was less than a mile from where ANTELOPE lived in Maida Vale.

"Congratulations," Shevchenko said as she removed her jacket. "The information you provided on Yezhov was outstanding. There was much at stake."

"Probably both of our jobs," ANTELOPE said in a dry tone. "Thank you. It's what you're paying me for."

"Yes indeed." It was precisely why on the first day of every month thirty thousand euros were transferred from an SVR account and deposited in ANTELOPE's numbered account in Zürich. So far, the agent had earned it.

"I am guessing that there was a nuclear explosion at Vauxhall Cross and Grosvenor Square when the news about Yezhov came through?" Shevchenko asked as she sat down in an armchair facing directly toward her agent.

Grosvenor Square in the exclusive Mayfair district was the site of the US embassy and CIA station in London, although work was already underway to move it to another location three miles away south of the River Thames, at Nine Elms.

"I hear it went ballistic," ANTELOPE said in a level tone of voice. "There is a witch hunt going on already for the source of the leak, as you might expect. But the fact that it was a joint operation does help to muddy the waters, so to speak. They don't know which direction to look in."

"Good. The strategy is working, from that point of view."

"Yes, there is a lot of embarrassment that such a valuable defector was not brought in successfully. It was a massive failure. But there is a downside to that too."

"What?"

"My understanding is that they have got an outsider to run an unofficial independent inquiry. I think they want deniability and don't want a full high-profile internal inquest going on, which might be more damaging if knowledge of it were to become public. They might have to brief the politicians. So they seem to have opted for something lower key but potentially dangerous. However, so far no progress has been made, as far as I understand."

Shevchenko didn't like the sound of this investigation. She poured a glass of water from a jug on the coffee table in front of her and topped up ANTELOPE's, then glanced around the room, silent for a few moments. The apartment was sparsely but comfortably furnished with flat-pack items mainly bought from IKEA. It was a typical SVR safe house, not designed for long stays but rather shorter meetings.

"Who is running the inquiry?" she asked eventually, leaning back in her chair.

"It's a strange one. He is a friend of Vic Walter, the CIA's new operations directorate chief. He's an independent war crimes investigator, used to work for the CIA years ago. Name of Joe Johnson. He has a strong track record. He got fired by the CIA in 1988 but then worked very successfully from 1990 to 2006 as a Nazi hunter for the Department of Justice in the States—their Office of Special Investigations unit. He's got unorthodox ways of working, apparently, which I also don't like."

"Why did the CIA fire him?"

"An operation in Afghanistan went wrong," ANTELOPE said.

"And war crimes? Why the hell would he get involved in this, then?"

"He was brought in for the planned debriefing of Yezhov because there was some information he apparently had relating to bomb attacks in Berlin in the '80s where a lot of Americans were killed or injured. The idea was that Johnson would tackle that aspect. It's his specialty. Then after Yezhov was removed from the equation, they seem to have somehow pressed him to investigate the leak. I don't know. Hopefully it won't come to anything, but you need to know."

ANTELOPE held out a phone and showed Shevchenko two photographs. The first was of Johnson, the second was of Vic Walter. "These are the two men."

Shevchenko recognized Walter, whom she had bumped into a couple of times at diplomatic functions, but not Johnson. She scrutinized the photograph, memorizing his features, and handed the phone back.

"Thank you, that is helpful. Now, what else have you got for me? Are there any more military secrets coming through?"

Since ANTELOPE had begun working for Shevchenko, a whole stream of military intelligence had been handed over. Most recently, this had included incredibly valuable advance information about the planned naval responses by NATO generally, and the US in particular to Russia's politically and militarily bold move to take over the Crimean Peninsula from the Ukraine.

ANTELOPE reached into a small black backpack and removed a micro SD, placing it on the table in front of Shevchenko. "Here. There's more details there of American and British plans to build up their military presence in the Black Sea. The documents show that the US may send in a destroyer, the USS *Donald Cook*, which has guided missiles, and at least one other, maybe more."

"When?"

"Very soon. It doesn't say precisely when. I will notify you if I find out."

Shevchenko leaned forward. *Dermo*, she thought. Shit. "Destroyers, or carriers?" She knew that one carrier, the USS *George H. W. Bush*, was in the Mediterranean. Since Russia's invasion and annexation of the Crimean Peninsula, completed only a few weeks earlier, there had been talk of the US sending it from there through the Bosporus Strait past

Istanbul and into the Black Sea within reach of the Crimea. The prospect of a military conflict there seemed very real.

"Carriers are highly unlikely at this stage," ANTELOPE said. "It would not be the most sensible move, and I do not think the Pentagon is at that point. The Bosporus is narrow. The carrier is nuclear-powered. It could get trapped; it could get attacked. Very dangerous. I don't think so. Read the documents. They spell it out. But the destroyers . . . that's another question. They could go through to the Black Sea. It would be a tough military statement by the US. Putin would be furious."

"What weapons does the *Donald Cook* carry?" Shevchenko asked.

"Like I said, guided missiles. There's Tomahawk cruise missiles. Dozens of them—with a 1,500-mile range. Also Harpoon antiship missiles."

Shevchenko nodded. "It's gold, this naval intelligence. The president will be highly delighted with it. If you hear any more about precise timings of moves by this destroyer, please inform me immediately."

She knew the material would be on Putin's desk within hours of her getting it to Moscow and would earn her another major step in her climb up the promotional ladder. She didn't need to spell out that the intelligence would enable Russia's air force and navy to prepare a response should US destroyers sail through the Bosporus. The city of Istanbul had been built on both the east and west shores of the narrow straits, which were only between a third of a mile and two miles across. It was an international waterway of great strategic importance and only about 320 miles from the Crimea.

ANTELOPE shrugged. "There's other material on the drive too. I won't go through it now. You can read it for yourself."

Normally Shevchenko sent her leaked documents to only

two people at Yasenevo: to Yevgeny Kutsik, the first deputy director in charge of Directorate KR, responsible for foreign counterintelligence, to whom she reported officially, and also to the overall SVR director, Maksim Kruglov, whose job she ultimately coveted and to whom she was close, much to Kutsik's annoyance.

However, these documents, plus some of the other information she had just gleaned from ANTELOPE, would go to one other person, too, who she knew for certain would be more than interested in the Black Sea military details and the information about the investigation into Yezhov's death.

Shevchenko glanced at her watch. "We should go. We've had long enough. There is one other thing I would like to discuss, and that is how we will handle you in the future."

ANTELOPE raised an eyebrow. "Go on."

"It is too dangerous for both of us to continue meeting in person like this for much longer. This investigation that is underway, the hostile atmosphere on the street, constant surveillance. It makes it difficult to operate. I want to put an illegal in charge of collecting this intelligence from you, and we can do some of it electronically too."

Shevchenko went on to outline in some detail what her plans were, how the illegal would operate, and how the information would be deposited by ANTELOPE and how it would be collected.

"When do you want to do this?" ANTELOPE asked.

"I should get the SRAC kit within the next few days or so from Moscow Center, and I will give it to you as soon as I get it. We will then have a short handover period before I withdraw to Moscow on April 14. That way you can get accustomed to using it."

"That sounds safer, I agree."

Shevchenko reached into her black backpack and removed a slim circular steel device with a USB port, an SD memory card port, and a couple of LED lights on the top. She showed it to ANTELOPE. "This is what you will get, one of these. I'll show you how to operate it."

She flicked a small black switch on the side of the SRAC device, then took the SD memory card that ANTELOPE had given her and pushed it into the port. Immediately, a red LED flashed twice, then held a steady red for about ten seconds. Then the green LED came on, flashed three times, and remained on.

"That's it. All loaded," Shevchenko said as she turned the device off. "Your files are on there now. All I need to do now is upload them wirelessly to the master device, and my illegal will pick them up once I give a signal. She'll put them on another encrypted SD card and leave it in a dead drop where a courier will collect it to take to Moscow."

It was a safe system. The idea of Shevchenko herself loading a dead drop site, given the surveillance she was under, was unthinkable. If an MI6 team spotted her, they would keep the site under twenty-four-hour watch, and then whoever unloaded the material would be a dead duck. The use of an anonymous illegal to do it instead was an excellent safeguard.

"So once I have an SRAC, I can upload wirelessly directly to the master," ANTELOPE said. "That streamlines the process, doesn't involve you, and is more secure."

"Correct," Shevchenko said. "I'd like you to do a couple of practice runs at some point, once we have the kit, to ensure it is all working properly. I will let you know when I have your SRAC. At present, we have only one base station, in Regent's Park, plus a backup there as well."

ANTELOPE nodded. "Anything else I need to know?"

"I am arranging for a second base station to be set up, also not too far from your apartment," Shevchenko said. "Somewhere where you might reasonably go for an evening stroll or drive past on a routine shopping trip. Another park, perhaps, or maybe near to the Regent's Canal towpath."

She knew that ANTELOPE's apartment was only a short distance from the Regent's Canal that wound its way through the Paddington and Maida Vale areas, and its towpath was helpfully secluded in certain places yet also very close to nearby streets. That would be an ideal location to bury a base station because it gave the option of uploading material either from the car or on foot.

Shevchenko leaned back in her chair. "When we've completed all that, you will be sewn up tight. MI6 and the CIA will never be able to trace you after that—and they won't trace me either. I will be back to Moscow."

* * *

Thursday, April 3, 2014
London

After leaving the safe house, Shevchenko walked back to Regent's Park, past the London Central Mosque, with its golden dome glinting in the afternoon sunshine, and along Hanover Gate with its statuesque plane trees and black iron railings. She made her way toward the park's boating lake, with its green-painted Boathouse Café and outdoor tables, but before she reached it, she turned sharply right along a footpath.

She continued along the footpath, which ran parallel to the lake to her left and the Outer Circle street to her right, for about four hundred meters until she came to a bench.

There she sat, took a pack of cigarettes from her bag, lit one, and leaned back to smoke and to observe. There was the usual crowd of mothers with strollers, dog walkers, and schoolchildren joking with each other and teasing.

But she was certain she remained black.

Shevchenko felt in her backpack and, without removing the SRAC device, found the switch with her fingertips and clicked it on. She counted silently to twenty, then opened the backpack and glanced inside, just to be certain.

The green LED light on top of the SRAC was glowing steadily. The transfer, which was encrypted and lasted no more than a couple of seconds, had taken place.

She waited a few more seconds, then pressed a button and the light went off.

The two-way base station that was buried in some evergreen bushes near a hedge ten meters behind her had collected the files wirelessly—the green light confirmed that the transfer had taken place.

Shevchenko's illegal, Natalia, would collect the files using a similar device.

The device had been buried six inches underground by a fellow SVR officer from the Russian embassy several months earlier. He had used a special hand tool to lift out a plug of soil, creating a cavity into which the base station could be placed. The soil plug was then deposited on top of the device. The job, carried out under the cover of night, was completed in about thirty seconds.

Once in place, it was virtually undetectable, and its range meant that either Shevchenko or Natalia could sit on the bench and deposit or collect the messages if they wanted.

Or they could simply drive past along Outer Circle, which was on the other side of the hedge. The base stations and SRACs operated at such a speed that they would work quite effectively from a car. The driver might need to slow down a little at the precise spot, but that would be the only requirement apart from the ability to steer steadily with one hand

and operate the SRAC with the other, probably by reaching inside a handbag or supermarket bag. A motorbike was another option, although that was not Shevchenko's style.

Sometimes, if Shevchenko wasn't certain that she had no surveillance, if she suspected that one of the casual passersby wasn't actually a casual passerby, she would abort by either not entering the park at all or just sitting on her bench and smoking her cigarette, as if it was part of her relaxation routines, without activating the SRAC. But that was simply her innate cautiousness.

Another identical base station had been buried at a different location on the far side of Regent's Park, near the children's playground at Gloucester Gate. But that was purely for use as a backup in case the primary device failed.

The base station was capable of transmitting messages left by Natalia to Shevchenko's SRAC device too. If such a message had been left a blue LED on her SRAC would have lit up. But today it did not.

Now Shevchenko needed to give her usual signal to her illegal to pick up the files, and she did that using a much more old-fashioned method

There were two table lamps on the window ledge in Shevchenko's second-floor apartment in nearby Dorset Square, next to Marylebone station.

When she got home she would turn both of them on, knowing that Natalia would check later in the evening by walking or driving past the apartment building.

One lamp meant it was fine to proceed at the normal pace —there was no need to rush. Two lamps was the signal for an urgent job. The files needed to be in Moscow as quickly as possible.

CHAPTER SEVENTEEN

Friday, April 4, 2014
Moscow

It was the first day of the year when the temperature was actually warm enough for Severinov to sit outside on his terrace, even if he did have to wear a jacket. Thirteen degrees Celsius, according to the enormous decorative thermometer that hung on the balcony of his $30 million residence in the Gorki-8 district.

The house, about eight miles west of the Russian capital, had uninterrupted views out over landscaped gardens that stretched down to the Moscow River, complete with a multi-level heated swimming pool, although Severinov was not an enthusiastic swimmer and rarely used it. But the views, along with the seventeen luxurious bedrooms, had been a major draw when he had bought the property in 2006.

As was his habit, particularly during the summer months, Severinov clutched a glass of his favorite Madeira wine from the Koktebel winery in the Crimea that his staff had left for him. It was usually either that or an ice-cold Beluga vodka.

He had only arrived back in Moscow's Vnukovo Airport the previous night, after a flight in his private Cessna Citation from the Krasnodar refinery at Tuapse. Until the previous year, he had leased a larger $50 million Bombardier Global Express, but that had been shot down by a Stinger missile in Kabul—thankfully not while he was on board—during his disastrous attempt to buy into Afghanistan's oil and gas fields. The Cessna was kept on standby at Vnukovo, about eleven miles from his residence.

Severinov's phone vibrated twice in his pocket. He took it out and entered a key in order to read the encrypted messages that had just arrived.

They were both from his occasional lover, in her native Russian. But neither of them were love notes. They were short and to the point. He clicked on the first message.

I have been told there is a CIA/MI6 investigation into Redtail. To be expected. But the man running the investigation will be of interest—a CIA freelancer, not staff, called Joe Johnson, ex-CIA war crimes investigator. I am certain he is the same man who caused you big problems last year in Afghanistan. He was brought in by Vic Walter, new head of CIA's operations directorate. Of course we know the first person he will try to speak to—Varvara. I suggest to negate that, take action against her first and urgently. A task for Balagula? Your decision.

Severinov swore out loud, his mind swirling with questions. Johnson again? But how and why had he been brought in to investigate the Redtail operation? And hadn't Vic Walter also been part of the Afghanistan debacle? He was certain he had.

He leaned back in his chair and stared at the blue skies overhead. Anastasia was right about Varvara, for sure. And if she was suggesting deploying Vasily Balagula, his former Spetsnaz special forces friend, she must think it was serious.

Balagula was a so-called wet work specialist, to be called in when lethal solutions were required. These days he worked as a freelancer for whoever needed him—whether the Russian government, the FSB, the SVR, or even occasionally the president's office.

He was one of a few good friends Severinov still had in key roles in both the FSB and the SVR, all of them long-standing colleagues from his time in the KGB with whom he had kept in touch and trusted, more or less. Most of them were in Moscow, with a couple based in St. Petersburg and other cities. They all called in favors from each other as required.

Balagula's last job had been an unmitigated success—it was he and a colleague who had delivered the coup de grâce on Redtail in Berlin, using a Spetsnaz special-issue suppressed sniper rifle, the VSS Vintorez, from a hotel window.

The weapon, in which Balagula had used a subsonic 9x39 mm SP5 cartridge, was specifically designed for covert operations. It could be stripped down very quickly and carried in an adapted briefcase, which was exactly how Balagula had transported it around Berlin.

A pity he wasn't just as successful with Johnson in Afghanistan last year, Severinov couldn't help thinking.

He clicked onto the second message.

Urgent military intelligence out of London tells me that US is about to escalate its presence in Black Sea for obvious reasons. I am told at least one destroyer, the USS Donald Cook, *will be sent in, maybe next week, from Mediterranean. It could affect shipping to/from your refinery operations. See attached document—read but then delete. This is of course going to Yasenevo, and the president may want to take action.*

Severinov tapped his foot repeatedly on the glistening

granite terrace, and his hand tightened around his wine glass, spilling some of the contents. This was the last thing he needed. He read the attachment, which was a photographed copy of a intel report from the United States Secretary of Defense, Anthony Everson, to a list of senior military and CIA officers in Washington and London.

It briefly outlined the strategy behind the decision to send in destroyers—to dissuade the Russian navy from taking hostile action against foreign shipping—and stated that the *Donald Cook* was now primed for action.

Severinov deleted the attachment, as requested, and drank the rest of his wine. He then stood and walked to the edge of the terrace, gazing out over his expansive seventy-five-hectare estate. Behind the magnificent house, tucked away beyond a thick screen of pines, were two helipads. The property also had a garage complex able to take up to sixteen cars, tennis courts, and a golf driving range.

For the past year, he had felt that all of it was at risk. Now it seemed those risks were mounting further.

All of his wealth had been built up since he had left the KGB when it was replaced by the SVR at the time of the breakup of the Soviet Union in 1991. Following high-profile KGB postings in Berlin and Afghanistan during the 1980s, he had made a name for himself and was able to capitalize on that once he started working as a private adviser to corporate clients on security matters.

He worked for oil and gas companies as a foreign affairs and security director, and under the economic reforms brought in by the new Russian president, Boris Yeltsin, he was allocated shares in some of those companies. Severinov made a lot of money and at the same time built a good network of contacts in Russia's political community.

The *siloviki*—Putin's gang of ex-KGB and military men who took charge of Russia—liked Severinov's KGB background, his business mind, and his political views. This helped him as he established Besoi Energy and paved the way for a quiet nod of the head when he wanted to execute a series of increasingly high-profile acquisitions.

That was how he had made his fortune. But now the hands that had helped him on the way up were the same ones that could push him back down if things went awry. It had already started to happen.

If a military conflict escalated in the Black Sea, shipping would be disrupted, which would almost certainly impact the flow of essential crude oil—the juice on which his hungry refinery fed in vast quantities every day.

But more than this, there would be close monitoring of vessels by the Russian navy, unannounced searches, checking of cargoes. And if he was found to be carrying arms destined for the Syrian rebels, and the president found out . . . well, it would be curtains.

On all fronts Severinov felt he was coming under siege once again. And all his instincts told him to follow the advice his father had instilled in him: when trapped in a corner, go out fighting. It was a lesson his father had learned from seven years working under Josef Stalin.

He walked back to his chair, took his phone out of his pocket, and dialed a number for Vasily Balagula. He might not be able to do much directly about the US destroyer in the Black Sea, but he could do something about Joe Johnson and the investigation he was starting. This time, he would not screw up.

* * *

Friday, April 4, 2014
Berlin

. . .

The small secure conference room had sealed doors and soundproofed walls, floors, and ceilings that isolated it from the rest of the CIA station. Johnson, Jayne, Vic, and Neal were ensconced in there discussing their next moves when Vic received a secure message from Nicklin-Donovan. He wanted them all to join him on a call, urgently.

On a call the previous evening, Vic had already given Nicklin-Donovan what he had termed "the good news and the bad news"—that the MI6 chief didn't have a mole in Berlin, as originally suspected, but that he definitely did have one in London. Predictably, the latter piece of information had not gone down well.

The team now teed up the call as requested, using a secure squawk-box conference phone in the room that was connected to a similar facility at MI6's Vauxhall Cross headquarters.

After the usual round of opening banter, which in Nicklin-Donovan's case related to the soccer team he supported, Arsenal, having beaten Wigan Athletic on penalties in the semifinal of the Football Association Cup, they got down to business.

"I still have limited progress to report in locating this mole," Nicklin-Donovan began in his rounded English tones. "But there are two things to report. First, the analysis of the various leaks we've seen in recent months, relating to timings and the logs we have of personnel arrivals and departures at the Russian embassy over recent months. As you know, the number and significance of the security breaches increased from September and October last year onward."

Vic leaned forward to speak into the microphone. "And what was the catalyst at that time?"

"I'm coming on to that. My current thinking focuses on a new arrival in July last year at Kensington Palace Gardens: the SVR's Major General Anastasia Shevchenko."

"She's the current *rezident*, right?" Jayne said.

"Indeed. She's number two in counterintelligence behind Kutsik and is seen as a potential director, in time. She's also a known recruiter, which is why we immediately covered her 24/7. But she's good. There have been a significant number of occasions when she's slipped surveillance, but always without it being obvious that that was what she was trying to do. It always looks like our fault in losing her, not her skill in evading us."

Vic shook his head. "Okay, get to the point, Mark. The Russians have a recruiter in the *rezident's* chair at Kensington Palace Gardens, and she's given surveillance the slip, as they do. It's her job. You think she might be the handler for the mole?"

"Yes, that's exactly what I think," Nicklin-Donovan said. "But we have also picked up some intelligence from an agent at the Russian embassy that Shevchenko is going to leave London on April 14. She's already made arrangements to head back to Moscow, apparently. It's a very early departure, given she only arrived last July."

"And?" Vic asked, catching Johnson's eye across the table and raising his eyebrows.

"An illegal replacement," Johnson murmured.

"What was that?" Nicklin-Donovan said, his voice sounding distorted through the loudspeaker.

"Joe said he thinks Moscow will put in an illegal replacement for her," Neal said, exchanging glances with Johnson, who nodded to confirm that that was precisely what he meant.

"Yes, exactly," Nicklin-Donovan said. "My concern—no, more than a concern—my worry, my panic, is that if she's been handling the mole in our midst and now she's leaving, then she's not going to abandon the mole. Of course not. Instead, she will replace herself with some illegal whom we are going to be desperately hard put to trace. It might be almost impossible."

There was silence in the Pariser Platz meeting room. There was complete logic in what Nicklin-Donovan was saying, Johnson thought.

Johnson sipped from a glass of water. "So, we've possibly got ten days to do this job."

* * *

Friday, April 4, 2014
   Berlin

The task now facing Johnson was simply too great and spread too wide geographically for him to continue operating together with Jayne. They needed to divide up the workload. It was vital to reach Varvara Yezhova in St. Petersburg but equally important to follow up on the leads they now had in London.

After they had finished the call with Nicklin-Donovan, it took the team little time to decide on their next course of action.

"You should go to St. Petersburg, Joe, and charm Varvara," Vic said. "That's your specialty."

"What, charming older Russian women?" Johnson asked. He had met a few Russian women he might like to charm, but he doubted very much that Varvara Yezhova would be one of them.

Jayne snorted, and a faint smile crossed Vic's face. On the other side of the table, Neal guffawed loudly.

"No," Vic said. "I meant pursuing the historic aspects of the inquiry. Although I have no doubt you're highly capable of both."

"He'd bloody well better not be," Jayne muttered.

"Jayne, you should head to London," Vic continued, ignoring her mock protest. "It's your home territory, and you can start mapping out a plan there with Mark."

Johnson glanced at Jayne and then nodded. What Vic was saying was logical.

"I need a good cover story and a good legend to go with it," Johnson said. "I've got an idea for that."

"What's that?" Vic asked.

"I need to put in a call to someone over in DC. Then I'll tell you if I get the green light from them."

Vic nodded. "We can get the team to beef up the legend and road test it to make sure it's robust and stands up under pressure, in case you get questioned."

Johnson scrutinized Vic. "What about you? Are you going to stay here?"

Vic shook his head. "No. I need to get back to Langley tonight. I've got an important meeting with the director tomorrow morning, part of which I will now spend updating him on developments here. We've got Neal here who can control the operation until I'm able to get back."

Neal nodded. "Yes, makes sense. We don't want Veltman complaining that all his lieutenants are living it up in Berlin."

Vic turned to Johnson. "When are you aiming to go?"

"I need to get this thing moving. I'm worried that the FSB thugs will realize that's likely to be our next move and get to Varvara before I do. So I am thinking as quickly as possible—ideally Monday. There is a big legal conference starting that day in St. Petersburg. I would like to attend it."

CHAPTER EIGHTEEN

Friday, April 4, 2014
Moscow

The smart-suited aide bowed at the heavy double wooden doors of the president's Kremlin office, his heels pressed tight together, then walked deferentially across the parquet floor inlaid with an intricate design of light and dark blocks and onto the hand-woven Russian Bokhara carpet that stretched across the center of the room.

"Mr. President, I have this from Mr. Kruglov's office, sir," the aide said. He placed the beige folder carefully on the glass-like polished wooden surface of the desk, bowed again, and withdrew.

Vladimir Putin picked up the folder, removed the report from inside, and settled back in his beige leather-covered chair. Behind him, the Russian national flag and the president's standard hung limply from their poles against a wooden paneled wall.

"*Dermo*. More shit from Kruglov," the president said to

his visitor, the Prime Minister Dmitry Medvedev. He glanced up and caught Medvedev's eye, a thin smile on his face.

Medvedev was sitting on one of two chairs that stood on either side of a small chess-style table that jutted out at right angles from Putin's main desk. The president used it for informal face-to-face discussions.

Putin received regular missives from Kruglov, whom he viewed with a healthy disdain—a perspective he shared with Medvedev. Although Putin had been a long time out of the KGB—twenty-three years, to be precise—he took a critical view of how his intelligence chiefs operated, and he still retained his old mind-set: the mistrust of everyone he met and everything he was told.

"Kruglov is deeply concerned about the Crimea," Medvedev said. "He is overanxious, in my view."

"Maybe. Actually, this report is about the Crimea," Putin said as he read. He sat up straight and placed the report on the desk. His eyes narrowed as he read.

"Is it significant?" Medvedev asked.

"Yes. It's about material received from ANTELOPE in London," Putin said, his voice level. "The Americans are considering sending at least one destroyer into the Black Sea soon. Maybe more."

Medvedev stiffened in his chair. "They will play their game, but it is meaningless. Is this solid information?"

"It appears concrete, yes. This report paraphrases naval documents seen by ANTELOPE, and it names the USS *Donald Cook*. Maybe it is meaningless. Maybe it is just postur-ing," Putin said, still reading the document. "But I am not going to allow them to get away with doing this unchallenged. They are trying to slap Russia in the face. To slap me in the face. It is our reputation at stake."

He continued to read, tracing his forefinger down the

page as he did so. Beside him, his secure cell phone vibrated on the desk, but the president ignored it.

"We will monitor this situation," Putin said. "If they send this destroyer in, we will take action. I want fighters and tactical bombers put on standby. We will then play the situation as it evolves. I am not making any decisions now, but I want all options to be open."

"I agree," Medvedev said. "But we'll need to clear the area of our merchant shipping if we do this. You can't be certain how the Americans will respond. They have a carrier in the Mediterranean within range with Super Hornets on board. We can't put container ships and tankers at risk in a conflict zone."

Medvedev was referring to the Boeing F/A-18E Super Hornet supersonic twin-engine fighter aircraft that operated from the carrier USS *George H. W. Bush*.

"The Hornets are for show," Putin said. "I think you can be certain how the Americans will respond—they will likely do nothing. But yes, get the whole Black Sea cleared from Tuesday onward. The oil and freight shippers will squawk about it, but that can't be helped."

"Yes, I will get this organized," Medvedev said.

The two men had worked hand in glove since the 1990s to bring about huge changes in Russia's political landscape. They effectively seized control when Putin became president in 2000 and used the power and far-reaching tentacles of the military, the FSB, and the *siloviki* to retain it.

Putin took a second report from the folder and scrutinized it. He shook his head as he read.

"Fools," he murmured.

"Also from Kruglov?" Medvedev asked.

"Yes. It's more information from ANTELOPE. The idiots at Langley and Vauxhall Cross are furious about Redtail. What did they think we would do if one of our senior SVR officers was defecting and going to destroy one of our top assets in the process? Did they just think we would stand by and watch Yezhov go with his secrets and his stack of confidential documents? It's a joke."

"What are they doing?"

Putin continued to read, turning the page and finishing the second sheet before answering.

"They are going to carry out some kind of off-the-books investigation. They don't have the courage to do anything that would leave them open to accountability. They are employing some freelancer to try and find out ANTELOPE's name, which undoubtedly Yezhov would have given them if he had made it. They also want this freelancer to try and source the other information Yezhov was carrying."

"A freelancer?"

"Yes, a US investigator, Joe Johnson. Ex-CIA, war crimes investigator, who—"

"Is that not the same man who ruined our Afghanistan oil and gas bid last year?" Medvedev interrupted. "The one who Yuri Severinov failed to eliminate, despite our instructions?"

Putin stared at Medvedev. "Yes, I believe you are correct. It's the same man." He tapped his fingers on the desk for a couple of seconds. "Well, if the Americans are going to employ some freelancer to try and decommission ANTELOPE, we can play them at their own game. Go and find Severinov and tell him we're giving him a chance to put right his screwup from last year. Tell him he needs to do whatever is necessary with this Johnson and any associates of his and put an end to this investigation that they are conducting. Understood?"

"Yes, it makes sense to have deniability," Medvedev said. "Especially given what's about to happen in the Black Sea. I will talk to Severinov."

"Good. But tell him he needs to operate on his own with

this one—I don't want to be seen helping him. He is not to contact us for assistance."

* * *

Friday, April 4, 2014
    London

ANTELOPE had decided from the outset never to copy sensitive files from a work laptop or desktop computer and load them directly onto a flash drive or SD card. That was far too dangerous and left too many electronic fingerprints.

Instead, a much safer albeit slower, alternative was to use a micro digital camera to photograph the documents on-screen.

The Japanese camera that ANTELOPE kept hidden at home in the Maida Vale apartment was less than one and a half inches long and stored its images on a micro SD card of a similar size to a phone SIM card. It was a flexible solution in that the portable card could be inserted directly into an appropriate SD port or card-reading device or, using an adaptor, could be plugged into a USB port on a computer.

ANTELOPE scrolled through the daily cluster of classified reports that arrived in batches during the day and gave updates on highly sensitive top secret operations across the globe. Only very senior officers had such access, and most of the documents had very secure distribution lists.

Every so often, ANTELOPE stopped and photographed a document or an intel report, then continued to scroll. There was no way all of them could be copied—that would be far too time-consuming. But the most important would go onto the SD card and then on to Moscow Center.

Today there was another update on the gathering crisis in

the Black Sea. A report from the US Department of Defense, classified as top secret—the highest level of sensitivity in US circles—noted that the USS *George H. W. Bush* had been ordered to delay its scheduled departure from the Mediterranean and instead push up into the Aegean Sea, just south of Istanbul, to put it within reach of the Bosporus Strait and to ensure its aircraft could reach the Black Sea in short order.

ANTELOPE, who was copied on a whole raft of Department of Defense program intelligence, photographed all three pages in that report.

The next document was also photographed. It was a UK Ministry of Defence document, stamped TOP SECRET STRAP3 UK/US EYES ONLY, that gave a perspective on the Black Sea crisis from the UK's secretary of state for defence, containing similar details as the US report. ANTELOPE only very occasionally saw documents marked STRAP3, which indicated the very highest level of sensitivity in the UK.

The fifth report that came up caused the skin to tighten a little on ANTELOPE's scalp. It was a short two-paragraph update from Vic Walter to Mark Nicklin-Donovan on the investigation into the failed Operation Blackbird and outlined the next step that Joe Johnson was to take. He had somehow obtained valuable information from an unnamed SVR agent in Berlin and was now planning to try and reach Yezhov's wife in St. Petersburg.

Yezhov's wife? Of course, ANTELOPE thought, reading through the material again. It made absolute sense for Johnson to visit her.

It was the first time ANTELOPE had heard of the St. Petersburg initiative. There was no detail on how or where Johnson would make contact with Yezhov's wife, or how or when he would travel, but nevertheless, this seemed like priceless intelligence.

And the SVR agent referenced in the report? Moscow Center would be desperate to find out who it was.

The camera made no sound as ANTELOPE depressed the shutter.

Another one for Shevchenko. They'll like this at Yasenevo.

CHAPTER NINETEEN

Monday, April 7, 2014
   St. Petersburg

The delegates filing out of the bus and beneath the magnificent central arch of the General Staff Building, on the vast
expanse of Palace Square, were in an upbeat mood. The idea
of two and a half days in St. Petersburg, ostensibly for the
city's International Legal Forum but in reality for a series of
convivial meals, some decent wines, and good company, was a
major attraction for legal professionals the world over.

They came from more than eighty countries, according to
the welcome pack. Most of those present were law practi-
tioners of one form or another—ranging from barristers in
Sydney to corporate general counsels from Madrid and Paris.
But there were also a few professors of law and other
academics.

The General Staff Building, built during the 1820s in a
580-meter bow shape in front of the legendary Winter Palace
of the Russian tsars, was one of St. Petersburg's iconic loca-

tions. The triumphal arch through which the delegates were walking was designed to mark the Russian victory over Napoleon's France during the Great Patriotic War of 1812.

All the delegates were arriving that evening for a semi-formal evening drinks reception prior to the official start of the conference the following morning.

Among those last to leave the bus was a man from the American University's Washington College of Law, William Cadman, who was the deputy director of the War Crimes Research Office.

At least, that was the name on his passport and on his conference registration form and entry pass.

But the passport bearing Cadman's name was carried by Johnson, along with a credit card, a bank card, and a driver's license. Johnson had acquired a pair of black glasses similar to the real Cadman and had cut his hair even shorter than normal.

Johnson paused for a moment after stepping off the bus and glanced around. The Palace Square, where part of the 1917 October Revolution took place, had been the scene of various bloody encounters over the years, including the 1905 Bloody Sunday massacre, when hundreds of protesters were killed by the Imperial Guard.

He had been late to confirm Cadman's attendance at the conference, having done so just before the deadline the previous Friday night following a series of secure calls between the Berlin team and Nicklin-Donovan in London.

Before Johnson and Jayne had departed from Berlin, they had set up GPS tracking devices so that each of them could monitor the other's position if needed. It was something they had used on a previous job in Afghanistan to extremely good effect, and both of them viewed it as a sensible insurance policy to deploy the technology again here.

The trackers, costing a few hundred dollars each, were

tiny: only an inch and a half square and very thin. They had a battery life of about two weeks and could be monitored anywhere in the world using an iPhone app.

The devices were concealed in a cavity cut into the honeycombed rubber midsole of their shoe heels and were undetectable unless the heel was dismantled. The system had enabled Jayne to mobilize a US Army unit to rescue Johnson from incarceration in a cellar in Kabul the previous year.

Apart from the trackers, the registration of Cadman for the St. Petersburg conference had triggered a flurry of other activity over the weekend within the CIA station at Pariser Platz, where arrangements had to be made at short notice to manufacture his passport and driver's license.

Johnson, Vic, and their tight team across both CIA and MI6 functions were determined to keep details of his visit to St. Petersburg as secure as possible, and distribution of the intel report about the operation was therefore kept confined. The report contained few details, with no accommodation addresses, no operational plans, and no details of aliases or cover stories. It was limited to the individuals who had previously been briefed on a need-to-know basis.

Nevertheless, it triggered requests for more details and explanations from a number of those people via emails or phone calls to Vic, Johnson, and Nicklin-Donovan. A few offered advice based on their previous experiences in Russia's old imperial capital.

But ultimately the flow of missives became irritating. When Johnson reported his list of contacts to Vic, his friend rolled his eyes and told Johnson he was of the mind to delete any further information requests and not answer his phone. He advised Johnson to do likewise.

When, eventually, Johnson arrived at passport control at St. Petersburg's Pulkovo Airport following his two-hour ten-minute Aeroflot flight from Schönefeld Airport south of

Berlin, his documentation under the Cadman alias was heavily scrutinized. But that was normal. There was no heavy interrogation, and he was allowed through.

Johnson's biggest concern was to check for any sign of surveillance as he journeyed by taxi to his hotel, the Taleon Imperial on Nevsky Prospekt, just a stone's throw from the General Staff Building.

A car followed him into the city from Pulkovo and had been easy enough to spot, but that had vanished after he had been dropped off at the Taleon, which was a former palace turned luxury hotel. During Johnson's short walk from the hotel to the General Staff Building and at the reception, any number of people could potentially have been observers from the FSB, Russia's Federal Security Service, which was responsible for internal intelligence and security within the country. Johnson assumed that some of them were watching.

He had an address for Varvara Yezhova that he had been given by the operations team at Pariser Platz. It was for a fourth-floor apartment on Bolshoy Prospekt, in the Petrogradsky district of the city, about a mile and a half northeast of the General Staff Building.

Johnson had no prearranged appointment with her, just a couple of photographs. Because of the security concerns about FSB surveillance, he had not even been able to notify her that he was coming. Although he had a phone number, he remained too worried to use it. Certainly the family of a defector who had just been assassinated—presumably on the directions of the SVR, or most likely the president's office—would be monitored around the clock.

Instead, he would have to find a way to reach her unannounced. Johnson had devised a plan. But first he needed to get black.

CHAPTER TWENTY

Tuesday, April 8, 2014
   St. Petersburg

It was a strategy that Johnson had used once before in Russia, many years earlier, when he needed a cover story and a plausible disguise while gathering evidence against an alleged war criminal who had subsequently obtained refuge in the United States under a false identity.

Johnson went along to the conference as scheduled on the Tuesday morning and signed in at the registration table. The sessions that followed, between nine o'clock and one o'clock, were a boring mixture of presentations about legal developments of global interest, mainly given by people who seemed intent on raising their own profiles as much as discussing the issues at hand.

But when the conference broke up for lunch, Johnson returned to the Taleon Imperial and embarked on his own private tour of the building—one that took him down to the hotel basements in search of a room, or series of rooms, that he knew existed somewhere.

There was nothing of the kind he was seeking on the first basement level, so he continued down another flight of concrete stairs, this time uncarpeted and less maintained, that echoed under his shoes.

Once on the second basement level, he went through a set of double swing doors and along a corridor until he found what he was looking for. Two doors, both marked in Russian: *Komnata dlya personala*. Staff room. One had another sign below that read *Muzhskoy*, men. The other said *Zhenskiy*, ladies.

He took a breath, then opened the door to the men's room and strode in, his head high. Swiftly, he took in the scene ahead of him. Metal lockers lined the walls, and around a line of benches in the center of the room, a handful of men were buttoning smart white shirts, donning black waistcoats, knotting ties, and polishing black shoes.

At the rear of the room was a long hanging rail with uniforms that had just come back from cleaning. They were hanging in flimsy polyethylene protective covers, all with labels attached.

Without hesitation, Johnson strode to the rail and, copying another man who stood there, rifled through the sets of uniforms. In his case, he wasn't looking at the name labels but rather the sizes. He needed one in large.

He grabbed a uniform from the rail and, like the others, moved to a bench and began to get changed. Within four minutes, Johnson looked like any one of the scores of hotel staff that lined the lobby, corridors, dining rooms, and bars of the Taleon. His waistcoat fitted snugly, and his tie knot was perfect.

Johnson put the clothing he had taken off inside the plastic cover, rolled it up, and nodded at a couple of other men on his way out. He took the staff elevator directly to the fifth floor, where his room was located. He emerged from an elevator shaft tucked away next to an emergency staircase at the rear of the building rather than the main guest elevators in the center.

As soon as he walked into his room, he caught a glimpse of his image in the full-length mirror that was attached to a wall.

"You look like a penguin," he said out loud to himself. "But I think this could work." He had noticed groups of uniformed hotel staff waiting for taxis at the rear of the hotel, presumably after completing their shifts. They had emerged from a staff door close to the kitchens. Providing he used the staff stairs and elevators, took the usual precautions, and checked for signs of coverage, the chances of being followed by FSB surveillance from the taxi stand were lower than by exiting the grandiose front doors through the lobby, he figured.

It was time to go.

Johnson sent an email to the legal forum's delegates coordinator, apologizing that he would not be able to attend that day's proceedings because he had been incapacitated with some kind of food poisoning after breakfast. There was little doubt that the FSB would eventually be notified of his absence.

Forty minutes later, a taxi dropped him in front of a men's clothing store on Bolshoy Prospekt, a broad street lined with five-story buildings housing a variety of smart restaurants, fashion shops, banks, and electronic goods outlets on the ground floors, with apartments above.

There seemed to be no shortage of disposable income for shopping in this area of St. Petersburg.

He entered the store. From his vantage point, where he stood examining a selection of jackets, the clothing shop gave him a perfect view of the apartments across the street where Varvara lived. There was a heavy wooden door at street level, sandwiched between a Greek restaurant and a music shop, with push-button buzzers to the right.

Every so often, pedestrians entered the apartments using their own keys, or cars or taxis pulled up outside and people got out and went in. It was a busy residential building.

Johnson, still wearing his hotel waistcoat and tie, spent some time moving from one shop to another, browsing and drinking the occasional coffee, all the time checking for any sign of surveillance. There was none. Any observer would probably have assumed he was an off-duty waiter or concierge.

A black Mercedes had been standing outside the apartments for a while, with a man in a dark suit in the driver's seat behind darkened windows. But it looked as though it was waiting for a resident to emerge.

After a while, Johnson was satisfied enough. He waited in the music shop next to the apartment's entrance until another taxi pulled up outside, then timed his arrival at the door to coincide with that of the woman passenger who got out.

Johnson exchanged a couple of good-humored words of thanks in fluent Russian with the woman, who was middle-aged and wearing what looked like a white nurse's tunic, insisting that she go first. He followed in her slipstream while she unlocked the door, pushed it open, and slipped inside.

Johnson headed past the elevators and through the door to the stairs at the rear of the entrance hall. He began to climb, his footsteps echoing up the concrete steps.

The stairwell had a strong smell of disinfectant and cement dust. It was obviously not well used, unlike the elevators, which Johnson noticed on the way past had well-worn call buttons set into a brass plate.

When he reached the third-floor landing, from somewhere out of sight above him came a crack that was almost explosive. Johnson immediately realized it was a door handle smashing back against the wall of the stairwell on the fourth floor above. Someone was on the move, and fast.

Then came multiple sets of running footsteps echoing down the stairs. Seconds later, two men dressed in black jackets and black trousers burst into view around the banisters of the next flight of steps.

They both hammered down the stairs toward Johnson. The first man was stuffing a bundle of black cloth into a pocket as he ran.

Johnson stopped still. He began to brace himself, and his heart rate automatically shot up as a flow of adrenaline rushed through him. These two were muscly, barrel-chested military types, with similar short-cropped dark hair.

The man in front ran straight past Johnson without a glance. The second, who was swarthier, with tufts of black chest hair showing where his top two shirt buttons were undone, threw Johnson a sharp look. But they didn't pause, rushing and clattering down the next flight of stairs toward street level.

A chill ran down Johnson's spine. Had his biggest fear about this trip just come true?

Shit.

Johnson turned to watch the men disappear. The second man's face had rung a bell in the back of his mind, but he couldn't place him. He made his way up to the next landing and opened the stairwell door.

Ahead of him was a dimly lit hallway next to the elevator shaft with corridors leading off at either end. At an open apartment doorway opposite, a woman lay on her back, her head inside the apartment, her bare legs spread-eagled across the doormat.

Johnson moved closer. He could see a stream of blood trickling its way across the terra-cotta tiled floor of the apartment. He recognized the face from the photographs he had seen: it was Varvara Yezhova. There was a bullet entry wound in the center of her forehead.

CHAPTER TWENTY-ONE

Tuesday, April 8, 2014
   St. Petersburg

Johnson hurried over to Varvara's body on the floor. Although he knew he was wasting his time, he knelt and felt her wrist for a pulse. The wrist was still normal body temperature, but there was not a hint of a beat.

She was gone.

"Shit," Johnson said out loud.

He put Varvara's wrist back down on the floor and for a few seconds considered what to do next. The two men he had seen running down the stairs had killed her.

Johnson's mind raced. Had someone leaked details of Johnson's plan to try to meet with her? Even more critical, did they know what secrets she might have been able to pass on?

Johnson looked up and down the hallway. He was surprised that no other residents had emerged from their apartments. Surely, they must have heard the gunshot. That is, unless the killers had used a suppressor, which was quite possible, because Johnson himself had heard nothing while climbing the stairs.

One thing was certain: he didn't want to just stay there and be caught next to a dead body. Should he drag Varvara's body into the apartment and see if he could find anything? Or just leave and abort the operation entirely?

Just then, the elevator doors behind him opened, and out stepped a slim young woman with shoulder-length dark brown hair. She took in the scene in front of her and let out a piercing shriek.

"Mother!" she screamed in Russian. "*Bozhe Moy*. My God, what did you do to my mother?"

Johnson stood, realizing as he did so that she was almost as tall as him. He spoke to her in Russian. "No, I just arrived and found her like this and—"

But the woman shrieked again, rushed to Varvara, and cradled her head in her arms, oblivious to the blood that was splattering over her jeans, black denim jacket, and white T-shirt.

Johnson swore inwardly. At this rate the entire apartment building would be emerging from behind their locked doors and blaming him for Varvara's death. So much for keeping his visit low-key.

"I promise you I did not kill your mother," Johnson said. "I just arrived to visit her, only a minute before you got here."

What the hell to do next?

"Call an ambulance. Call a doctor, quickly." The woman was struggling to get her words out between sobs. This was clearly the twenty-five-year-old daughter.

"I am so sorry," Johnson said. "She's gone, she's gone. There's no pulse. We can call a doctor, but they can't help her now. I am sorry."

Johnson knew he had to get the body inside and shut the

door as quickly as possible. He was by now fearful that someone else would arrive, and before they knew it, the police and the FSB would be called, and he would be thrown into a cell for questioning.

He also didn't want to introduce himself out in the corridor within potential earshot of other residents.

"Listen," Johnson said, trying to think of how to phrase the need to move her mother's body without causing an even larger scene. "I will help you to get your mother into the apartment. She shouldn't stay here in the doorway. You can decide what to do inside. Come on, I can help you. You must be Katya?"

"Yes, I'm Katya," the young woman wailed. She gently laid her mother's head on the floor again, which Johnson took as a signal of acceptance of what he had said. She stood and sobbed in the doorway, hands clasped to her head, tears trickling down her face and dripping to the floor. "Who are you?"

"I was coming to visit her," Johnson said as he stood. "I am a friend of your father, and I needed to talk to your mother about what happened to him."

At the mention of her father, Katya doubled up, and her sobbing became uncontrollable.

Johnson exhaled. Two bullets, two deaths a couple of weeks apart. And an entire family blown apart, literally.

Johnson took a hold beneath Varvara's armpits and pulled her body into the tiled hallway of the apartment, where he laid it to rest on a long, narrow red rug. Katya didn't offer to help, but she didn't object either; she backed into the hallway ahead of him, too overwrought to speak.

Johnson grabbed a roll of paper towels from a table and wiped the blood from the floor outside the apartment door as best he could. There were also splatters of red on the white plastered wall between the Yezhovs' apartment and the one next door, which he tried to clean with equally mixed results.

Finally, Johnson closed the apartment door. He walked to the window, opened it, and looked down into the street. There was no sign of police or other emergency services, no sirens wailing. The black Mercedes that had been parked outside the apartments had gone. His best guess now was that it had been used by the two men who had killed Varvara. He left the window open so they could hear if there was activity outside.

Katya, who was still crying, looked at Johnson. "Who are you?" she asked again.

Johnson decided to be honest; otherwise he would make no progress. She might assume he was from the FSB or the SVR. And now was the time to get her to talk, while she was still emotionally unbalanced, not when she had dried up in a day or two.

Plus, he needed to get out of there as quickly as possible. There was no time to waste. He either got some information now or whatever secrets the dead couple carried would be gone.

But he felt he could not speak out loud. The likelihood was that the Yezhovs' apartment had been bugged. He looked around, found a pad and pen, and instead scribbled a note in Russian.

I am Joe Johnson, an American investigator. I work for the US government. I was due to meet your father in Berlin a couple of weeks ago to speak with him. But things went wrong, as you must know.

Katya wiped her eyes with the back of her hand and, still weeping, tried to focus on the note. "We can speak in here. We had this apartment swept for bugs only yesterday. It is safe. How do I know you are telling the truth? Are you carrying identity papers?"

Johnson paused, momentarily taken aback by the young woman's evident grasp of security matters. "You can call me Joe. I'm not carrying my own US identity papers. I've been traveling under the name William Cadman. But I can prove my actual identity. I know where your father was going in Berlin and why—he was a good man who was doing the right thing. And I would like to help find out who killed him and who did this to your mother. Do you have any idea?"

"There were two men, both in black clothing, getting into a car outside. When I saw them my first thought was FSB."

"Yes, I saw them on the stairs," Johnson said. "I don't know if they are actually FSB, but I'm sure they killed your mother. Did your father or mother ever talk about being under threat from anyone? Before your father traveled to Berlin, I mean."

Katya looked down at her mother's body. She burst into tears again, then took a deep breath and wiped her eyes, seemingly struggling to breathe evenly. There was a pause lasting at least a couple of minutes.

Johnson reached out and put his hand on her shoulder. "Take your time."

"My father told us that he was going to defect because he knew things that were important for world peace. He never said what."

"He never told you what information he was going to pass on to us after he had defected?"

Katya shook her head. "No. He didn't confide in me with that type of thing."

Johnson exhaled. He hadn't imagined for a moment that Gennady Yezhov would have handed over highly sensitive material to his daughter, but he nevertheless felt his hopes deflate yet further.

"But one thing I am sure of," Katya said. "The information must have been something related to the intelligence service. My father had a lot of enemies in the SVR and the FSB, some of them dating back to the 1980s when they were called the KGB. Those people are my big concern now. I would not be surprised if some of them were the killers of my parents. We need to be careful—it is not safe to be here."

Johnson's initial impression of Katya was shifting by the second. Although in shock over her parents' sudden violent deaths, she seemed to intuitively grasp the political backdrop to what had happened.

"Who were they, your father's KGB colleagues, at that time?"

"One was Yuri Severinov, the billionaire, one of Putin's circle. Everyone knows he was KGB before he made money in the oil industry. Another was—"

Johnson felt his stomach flip over inside him. "Hold on a minute. Did you say Yuri Severinov?"

"Yes, he was my father's boss in the KGB at that time. Do you know him?"

Johnson nodded. "Yes, unfortunately I do."

He felt stunned. The same Yuri Severinov with whom he had gone head-to-head in Afghanistan the previous year? The same Severinov who had locked Johnson in a cellar in Kabul, only to have the tables turned on him after Jayne master-minded a rescue by the US Army? And the same Severinov who had escaped justice for his war crimes, his genocides, in rural Afghanistan?

He was someone whom Johnson had subsequently sworn he would ultimately see brought to trial for his crimes, although how that would happen, he had no idea. The International Criminal Court did not seem interested in pursuing war crimes committed in Afghanistan prior to 2001.

So—Severinov had been Yezhov's boss.

But it made sense.

Severinov had been a senior KGB officer in Afghanistan in the late 1980s, responsible for military intelligence, and Johnson knew he had done a stint in East Germany too.

It was then that the connection was made in his mind.

The second man he had seen earlier, running down the stairs, had been Severinov's thuggish sidekick whom he had last seen while incarcerated in the Russian's safe house in Kabul the previous year. His name was Vasily.

The recollection sent an immediate jolt of alarm through him: it must have been Severinov, then, who had been responsible for killing Varvara. He must have ordered Vasily to execute her.

Johnson felt suddenly certain that the look Vasily had thrown him while running past him on the stairs had been one of vague recognition, despite the black glasses that Johnson had been wearing. Something had clicked in the man's mind—he had seen it. Presumably he had been focused on getting out of the building as quickly as possible; he would have had no reason to expect to see Johnson there, and he had run on. But now Johnson felt that there was a significant danger that Vasily would put two and two together and return. He knew Severinov and Vasily wanted him dead.

He walked to the window and looked out. There were no cars parked along the street outside the apartment. He scanned the street, carefully checking the few pedestrians on the sidewalks. When he was finally satisfied there was no imminent danger, he turned, folded his arms, and scrutinized Katya.

"What is it?" she asked. "Why are you looking at me strangely like that?"

He pursed his lips. "I think the men who killed your mother were sent by Severinov. In fact I'm quite certain they were."

"What makes you say that?"

"I had a battle with Severinov and his men last year, in Afghanistan. I recognized one of his men running down the stairs as I came up. And I have a feeling he might have recognized me."

What Johnson didn't add was, if indeed it was Severinov's men who had killed Varvara, why had they done so? And why had they done it just when he was due to visit? It was the timing.

How did they know?

CHAPTER TWENTY-TWO

Tuesday, April 8, 2014
 St. Petersburg

The bare floorboards in the first-floor apartment creaked as
Yuri Severinov paced up and down. Across the other side of
the room, his former KGB colleague and longtime friend
Leonid Pugachov sat in an armchair, chain-smoking his
favorite LD cigarettes, a pack of which lay open on the table
in front of him.

The two men were waiting just a kilometer away from the
apartment building where, Severinov hoped, Vasily Balagula
should have completed the task he had been given by now. It
should have been the easiest of kills, but nevertheless,
Severinov was anxious as always to know it had gone
smoothly.

Pugachov, who at fifty-eight was a couple of years older
than Severinov, was a colonel in the FSB. Now with short
white hair and a mustache to match, he had studied
economics with Severinov at Moscow State University and

had joined the KGB at the same time in 1980. They did some of their initial training together and, although they subsequently ended up in different parts of the KGB, had always kept in touch.

The difference was that whereas Severinov had left the KGB in 1991 when the Soviet Union broke up and had thrown himself into business, Pugachov had stayed on, working in the new FSB, the domestic intelligence service based at the former KGB headquarters at the Lubyanka.

Pugachov had given Severinov assistance on various operations over the years since, in return for either generous transfers into a special numbered bank account that he held in Vienna or old-fashioned bundles of rubles.

This would be another one of those jobs, of which Severinov currently had two on his plate. He had found out about both within an hour or so just the previous morning.

First, he had received an update from London telling him that Joe Johnson was investigating Gennady Yezhov's death and as part of that was planning to visit his widow, Varvara. There had been no indication of timing.

The intention behind such a visit was clear, and just as clear were the risks to Severinov, who decided very swiftly that there was a quick solution to the problem: if Varvara was dead, Johnson would struggle to speak to her.

The second job on his list tied very neatly into the first: he had received a call from Dmitry Medvedev's slimy assistant, Mikhail Sobchak, passing on orders from the president's office that Severinov was to have Johnson eliminated by whatever means was necessary.

To Severinov's irritation, Sobchak had also told him that this was an unofficial job and that under no circumstances was he to request assistance from the Kremlin. The unspoken but unmistakable subtext was that the leadership was still mightily pissed with him following the Afghanistan debacle. Was the instruction a test of his loyalty? It felt like it.

Exactly how and when a hit on Johnson was to be arranged was an issue yet to be determined, although it would be another one for Balagula, that was for certain. Severinov would take this one step at a time: Varvara Yezhova would come first.

Within an hour of receiving the missive from London and the instruction from the Kremlin, Severinov made contact with both Balagula and Pugachov, who was also based in Moscow. On Monday afternoon he flew the two men to St. Petersburg on his private Cessna Citation. Most of the flight was spent making plans for Varvara, although Johnson was also discussed.

The plan was that for Varvara's execution, Pugachov would cover any local difficulties that might arise involving FSB or police, while Balagula would deal with the wet work.

Now Severinov and Pugachov were sitting in an FSB safe apartment that they were using as an operations center, less than a mile away from Varvara's apartment.

Severinov didn't generally prefer to get too involved in such operations—like most oligarchs with almost unlimited funds, he found it far easier to simply pay someone whatever was required to do his dirty work for him. But this case was different: it was deeply personal.

The front door security buzzer sounded—a long beep followed by four short ones. That would be Balagula and Roman Gurko returning. Gurko was one of Pugachov's trusted FSB men based in St. Petersburg who had been brought in for this operation. It was his job to act as cover for Balagula, if required.

Severinov strode to the apartment door and opened it, listening as Balagula's and Gurko's footsteps came up the wooden staircase; they walked slowly and in a relaxed fashion as instructed. He held the door open as they entered the apartment, then closed it swiftly behind them.

"Well?" Severinov said. "Is the job done?"

Balagula nodded and took off his jacket. His barrel chest stuck out, black hairs protruding above his shirt buttons. A python tattoo writhed down each of his forearms. "Easy. She answered the door, and it was all over in a few seconds. There was nobody else in the apartment—we checked."

"Nobody saw you do it? Her kids weren't there?" Severinov's eyes searched Balagula's. He had been concerned that one or both of Yezhov's children, Katya or Timur, would be there and cause complications.

"No—and the suppressor did its job, so little noise. No one came out of the other apartments." He paused. "Just one thing. On the way down the stairs, we were hurrying out, and we passed a guy dressed like a waiter, with a waistcoat and tie, who was coming up. I'm not certain about this, but I thought I recognized him."

"Who?" Severinov said sharply. He didn't like the sound of this.

"Johnson, I think."

"*Johnson?*"

"Yes. I think it might have been him. We were in a hell of a rush, and it didn't register with me immediately. I think he was wearing glasses, which threw me a bit too. I just put a name to the face on the way back in the car. A tall guy, mainly bald, with graying hair."

Severinov stood motionless. That figured if so. It was in line with what Shevchenko had told him, although Johnson had moved much more quickly than he had expected.

"How sure are you?" Now his voice was abrasive and rapid-fire.

Balagula shrugged. "I don't know. Maybe seventy percent."

"Where did you leave the body?"

"In the apartment door. We fired and ran," Balagula said.

"Were you wearing the balaclavas?" Severinov asked.

"On the landing outside the apartment door, yes."

"No, I mean when you saw Johnson, or who you thought was Johnson?" he snapped.

Balagula shook his head. "We took them off on the stairwell."

"So when Johnson saw you, they were off?"

Balagula hesitated for a beat. "Yes."

"Idiots."

During a planning phase, the group had held a long discussion about the merits of wearing balaclavas at different stages of the operation. Severinov had wanted the two men to wear them until they were back in the safe apartment. All the others had argued that they should be worn only while carrying out the actual killing. Pugachov's argument was that while they were useful to avoid being identified while firing guns, wearing them in other public areas would only set alarm bells ringing and attract attention.

Severinov tried to put his anger to one side, thinking quickly. If it was Johnson, it was unlikely that he would just walk away upon seeing a dead body. If he was trying to find out more about Yezhov and what he knew, then it was almost certain he would go into the apartment and search it.

His hand went instinctively to the Makarov pistol that he had stuck in his belt. This seemed like an unexpected opportunity to get both jobs on his list done together. "Let's get back to that apartment. Move, let's go."

* * *

Tuesday, April 8, 2014
   St. Petersburg

. . .

"You think Severinov ordered this?" Katya asked. "I don't understand why he would want to kill my mother."

"Probably because he thinks your mother knew something that he didn't want told," Johnson said. "Maybe the same thing your father knew."

The sound of a car engine and a slight squeal of brakes drifted through the open window from the street below. Johnson strode to the window and looked out. Down below, a black Mercedes had pulled to a halt outside the apartment building. Not two men, but four, all in black clothing, got out and moved in a businesslike fashion toward the doors.

Shit.

Johnson felt another jet of adrenaline spurt through him. He didn't wait to try and get a better view of who they were. He knew.

He turned to Katya. "Listen, we are in some danger right now. I think the men who shot your mother have just come back. There's four of them now. Can you help us get out of here—fast?"

Katya jumped to her feet and then looked at the body on the floor. "What about my mother?" She looked as though she was about to burst into tears again.

Johnson momentarily felt pulled in two directions. The girl's mother had just been murdered in front of her in cold blood, not long after her father had been killed, and he felt terrible about it. But then self-preservation took over.

"Katya, I will help you take care of your mother later, but if we don't leave right now, we will also be dead. They are coming back. We need to move—right now. We'll have to leave her."

Johnson thought quickly. If there were four men, and he had to assume they were all trained security services guys, they would know how to seal off a building. It was virtually certain that they would have checked out the apartments carefully before their operation to kill Varvara and would know the layout.

"How many sets of stairs and elevators are there?" Johnson asked.

"Two stairs, the main ones and the emergency escape stairs at the back of the building. And two elevators. The main one and a small service elevator at the rear."

"There's no exterior fire escape?" Johnson asked.

Katya shook her head.

Johnson assumed they would have one guy guarding the elevator doors and stairwells at street level at the front, another doing likewise at the back, and two that would most likely come to the apartment.

"Is there anywhere we could hide?" Johnson asked.

"There is a neighbor's apartment. An old couple. We keep an eye on it for them. They may be at home, but I have a key if not."

"Get it." He would have to hope the neighbors were not at home. If they were, they would have to act to keep them quiet if necessary.

Katya ran to a row of hooks above the kitchen countertop and grabbed a key. Then she turned back toward Johnson and stopped, her face visibly stressed.

"We have two pistols. Shall I bring them?"

This woman's tougher than she looks, Johnson thought.

"Yes. But quick," he said. A pistol would be hugely helpful.

Katya ran to a bedroom. There was the sound of some piece of furniture being dragged across the floor and then a squeak, followed by a loud smack as something was slammed shut. She reemerged a few seconds later holding two identical Heckler & Koch P7s, two spare magazines, and two slim black suppressors.

She offered a gun, a magazine, and a suppressor to Johnson and put the others in her jacket pocket. Johnson noticed that the P7s both had threaded barrels for the suppressors.

"Suppressors?" Johnson asked, again taken slightly aback. *Where the hell did she get those from?*

Katya's face tightened. "My father was an SVR colonel. They belonged to him."

Johnson glanced at the safety of the P7 she had given him to ensure it was on, then slipped the gun and magazine into one of his jacket pockets and the suppressor into the other.

"Let's get out of here," he said.

Katya led the way out of the apartment, glancing down at her mother's body on the floor as she went. Johnson took the key from the inside of the door and locked it as he left. If the Russians were looking for him, they would inevitably break into the apartment, see Varvara's body, and hopefully conclude that Johnson had put it there and had left the building in a hurry. Locking the door would at least slow them down.

The light indicators on the elevator panel showed that there a car was coming up, already at the third floor. Johnson could hear the elevator mechanism whirring.

Katya ran along the hallway past a few apartments and stopped at the next, Johnson close behind her. She bent down, pushed the key into the cylinder lock and opened it, then removed the key.

Behind him, Johnson could hear the clunking sound of the elevator doors beginning to open.

He followed Katya and gently closed the apartment door behind him.

CHAPTER TWENTY-THREE

Tuesday, April 8, 2014
  St. Petersburg

Severinov and Balagula emerged from the elevator door on the fourth floor of the apartment building, both with their pistols in hand.

The hallway was deserted and quiet. Severinov, the knuckles on his right hand showing white where he was gripping his Makarov, and his eyes darting, took in the scene.

"That one, presumably?" Severinov muttered, pointing at the closed apartment door opposite the elevators. There was a slight blood smear on the tiled surface next to the door and more blood specks on the white wall.

Balagula nodded. "They've moved the body."

Severinov strode to the door and knocked twice. There was no response. He tried the handle. It was locked. "This is the police. Can you open the door, please," he called. There was no reply, so he called again, this time more loudly. Nothing.

Severinov looked around and spotted a fire extinguisher cylinder hanging on the wall on the far side of the hallway. "Use that," he said.

It took Balagula less than a minute to use the bottom of the metal cylinder as a battering ram to smash open the door, splintering the frame as the lock gave way.

Severinov stood to one side of the door, providing cover with his gun as he did so, and both men flattened themselves against the walls to either side of the entrance as the door swung open.

The first thing they saw was the lifeless body of Varvara Yezhova lying on the floor. The lights were off, and there was no sign of Joe Johnson.

Severinov, holding his gun in both hands, his body taut, inched his way along the wall as gradually his view of the rest of the apartment opened up.

There was nobody in the living room, nor in the three bedrooms, nor the kitchen or bathroom. The rest of the apartment appeared to be deserted.

"*Dermo*," Severinov said. "If it was him, he's gone."

"I think it was him," Balagula said.

Severinov glanced around. On the mantelpiece was a photograph of Gennady and Varvara Yezhova standing next to the driver's door of a red Škoda sedan. Sitting in the driver's seat was an attractive girl, who Severinov guessed was aged in her midtwenties, with shoulder-length dark brown hair.

That must be Katya, the daughter, he figured.

Another photograph showed the couple sitting on a park bench with the same girl and a boy who looked to be in his late teens, with short blond hair, who was presumably Timur.

"Nice-looking kids," Severinov said.

"Yes."

"Do they live here permanently?"

"Yes."

Severinov paused for a few seconds. He was confident that the front of the building was effectively sealed off, with Pugachov guarding the elevators and the stairs at street level at the front of the building and Gurko the secondary set of stairs and entrance at the rear.

The likely conclusion was that Johnson had managed to get out of the building and away before they had arrived. Unless, that is, he was hiding somewhere else in the building.

"Let's try the other apartments on this floor and check if anyone saw Johnson," Severinov said.

They set off and began knocking on doors. Each time Severinov called the same thing. "Is anyone there? Can you open the door? This is the police."

There was no response at any of them. Most people would be out at work, he assumed. And even if people were in, it wouldn't be surprising if they didn't answer, given the noise they had made when breaking into the apartment. They were probably all hiding behind their doors, staring at him through their security fish-eye-lens peepholes.

But all he needed was to strike lucky—an old man or an old lady, who might have seen Johnson.

* * *

Tuesday, April 8, 2014
    St. Petersburg

"Katya! What are you doing?" The voice was cracked and reedy. A diminutive white-haired woman who looked to be in her eighties, perhaps even older, stood at the far end of the entrance hallway. "Who is that man?"

"Quiet, Nina," Katya hissed. "We are in danger. Some men are after us. My mother has been shot."

The old woman squealed, causing Johnson's heart to jump.

"Just shut up," Johnson muttered under his breath.

Nina belatedly clapped her hand to her mouth. "Your mother has been *shot?*" she whispered. "Dead, you mean? Here? And we heard nothing?"

"You are both old and deaf, Nina," Katya said. "Go and sit down. I will explain." She took the old lady by the arm and gently led her into a living room, leaving Johnson in the hallway.

From the corridor outside, Johnson could hear the faint sound of two men's voices. He picked up a few words, then heard a knock on a door, followed by someone speaking louder and quite audibly: "This is the police. Can you open the door, please?"

A short while later, there was a series of loud thuds followed by a crunching, splintering sound. As predicted, the Russians were smashing their way into the apartment. He was just going to have to hope that once they found it contained only Varvara's body, they would leave.

Johnson placed his ear to the door and tried to listen. The thuds had stopped, but the voices continued. He could not make out what was being said.

After several more minutes, he heard footsteps on the tiled corridor floor, followed by vigorous knocking on neighboring doors.

"Is anyone there? Can you open? This is the police," a loud man's voice said after each volley of knocking. No one opened their doors—either they were too frightened to do so, or everyone was out at work.

Johnson took the Heckler & Koch from his pocket and clicked off the safety.

As was often the case when Johnson found himself in such

situations, a large colorful image of his two children flashed across his mind.

Why do I do this?

The sound of footsteps grew louder. There came a sharp knock at the door that echoed down the hallway.

Johnson applied his eye to the fish-eye security peephole at the door and jumped a little as the distorted image of a man's face appeared in the tiny circular glass lens.

It was Severinov.

CHAPTER TWENTY-FOUR

Tuesday, April 8, 2014
   St. Petersburg

After knocking on about twenty-five doors, or it might have been thirty—he lost count—Severinov stopped. This was fruitless.

He tried to put himself in Johnson's shoes. If Johnson had arrived at the apartment and had found Yezhov's wife dead, what would he do?

Without doubt he was trying to find out more about the secrets her husband had been intending to pass to the West before the successful assassination in Berlin. So who else could he try? The children? Severinov thought it highly unlikely that Yezhov would have confided very much at all in Katya or Timur. Their father wouldn't want to put them at risk, and what they didn't know they couldn't be forced to give to the FSB or any other agency.

But that wouldn't stop Johnson from trying. He seemed a determined man and presumably wasn't going to just give up and go home. If anything, the sight of Varvara's body would make him even more inclined to believe that dark secrets were being covered up.

So Severinov concluded that Johnson would most likely return to the apartment at some stage.

He turned to Balagula. "We can't break into every place in the building. We'll get Pugachov to put Yezhov's apartment under round-the-clock surveillance. My bet is that Johnson will be back to speak to the kids."

"Yes, agreed, boss. He's empty-handed so far. The kids are his last hope, even if they know nothing."

Severinov nodded. He started toward the elevators. "We'll give the stairs, elevators, and the basement a search, and if we can't find him, our work here is done for now. We'll get Pugachov's gorillas to take care of him."

But their search ultimately turned up nothing, and when they met with Pugachov at the front entrance to the building, the FSB man was busy handing out cards with a hotline phone number to a group of residents who had emerged from one of the elevators. He showed his FSB identity card, described Johnson, and instructed them to call the number on the card if they spotted him.

It was a sensible move, Severinov thought as he watched. The psychology of informing on neighbors and complying with instructions from police and security services had been ingrained into most Russians, especially the older ones, during the communist era and was still prevalent. Everyone ran scared of the FSB.

One middle-aged woman, wearing a white nurse's uniform beneath a blue jacket that was unzipped, paused to scrutinize Pugachov's card. She looked up at him. "I saw the man you are describing earlier," she said. "On my way into the apartments. I came in through the front door, and he followed me in. It was as if he had been waiting for someone to enter to tail them in. He made some kind of a joke and insisted I go first. He spoke Russian but sounded foreign."

Pugachov frowned. He followed up with a series of questions about where the man had gone and what he had been wearing, but beyond describing his waistcoat and glasses and that he had gone to the stairs, she was unable to give anything of further use. He took her cell phone number, apartment details, and name.

Severinov stepped forward. "Where are you going now?" he asked the woman. She seemed like a useful witness.

"I am going to my car. I keep it parked at the rear of the building," she said.

"Where are you driving to?"

"I am a hospital nurse and I have a night shift," she said.

"Please, keep your phone switched on. We might need more information from you. And if you see the man again, please give Mr. Pugachov a call," Severinov said.

The woman nodded. "Yes, I'll certainly do that." She headed for the exit.

Pugachov turned to Severinov. "I have two more men on their way here. They will work with me and Gurko to keep this building under close surveillance. If Johnson comes back, we'll see him. I need to go back to the safe house. I suggest you come with me; then we can discuss what we do next."

Severinov nodded and turned to Balagula. "Vasily, you stay here with the FSB team. You know Johnson—if you see him, disable him. I don't want him dead at this stage, though."

Balagula grinned. "Don't worry. I'll make sure he's disabled."

"Good," Severinov said. He and Pugachov headed out the door toward the Mercedes.

* * *

Tuesday, April 8, 2014
   St. Petersburg

When Johnson had seen Severinov through the peephole, he
had briefly considered opening the door and putting a round
into him. But that was the nuclear option and would most
likely open up a whole can of worms and unintended consequences—probably nasty ones.

   Instead, he had remained utterly silent.

   During the following few hours, Johnson checked
frequently out the window of Nina's apartment to see
whether the black Mercedes was still parked outside. But it
did not move. Presumably Severinov and his cronies were
searching the building.

   Unlike the Yezhovs' apartment, which had been fully
modernized, including a kitchen with granite countertops and
most appliances seen in American homes, this one looked as
though it had not been touched since the Stalin era. It was
more like how Johnson imagined Russian apartments to be
outside the glitzy center of Moscow.

   All the walls and ceilings, including the kitchen and bathroom, were painted in a nicotine-colored brown that was
peeling in places. The kitchen consisted of a couple of
unpainted wooden cabinets attached to the wall, a freestanding electric oven, and a large fridge that had yellowed
with age. The only modern appliance was a gas boiler that
hung on the wall next to the cooker. The sofas were covered
in a worn floral pattern that had a number of holes.

   Nina's husband, Ivor, who had a mop of white hair that
made him look like an eccentric professor, did not move from
his armchair in the living room the whole time they were
there and only spoke briefly, when his wife asked him if he
would like tea.

Johnson watched as she heaped several spoons of dry tea leaves into a teapot and poured in boiling water from a rusting old electric kettle. Normally a coffee drinker, he sometimes enjoyed tea for a change. But the concoction that Nina produced was the thickest and darkest he had ever seen, even in Russia, where on previous visits years ago he had gotten used to the traditions of strong tea. He wondered whether Nina would have to cut it out of the pot with a knife.

After she had left it to brew for several minutes, she poured it into cups but filled them only halfway. Then she indicated to Johnson to top off his cup with hot water if he wanted to dilute it and to take his pick from cups of sugar and honey, and a lemon that had been cut into slices.

Johnson put a spoonful of honey and a slice of lemon in his tea. He had to admit, once diluted a little, it tasted better than he had expected.

As he sipped the brew, Johnson could not help recalling Severinov's parting words to him and Jayne the last time he had seen the oligarch at Bagram Air Base in Afghanistan. They were ingrained in his mind.

Don't come to Russia. I have friends deep inside the FSB and SVR—I will make sure you are both on their list.

He was glad that Katya had thought to bring the pistols, which now lay on the table between them.

"Do you know how to use those?" he asked, nodding toward the weapons.

"I'm Russian. My father spent a lot of time teaching me and my brother how to use guns, and I also used to go shooting in the woods with a couple of friends from university. One of my friends had a father who was special forces, a Spetsnaz member—she knew how to shoot and handle a gun. I learned a lot from her, I can tell you. Don't worry, I'm very good with them."

She explained that she had studied international relations at St. Petersburg University, and a handful of her cohort had also been the children of middle- or high-ranking FSB and SVR officers. They all took the view that learning how to use firearms and other self-defense techniques was a good idea.

Johnson was extremely tempted to dispatch a short text message to Jayne, who he assumed was now in London, and Vic, in Berlin, to update them. In fact, it was a pity she wasn't here with him right now. But he held back, concerned that the FSB would be checking all communications traffic in the immediate area. Even if they were unable to read his encrypted message, they might be able to identify his German cell phone number, pinpoint that it was being used from somewhere in the apartments, and start a new door-to-door search of the building. In any case, neither of them would be able to do anything to help him in his current situation.

Just after ten o'clock, Nina served them a large bowl of chunky beef and beetroot soup, served with a dollop of sour cream on the top and some brown bread. "I am sorry, it is all I have," she said. By that stage, Johnson's stomach was rumbling, and the meal was extremely welcome.

Johnson finished his food and walked to the window yet again. The Mercedes had gone, but two men in dark suits were standing on the sidewalk near where it had been parked. Even if Severinov and Balagula had left in the Mercedes, their sidekicks clearly hadn't.

Severinov might logically assume that with Yezhov and his wife dead, Johnson would want to do exactly what he was doing now—making contact with Yezhov's children. And presumably he would want to prevent that.

Johnson beckoned Katya to the window and pointed at the two men.

"FSB," she said as soon as she saw them. "They're guarding the place."

"We could try and make a move now, but maybe we should wait until early morning and go before sunrise," Johnson said. "Maybe by then they will have given up or dozed off. We can try and get some sleep here ourselves." He indicated toward the two spare bedrooms that led off Nina's hallway.

"Yes. I agree. It is a little risky to stay but riskier to try and leave right now. I do not think they will search every apartment in this building, just the public areas. Before sunrise is better."

Katya discussed the options with Nina, who agreed that they could stay overnight. She showed them the spare bedrooms. Both were furnished in a very basic fashion: one had a rustic wooden bed but the other just a mattress on the floor.

"I have been thinking we could take my father's old escape route out of the building," Katya said to Johnson. "He had it prepared in case of trouble and he needed to move quickly."

That sounded promising to Johnson. Katya described a route using the service elevator down to the second basement and out through a fire door to an alleyway that formed a narrow thoroughfare between Bolshoy Prospekt and the street that ran behind and parallel to it, Malyy Prospekt.

"My car is parked along the alley, near to Malyy Prospekt. We can use that."

"What happens if the elevator stops at street level on the way through and we find FSB guards there?" Johnson asked.

"Don't worry. I know how to override the elevator. Now I need to make a couple of calls to arrange our escape and to speak to Timur, my brother. Please excuse me."

"I hope your phone is secure."

"Yes. I bought the SIM card two days ago. I change them every week. My father insisted we all do that."

She disappeared into one of Nina's bedrooms and shut the door. Johnson could hear her speaking in rapid Russian but could not pick up what she was saying.

This girl was resourceful, Johnson had to say. But getting out of the building safely and bypassing the surveillance that was surely in place was only a first step.

When Katya reappeared ten minutes later, Johnson asked what the escape route would be. "Using your car is good, but there is the question of where we drive to. I am now assuming that if the FSB is involved, they may have worked out my false identity. So my hotel is a nonstarter, and they will probably also have alerted the airports and railway stations. I will now be the target of a hunting pack. Basically, I need to get out of the country."

Katya stroked her chin. "Mr. Johnson, my father—"

"Call me Joe."

"Joe, as you might expect, my father had a plan to get out of Russia in case he was ever blown," Katya said. "He never completely trusted the CIA's exfiltration procedures for use in case of emergency, which involved pickups by boats on the Black Sea or the Baltic. So he devised his own alternative as well. We will follow that same route. That is what I have just been arranging on the phone."

"What's the route?"

Katya paused. "I will tell you as we go along."

This one gives nothing away—she's far too well trained, Johnson thought to himself. He was tempted to remonstrate but checked himself. Could she be trusted? He was far from certain, but right now he had no alternative options. He would have to go along with it.

"You said 'we'?" Johnson asked. "You intend to come too? What about your mother? You will need to bury her. And what about Timur? Don't worry—you had better stay here, and I can go alone." He had had difficulty getting the image of Varvara Yezhova, lying dead in her apartment only just down the corridor, out of his mind, and it didn't take too much imagination to realize what might be going through Katya's mind.

"Yes, I said *we*. I will come with you. It's dangerous for me to stay. The exit route is complicated—you won't be able to do it by yourself," Katya said. She sounded confident, but the frown lines that creased her forehead and her cheeks told a slightly different story. "My brother is away in Moscow right now. I have just been speaking with him. It is not safe for him to come back here, of course, so he is going to Turkey. He has an escape route he can take via the Black Sea, and he will get some friends to take care of arrangements for my mother. Don't worry, we are used to this kind of thing. You will need me to guide you. I have the contacts. My father made sure of that. And your Russian, while fluent, would never pass for that of a native." There was a note of finality in her voice.

Johnson swiftly thought it through. What she said made sense. He needed a quick exit from Russia, and Katya appeared to provide that possibility. She seemed very switched on and aware of the need to take rigid precautions against FSB surveillance. But that was probably what he would have expected as the daughter of a defecting CIA agent who had operated successfully for many years within the SVR. She seemed to have been taught well, and it was entirely her decision whether to stay or go.

"All right. We go at four in the morning, then," Johnson said. "Let's pray that those FSB animals outside are asleep by then."

He just had to hope an early morning escape would work. It would mean his mission in St. Petersburg had failed: he was no further forward in discovering what secrets Gennady Yezhov was intending to convey to the West.

Johnson walked to the window and glanced out. As he did so, a thought crossed his mind.

"You said your father didn't confide in you what information he was defecting with, correct?" Johnson asked. He turned and leaned against the windowsill, his arms folded.

"No, nothing."

"But is there anyone whom he *did* confide in about these things? Someone I could speak to?" Johnson asked.

She looked down at the floor for a few moments, then back up at Johnson.

"There is a man. My father called him the Nazi's son."

Johnson jerked bolt upright and stared at Katya. "The *Nazi's* son?"

"Yes. My father said that if anything happened to him or my mother, and if anyone tried to find out what information he was taking with him, I was to tell them to talk to this man. That is all I know."

Now she tells me.

"Who is he, this Nazi's son?" Johnson asked. "Does he live here?"

"He is an old friend of my father's. He is not here—he's from Germany. From Berlin, I think, although I do not know if he is still there. They knew each other years ago, when my father and mother met there. They were in the KGB, but I believe the man worked for the Stasi."

Johnson tugged at his right ear. This sounded like a highly promising revelation. "Is he really a Nazi's son? Can't you give me his name?"

"I presume he is, but as for the name, we first need to get safely out of Russia. Then I will tell you."

"Katya—"

"No, Joe. What you don't know, you can't be forced to tell. I cannot risk the FSB finding out about him."

"And do you have his contact details?" Johnson pressed her.

"Only his name—in my head. I do not know where he lives—or even if he is still alive."

CHAPTER TWENTY-FIVE

Tuesday, April 8, 2014
London

For the fourth time in an hour, Jayne checked the GPS monitor app on her phone. The satellite map showed a blue dot that had remained stationary on Bolshoy Prospekt, St. Petersburg, for the previous few hours.

At first, she had been reassured that Johnson had reached his target address, and presumably the fact that he was remaining there for a while, rather than departing swiftly, was good news. She assumed that he had made contact with Varvara Yezhova and hopefully was making some progress.

But as the hours dragged on, her optimism turned to concern. She was certain that Johnson would intend to deal as quickly as possible with Varvara, both for his own security and hers. The longer Johnson remained "off grid" and away from the conference he was supposed to be attending, the greater the risk of discovery and intervention by the FSB.

Surely an hour with Yezhov's widow would have been

more than enough to secure the information he needed. Something had gone wrong; she was convinced of it.

Jayne had flown from Berlin to London the previous day, arriving during the afternoon, and had returned to her apartment on Portsoken Street. Since then, she had continued to work at home on plans for a special surveillance operation to be run against Anastasia Shevchenko.

She enjoyed the peace and solitude of her apartment and, two years after leaving MI6, also liked not having to go into an office each day.

Now, at half past nine in the evening, she was still awaiting the arrival of Nicklin-Donovan, who had been scheduled to arrive at seven. Her former boss at MI6 had decided to visit her on his way home rather than ask her to go to Vauxhall Cross. He wanted to keep her deployment on the Shevchenko and Blackbird operations as low-key as possible.

But Nicklin-Donovan had been delayed because a crisis had erupted at work over contingency planning for the conflict that was looming between Russia and Western military forces in the Black Sea.

Finally, the security buzzer mounted on the wall near her door rang.

When Nicklin-Donovan walked in, he had faint bags under his eyes and a gray pallor. He removed his jacket and immediately asked for a strong espresso.

Once he had the coffee in hand, he sat at Jayne's dining table and listened attentively as she ran through her plan for Shevchenko involving two new surveillance teams, which she had named B1 and B2.

"Why are you calling them B teams?" Nicklin-Donovan asked.

"So they don't get too arrogant," Jayne said with a faint smile. "I don't want them referring to themselves as the A team."

B1 would replace the unit that Nicklin-Donovan had been deploying against the Russian previously. Jayne could see that the operation had been run professionally, but her suspicion was that Shevchenko had either spotted the previous incumbents, which would explain why they had so far operated empty-handed, or that they simply were not good enough.

"They need to know when to back off," Jayne said. "We need to give her enough rope to hang herself. I don't know how the existing team has been working but maybe they have been too tight on her."

Nicklin-Donovan shrugged. "Not sure. Maybe it's just that Shevchenko is bloody good on the street. She's like a leopard looking out for poachers. The slightest whiff in the air, and she's called off the hunt."

The second team that Jayne proposed, B2, would keep watch on the motorbike dead drop parking location that Johnson had extracted from Schwartz, on the corner of Bread Street and Cannon Street near St. Paul's Cathedral. The idea was that they should put a tail on anyone they saw parking the bike or depositing or collecting items from the pannier bag.

The operation would run round the clock, twenty-four hours a day, seven days a week, for the next three weeks at least, covering the period beyond Shevchenko's scheduled departure to Moscow. Jayne's thinking was that with new developments surfacing every day in the Black Sea, and also with the counterintelligence hunt heating up, the SVR mole who was feeding information from inside Western intelligence would effectively force Shevchenko to act very soon to get her new material to Moscow Center. Shevchenko would not be able to just sit on time-sensitive information for long. And that would be the surveillance teams' opportunity.

Having given a broad outline of her intentions, Jayne then went over the finer details of the operation that she had strung together over the previous couple of days. She ended with her thinking that she herself would play a part in the operation but not lead it, given she was now an MI6 outsider.

Nicklin-Donovan nodded. "It looks comprehensive. Let's firm it up and press the button. I've got a surveillance team in mind that we could use, and a guy named Gary Bennett to lead it. I'll send them a message tonight and get them moving tomorrow first thing. We'll make an early start—I'll get a safe house prepared overnight."

Jayne smiled, relieved that he had accepted her ideas. She had been expecting more pushback. She rose and made him another espresso.

"Thanks," Nicklin-Donovan said as she pushed the refilled cup across the table to him.

"I suggest we keep this operation very tight," Jayne said. "No reports circulating to anyone describing what we are doing. No update meetings, even internally at any level. We can't afford for it to leak. I think there should be nothing written down, as far as possible."

Nicklin-Donovan exhaled. "Agreed, even though it could get me fired if it goes wrong. We have not circulated any details of the surveillance operation on Shevchenko so far anyway, and that will continue. If anything, we'll make it even tighter. I was already thinking along those lines." He paused for a moment. "Listen, I will have to inform C, of course, but that will be it. I will just have to hope he backs me and that he doesn't inform anyone else himself."

"And is there any news from St. Petersburg?" Nicklin-Donovan asked, taking a sip of coffee. "I'm assuming you've not heard from Joe—otherwise you'd have told me."

"No, and that's the problem," Jayne said. She showed Nicklin-Donovan the tracker app, which was still displaying a blue dot at Varvara's apartment building, and outlined her concerns.

"Hmm. Let's not jump the gun," Nicklin-Donovan said, his forehead creased, as he sipped his coffee. "We don't know for sure that something is wrong."

Jayne shrugged. "That's true."

"You're quite concerned about him, aren't you?"

"A little. I'm sure he can look after himself, though."

Nicklin-Donovan scratched his temple and gave Jayne an oblique glance. "Are you two getting close again?"

Her old boss knew that they had once been a couple for a short time, many years ago in Islamabad. But she hadn't expected him to suddenly raise the topic out of the blue, and caught unawares, she felt the color rising a little in her cheeks. It was unusual for her to blush.

He would without a doubt have noticed her slight embarrassment, of that she was certain. "We're close in terms of work, but that's all, Mark."

It was true in the literal sense, but she had to admit, she had increasingly been having what-if moments. She liked Johnson a lot, and after a few failed relationships she still hadn't given up on the idea of finding someone whom she could settle down with.

Johnson was still single, nine years after his wife had sadly died. However, he lived in Portland with his two teenagers and she was based thousands of miles away on the other side of the Atlantic. Could it work? She kept asking herself the question, and always the answer came back from somewhere inside her head: if she didn't try, she would never know. She suspected that Johnson might feel the same way, although they had both somehow avoided discussing their relationship, past and present.

For a short while, she had suspected that he might have feelings for one of his old flames, a Washington, DC–based journalist, Fiona Heppenstall, with whom he had a brief relationship a year or so after his wife had died. Johnson and

Jayne had worked with Fiona on a couple of investigations. But there had been no sign that relations between them these days were anything other than professional and just friendly.

Often Jayne blamed herself for being overly independent and thus making it difficult to build lasting relationships, but she told herself that that was the way she was. She couldn't change her personality. One thing that encouraged her in terms of Johnson was that he was an equally independent type of character. *Perhaps we would fit well together?*

"I hope you didn't mind me asking," Nicklin-Donovan said. "Just curious, that's all."

"It's fine, no problem," Jayne said.

"Good. There was something else I wanted to ask you as well."

Oh God, now what? she wondered. "Go ahead."

Nicklin-Donovan paused. "Are you happy working as a freelancer? You were inside Vauxhall Cross for a long time, and before you left you still seemed quite motivated."

What's brought this on? Jayne thought.

"There's a difference between being happy and being motivated," she said. "I left because I wasn't happy. Why are you asking?"

"We've lost a lot of people in the past eighteen months. A lot of skills and knowledge have gone out the door." Nicklin-Donovan raised an eyebrow. "Yours included."

"What kind of skills do you mean?"

Is he trying to hint he wants me back?

"Putin is starting to cause a lot of concern, as you can see from the current operation we're running and what's going on in the Crimea and the Black Sea. C is coming under pressure from the prime minister and from Westminster, and other things have been happening inside the tent that I can't share with you. To be blunt, our Russia expertise is depleted."

Jayne had heard on the grapevine that since her departure,

MI6 had lost a few more key people, both inside Russia and at headquarters. But she shook her head. "No, I'm not coming back in. I'm enjoying my freedom too much to go back to a regular job. I like the variety."

Nicklin-Donovan nodded. "Fair enough. If you ever want to talk, though, let me know." He stood and put on his jacket. "I need to go. My wife will wonder where I am."

Jayne also stood and showed him to the door.

"And I wouldn't worry about Joe," Nicklin-Donovan said as he reached for the door handle. "Maybe he is simply getting a bigger download from Varvara than we expected."

"I doubt it," Jayne said. "It just wouldn't take that long. I know how Joe operates. He would want to be quick."

"I guess he would," Nicklin-Donovan said. He kept one hand on the door handle but turned to face Jayne. "But even if he is in some sort of difficulty, we can't exactly expect Washington to send in an army helicopter to St. Petersburg and exfil him this time, can we?" It was a reference to the rescue mission Jayne had instigated for Johnson in Kabul the previous year.

Jayne shrugged but said nothing. Nicklin-Donovan was right. They might know where Johnson was, but they couldn't easily fish him out this time. He was on his own.

CHAPTER TWENTY-SIX

Wednesday, April 9, 2014
St. Petersburg

Johnson managed no more than a couple of hours sleep on the mattress on Nina's spare bedroom floor. He woke a few times and on each occasion walked to the living room window to check whether the FSB guards were still outside the building. At one o'clock in the morning, they were still there, but by quarter past three they had gone.

Johnson did not sleep again after that and waited for Katya to wake up, which she did at about quarter to four.

He pushed the H&K into his belt and put on his jacket, covering up the gun, then thanked Nina, who was hovering in the living room, still in her day clothes. She also appeared to have had little sleep but showed no surprise or irritation at the subterfuge taking place in her apartment. Maybe she was used to this kind of thing, Johnson surmised.

It was still dark outside when Johnson and Katya left. Before they did so, Katya screwed the suppressor onto the barrel of her H&K. She noticed Johnson looking at her and shrugged. "We might need it," she said. Johnson decided against attaching his; in his experience of using suppressors on H&K pistols, they did reduce the noise but not dramatically so. He preferred to be able to keep the gun tucked in his belt, which he couldn't do if the suppressor cylinder was screwed on.

They got Nina to check the corridor outside her apartment first, but there was no sign of anyone there, so they followed the corridor around to the service elevator at the rear of the building.

Once in the elevator car, Katya pressed the button for the second basement and simultaneously kept her thumb on the Close Doors button, holding her gun in her right hand. She continued to push the two buttons as the car descended. Sure enough, it continued through all floors without stopping.

The second basement had one dim lightbulb illuminating the short corridor onto which the elevator door opened. The floor was bare concrete, and there was a set of double swing doors at the end of the corridor. Without hesitating, Katya led the way through the doors and into a darkened room. She flicked on the flashlight on her cell phone and covered the light with a finger to minimize its beam.

The room was about fifteen yards long, ten yards wide, and completely filthy. It stank of diesel fumes, and the bare brick walls were covered with dirt and cobwebs. A loud humming came from what Johnson assumed was an electricity transformer that stood behind a wire mesh barrier in one corner. In the center of the room was a large diesel tank next to a generator that was not functioning. Presumably this provided backup power in the event of an electricity grid failure.

Katya did not pause. She strode across the room to

another set of double doors on the far side and passed through them.

Now they were in another smaller hallway that was empty apart from a rusting old bicycle that stood against one wall and four garbage cans.

Katya pointed toward a set of twin fire doors, painted black, with horizontal bars that needed to be pushed downward to open the doors.

"We go out there, then up some steps to street level. Follow me," she said.

"Wait," Johnson cautioned. "Slowly. We'll need to check carefully for anyone out there. Don't charge ahead; let me do the checking. We can't afford to blow this. How far is it to your car?"

"Two minutes' walk, maximum. Maybe one minute."

Johnson nodded and indicated for her to continue. He hoped the fire doors were not linked to some kind of alarm.

Katya pushed one of the bars down and gently pushed the door a few inches outward. A rush of cool air came in. She slipped through the gap, with Johnson close behind, and moved to the left of the doors.

No alarm sounded. Johnson pushed the door closed behind him but didn't click it shut. They might need to go back.

They were in a small courtyard, no more than a couple of yards wide and ten yards long, paved with concrete slabs and located at the bottom of a kind of pit. The fire doors from which they had emerged were right in the corner. Behind them the vertical wall of the building stretched upward; in front was another steep brick wall with a set of steps cut into it leading up to ground level. There was a handrail down the right-hand side.

Johnson took several moments to survey the steps and

listen. There was no sound other than the distant hum of traffic. No footsteps rushing toward them, no voices.

With no warning, the fire door behind them squeaked and rattled. Johnson whirled around and instinctively flattened himself against the building wall so that the door hinges were immediately to his right. Katya soundlessly did likewise.

Simultaneously, Johnson pulled out his pistol and flicked off the safety. He heard a faint sound to his left as Katya did the same.

The door opened slowly and silently, swinging back inch by inch in their direction. Someone must have followed them into the basement, although Johnson had heard nothing. This had to be one of the FSB gorillas.

Eventually, the dark outline of a man's head appeared at the side of the fire door. He was looking the other way, scanning the small yard.

Johnson's thoughts raced. Did he want to shoot the guy, thus making a noise that could alert other security guards nearby? The answer was no. Instead, he raised his pistol, preparing to club it down hard onto the man's temple.

But as he did so, there came a loud bang right next to him, making him jump involuntarily.

The man's head whiplashed back. His arm stretched out, and his body catapulted backward. The man, who wore a black jacket and trousers, slumped to the ground and lay motionless.

Johnson felt a hand grasp his arm. He turned to see Katya holding her H&K and signaling urgently to him with the barrel that they should go up the steps and away.

Shit, Johnson muttered inwardly. *Who is this woman?*

She moved to the bottom step and started climbing, taking them two at a time, using the handrail to help haul herself upward.

His first reaction was to be angry. The gunshot had been

far louder than he would have expected with a suppressor—certainly not the muffled *thwack* that emerged from certain other models. It had possibly been magnified by the quiet of the night, but either way, it would almost certainly have woken people in the apartment block: they were probably scurrying to their windows right now. It must surely also have alerted the man's colleagues, assuming he had some nearby. But Katya had not given him the option.

Johnson too set off up the steps after Katya. The stairs were steep and all the steps were shallow, leaving little space for footholds. But Johnson climbed as quickly as he could, also taking most of them two at a time and clinging to the handrail as he went.

By the time he reached the top, he was breathing hard. Katya had veered right and was ten yards ahead of him, jogging across a small concrete parking lot toward a narrow access street, no more than an alleyway, that ran parallel to the rear of the building. She unscrewed the suppressor from her gun as she went and stuffed both items into her jacket pocket.

Johnson glanced to his right and left. There was no sign of anyone running, no shouting. Behind him, he heard what sounded like a window creaking open, but he didn't turn to look.

Their only option now was to get to the car as quickly as possible and away. He too began to run and caught up with Katya in the street. They continued another twenty yards and then she wordlessly turned left onto another narrow street, where they slowed to a brisk walk. At the far end, four cars were parked in a bay to the right of the street that was illuminated by a streetlight. A fifth car, a blue Volkswagen, was reversing into the space nearest to them.

"Mine's at the far end," Katya said.

As they drew near to the row of cars, the driver's door of

the Volkswagen swung open, and a woman stepped out. Johnson immediately recognized her as the same woman whom he had tailed into the apartment building hours earlier.

The woman shut the car door, clicked on her key fob to lock it, and then turned and started off in Johnson's direction. She was wearing a blue jacket that was unzipped, showing a white tunic-style nurse's dress beneath.

The woman looked up, saw Johnson, and stopped momentarily before appearing to gather herself and walking on.

Johnson swore beneath his breath but continued past her, deliberately not making eye contact or showing any kind of recognition.

What to do now? Wait until she was out of sight before jumping into Katya's car, or just go as quickly as possible? His gut instinct was to not let the woman see his getaway vehicle. But hanging around would seriously increase the risk of any FSB surveillance catching up with them—he estimated that every second counted following the gunshot—and would also look suspicious.

Johnson decided to say nothing and just go. Katya opened her car, a red Škoda Octavia, got into the driver's seat, and immediately started the engine. Johnson climbed into the passenger seat.

As Katya pulled out of the bay, Johnson could see the woman from the Volkswagen turning the corner toward the apartment building. She glanced back briefly in his direction, then continued.

Katya turned right onto Malyy Prospekt, a broad street lined with apartment buildings and offices, and accelerated hard past a stationary garbage truck, causing her tires to squeal a little as she let out the clutch.

Johnson turned and glanced behind, his heart now racing.

Beside him, he could hear Katya was breathing heavily, her knuckles showing white as she grasped the steering wheel.

Johnson could see no pursuing cars, but in the distance he heard a siren begin to wail.

* * *

Wednesday, April 9, 2014
   St. Petersburg

Severinov watched as Pugachov flipped open his laptop in the safe house and went through three layers of security before he was able to access his FSB account.

"I'm going to put an alert out to local police," Pugachov said. "We'll get them to keep a tight watch over the rail station, airport, and the highways out of St. Petersburg. Don't worry, we'll track Johnson down."

He began to type in staccato fashion, using two index fingers.

As he did so, Pugachov's phone rang. He answered it, then listened, beads of sweat appearing on his forehead. He stood and walked slowly around the room, the phone pinned to his ear.

"Shot *dead*? *Pizdets*, dammit," Pugachov said. He let rip with a stream of curses. "Where?"

Severinov picked up the gist of what had happened from Pugachov's end of the conversation. He stood and waited with his hands on his hips, listening. He could feel his blood pressure rising.

How the hell had Johnson managed to get the better of the FSB team that Pugachov had put in place at the apartments? And where had Balagula been? He assumed that the FSB had pulled rank over him—it was highly unlikely that

Balagula would have made the kind of error that apparently had occurred. He was too professional for that.

Pugachov gave a stream of instructions to whomever he was speaking to, who Severinov assumed was at the FSB headquarters in the Lubyanka in Moscow. Eventually he ended the call.

"Johnson's shot dead one of my surveillance team outside the apartment block," Pugachov said. His voice croaked a little, and a bead of sweat dripped down his cheek. "They found his body outside the basement fire doors. Johnson was apparently with a woman; they've left by car."

"A *woman*?"

"Yes. He was with her, and they got into a red Škoda. One of the women from the apartments—the one I spoke to—spotted them leaving in it and called the information desk number I gave her."

Severinov realized instantly what had happened. "That's most likely the daughter Katya's car," he said. "I saw a photograph in the apartment of her sitting in a red Škoda with her parents. Do we know how your officer spotted them?"

"Apparently he was guarding a service lift at the rear of the building and noticed a car coming down from the fourth floor. He pressed the elevator call button to intercept it, but the car shot straight through and down to the basement. He realized something was wrong, radioed for assistance—which is how we know about it—and chased down the stairs to try and track whoever was in the car. We now know it was Johnson and the girl. My officer must have caught up with them outside the building where Johnson shot him. At least, we assume it was Johnson who did the shooting."

"So either Johnson must have returned to the apartment to meet the daughter, or—"

"More likely they were hiding in the building somewhere," Pugachov said. "You could argue we should have searched more thoroughly, but we couldn't break into apartments if nobody was answering."

Severinov paused for a second, thinking. "Can you check whether there is a Škoda of that type registered to the Yezhovs' apartment address and get the plate number?" he asked.

Pugachov nodded. "We'll get the plate number and put an alert straight out to police to intercept it." He quickly dialed a number and fired off another volley of instructions.

There were probably hundreds of red Škodas in St. Petersburg, Severinov thought. Getting the plate number was essential.

"We need to be ready to move fast as soon as we get word of any sighting," Severinov said.

"Agreed," Pugachov said. "If Johnson's killed an FSB officer, we get a free strike at him as far as I'm concerned—he's a target."

Severinov took out his phone and dialed Balagula's number. The call was answered inside two rings.

"Vasily, I'm not going to ask what went wrong, but—"

"I'll tell you what went wrong. The FSB are a useless bunch of bastards. Amateurs. That officer got himself shot chasing after Johnson and that young girl. Pssht. My grandmother could have done better."

"I'm sure you're right. Listen. As soon as we get word where the daughter's car has gone, I'm going with Leonid to head after them. For the moment, you stay at the apartments in case Johnson and the girl resurface there. We'll come and collect you if we need you. And I'm changing my instructions: if you see Johnson, kill him. Understood?"

"Understood, boss."

CHAPTER TWENTY-SEVEN

Wednesday, April 9, 2014
  St. Petersburg

Katya drove northeast over a couple of road bridges that spanned the broad expanse of the Neva River. She accelerated hard and overtook two white vans and a truck on the second bridge; then, as she reached the north bank of the river, she cut back into the right-hand lane and braked when she saw a white car parked at the side of the street. It had a distinctive blue stripe along the side and a red-and-blue lights bar on the roof.

"Police," she said, unnecessarily.

As they passed it, Katya glanced in her mirrors, but the police car remained stationary.

"That's my worry," Johnson said. "They will be on red alert very soon. That woman saw us getting into this car. You can almost guarantee she would have been stopped and questioned on her way in—they must have found that guy's body by now. She can't fail to mention she saw us. You shouldn't have killed him. It was unnecessary."

Katya shrugged. It didn't seem to bother her in the slightest. "You are right. We probably have twenty minutes maximum."

"So, what then?"

"I have a solution," Katya said. "Don't worry. This was my father's escape plan." She patted her jacket pocket. "I have keys here for another car. We will swap."

"And the plan is to go where?" Johnson asked.

"We are going north, to cross the border into Finland," Katya said.

"But the border police and customs will be on the lookout for us long before we get there," Johnson said. "You've shot an FSB officer—you'll be on every watch list there is, and I will be too."

"That is not a problem," she said.

"How do we cross the border, then?"

"I can't tell you. Not yet. Do you have an EU visa?"

Johnson explained that he did not need an EU-wide visa, known as a Schengen visa, for a visit of less than ninety days under the agreement in place between the US and Europe.

"Ah yes, of course," Katya said. "We Russians do need one, which I have. I got it when I learned my father was planning to defect."

"Why can't you tell me how we cross the border?" Johnson asked. His voice now took on a slightly irritated tone. He was pleased to see that she had security at the top of her mind, but she did seem a little too dogmatic about it sometimes.

"I can't tell you in case we get stopped and interrogated," Katya said. "It's the same as with my father's contact—if you don't know, you can't tell them. It's how we operate in Russia, given the risks we face and the kind of interrogation we might face if arrested. They are brutal. But don't worry, it will be fine."

By now it was getting light. Katya followed a tight loop before heading west along the busy Primorsky Prospekt, laden with traffic across all three lanes, that ran along the north bank of the river. Here the highway was lined with a series of elegant, well-spaced apartment and office buildings set back behind trees.

She drove for a few minutes, past the distinctive yellow-painted circular domed structure of the Church of the Annunciation, and then cut a sharp right. Soon they were in an area dominated by apartment buildings, interspersed with badly maintained parks.

Katya did another right turn onto Serebryakov Pereulok, then slowed as she drew level with a tall, ugly redbrick apartment building, eight stories high. She turned through an archway beneath the building to a parking lot at the rear. There she pulled into an empty space and switched off the engine.

Two large dumpsters stood in a metal enclosure, filled with plastic trash bags from the apartments, which surrounded the parking lot on three sides. Johnson looked up. A man stood on a balcony outside one apartment wearing a white vest, smoking a cigarette and staring at them. On another balcony, two young children were riding a small plastic tricycle, laughing and giggling. The concrete paving slabs from which the lot was made were cracked and broken in places, but the cars parked there were mainly new, expensive models—Volvos, a BMW, and a couple of Audis.

"We leave the car here. Police are unlikely to come in here. Come, our other car is across there." She pointed to a row of vehicles in the next bay, then got out of the car, locked it, and led the way to a gunmetal-gray Lada Kalina, a five-door hatchback.

Johnson figured that it was at least a better, far more anonymous option than the red Škoda. Ladas were easily the most common car in Russia, where they were built.

Katya explained that the Lada belonged to one of her father's friends who had moved to Hong Kong to work for a couple of years and had left the car and his apartment in Katya's care while he was away.

"I drive it once a week to keep it going. Now it will get a longer run, it seems," she said as they climbed into the vehicle.

Five minutes later, they were back on the highway—the Western High Speed Diameter toll road—heading through the northern suburbs of St. Petersburg. The speedometer indicated a steady 110 kilometers per hour—exactly the limit that showed on the digital displays mounted on overhead gantries.

This was a very new high-quality, fast highway, with three lanes in each direction and lighting mounted on arches that curved over the traffic like giant elephants' tusks. Metal barriers on the right side of the road blocked the traffic noise from reaching nearby housing.

Soon they were out of the city; the highway was now flanked by green fields and trees that stretched across a flat, featureless landscape to the east and west.

After about thirty kilometers, Katya slowed as they approached a set of eight tollbooths that stretched across the highway. She headed for one of the five booths that required payment by either cash or credit card. She stopped next to the booth, wound down her window, and leaned out to insert several coins into the machine.

Within seconds, the red-and-white boom had lifted, and they were on their way again. Soon they filtered right to join the M10, the highway that ran right up to the border with Finland.

"We travel fast, and we are long gone by the time they realize we are in a different car," Katya said. "That's if they realize at all. The police here are idiots. It will take them twenty-four hours at least. Maybe a couple of days."

Johnson said nothing. But he could not help thinking that though the police might be idiots, Severinov definitely was not.

CHAPTER TWENTY-EIGHT

Wednesday, April 9, 2014
St. Petersburg

Frustratingly, it took more than an hour for the FSB's head office at the Lubyanka to pinpoint the license plate for a red Škoda Octavia that was registered to Katya Yezhova. Once he had it, however, Pugachov wasted no time in ensuring that his senior police contacts had distributed it to all patrols across the city of St. Petersburg and the sprawling Leningrad oblast, or political region, that surrounded the city in all directions.

Severinov refrained from expressing his irritation at the delay. It wouldn't help, and it was better for him to focus his energies on trying to outthink Johnson rather than worry about bureaucratic tangles at the FSB or police service—or indeed the consequences from the Kremlin if he failed to deliver on the president's instructions.

He paced up and down the hallway of the FSB apartment, leaving Pugachov in the living room on a long call with his headquarters team.

What route will Johnson and Katya use to get out of Russia?

The airports and ports had been locked down—all officials and security people there had been given Johnson's details and photograph. He couldn't get through that way. So what was their plan?

Severinov stopped and stared out the window at the far end of the hallway at the line of cars and vans streaming along the street below, but he wasn't focusing. His thoughts were still crystallizing.

The pair could be headed south to Moscow or even right down to the Black Sea, where the options for escape by water opened up. But the Black Sea would be a three-day drive, and that would not be feasible with the FSB and police closing in.

Rather, the overwhelming probability was that the pair was headed for the land borders with Finland, Estonia, or Latvia, Severinov figured. They were the nearest. It was possible to get to the Finnish border, about 140 kilometers away, in roughly two hours and the slightly more distant Estonian border in maybe two and a half hours.

But Pugachov had already alerted the FSB's Border Service, the heavily armed security division responsible for preventing illegal entry into and exit from Russia, as well as customs and passport control.

Checks by Pugachov had shown that nobody by the name of Joe Johnson or Joseph Johnson had recently entered Russia, so he was obviously traveling on a false passport. Pugachov had instructed his teams to work with police and immigration officials to find out what identity Johnson had used to get into the country, but no progress had yet been made.

Severinov knew that unless Johnson and Katya had a way of smuggling themselves in a vehicle, they would be unlikely to try crossing at one of the official checkpoints. They would rather look for an illegal route through, which would be far from easy.

The 1,300 kilometer border with Finland had a seven-and-a-half kilometer security zone on the Russian side. Entry to the zone required a special permit, and it was covered by a mix of surveillance, both electronic and human. Very few attempts at illegal crossings were successful, and there were tough controls at the official border checkpoints at Vaalimaa and Nuijamaa.

The Latvian border was shorter, at about 214 kilometers, and although there were seven official checkpoints, surveillance at the crossings and in the security zone was just as tough as along the Finnish border. Severinov dismissed the likelihood of them getting right up north to the Norway border—it was just too far. Belarus was a possibility, but the border was about 300 miles away from St. Petersburg.

The other question was, How would they travel?

Severinov assumed it would be obvious to Johnson that his chances of making it in Katya's red Škoda were probably zero. The car would be easily traceable. So, what would he do in Johnson's position? He would switch to another vehicle.

Would he and Katya buy a car? Severinov considered it unlikely, unless they made a cash purchase and didn't register the vehicle. They wouldn't want to leave an electronic footprint of the transaction. But buying a car would be time-consuming, and time was not a commodity they had much of.

Would they steal one? That would be a quick solution, but again, not very likely since, unless they were lucky, the owner would report it stolen and alert police very quickly, raising the likelihood of being caught.

No. The most likely scenario, in Severinov's view, was that Katya would borrow another car from someone she knew. And that would be someone in St. Petersburg.

But who?

Another thing that was puzzling Severinov deeply was why Katya Yezhova had teamed up with Johnson and was helping him to escape. By doing so, she must know she was putting her life at risk.

It was of course possible that Katya's father had given her information that would be of use to foreign intelligence agencies, which she could pass on to Johnson, Severinov thought.

But he very much doubted it. Surely, Gennady, as a defecting SVR officer, would not put his family members in danger by entrusting them with secrets that could see them tortured or worse—with the inevitable result that the secrets would eventually be given up. No, that wasn't likely.

So if she didn't have such information, why was she doing it? That was a difficult one.

Had this been some sort of prearranged meeting in which Johnson had come to St. Petersburg in order to exfiltrate her? Probably not. Johnson was almost certainly trying to reach Varvara, not Katya; he would not have known that the mother was dead.

The more that Severinov thought it through, the more he was inclined to believe that Katya must be taking or directing Johnson toward someone else who could help him or who had the information he required.

Katya would be furious at her father's death and would know that the long arm of the SVR or FSB lay behind his murder. For that reason, she was likely willing to do what she could to help a genial, likable Westerner, which Severinov had to begrudgingly admit was the way Johnson presented himself.

Severinov had an idea. He strode back to the living room, where Pugachov had finished his call.

"Leonid, if anyone is going to help these two escape, it's probably going to be someone in her father's network around here—people with resources and money," Severinov said.

"Can we get a list of the candidates and get them checked out?"

Pugachov sat up straight. "I was thinking of that too. We already have a list of that kind—a counterintelligence standard process."

"It might be a good idea to use it, then." Severinov felt a flash of irritation—it was a knee-jerk reflex that he always felt when he perceived someone to be not moving proactively enough.

Pugachov glanced at him. "We've only just started this process and—"

"How many on the list?"

"About twenty. There might be more."

"Can you get the police to visit them all?"

Pugachov nodded and grabbed his phone.

CHAPTER TWENTY-NINE

Wednesday, April 9, 2014
Leningrad Oblast

The strip of flat, recently laid tarmac that comprised the M10 highway curved northeast through a flat expanse of fields and pine trees that stretched as far as Johnson could see, beneath a chilly ice-blue sky. Despite the warmer spring weather, there were still patches of snow on the fields, particularly up against the hedges, where it had drifted.

A blue signpost read Vyborg 56, Helsinki 311. Katya kept the Lada moving at a steady 110 kilometers an hour. Once they had reached beyond the city limits of St. Petersburg, the traffic had become light; there was little to hold them up.

Johnson checked the map on his phone. From the town of Vyborg, situated near the head of the Gulf of Finland, it was about sixty kilometers to the border crossing at Vaalimaa and about forty kilometers to the other main border post at Nuijamaa.

But by now he was becoming anxious and irritated at her

continued reluctance to tell him her planned route out of the country. It seemed a dogmatic approach, doubtless something that her father had ingrained into her rather than something she was actively thinking about in the current situation. She was young, and he had to assume she had little experience in assessing and dealing with potential threats from Russian counterintelligence officers.

On the other hand, she obviously did have a proper plan that had been set up by her father, who had known what he was doing.

They bypassed Vyborg to their left and then, rather than continuing along the M10 to Vaalimaa, Katya turned right onto the 41K-84, which led to the alternative Nuijamaa border post.

To their right lay the silvery waters of the head of the Gulf of Finland, which by that stage was no more than a series of lakes connected by narrow channels.

At a Tatneft gas station on the left side of the highway, a solitary customer was standing next to his pickup beneath a large overhead canopy. A pump assistant who was filling the truck with fuel for him looked up at the sound of the Lada's engine—there were few cars on the highway, and he was probably hoping for another customer, Johnson surmised.

But Katya braked hard opposite the gas station and, with a slight squeal of tires, turned off the highway and accelerated sharply in the opposite direction, down a narrow tree-lined lane.

They rounded a bend, and there in front of them to their right was the lake, with a long jetty that stretched far out into the blue-black waters.

To Johnson's surprise, moored to the jetty and dwarfing everything around it was an enormous ship, which he esti- mated must have been about 240 feet long and 30 feet high. He stared at the ship—a boat of this size was the last thing he had expected to see in the middle of rural Russia, surrounded by trees. The ship was heavily laden with timber; tree trunks were stacked high on deck, dwarfing the men he could see walking alongside them.

To their left was a canal lock, perhaps forty or fifty feet across—this was a an industrial-sized lock the scale of which far eclipsed the smaller versions Johnson had seen in the States. A crane stood on the jetty.

Johnson glanced at Katya, who drove straight over a hinged road bridge that spanned the canal beneath them. It could obviously be raised to allow tall ships, such as the one currently moored at the jetty, to pass through. A large sign on the side of the bridge read Brusnitchnoe.

"What's this?" Johnson asked.

"Saimaa Canal," Katya said. "It runs from here north into Finland."

"A *canal?* And that is—"

"Yes, the Saimaa. This will be our route out. This is Brus-nitchnoe lock—the first one heading north."

"Right," said Johnson. "But explain how that works."

"Don't worry. We will get over the border. As for how we will do it, I will show you later."

Johnson pressed his lips together but said nothing. He considered sending a quick text message to Jayne to update her but continued to hold back given the likelihood that all cell phone activity was being monitored by the FSB.

Katya drove on down the lane, the lock now out of sight behind them. After about a kilometer, she turned left off the pavement down a rough dirt track between the trees, which she followed for a few hundred meters, then made a right along a similar track. After a few minutes, she stopped outside a single-story wooden shack built in a clearing in the woods with a long double garage next to it, also made of wood. The shack looked deserted, although it was in good condition and had clearly been used. There was an old chair on a narrow veranda and a pile of firewood stacked beside the door.

"Get out. We're leaving the car at this *dacha*," Katya said. Johnson complied.

"Who does this belong to?" Johnson asked.

"The same friend of my father who owns this car—the one in Hong Kong. It's his vacation *dacha*. He loves his boats; he sails them on the lake and the canal."

"It looks a bit run-down," Johnson said, gazing at the shack.

"It's an old one, built during the 1970s—there were strict restrictions on the size you were allowed to build and also on what you could put in them at that time during the communist era. No permanent heating, all that kind of thing. They didn't want people living out of the cities for long. There was no point spending a lot of money on them."

Katya went to the garage, opened a padlock on the double doors, and swung them open. On the left side was a small sailing boat on a wheeled trailer, its mast folded down. Presumably the owner towed it to the lake and launched it from there. There was also a workbench down the right-hand side, along with two dusty mountain bikes. She pushed the bikes out and leaned them against the garage wall, then drove the Lada in, walked out of the garage, and padlocked the doors shut.

"Now we ride back to the ship," Katya said.

"That timber ship?"

"Yes," Katya said, a note of impatience in her voice. "Its owner is expecting us."

* * *

Wednesday, April 9, 2014

St. Petersburg

Severinov found his hopes rising every time Pugachov received a message to update him on the search for the red Škoda, but so far, hope had not been translated into positive progress.

Police were working their way down the FSB's list of Gennady Yezhov's close acquaintances in the St. Petersburg area. Officers were grilling the individuals and searching the areas around their properties for any sign of Katya's car. After checking thirteen of the twenty men on the list, they were still drawing blanks.

Police patrols on the main highways had also not reported any sightings of the Škoda.

By this stage, another hour had passed, meaning that if Johnson and Katya were heading out of St. Petersburg by road, they had at least a two-hour head start. Severinov could feel his anxiety levels mounting.

There was little they could do apart from wait.

"That car will turn up," Pugachov said. "It's just a matter of time."

"It could be in a garage, hidden away. Then we are screwed," Severinov said. His hope was that given most of the people listed were at addresses in apartment buildings, they would not have garages. And if Johnson and Katya were in a hurry, which he was certain would be the case, they might not have the time or the means to quickly find a secure hiding place for the Škoda. They would likely just dump it.

Twenty minutes later, Pugachov's phone rang. He answered it within two rings and listened carefully to the caller, fingering his white mustache as he did so.

"Thank you, my friend. We will get there immediately," Pugachov said as he ended the call.

Severinov took a step nearer to his old colleague. "They have found it?"

Pugachov nodded. "Yes, in a parking lot at some apartments in the north of the city, not far from the river. We will go there now."

En route in the Mercedes, Pugachov continued to make calls to his headquarters staff, who were now tracing other vehicles registered to the address where they were heading on Serebryakov Pereulok.

The street outside the redbrick apartment building was alive with St. Petersburg police vehicles, roof lights flashing red and blue, when they arrived. A group of kids stood watching as the two men climbed out of the car and walked through an archway beneath the apartments that formed an entrance to the parking lot.

There, standing in a bay and surrounded by several officers, was a red Škoda Octavia. The car doors were open, and another officer sat inside. Presumably the police had forced their way in, Severinov thought.

Severinov held back and watched as Pugachov made his way to a senior police officer whom he appeared to know. They held an animated conversation, and Pugachov returned holding a piece of paper.

"Well?" Severinov asked.

Pugachov waved the paper. "My police friend there, Fedot, has got the license plate and the model."

"Now we're making progress. How did you get it?"

"The known associate of Gennady Yezhov who lives in these apartments is currently working in Hong Kong. His car is not visible around here, but neighbors whom Fedot's team have interviewed say it normally is parked in these bays. It is a gray Lada Kalina, a hatchback. The neighbors also say that sometimes a girl comes here and visits the apartment and drives the car. Maybe that is to check everything and just keep the car going, I don't know. But I assume the girl is probably Katya Yezhova. Fedot thinks that the Lada is the vehicle Johnson and the girl have left in. They have put out an urgent search call for the vehicle and are checking the inputs from their license plate cameras at various places in the city."

Severinov nodded. "I think they will head for the Finnish or Latvian borders. It's got to be one of those."

As he spoke, the police officer with whom Pugachov had been talking strode through the archway toward them.

"We have picked them up," the officer said to Pugachov. "They went up the Western High-Speed Diameter, heading north. Cameras at one of the tollbooths recorded the license plate. Another camera then caught them turning north onto the M10. We're alerting patrol cars in the areas they're heading toward."

"Good work," Pugachov said as he turned to Severinov.

But Severinov was already climbing into the Mercedes.

"It *is* the Finnish border, then. I was right. Let's get moving," Severinov said. "I'm thinking we should take Vasily with us—he is the best when things get messy."

Pugachov shook his head. "If we go back and fetch him now, that will cost us three quarters of an hour. It could be critical."

Severinov pursed his lips. "Sure. Let's just go. We can't afford for them to get out of Russia."

PART THREE

CHAPTER THIRTY

Wednesday, April 9, 2014
Saimaa Canal

The Saimaa Canal is a key commercial waterway that links the Russian segment of the Gulf of Finland, at the eastern end of the Baltic Sea, with Lake Saimaa and a massive network of inland canals and lakes that spreads out across the southeast and south-central part of Finland.

The canal stretches for almost twenty-seven miles between the cities of Lappeenranta, in Finland, and Vyborg, in Russia. When construction was completed in 1856, it was entirely within the Grand Duchy of Finland, as it was known then. But the Moscow Peace Treaty of 1940 saw the territory that included the southern part of the canal and Vyborg given to the Soviet Union.

Since 1963, Finland has leased the Russian portion of the canal and controls its operations and staff, although each country has separate customs and passport control checkpoints. These are at Brusnitchnoe lock at the Russian end and Nuijamaa, on Lake Nuijamaanjärvi, at the Finnish end.

It is possible for ships of up to 271 feet long and 41 feet wide to use the canal. This means that large commercial ships with cargoes of more than 1,400 tons can navigate the waterway.

The ship moored at Brusnitchnoe, the *Sanets,* was one such vessel.

"We drop the bikes in the trees," Katya said as she dismounted about two hundred yards short of the lock. "Then we walk through the trees. It is less obtrusive and means the customs officers will not see us."

She paused and tapped a text message on her phone. "I am sending a quick message to the ship's owner. He is on board and will meet us."

Katya then wheeled her bike about forty yards into the undergrowth and pushed it behind some evergreen bushes on the edge of a small clearing amid the pine trees, out of sight of anyone passing along the lane. Johnson followed and did likewise.

They made their way on foot through the trees until they came to a narrow dirt path that emerged behind a hut at the quayside. Without pausing, Katya strode along the quay.

Johnson stood still for a few seconds and gazed at the ship, which was painted a dark blue at the top. It had two large red-and-white engine funnels at the stern and a white double-story deckhouse at the bow with a radar scanner, communications aerials, foghorn, and other equipment all mounted on the roof.

On the main deck, between the deckhouse and the funnels, were what Johnson estimated to be thousands of pine tree trunks stacked horizontally. They were piled at least twenty-five high, up to the same level as the roof of the deck-house, and nine end to end. A series of vertical poles spaced at intervals along each side of the ship prevented the timber from rolling off into the water.

The boat appeared to be fully laden, with only a narrow band of the red-painted ship's bottom visible above the waterline. Streaks of orange rust ran down the side of the hull.

Johnson glanced back down the lake that stretched south behind the ship toward Vyborg. Another ship was approaching that looked similar to the one they were about to board and was also laden with timber. There were three other smaller vessels—two luxury yachts and a rusty old barge —waiting to use the lock.

He studied Katya for a few seconds. She was confident, but he hoped she knew what she was doing and that this was going to work. He badly needed the information she was keeping from him—her father's ex-Stasi contact—and he badly needed to get out of Russia intact. Boarding a ship from which exit options were limited felt risky.

But Katya walked without hesitation straight up the first of two narrow gangways that led up to the deck at the bow of the ship, next to the deckhouse. Johnson followed behind.

At the top of the gangway was a broad-shouldered man with an unkempt iron-gray beard and hair, leaning his barrel-like physique against the gunwale. He was wearing a thick jacket with a logo on the breast that read Saimaa-Baltic Shipping, and Johnson couldn't help noticing his hairy, weather-worn hands, which were probably the largest he had ever seen.

Next to him was a much younger, slightly taller, and equally heavily muscled man with a shaved head, also wearing an identical jacket with the shipping company's logo. The older man stood up straight as they approached and glanced to his left and right, as if checking for something.

"Katya, come this way," the older man said in a low-pitched voice. "You got here just in time. We have been waiting for more than an hour, and I was about to give the order to leave."

He glanced at Johnson but made no attempt to introduce himself or welcome them, then turned and walked toward the deckhouse, his younger colleague close behind.

Two uniformed security guards, both carrying pistols in holsters, stood on deck, one on the port side of the deckhouse, the other on the starboard. A number of other crew members were busy carrying out various tasks on deck.

The older man opened a door into the deckhouse, stepped inside, and went through another door marked Bridge, then up a flight of steps.

When Johnson got to the top of the stairs, Katya and the older man were standing in a semicircular bridge area with windows that stretched around 180 degrees looking out over the bow of the ship. Next to them was a bank of navigational switches, controls, and monitor screens mounted on a long central console.

"This is Oleg Rudov," Katya said. "He is the owner of the shipping company that owns this boat and four other similar vessels. He was a close friend of my father."

Johnson stepped forward and shook Oleg's hand. "Good to meet you. I understand you might be able to get us out of the country."

"Yes, if you do exactly what I tell you," Oleg said. He indicated toward his younger colleague. "This is Yaroslav. He is the captain of this ship. He is very good. I am just here for the ride on this trip." He gave a faint smile.

Johnson shook Yaroslav's hand. "I am pleased to meet you." The Russian grunted in acknowledgment but said nothing.

"As you can see," Oleg said, "this is a big ship, and there are places we can hide you. However, we need to be extremely careful before we leave Russian territory. I have a family to look after, and I own several ships and have a responsibility to my employees. Have I made myself understood?"

"I understand," Johnson said.

"Good," Oleg said. He pointed through a window at the rear of the bridge toward the other timber ship that Johnson had seen approaching earlier. "That is also one of my vessels, identical to this one," he said. "We go through the canal first, and she will follow. We leave in twenty minutes. Come with me."

He led Johnson and Katya back down the steps and at the bottom opened a door that led to a changing room, full of wet-weather gear, boots, lockers, and towels. In the corner, four scuba diving suits were hanging on pegs next to a rack containing oxygen tanks, masks, and flippers.

Oleg opened what looked like a tall locker, similar in size to a wardrobe, to reveal more waterproof clothing hanging on a horizontal rail. He swept the gear to one end of the rail, then bent down and pushed a collection of boots and shoes to one side. He reached up and removed a thin, flat piece of metal from the top of one of the lockers, then inserted it into what looked like a narrow crack between the wall and floor of the locker.

There was a faint click, and the entire floor of the locker dropped by two inches at one end. Johnson could now see that there were hinges at the other end and the whole floor doubled as a tightly fitting, flush hatch that could be lowered and opened. Oleg reached with his fingers beneath the hatch door at the open end, released some kind of catch, and then fully lowered the door to reveal a narrow set of steps no more than a foot wide leading down into a black hole. It seemed impossible to detect that the floor was a hatch there until Oleg released it.

"This is where you will hide," Oleg said. "It is unlikely that you will be found here if the ship is searched, which is doubtful. He took out his phone, switched on its flashlight, and shone it down into the cavity.

"Come down and look," Oleg said. He climbed down the steps backward and beckoned to Johnson and Katya to follow.

The cavity was no more than seven feet long and four feet wide. The ceiling was only four feet high, requiring them all to remain kneeling to avoid banging their heads. The floor was covered by soft rubber matting. Two rolled-up sleeping bags lay at one end, while at the other was a bucket, presumably for toilet purposes, together with two jugs of water, two cups, and a battery-powered lamp.

"This is built in the cavity between two bulkheads and would not be detectable from outside without a minutely detailed plan of the ship," Oleg said.

Johnson surveyed the hiding place. "Do all your boats have these hiding places?" he asked.

"No, only three of them. I had them built in." Oleg's eyes narrowed a little, and he scrutinized Johnson for a couple of seconds.

Clearly this was not a one-off favor he was doing for Katya. If the grizzled ship owner was involved in regular trafficking or illegal transport of people across the border, then it was reassuring in some ways that he knew the ropes, but Johnson hoped that it didn't also mean he was on some kind of FSB or police hit list. He knew that transporting asylum seekers from countries all over the Middle East and North Africa into the European Union, of which Finland was a member, was a big and often lucrative business.

"Are there any other hiding places?" Johnson asked Oleg. "If the ship is searched, it would be useful to know if there are any other options."

Oleg hesitated. "Not really," he said. "Although there is

something. There is a space in the center of the cargo, between the timber logs."

"Show me," Johnson said.

Oleg nodded. He led the way out of the hiding place and back onto the main deck, then along the gangway between the timber cargo and the gunwale. Halfway along, he stopped and edged his way into a narrow gap that had been left between one pile of logs and the next, no more than sixteen inches wide and in some places less, because the ends of some logs were protruding into the gap. He sometimes had to move sideways—there was not always enough space to walk through the gap facing forward. Johnson and Katya followed while Yaroslav remained on the gangway and watched. After about four yards Oleg stopped and pointed downward.

Between the logs there was a frame made of steel beams bolted together to form a cube-shaped enclosure, no more than six feet long by three feet wide and three feet high. Sheets of steel were attached to the top and sides. Johnson could not help thinking it was like a child's hiding place amid the logs, which rested on top of the frame and pressed up against both sides. Inside were a few coils of thick rope, a couple of large tins of paint that had been opened, and a few dirty brushes.

"We keep bits of kit in there when we are working on deck when the ship is not loaded. But it can also be a refuge," Oleg said.

Johnson nodded. "It is a good hiding place. We could use it, but the underfloor cavity is better concealed." He led the way back to the deckhouse.

"How long does it take to get over the border?" Johnson asked. He unconsciously ran his fingers over the butt of the Heckler & Koch that was stuck into his belt beneath his jacket.

"It will take a few hours, maybe five or six."

"And where are the danger points in terms of possible searches?" Johnson asked.

Oleg hesitated. "There are five locks on the Russian side, then another three on the Finnish side. They are necessary because the water level in Lake Saimaa is about seventy-five meters higher than it is here. Sometimes we have to wait our turn for the locks, and the canal can get busy. The five Russian locks are the danger points. We are stationary and we are susceptible."

Johnson had been trying to remind himself that although they were close to the border now, there was actually still a long way to go. Oleg's comments underlined his thoughts.

Oleg stroked his beard and eyed Johnson. "Look—I know everyone on this canal. I have been sailing it for many years. The people who operate the locks, the customs people, they are all my friends." He rubbed his fingers and thumb together, as if wrinkling banknotes, in a gesture that Johnson knew to mean they were in his pocket.

But then Oleg added, "Despite that advantage, we have other things against us. When we are in the locks, we cannot turn, we cannot go back, we cannot move. If the higher authorities come, that is when we hope for the best."

CHAPTER THIRTY-ONE

Wednesday, April 9, 2014
Leningrad Oblast

The speedometer needle was touching 145 kilometers per hour—well above the limit—as Pugachov's Mercedes hammered its way north up the Western High-Speed Diameter.

"We need to get someone to go through any CCTV footage available," Severinov said. He was sitting in the front passenger seat poring over a large-scale map of the Leningrad oblast region while Pugachov hunched over the steering wheel, his forehead creased in concentration as he weaved in and out of the St. Petersburg commuter traffic.

"There won't be much north of the Diameter," Pugachov said. "It's open country up there."

The secure radio mounted on the dash emitted a loud squelch break. A few seconds later there was a crackle, and Fedot, the police chief, came on, his voice tense and clipped. "Leonid, we have four patrols at different spots along the

M10. I am sending two up the 41K-84 toward Nuijamaa and the other two toward Vaalimaa. Do you agree?"

"Agreed," Pugachov said.

"I think the Nuijamaa crossing is the priority," Severinov said. "It's closer. We must take that route. We will follow behind the patrols."

"Understood," squawked Fedot's voice from the loudspeaker.

"And get your officers to check all the gas stations," Severinov said. "They might have seen the Lada if it called in for fuel."

"They already have that instruction," said Fedot, his voice now showing more than a trace of irritation.

Pugachov veered right off the Diameter, and he accelerated again up the M10.

Severinov was now more confident that with police patrol cars monitoring the M10 and 41K-84, Fedot seemed to have the main routes to the border covered. The customs checkpoints were on full alert, and the net appeared to be closing on Johnson, despite his head start.

However, Severinov knew he couldn't relax yet. He had underestimated Johnson before, to his cost, and he wasn't about to do the same again.

Just over fifty minutes later, the Mercedes flew past Vyborg and reached the junction with the 41K-84, where Pugachov took the exit.

They had gone no more than a kilometer and a half along the highway when Severinov saw a BTK gas station and adjoining café on the left.

"Pull in there," Severinov said. "We'll check if they saw anything."

Pugachov braked and parked outside the gas station shop. Severinov trotted into the shop, but the cashier, an elderly woman, claimed not to have seen any sign of a gray Lada in

the previous couple of hours, nor did the station have any
CCTV cameras.

He hurried back to the Mercedes. "No luck," Severinov
said. "What if they have changed cars again somewhere?"

Pugachov shrugged. "I think two changes would be difficult. What is the likelihood of them having someone out here
in the wilderness who could provide another car? I don't see
it. Neither do I see them stealing another car. Let's keep
going."

He set off along the highway again. After a couple of kilometers, another gas station appeared, also on the left side of
the road, this time carrying the green-and-red branding of
Tatneft on the canopy that protected the gas pumps from the
elements.

"We'll try this one," Severinov said.

"It's not worth it," Pugachov said. "I say we carry on.
We're wasting time."

"No. Pull in," Severinov insisted. "You come with me to
the cashier. Maybe some FSB identification might help."

Pugachov grumbled again but complied.

Severinov jumped out and walked to the cashier's desk
inside a white-painted café with chairs, tables, and standing
umbrellas outside, Pugachov close behind him.

A wiry dark-skinned man with circular glasses looked up
at the two men from behind the desk.

"Fuel?"

"No," said Severinov. "We are trying to trace a car, a gray
Lada Kalina, that we think passed through here perhaps two
hours ago. There might have been a man and a woman in it.
Can you help?"

Pugachov removed his FSB identity card from his jacket
and laid it on the counter. The man studied it for a second,
his eyebrows flicking upward; then he looked alternately at
Severinov and Pugachov, a twitch crossing his face.

"I think I might have seen this vehicle. There have been very few cars passing today, and I was out on the forecourt, filling a customer's car. There was a gray Lada—it was the only one of that description I have seen today. It was going quite fast along here from the Vyborg direction. It braked hard just near the entrance, and I thought it was coming in for fuel."

"Did it come in?" Severinov asked. He clenched his fist on the counter as his adrenaline began to pump a little.

The man shook his head. "No. It didn't come in. But it did turn off the highway—it went down the lane opposite." He pointed toward the track that led off the main highway through some trees. "I remember it because it braked so hard, and then the tires squealed a bit as it accelerated down the lane. It seemed to be in a real hurry."

"Thank you. That is very helpful," Severinov said. "Do you have cameras on the forecourt that might have captured the car as it passed?"

"There are no cameras here," the man said.

"What is down that lane?"

The man shrugged. "Nothing. Only the canal lock."

"The canal lock?"

"Yes, the Saimaa Canal. It's the Brusnitchnoe lock."

"Ah yes, of course," Severinov said. He knew about the canal but had not realized they were so close to it.

He glanced at Pugachov and inclined his head toward the Mercedes outside, indicating they should move.

They hurried back to the car and seconds later were speeding down the lane toward the canal.

Severinov leaned forward in his seat as Pugachov braked to a halt a few meters before reaching the movable bridge that spanned the water.

To his left was a deep canal lock from which an enormous ship carrying a load of timber logs was exiting in a northward direction. To his right lay a lake and a jetty from which a similar ship, also carrying timber, was edging slowly forward, clearly preparing to enter the lock.

"Why would Johnson and the girl come down here?" Pugachov asked.

Severinov turned to his colleague. "I don't know. But can you get checks done on whether anyone in Yezhov's circle has anything in this area—property, boats, whatever. Anything that might be a hiding place. And get the police patrol officers off the highway and down here instead. We might need them."

"Good thinking," Pugachov said. He reached for his radio and pressed a couple of buttons, which triggered a series of crackling static noises until he managed to get a connection to Fedot once again. Then he issued a series of staccato instructions, including a call for the police patrols that had gone toward the Vaalimaa border crossing to be sent back to Brusnitchnoe instead. "This is extremely urgent," he added before ending the call.

Severinov gazed at the departing timber ship, which was now gathering speed away from them along the canal after exiting the lock. A slight wake from its bow was breaking against both banks of the canal. It dwarfed a couple of smaller leisure boats that were coming toward them in the opposite direction.

"The canal runs from here into Finland, doesn't it?" Severinov asked.

"Yes, correct," Pugachov said.

"You don't think Johnson might try and get over the border by boat, do you?"

Pugachov shrugged. "Don't know. If it was me, I might think about it. But he's not going to get on these big ships— they're commercial, on-board security is tight, and they are very slow. More likely to be a small, faster boat that will get him there at speed. Like those ones." He pointed toward the leisure craft beyond the lock.

"A boat might be easier than going by car," Severinov said, "but if they are doing that, a small boat might not necessarily be the best. They'd be too exposed. It might be easier to hide on a large ship."

He thought furiously for a few moments. Had Johnson come down this lane to hide somewhere or to jump on a boat? If it was the former, then it was simply a staging post before trying to get over the border, either by land or water; he was convinced of that. If Johnson planned to jump on a boat, then either the whole canal needed to be shut down to traffic or search parties needed to be sent aboard the various boats and ships using it.

Behind them came the whining sound of powerful car engines being thrashed in low gear. Severinov turned around to see two police patrol cars pounding down the lane behind them. They screeched to a halt just behind Pugachov's Mercedes.

"At least we've got reinforcements now," Severinov said. "I suggest we wait and get feedback from Fedot before we decide our next step. But he needs to hurry. Time is short. Give him half an hour, then call again and put a bomb under his ass."

CHAPTER THIRTY-TWO

Wednesday, April 9, 2014
London

The surveillance team, labeled B1, that Nicklin-Donovan had convened to tail Shevchenko had started early that morning, forcing Jayne to get up earlier than she would have liked and make do with a quick coffee and a banana for breakfast.

She then rushed to join Nicklin-Donovan and the B1 team's leader, Gary Bennett, in a safe house—actually an apartment—on the ground floor of a building on Rossmore Road, a few blocks away from the Baker Street underground station and Regent's Park.

Bennett had been on the team running surveillance on Shevchenko previously, and it made sense for him to stay there, providing continuity; it didn't matter if the team leader was unchanged, since he never went on the street.

They listened on a secure link as continual updates came in from the surveillance team. A middle-aged woman wearing a business suit and constantly checking her phone had tailed

Shevchenko as she left her apartment in Dorset Square, three blocks from the safe house.

Then a fake London taxi had followed Shevchenko as a driver ferried her to the Russian embassy at Kensington Palace Gardens.

Shevchenko disappeared into the embassy and the B1 team went into standby mode, waiting in nearby parks, stores, and coffee shops.

Jayne took the opportunity to retreat to a corner of the room and check the GPS tracker monitor app on her phone.

Where are you now, Joe?

To her astonishment, the monitor was showing that Johnson was no longer in Bolshoy Prospekt. Instead, the blue dot was located right in the middle of a waterway, the Saimaa Canal, about eighty miles northwest of St. Petersburg, and was moving very slowly.

Jayne swore to herself. Was this good news or bad? She knew of the Saimaa Canal from her time in Russia, but she had never had a reason to visit it.

She wandered over to Nicklin-Donovan to show him the tracking app; he scrutinized the phone screen and scratched his head, ruffling his neatly parted hair.

"What the hell's he doing there?" Nicklin-Donovan said. "And presuming that he's not swimming, why and how is he on a boat?"

Jayne shrugged. "He's got to be heading for the border with Finland—there's no other logical explanation."

"So, it's definitely gone tits-up in St. Petersburg, then."

It was a statement of fact, not a question. Jayne didn't reply.

She didn't need to. There was no doubt now—Johnson had run into trouble. If the meeting with Varvara Yezhova had gone according to plan, he would have been on a flight from Russia's second-largest city back to Berlin by now.

Still there was no message. He had obviously taken the view that communications were too risky. Jayne had been toying with the idea of sending him an encrypted text but decided against it.

She was hoping that Nicklin-Donovan would not raise the topic of her personal relationship with Johnson again. She had found it awkward when he had done so the previous day, and now she wanted to focus on doing all she could to preserve Johnson's security. She didn't want to feel mentally distracted by having to navigate around his questioning.

The truth was, the fact that Johnson was in danger was crystallizing the feelings she had toward him: she realized he meant a lot to her. On waking that morning she had found herself wondering how she would feel if he didn't come back. It was an outcome that seemed very difficult to contemplate at this stage.

Now, after several more hours with no communications from Johnson, those feelings were even more magnified.

Bennett called from across the other side of the room. "She's on the move, leaving the embassy again by car."

Jayne and Nicklin-Donovan walked over and listened to the voice feed coming over Bennett's squawk box as one of the team, traveling in another fake taxi and using a hidden microphone taped to her bra, very briefly described how the Russian was being transported back to her apartment the way she had come earlier.

Shevchenko then jumped into her black BMW 5 Series sedan and drove northwest around Outer Circle, the street that ran around the fringes of Regent's Park, to a newsstand in St. John's Wood, where she parked, went inside, and bought some cigarettes. She then drove back the way she had come, parked her car, and walked to the Baker Street underground station, where she made her way inside.

"Why did she drive to buy cigarettes?" Jayne asked. "She

could have got the embassy driver to stop somewhere, or she could have bought them in a kiosk at the underground since she was heading there in any case."

"Good question," Nicklin-Donovan said.

"There's got to be a good reason," Jayne said. "If we're following her in a car, I'd like to get some video analysis of her journeys, even if it's from some distance behind. Is she dropping data somewhere with an SRAC? Is there something going on at the news kiosk? Or is it simply that she gets her favorite Russian cigarettes brand there?"

"Yes, worth a try to see if we can spot anything," Nicklin-Donovan said. "We've got video recordings but haven't had them all analyzed yet. I'll get the team to finish that work as quickly as possible."

He turned to Bennett. "Gary, can you do that?"

Bennett nodded. "Sure."

"Thanks," Jayne said. "I'd like to see the videos, especially if there are any anomalies showing up. Variations in driving speed, unexplained stops, and so on." Any of those might signal that she was depositing data into an SRAC—Jayne had used similar systems herself before.

They listened to the feedback from the surveillance team for a few more minutes as they described her movements to the southbound Bakerloo line platform at Baker Street.

"She's definitely on an SDR," Nicklin-Donovan said quietly, when the squawk box went briefly silent. "I've seen from previous surveillance operations that her starting point is sometimes Baker Street. Paddington station is another favorite because it's large and complex."

Jayne nodded. "Yes, it's easy to jump on different lines, take different exits, walkways, staircases."

Sure enough, Shevchenko spent the next hour and a half taking a variety of underground trains, walking around stations, and ducking into shops and cafés.

The three people tailing her changed appearances on several occasions, using props in their bags, backpacks, and pockets.

Eventually, however, Shevchenko somehow evaded her tail in Covent Garden amid the plethora of shops with multiple entrances, walkways, and crowds of tourists.

According to the B1 team, Shevchenko had given no sign that she had detected coverage, but then again, Jayne wouldn't have expected her to do so even if that had been the case. She was too much of a pro.

It wasn't a good start for B1. The slightly embarrassed Bennett tried to shrug it off. "She's just damn good. It seemed so natural that she just melted into the crowds. But better we lose her than get too tight, in which case she actually knows she's being tailed and completely changes her approach."

"She knew," Jayne said. "She must have."

"Maybe, maybe not," Nicklin-Donovan said. "She doubtless assumes she's under constant surveillance, until she gets to the point where she thinks for certain she's not. There's a difference between assuming and knowing."

"We'll do better next time," Bennett said, turning and looking over his shoulder at Jayne, his lips pressed together. "We just need to get lucky once. She can't afford to ever make a mistake. I'm going to get some computer analysis done overnight on her previous runs—there may be a trend in her movements."

"Yes, good idea," Jayne said. She placed her hands on her hips, surprised they hadn't done that before. "Maybe it's best not to rely on luck. And we don't have long to play with. We know she's headed back to Moscow in five days."

CHAPTER THIRTY-THREE

Wednesday, April 9, 2014
Saimaa Canal

As it happened, it was only twenty minutes before Fedot came back onto the radio. His team had discovered that Gennady Yezhov's comrade who owned the Lada Kalina also had a small holiday *dacha* near to the Saimaa Canal, just two or three kilometers away from the Brusnitchnoe lock.

"It is in the middle of some woodland, down some dirt tracks, according to the satellite map I've just been looking at," Fedot said. He gave Pugachov the coordinates.

"That's got to be it," Severinov said. "There's no other reason he and the girl would have headed this way otherwise. Let's go check it out."

Pugachov asked the two officers in one of the police cars to follow him, then drove over the movable bridge that spanned the canal and, using his satnav to guide him to the spot identified by the coordinates, set off along the lane with a screech of tires.

After a kilometer, he turned down a dirt track into the woods and eventually took a right. After a few hundred meters, they came across a wooden shack, set in a clearing amid the trees.

"This is it," Pugachov said. He braked to a halt, as did the police car following behind him, and climbed out of the car.

The shack appeared deserted, with closed shutters and curtains, although a chair on the veranda and a pile of fire-wood hinted at recent use. The only audible sound in the woods was birdsong.

Pugachov instructed the two police officers, both of whom were armed with GSh-18 semiautomatic 9 mm pistols, to check out the house while he and Severinov watched.

One of the officers began kicking at the door with his heavy boots. It burst open on the third attempt, slamming back on its hinges and shattering one of the panes of glass. However, the two men reemerged from the shack a few minutes later to report that the house was completely unoc-cupied, with no sign that anyone was currently using it.

"There's no food, no milk, nothing, not even a cigarette butt, sir," one of the officers said.

Severinov indicated toward the garage. "Can you get into that too?" he asked.

The officer nodded. He walked to the car and returned with a crowbar, which he used to wrench off a large padlock that secured the large double doors at the front.

He swung open one of the doors, and there inside was a gray Lada Kalina. Next to it, on the left, was a boat on a trailer.

Severinov swore and went to feel the Lada's hood. It was still slightly warm. He was not surprised to see the car, but while the two police officers immediately began combing through the vehicle, his mind was focused entirely on where

Johnson and Katya Yezhova had disappeared to. There was no sign of them.

He walked from the garage back to the dirt track that ran past the property and looked in both directions.

It was then that he noticed twin sets of bicycle tire marks in the dirt just off the side of the track. Upon closer examination, it was clear that they had either gone to or come from the garage. Yet there were no bikes in the garage.

"Leonid, come here. Look at these," he called to Pugachov. He pointed to the tire tracks. The two men followed the tracks for a short distance along the dirt track.

"They've headed back toward the lock on bikes," Severinov said. "I think they're on a boat, my friend. Where else would they go on bikes? There's nowhere else around here. They're not going to cycle to the border, are they?"

Pugachov shook his head. "Maybe, but I doubt it."

"So they've dumped the car, and they're getting on a boat. That's my view," Severinov said. "We need to get all northbound boats stopped and searched. Let's get this canal closed down—I want it locked up tighter than a duck's ass."

Pugachov took out his phone, dialed a number, and walked away along the track, deep in an animated and heated conversation with someone, who Severinov assumed was at FSB headquarters. At various points during the conversation, he heard Pugachov swearing at whoever was on the other end of the line.

Eventually, the FSB chief returned, his face flushed and his black eyes glittering. "The damned idiots at the Border Service and customs control are refusing to shut the canal. They have told me it's the Finnish authorities who decide that—they operate the canal. But if we can identify which ship or boat Johnson and the girl are definitely on, they will ask the Finns to stop it. Otherwise they say their checks are more than tough enough—they are looking out and say there is no chance of them getting through undetected. Their argument is that they have a long queue of traffic coming through in both directions, and they can't afford to shut down. It would cause chaos."

"They will have to," Severinov said. "It is critical."

"No chance," Pugachov said. "They say they have had this situation before, most recently four days ago, and the transport minister has instructed them to keep the canal open. They say if we want to override it we will have to contact the Kremlin."

Severinov stood motionless. That meant Putin's office. Given his current relations with Putin and Medvedev and the specific instruction he had received not to involve them in his task of eliminating Johnson, that was one route pretty much closed off to him.

"Listen. If they are on a boat, which we don't know for sure, I think we can head them off ourselves," Pugachov said. "The highway follows quite close to the canal almost all the way up to Nuijamaa, although in some parts it is farther away. But we should be able to get to some of the locks farther north and catch them. We can drive faster than they can sail."

"But if the border guards say they can deal with it, why not just let them do it?" Severinov asked.

Pugachov shook his head. "No way. Not unless you want the whole operation screwed up. They are useless. I guarantee you, they will screw it up. Trust me, I've had to deal with them many times before, and they are bungling amateurs. We will handle it with these police officers. When we find out which boat they are on, we can call the border authorities then."

"All right, let's try that," Severinov said. He waved at the two police officers, indicating to them to follow, and strode back to the Mercedes.

* * *

Wednesday, April 9, 2014
  Saimaa Canal

About a mile and a half north of the *dacha* in the woods, Johnson was standing on the deck of the *Sanets* as the ship rose slowly inside the narrow rectangular concrete enclosure of the Iskrovka lock, the walls of which towered above him like some Soviet-era prison yard. The enormous black lock gates had closed behind them after they had entered, and now water was gushing steadily in from the northern end. According to Oleg, this allowed the ship to rise about eleven meters up to the level of the next stretch of the canal.

The crew had moored the ship to a series of moving hooks that were built into the lock wall and rose up and down as the water level changed.

It was the second lock the ship had been through, including Brusnitchnoe, which had a ten-meter rise. Oleg's other ship, the *Osa*, had followed them up the canal and was now waiting for the *Sanets* to complete its passage through the lock so that it could enter.

Johnson had been slightly surprised at the sophistication of the entire canal operation. Starting from the south, the first three locks and movable road bridges were controlled remotely from the operating center at Brusnitchnoe, according to Oleg, who had to remain in contact with staff there by VHF radio. The other five were controlled from a remote control center at Mälkiä lock, farther northwest.

The locks were illuminated by bright streetlights on lampposts, and were neatly landscaped, with areas of lawn and rose bushes growing in beds.

But otherwise, the territory through which they were

traveling was a kind of no-man's-land, with no houses or other settlements and no infrastructure apart from the highway and the locks.

Johnson and Katya had remained hidden in the compartment beneath the changing room floor until the ship had been cleared by Russian customs checkpoint officers at Brusnitchnoe lock. Although the ship had been subjected to a search, it had lasted no more than ten minutes and did not come remotely close to discovering the underfloor hiding place.

Twenty minutes after they had left the Brusnitchnoe customs post, Oleg permitted Johnson and Katya to come out on deck.

This was a relief to Johnson, whose principal concern was that somehow Severinov would work out what their escape plan was and track them to the canal before they were over the border. Therefore, wherever possible, he wanted to keep a close eye on the highway for any sign of police or FSB vehicles. The highway came close to the canal in some places, while in others the two were separated by the thick pine forests that covered most of the area right up to the canal banks.

Because of the regular movable road bridge closures to allow boats and ships through the locks, the vehicles in both directions tended to travel in bunches that had built up as they waited for the bridges to be lowered again.

Most of the northbound vehicle traffic consisted of commercial trucks and vans that were presumably heading into Finland to deliver or collect goods. There were only a few cars, and most of them were older models, some quite battered.

Oleg noticed him and Katya watching the traffic. "This is not the danger point," he said. "The next three locks, Cvetotchnoe, Ilistoye, and Pälli, are the difficult ones, where the highway runs next to them or over them. Pälli is the Russian border checkpoint, so if we can get through that, we're clear and through."

Johnson tugged at the old wound at the top of his right ear and explained his concerns about Severinov. "What if they catch up with us?"

Oleg gave first Johnson, then Katya a sideways glance and stroked his bearded chin. "We have a few options." He indicated toward some of his ship's crew, most of whom were heavily muscled and bearded. "We can rely on these men for help if needed. Another question: Can you both swim?"

"Of course," Johnson said. Katya nodded.

"Do you know how to use diving gear? Scuba diving kit?"

Johnson didn't like the sound of this, but he did know how to dive at a basic level. He had done a lengthy scuba course several years earlier back home in Portland Harbor and had also dove while on holiday in the Red Sea, to view the coral reefs there.

"Sort of, I guess," Johnson said. "I am not very good at it."

"I also don't like it," Katya said, "but I have learned it in the Baltic, near St. Petersburg, yes."

"Good," said Oleg. "I'm not saying you will need to dive, but it does give us an option if required. We also have the *Osa* as a backup." He indicated toward the *Sanets'* sister ship behind them.

Katya tapped the Heckler & Koch pistol that she, like Johnson, had tucked into the waistband of her pants. "I too have a backup," she said, glancing alternately at Johnson and Oleg. For a second, Johnson thought about laughing, but he could see that Katya did not intend the comment in a light-hearted way. He just hoped that if she intended to use the weapon again, she would do so in a disciplined manner this time.

After leaving Iskrovka, on the long stretch toward the

next lock at Cvetotchnoe, seven and a half kilometers north, the canal entered an extensive natural lake. However, the main fairway—marked with white buoys to indicate where the canal bed had been dredged deep to allow larger ships adequate bottom clearance—remained only wide enough to allow two vessels to pass each other, no more.

A group of birds, which Oleg said were black-throated loons, were busy diving into the water, often emerging half a minute later with small fish in their beaks.

The highway ran to the left of the canal during this stretch, sometimes concealed behind trees but visible in several places.

Johnson and Katya stood on deck on the port side of the ship to keep a close eye on the traffic heading north. A convoy of four white vans sped past. Close behind came a couple of large semitrailer trucks and a few cars.

At Cvetotchnoe lock, the highway toward Finland passed over a movable bridge positioned right next to the lock, similar to Brusnitchnoe, and then continued straight through the forest to the north at a ninety-degree angle to the canal, taking vehicles well away from the water.

As the *Sanets* drew closer to Cvetotchnoe, Johnson saw the movable bridge start to rise. The four vans had gone through, but the semitrailers and the cars were forced to stop and wait.

That was when he noticed a police car barreling up the highway left of the water, traveling at high speed and then braking hard as it came up to the rear of the line of vehicles waiting at the bridge. It came to a halt, and two men jumped out, both dressed in uniform.

"Shit," Johnson muttered.

He felt a surge of adrenaline go through him and immediately ducked down out of sight behind the gunwale, pulling Katya with him.

He peered over the top and watched as the policemen walked to the edge of the highway, looking out over the canal. One of them pointed at the *Sanets*.

Twenty seconds later, a black Mercedes came into view, also speeding northward. It braked to a sharp halt behind the police car and another two men got out, both dressed in black. Without hesitating, they walked over to the two police officers and began an animated conversation, glancing occasionally in the direction of the ship.

CHAPTER THIRTY-FOUR

Wednesday, April 9, 2014
Saimaa Canal

"We'll start with these two ships," Severinov said to the two police officers in a tone that stated there was to be no argument. He indicated toward the timber-carrying ship entering Cvetotchnoe lock ahead of them and another farther back on the canal to their right.

"I'm hoping that Johnson and the girl won't have gotten any farther north than this, so we begin here," Severinov said. "You two go on board the first one and search it. We will stay on the quay and keep a watch—if they are on the boat, I don't want to take the risk of them escaping while we're below decks."

The policemen nodded their agreement, and Severinov terminated the short impromptu roadside meeting before climbing back into the Mercedes. Pugachov did likewise, installing himself behind the steering wheel.

As the first ship came to a standstill in the lock, the enormous lock gates behind it closed, and the movable bridge slowly began to descend again. Water began pouring into the lock from the northern end of the structure, and the vessel, which Severinov could now see was named the *Sanets*, began to rise.

Within a couple of minutes, the line of traffic began moving again. The police car ahead of them nosed into a small parking lot next to the lock, and Pugachov piloted the Mercedes into a space beside it.

Severinov, Pugachov, and the policemen climbed out of their vehicles and began to walk toward the quayside. The blue-painted port side of the ship's hull was rising slowly ahead of them. A group of four men were standing next to the ship on the quay. Two of them looked like canal workers in fluorescent yellow jackets and the other two were clearly ship's crew who had disembarked; they were wearing thick jackets that bore the logo Saimaa-Baltic Shipping.

"Leonid, you show them your ID and get these two on board," Severinov muttered, indicating toward the policemen next to them.

Pugachov strode up to the group and flashed his FSB identification.

* * *

Wednesday, April 9, 2014
    Saimaa Canal

The angle of visibility out of the small porthole at the port side of the deckhouse was a narrow one, maybe no more than forty degrees. But it was enough.

Johnson felt his bowel flip inside him as he eyed the four

men who were standing on the side of the quay at Cvetotchnoe lock.

Shit, Johnson thought. He turned toward Katya and Oleg, who were standing behind him. "It's Severinov. I thought this was going too well to be true."

Katya bent down and looked out the porthole. "*Svolach*," she said. "Scum. Two police with him as well."

Oleg swore softly. "We will deal with this."

Yaroslav, wearing a shipping line jacket, appeared behind them. "Oleg, I have just been speaking to some men on the lock."

"Yes, I've seen them," Oleg said, turning to face him. "They're police. What the hell do they want?"

"Yes, there are two police officers and two other men. One of them is FSB—he showed me his identity card, and he wants to see our ship's registration papers. The police want to come aboard to search the ship. They are both carrying guns. What do you want me to tell them?"

Oleg shrugged and looked at Johnson. "They can see the papers—I will get them in a few minutes. And we will have to let them on board. We have no choice. I will try and talk them out of doing a search, but I am certain that will not work. You two need to get into the hiding place right now. Move." He pointed Johnson toward the door behind them that led into the crew's changing room, where the hatch leading to the underfloor cavity was concealed.

"You go in there," Katya said. "I'll go in the refuge on deck. It's better we are separate."

Johnson shook his head. Although the idea of being separated was a good one, the refuge on deck was not concealed well enough, in his view.

"No," Johnson said. "They are more likely to find you there. It's not such a good place. Why do you want to go there?"

"If they find this underfloor hole, we are sitting ducks together. We are both finished. But if we are separate, it is different. If they find you, I will take them out. And if they find me, you can take them out."

"I don't think so. I'm not going to let—"

But before he could complete his sentence, Katya interrupted. "Don't worry about me. I can look after myself." Without a further word, she turned and headed out the deckhouse door.

Johnson instinctively started to go after her, but Oleg put his hand up, indicating that he should stop.

"No," Oleg said. "There's no time to argue. We need to move. Let her go out there if she wants; it's her risk. You go inside. She may be right—if they did find this hiding place, you would both be sitting ducks, as she calls it." He opened the door to the crew changing room and pulled Johnson inside, then reached up to the top of the lockers and removed the metal catch release for the underfloor cavity hatch door, which he opened.

"I will get you when we are all clear," Oleg said. "Just remain extremely quiet, and don't move."

The urgency in Oleg's voice clearly said there was no time to waste, and Johnson knew he was right. The Russian couldn't delay going to see the police officers any longer. He just hoped Oleg's affable manner and plausible arguments would be enough to persuade them that a cursory search of the ship would be sufficient. He also hoped that his instinct to trust the ship's owner was the correct one.

Johnson descended into the cavity and sank to his knees on the sleeping mat covering the floor. He had just switched on the battery lamp when the hatch door above him clicked shut.

* * *

Wednesday, April 9, 2014
  Saimaa Canal

It was the situation Katya had always feared being in. Backed into a corner with no obvious means of escape. She knew that if the police officers who were trying to board the ship, or the FSB, for that matter, were to trap her now, she would face an extremely grim fate, not least given her father's track record and the fact that she had the blood of an FSB officer already on her hands.

Some of her friends had eventually returned following various ordeals in the subbasements of the Bolshoy Dom, the monolithic FSB and former KGB office building on Liteyny Prospekt in central St. Petersburg, and had never been the same again. Some of their stories of torture and beatings had given her nightmares. Two of them had not returned—their bodies were never recovered.

To her ongoing surprise, Katya had never been hauled in for interrogation, but if the officers got their hands on her now, she knew it would likely end in only one way.

That wasn't going to happen. Not if she had anything to do with it. If they came close to finding her, she would go on the offensive. As a last resort, it would be better to die fighting rather than be captured helpless down some rabbit hole of a hiding place. That was what her father had instilled in her. For what they had done to her parents and her friends, she would rather take as many of them with her as she could.

Katya moved swiftly along the gangway on the starboard side of the ship, out of sight of the policemen who were standing on the other side of Cvetotchnoe lock. She walked between the gunwale and the towering piles of timber stacked on the main deck and eventually reached the narrow gap between the pine trunks that led to the steel refuge.

Katya slipped into the gap and crawled into the refuge. There she removed the Heckler & Koch from her waistband and the suppressor from her jacket pocket and screwed the suppressor onto the barrel.

Then she sat silently to wait. She was completely certain of one thing: she wasn't going to be the third member of her family to be gunned down by these bastards. She was also certain she would do everything in her power to prevent Joe Johnson from also being gunned down—he seemed the best chance of getting some justice for what had happened to her father and mother. Perhaps she could help him finish what her father had intended to do.

After several minutes, Katya heard the sound of voices coming from the port side of the ship. It was difficult to hear much, but she did make out Oleg's low-pitched, gruff tones saying something about there being nobody unauthorized on board the ship.

Then came another man's voice, a brusque, commanding one. The only audible part of the conversation was when he demanded to see the rear of the ship.

The voices rapidly faded, presumably as the men moved to the ship's stern.

What seemed like an eternity later, but in fact was probably no more than ten minutes, she again heard the same voices coming from the same direction. This time they were louder.

"What is down here?" a man asked from somewhere out of sight.

"Nothing," came Oleg's voice. "It is just a gap between the timber cargo."

"We will have a quick look. Then we will search the deckhouse and the engine room. Come this way, Ivan."

Katya assumed that Ivan must be the man's police colleague.

Next came the sound of multiple footsteps and the brushing sound of clothing rubbing against the pine trunks as the officers began to make their way down the gap between the logs.

Katya knew what she was going to do next: it was them or her. She wasn't going to give them a chance to take her out.

She flicked the safety on her P7 to off and inched forward on her knees. Then in one movement, she pushed herself out into the gap, took aim, and fired three rounds in quick succession.

As she moved, she could see the first officer reaching for his gun. But he was too slow.

The first two rounds hit the officer in the chest. As he fell, the third round hit the second policeman in the head.

Bull's-eye.

Behind them, Oleg stood, his eyes wide, his mouth open, and his hands raised.

"Don't shoot," he called.

CHAPTER THIRTY-FIVE

Wednesday, April 9, 2014
Saimaa Canal

Johnson heard the squeak of the door to the crew changing room above his hiding place as someone opened it. Then came a prolonged scraping, scratching noise as something was dragged across the floor, followed by a slight thud. There was a pause, followed by another similar series of sounds.

Three knocks sounded on the hatch door above his head, followed by a click, and it sprang open a couple of inches before its fall was interrupted by the safety catch.

Johnson reached up, unclipped the door, and lowered it fully. Above him stood Oleg and Katya. Both were slightly out of breath. Behind them was Yaroslav.

"What's happening?" Johnson asked as he looked up at them.

But Oleg ignored the question. Instead he spoke quickly in a low, urgent tone. "Get these two down there, quickly, before the others come." He indicated with his hand toward something that was out of Johnson's line of sight from below.

Johnson guessed what was there. He took two steps up the ladder. Then he saw the motionless bodies of the two Russian policemen.

"Oh shit," Johnson muttered. His first thought was of the potential consequences of killing two Russian cops on Russian soil. He looked at Katya. It was obviously her who had done it: she had a determined glint in her eye.

Oleg must have caught the nonverbal exchange. "Ask questions later," he said. "Just get them down there. Quickly."

He grabbed one of the bodies beneath the armpits and hoisted it toward the hatch opening, then swung the man's legs down into the cavity. Johnson grabbed the legs while Oleg supported the torso, and slowly they maneuvered the body down onto the sleeping mat. Johnson pushed the corpse to one side, then reached up to repeat the exercise with the other body, which Oleg was already lifting into place.

Johnson was suddenly grateful for the ship owner's loyalty to Gennady Yezhov and his family. It obviously ran deep. He could have simply turned him and Katya over to Severinov, the FSB officer, and the police and saved himself a world of trouble; but he had chosen to do the opposite.

Johnson took the radios and phones from the policemen's pockets and belts and removed the batteries and SIM cards. He didn't want them to be tracked to the ship's position.

Katya found a couple of cleaning cloths in the changing room and began wiping up the blood that had been smeared across the blue linoleum floor.

"Did you have the suppressor on?" Johnson asked as he climbed up out of the hatch door. He had not heard any gunshots, but his first thought was that Severinov and his FSB colleague on the quay might have.

Katya nodded. "Of course."

Johnson glanced at his watch. "The other two will be on the ship soon, once they realize something has happened to their men."

"We'll have to make a plan," Oleg said.

"Yes, we need one," Johnson said. He looked Oleg in the eye. "I appreciate what you are doing."

"Gennady was my friend, which makes you my friend too," Oleg said. "And Katya is his daughter. He was a good man. Our loyalty runs deep, my friend. And I hate the authorities here."

He turned to Yaroslav. "Now, a plan. The FSB officer wants to see our registration documents and the crew list. I have them. We will both go and show them to him on the quayside, and we will tell him that the two police are still searching the ship. Then we will surprise them—we will deal with them."

Oleg briefly lifted his jacket at the hip, revealing a pistol that was stuffed into his belt.

A slight tremor of alarm went through Johnson. Yes, they were backed into a corner and needed to get out of Russia as quickly as possible. But things were starting to spin out of control. "I don't think you can afford to kill those two as well. If we're caught, it will make things even worse."

Oleg eyeballed him. "What else do you suggest, then?"

"Can you disable them? Incapacitate them? That would give us some options about what to do with them."

Oleg glanced at Yaroslav. "We will go by instinct," he said with a note of finality in his voice. "Come on. Let's go." He turned back to Johnson and Katya, his black eyes now glittering like quartz crystal. "You two wait here. Watch us through the porthole and get back down into the hiding place if you need to."

He led the way out of the changing room door, Yaroslav following close behind.

"Let him deal with it his way," Katya said when they had gone. She folded her arms firmly across her chest. "That is best."

"Maybe it is best," Johnson said. "But I am working for American intelligence here. And one of the guys out there is FSB, and the other is ex-KGB. We tend not to go around shooting each other if we can avoid it. Otherwise it tends to lead to serious repercussions. An eye for an eye and all that kind of thing."

Katya did not reply.

Johnson bent down to peer out of the small porthole window that looked out from the port side of the ship.

The previous time Johnson had checked, two canal employees had been working on the lock, dressed in fluorescent yellow jackets. But they were now nowhere in sight. He assumed that Oleg must have paid them to disappear.

However, Severinov and the FSB officer were still standing on the lock side. Severinov checked his watch, then said something to the FSB officer and pointed at the ship. They were clearly becoming impatient. Severinov then removed a pistol from a holster at his waist and held it in his right hand. This didn't look good. Were they going to come on board and carry out a gunpoint search for the police officers—and for Johnson?

A minute or so later, Oleg and Yaroslav came into view, striding toward the two men across the concrete surface. Severinov raised the pistol and said something, at which point Oleg, who was holding a few sheets of paper, stopped and threw up his hands. He was clearly objecting to Severinov's gun.

Severinov eventually relented and lowered the gun, but he kept it in his right hand while they spoke. Oleg then pointed back at the ship and shrugged. Presumably he was referring to the two policemen. He held out the papers in front of

Severinov and pointed to something on the sheets while Yaroslav positioned himself slightly behind the FSB man.

Severinov, still holding the gun, peered forward at the papers that Oleg was holding. While he was doing so, Oleg, without warning and without much windup, delivered a short jab with his right fist straight into Severinov's face and then immediately grabbed Severinov's right wrist with his left hand, twisting it sharply sideways.

Simultaneously, Yaroslav appeared to swing the side of his hand straight into the FSB man's neck, somewhere around his Adam's apple, causing him to buckle to his knees.

As Oleg grappled with Severinov, the oligarch's gun went off with a crack that echoed around the lock and caused Johnson to jump slightly. But the round must have hummed off harmlessly away from Oleg, because he continued to pressure Severinov's wrist, eventually causing him to drop the gun.

As soon as the gun dropped, Severinov, whose nose was streaming blood, tried to punch Oleg with his left hand. But Oleg ducked out of the way and followed up with another sharp right-hand blow to Severinov's solar plexus, at which point Severinov doubled up and fell backward. As he tumbled, Oleg landed another blow somewhere on his face.

Within seconds, both Severinov and the FSB man were on the ground. Oleg delivered another blow to Severinov's neck area, and the Russian collapsed onto his back. The FSB man was still on his knees, and Yaroslav punched him again in the face, causing him to also topple onto his back.

Oleg jumped on top of Severinov, flipped him over and pinned him to the ground, his hands behind his back. Then he pulled some heavy-duty cable ties from his pocket and lashed Severinov's hands together, followed by his ankles. Yaroslav performed a similar maneuver on the FSB man.

The speed and ferocity with which the two Russian

mariners had acted took Johnson by surprise—not to mention their bravery, given Severinov had been wielding a pistol. They were clearly well trained and well practiced.

Oleg went through both men's pockets, removing two pistols, phones, wallets, and keys, which he shoved into his jacket pockets.

Next he turned in the direction of the ship's gangway and beckoned to someone who was out of Johnson's line of sight. Two other men appeared and together the four of them picked up Severinov and the FSB man by the legs and under the armpits and carried them out of sight toward the gangway onto the ship.

A few minutes later, the door to the changing room swung open, and the four men and their captives appeared. Severinov and the FSB man were both yelling a string of foul-mouthed obscenities in Russian, for which Johnson did not need a translator.

Oleg and his colleagues were by now sweating profusely from their efforts. Yaroslav's hand was bleeding, had turned purple, and was visibly swollen as a result of the blows he had delivered, but he seemed to register no pain.

They dropped their captives next to each other on the linoleum floor and stood back, breathing heavily.

Severinov rolled over and immediately saw Johnson standing there.

"*Ublyudok*," Severinov said. You bastard.

Johnson tried to remain expressionless, although he was sorely tempted to grin at the Russian. It had been barely ten months since the boot had been on the other foot and Johnson had been held captive by Severinov in Kabul.

"You deserve everything you get," Johnson said to Severinov. "If I was a Russian, I'd doubtless put a bullet in the back of your head now—and you'd deserve that too."

Johnson paused. There was a question he badly needed to

ask Severinov, but doubted he would get an answer. "But
given that I'm sparing you the bullet, what I want to know is,
why did you kill Varvara Yezhova, and why are you now
pursuing this lady?" He indicated toward Katya.

A faint trace of a smirk crossed Severinov's face, then
disappeared again. "*Poshël ty*." Piss off.

Johnson shook his head. He had to try.

He turned away and shook Oleg's hand. "That was a clean
job. Well done. Can we discuss what we do with these two?"

Oleg nodded and opened the door onto the deck. The
two men stepped outside.

Johnson asked Oleg for the men's phones, which he
handed over. Johnson checked the contents of both, but as he
had half expected, there was nothing sensitive stored on
them. They had both been careful. Instead, Johnson removed
the SIM cards and batteries and threw them all into the lock,
together with the radios and phones he had removed from
the policemen. That would at least reduce the likelihood of
the FSB pinpointing the two men's whereabouts.

"We need to move immediately and get out of this lock,"
Oleg said. "We have already been stationary here for twenty
minutes. I radioed to the control center that we had a slight
mechanical problem but that it was being fixed. If we stay
any longer they will start asking awkward questions because
other boats are approaching. Are you sure you don't want me
to put a bullet in their heads and sink them to the bottom of
the canal along with the two policemen? It would be the
safest thing. In Russia, if you disappear, you disappear. People
do not ask many questions, even if the disappeared are
police."

Johnson was sorely tempted to give him the go-ahead, but
if he was being given a choice, he couldn't take that option.
He knew that.

"You must do what you must do with the policemen. But

personally, I don't want any more unnecessary deaths. I will tell you what I was thinking of doing."

Johnson began to detail what he had in mind.

* * *

Wednesday, April 9, 2014
  Saimaa Canal

Ships on the Saimaa Canal were restricted to a speed of nine kilometers per hour to avoid damage to the banks and infrastructure. Yaroslav pushed the *Sanets* speed right up to the limit as they finally left Cvetotchnoe lock and forged north toward Ilistoye lock, a little over a mile away and still well within Russian territory.

After a lengthy discussion, Oleg and Johnson agreed on a plan to deal with the dead policemen as well as Severinov and the FSB man, whose identity card showed he was a senior officer named Leonid Pugachov.

About halfway between the two locks, the canal fairway passed through a small lake. Just after they reached the point where the lake broadened and they were out of sight of the locks, Oleg instructed Yaroslav to slow the *Sanets* to a crawl.

Johnson stood next to a lifeboat at the stern of the ship and watched, his arms folded, as two crewmen strapped heavy steel tubing to the bodies of the Russian policemen and threw them into the water.

Despite further grumbling from Oleg, who was still favoring a bullet in the back of their heads, Johnson had convinced him that for diplomatic reasons, the lives of Severinov and Pugachov should be spared.

Johnson suggested a simple enough plan to deal with them.

Once the policemen's bodies had sunk out of sight, making it impossible for Severinov and Pugachov to witness what had happened to them, the crew carried the duo up from below deck to the stern of the ship.

Once Severinov and Pugachov were at the stern, the crew untied their arms and legs and threw them both into the water.

There were no backward glances from the crewmen as the pair hit the water; it looked as though they had done it before.

"Are they going to survive in this water?" Johnson asked Oleg. He wanted to seriously inconvenience and delay them, not kill them.

The shipowner shrugged. "If they swim fast, unfortunately they probably will survive. It's probably three or four degrees above freezing."

Severinov had let fly with a stream of obscenities, mostly relating to Johnson's mother and his parentage, as he was deposited into the inky black canal. But he immediately began to swim using a slow crawl stroke toward the lake shore, which was perhaps three hundred yards away. Pugachov looked less confident in the water and thrashed around, deploying a rudimentary doggy paddle.

Johnson could see that, even assuming they made it to the shore, the pair would also need to scramble probably another half a mile, if not more, through the forest before reaching the highway.

But he had already checked with Oleg the likely timings for the *Sanets* to pass through the remaining locks and the customs post and get over the border.

"The water is very cold," Oleg said. "They will not be in a good state when they reach the shore and will not be able to move fast. The forest is thick. Don't worry. We will have plenty of time to get through Ilistoye and Pälli."

Johnson was reassured, but he still remained worried. His initial instinct had been that Severinov and Pugachov must surely have notified the border authorities that they were pursuing two fugitives who were escaping by ship. But if so, why hadn't the canal been closed down? Maybe Pugachov hadn't been sure that Johnson and Katya were on a boat and had either not put the calls in or had not been able to persuade the authorities to close the canal without knowing for certain. He and Severinov had not given the impression at Cvetotchnoe lock that they knew their targets were on the *Sanets*—they had sent the policemen on board for what seemed like a speculative check.

Meanwhile, the crew set to work to clean up any traces of blood from the deck, the changing room, and the underfloor hiding area.

As the *Sanets* neared Ilistoye lock, which like Cvetotchnoe was controlled remotely, Johnson and Katya retreated into the hiding place.

They remained there in silence in the dark, the light switched off, as the ship traveled the remaining kilometer and a half to Pälli lock, where the Russian border checkpoint was located. Johnson felt the ship bump slightly on the steep concrete sides of the lock as it entered and then sensed it moving upward as the water level inside the lock slowly rose.

After the *Sanets* came to rest in the lock, there was silence for at least five minutes. All Johnson could hear was the distant faint rumble of the idling giant diesel engines at the far end of the ship.

Then came the sound of footsteps on deck and voices that grew more distinct.

A creak came from above as the door to the crew changing room was opened. The voices were now loud, the footsteps echoing like irregular drumbeats on the floor above them. Oleg was conducting a tense-sounding discussion with a man who was clearly from the Russian border authority and who was asking a string of questions about the cargo and crew members.

The official asked to see the crew's passports. Oleg replied that the documents were upstairs on the bridge, and at that point the door creaked again, and there was the sound of retreating footsteps.

Johnson found it impossible to relax. He could feel his heart hammering in his chest. Every sound was magnified, and every voice seemed a potential threat. The ship remained stationary.

CHAPTER THIRTY-SIX

Wednesday, April 9, 2014
  Saimaa Canal

The water was only a few degrees above freezing. Severinov knew that because of the sharp involuntary gasp he had given upon hitting the water, the stinging pain from the cold, and his racing heart as he hyperventilated for a minute or so.

He continued to swim, but after a while he could no longer feel his feet or hands. His arms and legs felt incredibly heavy and were barely doing what he was trying to coax them to do.

The cold had penetrated his nose, sinuses, and his temples, which initially felt as though sharp needles were stuck into them but were now just numb.

But the Russian oligarch was a survivor—his instinct for self-preservation was not going to allow him to surrender. He was not a swimmer, but he somehow continued to turn his arms over and pull back in a crawl that was scarcely functional.

It crossed his mind that if he removed his jacket and pants, he might be able to swim more easily, but he knew his numb fingers would prevent him from undoing buttons and zippers and that he might drown while trying to undress. The water-logged clothing was heavy, but perhaps keeping it on might give him some insulation against the cold. It was easier to keep going.

The distance from where he had been unceremoniously thrown off the stern of the timber ship to the safety of shore felt much farther than it actually was. It took Severinov more than fifteen minutes to complete.

Several times he sucked in water instead of air and was left spluttering and coughing in an attempt to clear his lungs.

When he finally beached himself on a stony, muddy stretch of the shore that was covered in bird droppings, Severinov collapsed and lay there motionless.

He felt furious with himself for not anticipating better, furious that he had let his guard down on the side of the lock, and furious that he had not kept the ship's officer at a distance while examining the papers. It had been deeply unprofessional. He knew that in his KGB days, he would have fired a subordinate for such an operational failure.

That was quite apart from the fate of the two policemen who had boarded the ship and appeared to have vanished completely. Severinov suspected he knew exactly what had happened to them: either Johnson or the Russian crew members had probably shot both of them and thrown them overboard.

Severinov swore to himself.

Eventually he turned to see what progress his friend and colleague Pugachov was making.

The FSB officer was still floundering thirty meters offshore, but his slow doggy paddle was pulling him incrementally nearer with every splash.

After another few minutes, Pugachov collapsed onto the mud bank next to Severinov.

Neither man spoke for a couple of minutes. Finally, Severinov hauled himself to his feet and stared at the thick pine forest that lay ahead of him. His body was shivering uncontrollably.

"Come on, get up. We'll die of hypothermia if we stay here. We need to get through this shit and get to the highway. We need to call the border guards—stop that bastard Johnson."

He reached down, grabbed Pugachov beneath the armpits, and pulled him upward.

* * *

Wednesday, April 9, 2014
    Saimaa Canal

It took more than twenty minutes before the distant hum of the *Sanets'* diesel engines turned into a throatier roar. Johnson, in his darkened hiding place, felt the ship begin to move, and finally it was on its way out of the Pälli lock, heading northward toward Finland.

However, Johnson knew from his conversations with Oleg that there was still a stretch of more than two kilometers of canal that ran immediately next to the highway inside Russian territory, and then at least three kilometers of open water where the canal fairway ran into and through Lake Nuija-maanjärvi until they reached Finnish waters, roughly halfway across the lake.

Johnson glanced at his watch and fingered the small hole at the top of his right ear, as he sometimes did when feeling anxious. Katya, next to him, had remained completely silent as they waited.

Despite the challenging swim and passage through the forest that they had given Severinov and Pugachov, he remained concerned that the two men would reach the highway and get an alert to a Russian Border Service patrol vessel before they could reach the Finnish border control point at the Nuijamaa customs quay on the northwest side of the lake. However, they had no choice but to release them at the point that they did.

The unknown factors were Severinov's and Pugachov's swimming abilities and resilience in extremely cold water.

After Oleg sent a crewman down from the bridge to open the hatch for them, Johnson and Katya climbed out into the changing room but left the hatch door open in case they needed to make a hasty retreat in the event of such an inter-ception.

Johnson glued himself to the porthole on the port side of the boat, while Katya kept watch on the starboard side.

Now Johnson guessed that the ship was back up to the maximum permitted speed of nine kilometers per hour. He glanced at his watch, willing the ship—and the time—to go faster.

Fifteen minutes later, Oleg opened the changing room door. He gave a faint smile. "I think you are safe now," he said. "We are over the borderline, and we are about to reach the Finland customs quay at Nuijamaa."

It was only then that Johnson felt confident enough to emerge onto the deck. By the time he did so, the *Sanets* had slowed to a crawl as it approached the customs quay, a long, slim concrete jetty that protruded out into the lake and was clearly marked by signs along the fairway.

"Thank you for what you have done, but I am worried

about you," Johnson said to Oleg. "You will have to return to Russia. What happens then, given the incident at Cvetotchnoe lock?"

Oleg gave a slight shrug. "You do not need to worry about me," he said. "I'm done with Russia."

"What do you mean?"

"I mean that I am leaving. My other five ships are all out too, once the *Osa* is through customs control." He pointed toward the second of his timber ships, which was visible half a mile or so behind them, forging its way toward Nuijamaa. "My other ships are all operating in Finland. I set up a company there some time ago and have registered the boats there. I do most of my business in Finland and in Norway now. I do not like the Russian business environment, and I don't like the leadership. What happened to my friend Gennady was the incident that finally decided everything for me. I can look after myself in Finland—I'll be fine. I've been preparing for this for a long time, offshoring all my assets and so on. All this just means accelerating my exit slightly but that's not a problem."

That explained that, then, Johnson thought. He had been wondering what Oleg's motivation was, apart from assisting the daughter of an old friend.

He pulled his Heckler & Koch from his belt and handed it to Oleg, along with the spare magazine and the suppressor that Katya had given him. Katya did the same with her gun.

"There you are," Katya said. "Two thank-you presents from us. You deserve much more, but it's all I have. My father would have been very proud of you for all the help you have given us."

"And we can't take those guns through customs very easily," Johnson said.

Oleg accepted the two weapons, giving a slight snort and a

thin-lipped smile as he eyed the suppressors. "You think we are assassins?" he asked. But he pushed all the weaponry into a cupboard and closed the door.

Two uniformed officers, one from Finnish customs and one from passport control, boarded the ship as soon as the crew had moored. After shaking hands with Oleg, who they appeared to know well, they began checking the crew and passenger list that he had handed over.

To Johnson's relief, his US passport in the name of William Cadman merited little more than a passing glance. As an American citizen, he didn't need a visa for entry into the EU, provided he stayed less than ninety days.

Katya too passed through without challenge. Her precaution in obtaining a Schengen visa well in advance had proved a valuable one.

After the officials had departed, Johnson turned to Oleg and thanked him once again. The Russian shipowner had saved their skin—there was no doubt about that.

"Where are you going to now?" Oleg asked.

"We need to get to Lappeenranta Airport," Johnson said.

"The canal goes to Lappeenranta and into Lake Saimaa. We can take you."

Johnson shook his head. He had seen enough of the Saimaa Canal, and grateful though he was for the escape from Russia that Oleg and the *Sanets* had given him, he knew that the FSB would have agents inside Finland that they could deploy. He guessed that by now, either Severinov or Pugachov or both would have reached the highway and found a way to call or get messages to FSB headquarters.

"We will both take a taxi from here. Tonight we will stay in a hotel, and then tomorrow morning we can fly out."

The city of Lappeenranta was only about half an hour's drive from Nuijamaa. Johnson had used his phone to check flight departures, and although Lappeenranta was one of Finland's smaller airports, it did have flights to Berlin.

Johnson and Katya shook hands with Oleg, then walked toward a line of taxis waiting outside the passport checkpoint.

Suddenly Johnson felt extremely tired. After only a couple of hours' sleep the previous night and a stressful, long journey that had lasted almost the entire day, he needed a bed.

But before he could think about bed, his concern was to get safely to a hotel. Lappeenranta was only thirty kilometers from the Russian border and though they were undoubtedly far safer here than inside Russia, he knew that it would be a potentially fatal error to become complacent.

Johnson needed to be as sure as he could that there was no surveillance tracking them before they checked into a hotel. He therefore instructed their taxi driver to take a circuitous route around the fringes of Lappeenranta.

They started with the airport, which had busy highways running parallel to the single runway on either side, less than five hundred meters away.

They then drove through the city's two universities and paused for a while next to a marina filled with yachts and boats on the edge of Lake Saimaa. Twenty minutes later, they stopped again in a drive-through burger restaurant's car park next to a mall, where they got out and wandered in and out of a few shops. But there was no sign of any surveillance, no repeating faces or cars, and nobody sitting in parked cars or loitering on motorcycles.

After fifty minutes and another stop at a cell phone store to buy two burner phones and SIM cards, one for himself and the other for Katya, Johnson was satisfied. He told the driver to take them to a hotel he had found online, the Original Sokos Hotel Lappe, in the city center.

Johnson and Katya checked into adjoining rooms at the

hotel, a modern two-story building that was tucked away in a pedestrianized plaza that also housed the town hall, government offices, and a police station.

After showering, Johnson used one of the burner phones to book two seats on a budget flight leaving the following morning for Berlin's Schönefeld Airport.

For the first time since his arrival in St. Petersburg two days earlier, Johnson felt safe enough to call Vic and Jayne to update them, again using the burner. He kept it brief and gave only vague details of their hotel and flight plans. Johnson also sent a text message to each of his children and to his sister, Amy, to let them know he was safe and that he would call and have a proper conversation as soon as he was able to do so.

There came a knock at Johnson's door. It was Katya, also freshly showered, and carrying a bottle of Moskovskaya Osobaya vodka that she had procured from room service.

She entered Johnson's room and poured two large glasses of the vodka.

"*Za tvajo zdarovje*," she said, raising her glass. "To your health." She downed the measure in one gulp and smiled. It was a broad, white-toothed smile, and Johnson realized that it was the first time he had seen her smile since he had met her, next to the bloodied body of her mother outside her apartment in St. Petersburg.

Johnson returned the toast. He badly needed a drink, and Katya yet again had gone up in his estimation, even if he would have preferred to be having a drink with Jayne in that moment.

"I owe you," he said. "I doubt I would have gotten out of St. Petersburg without you."

Katya nodded. "We Russians have our uses," she said, smiling again as she poured out another two measures. They sat on armchairs on either side of a small table next to the hotel window. Outside on the plaza a few tourists were taking photographs in front of the town hall. This time she sipped her drink more slowly.

"What will you do about your mother and your brother?" Johnson asked.

Her smile vanished. "I have just spoken to my brother," she said. "He is at the Black Sea, waiting for a boat to take him to Istanbul. He will ask someone to arrange things for my mother's funeral. He is safe."

Johnson looked at the floor. Both Katya and Timur had been forced to leave their homeland because of his arrival in St. Petersburg. Now, with the blood of an FSB officer and two policemen on her hands, she would not be able to return. That was for certain.

"There is another thing," Katya said as she took another sip of her vodka. "I think it is now safe for me to tell you."

Johnson glanced at her. "The name, you mean? The Nazi's son?"

During the entire escape from St. Petersburg, he had constantly worried that something might happen to Katya before she could give him details of her father's contact in the Stasi.

"Yes. His name is Ludwig."

"Ludwig? And what is his last name?"

"Helm. Ludwig Helm."

Johnson felt his face muscles tighten. "And he is definitely ex-Stasi?"

"Yes, I already told you that."

"Why 'the Nazi's son'? Was his father in the SS?"

"I have no idea. My father never gave me details. It must have been for the obvious reason, I guess."

"Do you have his contact details?" Johnson pressed her.

Katya shook her head. "Unfortunately not. Only the name."

Johnson exhaled sharply. The trip to St. Petersburg had not gone according to plan, and he had several times wondered whether it would be worth all the hassles and dangers.

Now all he had was a name. It didn't seem like much.

CHAPTER THIRTY-SEVEN

Wednesday, April 9, 2014
London

It had taken a long time for Shevchenko to be certain she was black. A protracted surveillance detection route had taken her up and down the Bakerloo line, along Oxford Street with its crowds of tourists and shoppers, and eventually into Covent Garden. After emerging into the Strand and walking through the Savoy hotel, where she exited via a rear door and ended up on the Embankment, she finally felt secure enough to make her way back to the safe house in the St. John's Wood apartment building in a taxi.

As was usually the case, ANTELOPE had arrived well before her. But then, her agent wasn't under the same surveillance pressures; nobody from MI6 was attempting to follow ANTELOPE every minute of every hour.

Shevchenko held up a hand in apology and removed her jacket. "I am sorry I am so late. They are watching me even when I clean my teeth now. Probably even when I change my knickers. I have to be careful."

ANTELOPE gave a slight smile. "In that case, let's hope they don't catch up with me. I'd better buy some new underwear, just in case."

Shevchenko inclined her head in acknowledgment of the joke as she sat in an armchair opposite ANTELOPE, but she didn't laugh. "You must be very careful."

ANTELOPE was a prize asset in Western intelligence, and the last thing Shevchenko wanted, having done all the hard work in getting the agent established, was for the entire operation to be blown through some careless mistake.

But the fact that ANTELOPE was feeling somewhat disgruntled and unappreciated at work had opened the door for Shevchenko to work her magic.

That was why a campaign that had lasted many months eventually bore fruit: ANTELOPE decided to take the money on offer. The decisive factors when recruiting assets in foreign intelligence or military organizations had remained remarkably constant: unhappiness for whatever reason in a work situation, the lure of a numbered bank account in Zürich, and the prospect of an early, very comfortable retirement.

"Now, what have you got for me?" Shevchenko asked.

ANTELOPE handed a micro SD card to Shevchenko and explained that it contained a number of top secret NATO documents that had been circulated late the previous evening.

One document detailed how three French navy vessels were under orders to proceed immediately to the Black Sea as part of the reinforcement of NATO positions following the annexation by Russia of the Crimean Peninsula.

One of the vessels was the intelligence collection spy ship the *Depuy de Lôme*, which was expected to pass through the

Bosporus Straits within the next couple of days. The ship, equipped with satellite communication interception technology, would be capable of collecting intelligence and electronic data transmitted well into Russia once she had reached her destination, the report indicated. The ship also had a helicopter landing pad that might be used to operate small intelligence-gathering drones.

The *Depuy de Lôme* would be joining another French vessel the *Alizé*, which was an auxiliary support ship for divers and was primarily used by the French intelligence agency, the Direction Générale de la Sécurité Extérieure, the DGSE, which was France's equivalent to the SVR or CIA.

The third French vessel, a destroyer, was the *Dupleix*, which was also expected to arrive in the Black Sea over the following few days.

Shevchenko listened to ANTELOPE's summary and leaned back in her chair, deep in thought.

"Is there any update on the timing of the US destroyer's arrival, the *Donald Cook*, in the Black Sea?" Shevchenko asked.

"No, nothing yet. I will tell you if I hear any more on that."

"Fine. This seems to me like a significant buildup of NATO military capability," she said. "Sending two spy ships and a destroyer is a provocation, particularly when you look at what the Americans are also doing in that region."

"No doubt Washington, London, and Paris think invading the Crimea and taking it off the Ukraine is a provocation."

Shevchenko ignored the comment. "The president will be furious. I will transmit a short summary to Yasenevo and the president's office immediately after we have finished here, and then the entire set of documents can go via the usual route as quickly as I can arrange for my illegal to collect the SD card."

"Good," ANTELOPE said. "There will almost certainly

be a constant stream of these NATO military updates coming through during the next few weeks."

"Indeed," Shevchenko said. "Which is why I have this for you. It came a few days earlier than I expected. You can send the next batch of documents yourself."

She reached into her bag and removed a slim cardboard box that she opened and handed to ANTELOPE. Inside was a circular silver SRAC transmitter receiver.

"Thanks. That's good work," ANTELOPE said. "Now I need to know exactly where the base station is."

Shevchenko took out her phone and opened a maps app set to satellite mode, then showed ANTELOPE the precise location of the SRAC base station in Regent's Park and described the landmarks on the street and in the park to look out for when identifying where it was. That gave ANTE-LOPE the option to drive past the SRAC base station, which was the safest option, or operate on foot.

"If you are driving, don't go flying past; just take your foot off the gas a little. You need to be traveling at around twenty-five miles per hour. No faster. The SRAC will connect quickly, but don't take a chance. On the other hand, don't slow too much, or else if you have surveillance they will spot it."

"I am certain I've not had surveillance," ANTELOPE said.

"Fine. You need to be one hundred percent sure. And even then, when you transmit, you are in danger because you will need to reach into a bag on the seat next to you with one hand and operate that. You press this button and hold for three seconds." Shevchenko pointed to the SRAC device.

"They may be watching you from a vehicle through binoc-ulars or filming you to analyze later. So you need to be able to drive completely straight during that three-second hold," Shevchenko continued. "You must also sit straight, not turn your shoulders while you are operating the device, or do anything else unusual that might give you away. Do I make myself understood?"

"Completely understood."

"Good," Shevchenko stood. She wanted to get out as quickly as possible.

"I will think through which is the best way of doing the drop," ANTELOPE said.

Shevchenko nodded. "I will leave it up to you which option you choose. Just make sure that either way, you send me a short 'okay' message, a secure text, once the data has been uploaded."

"Of course. You don't need to worry," ANTELOPE said. "There's just one other thing. I heard that Joe Johnson has been into St. Petersburg and out again. He's over the border into Finland."

Shevchenko swore. "The FSB are losing their touch. Thankfully Yezhov's wife is dead."

"Yes, but his daughter is very much alive. Johnson is apparently with her. I don't know much more, but I heard that."

As she put her jacket back on, Shevchenko stared out the ninth-floor window over Lord's Cricket Ground, where another match was being played.

She had not expected Johnson to emerge unscathed from Russia, let alone with a potential lead. That did not sound good.

CHAPTER THIRTY-EIGHT

Thursday, April 10, 2014
  Berlin

"Ludwig Helm? One of the Nazi's sons?" Schwartz asked with a wide grin. "Yes, I knew him—I used to work with him for the Stasi. I could have told you that. And what's more—"

"What do you mean you knew him?" Johnson snapped. He felt irritated. Schwartz was putting on a performance, being overly chatty, clearly enjoying the fact that Johnson had been all the way to St. Petersburg to find out something that he could have told him in Berlin.

Schwartz shrugged. "I mean what I said. I knew him. I worked with him."

He glanced alternately at Johnson, then at Katya, who sat next to him on the leather sofa at the CIA safe house on Limonenstrasse.

"So tell me why you call him 'one of the Nazi's sons,'" Johnson went on.

He had heard Katya's version and now wanted to see whether it tallied with Schwartz's account.

Schwartz narrowed his eyes. "That's what he was. We used to call both him and his brother, Christoph, *die Söhne der Nazi* —the Nazi's sons. Their father, Heinz, was some senior officer in the SS. A Gestapo chief. He vanished off to South America somewhere after the war and left his family behind. The boys were in the SS, too, at a much lower level, and they both got jobs with the Stasi."

"It would have been helpful if you had told me before," Johnson said, although more out of annoyance than anything.

The corner of Schwartz's mouth turned up. "Well, Herr investigator, why would I? And anyway, you never asked."

Johnson had to admit to himself that there was indeed no reason why Schwartz should have mentioned Helm. He stood and walked out to the kitchen. He needed a drink of water.

As he went, he couldn't help recalling his son Peter's question before he had left Portland, and his response.

"So will you be hunting Nazis this time, Dad?"

"No, not this time. No Nazis involved."

Johnson and Katya had arrived at Berlin's Schönefeld Airport just after lunchtime. By that stage, after nine hours' sleep and a few coffees, both of them were feeling significantly better. They had been collected by Neal and his driver, who took them back to Limonenstrasse after a lengthy surveillance detection route.

After drinking the water, Johnson put his head around the door of a meeting room next to the kitchen. In there, Neal was busy delegating to Mary Gassey the task of working out a settlement plan for Katya somewhere in the West: it was likely to take some considerable time. It had to be somewhere that Katya was comfortable with and that gave her sufficient anonymity and security. The tentacles of Moscow

Center reached far, and there was no way she was going back to Russia.

The biggest issue in Johnson's mind was whether Katya was a safe person for resettlement, given he had witnessed her kill three men. But the shootings were all in extreme circumstances, and given that Johnson owed her his life, he decided to disclose the kills she had made in Russia only to Neal, who understood immediately. The decision was made to give her a chance.

The favored location for resettlement was not Germany but the United Kingdom: probably some small village tucked away in the countryside many miles from anywhere the SVR would think to look. However, achieving that and establishing an appropriate false identity involved a lot of red tape and multiple discussions with civil servants. Johnson was glad he didn't have to get involved in the process.

Katya was going to miss her father's memorial service in St. Petersburg, scheduled for the following week, as would her brother, who was now staying temporarily with friends in Istanbul. It remained unclear whether Gennady's body would be returned to Russia for burial: it was lying in a Berlin morgue, where forensic pathologists still had not completed an extensive round of tests.

Varvara Yezhova's funeral was also still to be arranged somehow, but there was no way either Katya or Timur would be able to attend that service either. Johnson felt deeply for them both.

While Johnson was away, Neal had decided that despite his mounting concerns, they should continue to detain Reiner Schwartz, although not under the same duress as during his initial few days in CIA custody. It was certain that Schwartz would vanish out of Germany, probably to Moscow, the moment he was released, and they could not yet afford for that to happen. Vic, however, remained paranoid that the SVR would discover his whereabouts and try to launch some kind of operation to rescue him.

Johnson walked back into the interrogation room and sat down on the sofa. A CIA guard holding a Beretta was sitting six feet behind him, next to the wall.

"I need to know where this man Helm is," Johnson said. "Do you have any clue?"

"No." Schwartz shook his head. "We are not in contact."

But Johnson wasn't going to give up that easily. He knew Schwartz had more useful information about Ludwig Helm in him.

Johnson realized he was probably going to need some leverage to persuade Ludwig Helm to give him what he needed. He recalled that a significant number of SS officers had found work at the Stasi.

Johnson leaned forward. "You said that Ludwig Helm was an SS officer during the war, as was his father."

Schwartz yawned and nodded. "Yes. A junior officer. A *Junker*. He had just gone to one of the training schools, the *Junkerschulen*, when the war ended. I remember him mentioning it to me and saying in a joking way that his father had high hopes for him—he seemed disappointed that his ambitions were terminated. He became a musician instead."

Johnson knew that the *Junkerschulen* had been set up to train SS cadets to become leaders for the future. Getting a place in the schools was a significant first step on the career ladder.

But even at that level, any SS officer might have been a candidate for prosecution after the war ended. In line with guidance from Moscow, the German Democratic Republic was anti-fascist—at least officially, if not in practice. The GDR convicted more than eight thousand former Nazis, many of whom received death sentences. If they weren't prosecuted, they were often coerced: a significant number were blackmailed into working for the Stasi as spies, interrogators, and in various other roles, both in East and West Germany. Others joined of their own accord, having concealed or downplayed their time in the SS, and applied through normal channels, desperate for any sort of employment amid the economic wreckage of the postwar years.

Johnson tugged at the old wound on his right ear. "Presumably the Russians, the KGB, did not know that Helm was SS?" he asked.

Schwartz shrugged. "I doubt it. He had only just started in the training center when the war ended, and he would have hidden that fact to get his job with the Stasi. The Russians would not have been able to get into the Nazi Party files because you Americans had them."

Johnson knew very well that was true. In April 1945, as the war ended, the Nazi leadership sent their entire portfolio of ten million party membership card files to be pulped.

But a paper mill manager, instead of pulping the documents, hid them under wastepaper until US Army archivists obtained them in October 1945. Eventually, they were moved to a Berlin document center, and microfilmed copies were made for use at the National Archives in Washington, DC. The copies of those files later became vital evidence in the prosecutions of Nazi war criminals, including at the Nuremberg trials. Johnson himself had used them on many occasions while working at the Office of Special Investigations when he needed evidence against certain war criminals who had taken refuge in the United States.

All this gave Johnson an idea.

He quickly wrote an email on his phone to a former colleague at the OSI, Ben Veletta. Since 2010, the unit had been part of a new division of the Department of Justice, known as the Human Rights and Special Prosecutions section, of which Ben was now deputy chief historian. Johnson had kept in touch with Ben over the years and had occasionally asked him for help. Now he asked Ben if he could obtain copies of Ludwig Helm's and Heinz Helm's Nazi Party files, which with any luck would be with all the other files at the National Archives in Washington, DC.

After dispatching the email, Johnson began making checks on Ludwig Helm's whereabouts. There were four people of that name listed in the online German Telefonbuch phone directory. But it was obvious after a few searches online, including checking their social media accounts, that none of them were the former Stasi officer he was seeking. Neither was there any trace of him elsewhere.

In the end, it required an afternoon's work by Jayne's contacts at GCHQ to track him down to an address in the city of Leipzig, almost a hundred miles southwest of Berlin.

At the same time, Nicklin-Donovan's office unearthed a brief MI6 file on Ludwig Helm dating from 1989. The short memo inside noted that MI6 had tried to persuade him to go on the payroll, but the attempt had not been successful. At the bottom was a list of some of his known colleagues, contacts, and acquaintances in both the KGB and the Stasi. Among them was a Gennady Yezhov, a Varvara Menshikova— so Menshikova must have been her maiden name—and Reiner Schwartz. It gave his birth date, December 2, 1924, but there was nothing about Helm himself having been in the SS or a Nazi Party member.

However there were several paragraphs about Helm's father, Heinz, and his Nazi background. This was of significant interest to Johnson, given his background as a war crimes investigator. It turned out that Heinz Helm, who held the rank of *SS-Gruppenführer*, was a very senior Nazi Party official, third in command of the secret state police, the

Gestapo, and played a major part in planning the Holocaust. He was one of the top Nazis who had never been captured nor confirmed dead. There were reported sightings of him in Buenos Aires, Argentina, in the 1950s, but nothing after that. He had, as Schwartz had indicated, apparently vanished, leaving his family behind in Leipzig.

Nicklin-Donovan had also included a separate, much larger file on Heinz Helm, likely knowing Johnson would find it interesting to see. The elder Helm must have died many years ago, though, given he was born in 1902, so Johnson turned his attention back to his son Ludwig.

Finally, at around half past nine in the evening, a secure email arrived from Ben at the HRSP containing the Nazi Party files on Ludwig and Heinz Helm. The files corroborated all that was in the MI6 file and what Schwartz had told Johnson: Ludwig had been in the *Hitler-Jugend*, the Hitler Youth, and then attended *Junkerschule* as the Second World War came to an end.

Although there was no indication that Ludwig had been involved in any activity that might trigger a war crimes prosecution, Johnson nevertheless had the ammunition he needed to put his idea into action.

Johnson immediately arranged for a US embassy car and driver to take him to Leipzig the next day. He also reclaimed the Beretta M9 from the weapons locker at the CIA station that he had deposited before departing for St. Petersburg.

"Let's hope our friend Ludwig proves less obstructive than he was in 1989," he said to Neal.

Johnson pointed toward Schwartz, who was still on the sofa under the CIA guard's watchful eye. "I think we should let him go now. We've bled him dry."

Neal nodded. "Yes, I agree. Kiss him goodbye." He called the guard over and instructed him to have Schwartz ready for release first thing the following morning.

"Make sure he's taken back to his house in a blacked-out car," Johnson said. "It's obvious the Germans still don't know we're holding him, but nevertheless, I don't want to run the risk of him being arrested by the police outside our embassy or something. That would be a PR disaster, and the ambassador would kill us."

CHAPTER THIRTY-NINE

Thursday, April 10, 2014
Moscow

The fragments of broken glass that lay on the floor in front of the three-meter plasma television screen and the fist-size hole in the center of the screen itself gave a small clue as to Severinov's state of mind after he arrived back home from St. Petersburg.

Of course, the news bulletin on his television, detailing American navy moves in the Aegean Sea, near the Bosporus, in response to the reclaiming of the Crimea by Russian forces, had been but the final straw. He had catapulted the drinking glass he had been holding and the sparkling water it contained against the giant screen attached to his living room wall.

He wasn't surprised that the house staff at his residence in Gorki-8 was giving him a wide berth. He had no doubt that word had quickly got around: something had gone wrong on his trip, and the boss was in a foul mood.

It would have been difficult to deny. His nose was badly bruised, dried blood clearly visible, his lip was cut, and his face had a number of scratches from scrambling through the forest.

None of his staff were prepared to ask for the precise details, but Severinov guessed that someone would have given the rest of them the general outline of what happened in the Saimaa Canal. It was most likely a member of his aircrew who had flown him, Pugachov, and Balagula back to Moscow from St. Petersburg.

Severinov glared at the pile of glass on the floor, then retreated to his study and tried to think through what to do next. The mission to assassinate Varvara Yezhova had been completed successfully. Likewise with her husband. But after the unexpected appearance of Joe Johnson in St. Petersburg, Severinov had certainly not anticipated coming off worse in the ensuing tussle—not on his home turf.

In retrospect, Severinov felt he had made a fairly fundamental error in not taking Balagula with them in pursuit of Johnson and Katya toward the Finnish border. The decision to leave him behind in St. Petersburg had been made on the spot. He had allowed himself to be influenced by Pugachov, and it had been wrong: it might have taken a bit of time to fetch Balagula, but the debacle at Cvetotchnoe lock almost certainly would not have occurred had he been there.

He and Pugachov had eventually made their way through a dense forest to the highway and had halted a truck. The driver was visibly horrified at the two men's appearance— soaking wet, half frozen, bloodied, and scratched.

Pugachov had used the driver's cell phone to call the Border Service. But it had been too late. Johnson and Katya Yezhova had already gone through and were over the border into Finland. Quite apart from the discomfort and indignity inflicted on Severinov and Pugachov, the fugitives had the

deaths of two Russian policemen and an FSB officer on their
hands. If Severinov had anything to do with it, the pair of
them would pay heavily in the end for all of it.

Severinov and Pugachov had returned to St. Petersburg in
the back of a police car. En route, Pugachov received a
message saying that the police had managed to determine the
false identity under which Johnson was traveling: it was that
of William Cadman, a law lecturer from Washington, DC,
who had a place at the St. Petersburg International Legal
Forum but had failed to turn up to any sessions apart from on
the first morning.

Severinov snorted in disgust when Pugachov passed on
the details.

What use is that now?

He felt as though his pride and his professionalism, as
well as his body, had taken a severe knock.

Severinov felt certain that Johnson would now be fired up,
full of adrenaline, and probably more determined than he
previously had been to get to the bottom of his investigation
into Gennady Yezhov's death.

He knew he had to put a halt to it. But how?

What would Johnson's next step be, after his failure to
speak to Varvara? Although the American was presumably
still with Yezhov's daughter, Katya, Severinov still doubted
that the daughter would have been fully briefed by her father
on highly classified matters relating to national security. He
knew how the likes of Yezhov thought. Secrecy was hard-
wired into the old KGB culture of which Gennady was a part,
despite his eventual defection.

However, there was a definite risk that the girl could
point Johnson toward others who were better placed to help
him in his investigations. Among them would be people who
had been in the same circle of KGB and Stasi operatives
during the 1980s. He ran through a mental list of them, but

there only a couple of men really mattered, both of whom had been in the Stasi but had worked closely alongside the KGB.

What decided it for him was the arrival of a secure message from Anastasia in London, relaying details picked up from her agent ANTELOPE, who was trying to keep a close watch on Joe Johnson's investigation. Details were sparse because ANTELOPE was not in the loop on everything. But apparently, Johnson had gotten back to Berlin, along with Katya Yezhova, and was heading to Leipzig the following day.

Severinov thought he knew exactly who he would intend to visit there, although there was no confirmation of that from Anastasia.

He also knew for certain that unless he acted now, he would be effectively hanging himself out to dry.

He checked his laptop: yes, he still had addresses for both men. He just hoped they were still current, as it had been a long time since their last contact.

Severinov did a quick mental calculation. If he got Balagula on a plane that evening, he could be in Berlin by midnight and operational first thing in the morning for the two tasks that he had in mind.

After all, dead men could tell no tales.

He picked up the phone and dialed.

* * *

Thursday, April 10, 2014
London

The breakthrough came just after three o'clock on Thursday afternoon, when the B2 surveillance team that was stationed near the Bread Street motorbike bay saw a woman walk up to the motorbike they were watching.

The team of four was staked out in two nearby buildings and the adjacent streets.

The building across the street from the motorbike belonged to an investment company where a female B2 member, Zara Ashwin, was sat at a corner desk on the ground floor. One of Bennett's "fixers" had forged an arrangement to use the desk with the investment company's managing director, telling him only that they were following up on a lead on a suspected illegal immigrant.

The second building, where the fixer had made a similar arrangement to temporarily use a desk with a view of the motorbike bay, lay on the other side of Cannon Street and belonged to a law firm. Ashwin could actually see her B2 colleague from her vantage point.

The other two members of the team loitered nearby, drinking coffee in cafés, sitting in parks, browsing in shops, and waiting in line for buses. They changed their disguises frequently, and Ashwin occasionally amused herself by trying to spot their next appearance in the vicinity.

Ashwin herself spent most of her time on her laptop computer surfing the internet but with her attention mainly focused on the bike, a Yamaha.

As soon as Ashwin saw the Southern European woman take out a key and unlock the Yamaha's pannier bag, she calmly closed the lid of her laptop, placed it in her bag, and walked out into the investment company's rear courtyard that led onto Bread Street via a pair of heavy wooden doors.

Ashwin exited the doors onto the street and found herself about thirty yards away from the motorbike. She was just in time to see the woman place something in the pannier and lock it again. Ashwin lit a cigarette, as if on a break from her work, and called Bennett on her secure cell phone.

"Gary, the drop's been activated," she muttered. "Am starting foot surveillance immediately. It's a Southern European–looking woman, possibly Spanish or Italian, shoulder-length black hair, dark jacket, jeans, with a beige shoulder bag. She's about five feet six inches tall, olive skin, medium build. She has placed something in the Yamaha's pannier, presumably a flash drive or similar. Please launch backup team."

"Thanks, Zara, will do," Bennett said. The arrangement was that the other three members of the team would now operate together to tail the woman as she left the scene.

Ashwin ended the call.

* * *

Thursday, April 10, 2014
London

Jayne could hear only silence at the other end of the secure phone connection as Johnson digested what she had just told him.

The good news she had to report from London was that the B2 team had spotted the illegal, a Southern European woman, while she was placing material in the motorbike dead drop near St. Paul's Cathedral and had now put her under surveillance.

The bad news was something that occurred to Jayne in response to Johnson's news that he was heading to Leipzig the next morning to chase down Ludwig Helm.

Having gone over the documents that had been circulated to the joint CIA-MI6 team over recent days, and which therefore might have been leaked to Yasenevo, Jayne had realized that one of them, dated April 4, was a short update from

Vic Walter to Mark Nicklin-Donovan that mentioned Johnson's intention to travel to St. Petersburg to locate Varvara Yezhova.

It stated that this followed intelligence sourced from an agent in Berlin, an unnamed SVR officer.

"That's how the FSB got onto your trail in St. Petersburg," Jayne said. "They saw the leaked report."

"Yes, maybe, but that's not going to impact my Leipzig visit," Johnson said. "They won't know about that."

"They might not know, but they could work it out. If Moscow Center knows we have been getting our information from one of their SVR people, it won't take them long to work out that it's Schwartz, and then—"

"They have lots of people in Berlin—they might not deduce it that quickly," Johnson interrupted.

"Who knows? And if they then realize that Schwartz and Helm were connected in the '80s, they could put two and two together and work out that Helm was next on your list for a visit."

"That's a very long shot."

"Yes, but they're good at long shots."

Another silence from Johnson. Jayne knew that maybe her mind was working overtime, but that's what she was paid for and why she had delivered such good results over more than two and a half decades in the intelligence community. In her experience, a little paranoia kept the adrenaline flowing and often put her one valuable step ahead.

In this case, she realized that her concern was due to more than purely professional reasons.

"Joe, from what I've heard, it sounds as though you've almost used up your cat's nine lives on this operation. Just be very careful. I want you back. I was worried as hell when you went off the radar in St. Petersburg."

Johnson chuckled a little. "Good to know someone cares.

I wish I'd had your levelheaded companionship and humor in Russia—unlike the loose cannon I was with. Although to be fair, she saved my skin. I'll be back. I'm looking forward to seeing you too. Listen, I've got to go. I need to call Vic and update him."

Jayne ended the call and sat staring at the ceiling of the Rossmore Road safe house. She was getting a bad vibe, and Johnson's reassuring words hadn't shaken it off.

CHAPTER FORTY

Friday, April 11, 2014
  Berlin

Reiner Schwartz stood on the sidewalk outside his house. He watched the unmarked gray CIA car that had just dropped him off skirt around a white Volkswagen parked a few meters farther along the street and disappear around the corner. Then he turned and made his way up the narrow driveway that ran alongside his house.

The whole episode seemed like a nightmare. Maybe if he went inside and poured himself a large tumbler of brandy, he might wake up.

But the twelve days' worth of beard growing on his face and the kilos he had lost were evidence that it had been no bad dream.

Those bastards in the CIA and their British sidekicks were as bad as the damned SVR. How dare they imprison him in some safe house for nearly two weeks.

How dare they.

He felt anger rising up inside him like a wave. Anger at himself, for being so stupid and careless as to be captured in the first place, and anger at everyone else. *People. He hated people.*

The problem he now had was what to do next. His job at the ministry was finished; he knew that. Quite apart from the fact that he hadn't been into the office for two weeks without contacting his boss, he knew that the Americans would have to pass along their intelligence about his role with the SVR. They would have to—if they didn't, their friends at the BND would find out at some stage anyway.

He was also finished in Germany for the same reason. If he stayed, he would be inside a prison cell before he could blink. So he needed to get out, and the only place he could realistically go now for refuge was Moscow.

As Schwartz turned right to go along the path that led to his rear door, he heard a car door click shut out on the street.

He turned to look. A barrel-chested, muscled, military-looking man was striding up the drive toward him, dressed in a dark jacket and trousers. Black chest hairs were showing at the V where his shirt buttons were undone.

Mein Gott. My God.

As the man drew near, he put his hand inside his jacket. It was obvious what was hidden there.

"Go inside," the man said in German. But Schwartz immediately picked up on the Russian accent.

They must know what I've done, what I've given away.

Schwartz hesitated for a beat, then walked slowly along the path to his door. He knew this was the end. Somehow the Russians had found out he had been talking to the CIA. They wouldn't be interested in why he had talked, how he had been captured, or the torture he had faced. He looked briefly up to the sky—he would likely need a miracle to save him now.

"Open it and go inside. Do not try anything stupid," the man said.

"I must take my key from my pocket," Schwartz said.

"Yes. Do it slowly."

Schwartz removed the key from his jacket pocket, inserted it into the lock, and opened the door. He couldn't help noticing that the daffodils in his flower bed, which had been yellow and thriving when he had been taken away, were now brown, their heads drooping.

"Walk into your kitchen and stand in front of the fridge," the man said. "Then raise your hands above your head."

Schwartz did as instructed.

The man positioned himself about two meters in front of Schwartz and raised his handgun, which Schwartz could see was a Makarov with a suppressor screwed into the barrel. He pointed it directly at Schwartz's head.

"No! Don't do that. Please! I can—" Schwartz shouted.

There was a muffled thwack, and Schwartz's world went black.

* * *

Friday, April 11, 2014
    Leipzig

The apartment building was a five-story stone property overlooking a cobblestoned square that housed an old church, Thomaskirche—St. Thomas Church. The church's white tower, imposing vertiginous stone walls, and tall arched stained-glass windows dominated the square, where two solitary trees were showing the first signs of spring growth.

Johnson gained entry to the building by tailgating a teenage girl who was entirely focused on the music blaring from her headphones, not on the middle-aged balding man who followed her in through the main entrance.

From there, it was a straightforward matter to take the elevator to level two, where Ludwig Helm's apartment, number thirty-six, was located halfway along a dismally lit high-ceilinged corridor with faded dark-green carpet.

Before approaching the apartment, Johnson checked out his exit routes, as he always did when visiting a new building. Apart from the twin elevators, which were located in the center of the corridor, there was also a main staircase next to the elevator shaft, and at the far end of the corridor there was a sign marked Fire Escape.

He wandered along to check the fire escape, the door to which was set back from the main corridor in a recess. Unlike the main staircase, which was wide and carpeted, this one was narrow and consisted of bare concrete steps and landings.

Satisfied, Johnson pushed his Beretta down into his jacket pocket and checked that the handkerchiefs he had positioned to disguise the gun's outline were still in place. Then he walked back to Helm's apartment and knocked on the door.

The stooped man who answered had an unruly mop of white hair, a gray complexion, and round metal-framed glasses.

So this is the Nazi's son.

Johnson, telling a few half-truths, deployed his fluent German to claim that he was an American historian who was carrying out anonymous interviews with former senior members of the Stasi for a book and a film that was planned to mark the twenty-fifth anniversary of the fall of the Berlin Wall.

Helm's lip curled up when Johnson told him he was American. "So will this be a well-balanced view of the Stasi? I haven't seen one yet from your side of the Atlantic," he said. But after Johnson deployed some of his well-practiced doorstep charm and a little persuasion, Helm eventually let him into the apartment.

A grand piano that looked like a museum piece stood beneath a window at one end of the lengthy living room. The lid was covered in scratches, the varnish was peeling off in places, and some of the white keys were chipped. Piles of yellowed sheet music lay on top of it.

"Do you play it?" Johnson asked.

"Of course," Helm replied as he walked stiff-legged to the piano. He tapped his hand on the lid. "Everyone in this city plays music. I was the organist at Thomaskirche across there for a few years in the '90s." He indicated through the window at the church across the square. "And I also used to be chairman of the Leipzig Bach Festival—one of the biggest music festivals in the world. Did you know Johann Sebastian Bach was *Kapellmeister*, music director, at Thomaskirche in the eighteenth century?"

Johnson admitted he didn't know that. This story was becoming stranger with every revelation. *An ex-Nazi, ex-Stasi turned church organist?*

Helm gave him a short unprompted lecture on the famous composer's twenty-seven-year tenure at the church. "He wrote more than three hundred cantatas and his famous Mass in B-minor here, and the St. Matthew Passion," Helm said. He pointed out a large statue of the composer that stood on a stone plinth in the square in front of the church, between the two trees.

"Anyway, enough of Bach." Helm pushed his glasses up his nose and smiled. Despite being eighty-nine, he was clearly still bright and switched on. This was promising.

He indicated to Johnson to sit in a faded leather armchair and took his place in a matching chair that faced Johnson's. "How can I help you with your book? I don't get many people who are interested in the Stasi these days, thankfully. Everyone tries to forget those times, including me."

"I'm actually interested in two quite narrow aspects of the Stasi," Johnson said. "The first relates to the Stasi's links with the KGB and to one person in particular. The second is to do with a terrorist attack."

Helm's smile disappeared. "The KGB? Which person are you talking about? And which terrorist attack?"

"The person was a KGB officer, Gennady Yezhov, who I understand was a friend of yours, and the attack I am interested in is the La Belle discotheque."

Helm's eyebrows flicked up, and he visibly stiffened in his chair. There was silence for several seconds.

"I don't want to talk about this," Helm said eventually, his voice now quavering a little. "It was a long time ago, and I can't remember a great deal."

"Listen," Johnson said. "This is an anonymous conversation. I can assure you of complete discretion, and your name will not appear in any publication or article I might write. As you say, it is history. I need to tell you that Gennady Yezhov was murdered recently in Berlin by his former colleagues in the SVR as he was in the process of defecting. He was shot dead in the street. My understanding is that he was to inform Western intelligence services about many things, some current, some historic, but among them was information relating to La Belle and the events of early April 1986 when that disco was blown up. Gennady gave his daughter your name as a person to contact if anything happened to him."

Helm's eyes narrowed, and he scrutinized Johnson. "Gennady has been killed?"

"I am sorry to report that yes, that is true. It happened on March 21 near to Friedrichstrasse station. I can prove it to you, if you like. There was a lot of news coverage, but his name was not released."

Helm looked at the floor. "Yes, I remember the TV news bulletins, now that you mention it. I am sorry to hear that. Very sorry. He was a good friend."

After a few seconds, Helm looked up. "You're not writing a book, are you? *Das ist doch Quatsch*. That is bullshit."

Johnson raised his hands, as if to admit defeat. "No, I am not writing a book. I am carrying out an investigation into Gennady Yezhov's murder and the reasons why that happened."

There was fear in Helm's eyes now. He shook his head. "No, I cannot help with this."

Johnson had a feeling that was going to be Helm's reaction. Fear of the state still ran deep in these eastern areas of Germany. "Let me just assist you with your decision about this. Let's go back in time a little, shall we? Back to the Second World War, when it is my understanding that you were a member of a certain organization—the Nazi Party. You joined the *Schutzstaffel*, the SS, and you were following firmly in your father's footsteps, weren't you?"

Helm tightened his fists so his knuckles were showing white through his mottled pink skin. He pressed his lips together. "I didn't. No. I wasn't anything like that. You have got it wrong."

"And at the end of the war, you became a *Junker*. You joined one of the *Junkerschulen*, and your aim was to become an SS officer, again in the mold of your father, Heinz."

There was a shake of the head, and Helm's Adam's apple bobbed up and down as he swallowed hard.

"It's all in your Nazi Party file, Mr. Helm," Johnson said. "I have seen it, and I have seen your father's file. I have copies of both of them, actually, on my phone, if you would like to look at them."

The German's eyes widened a little as he stared at Johnson. But he said nothing.

"It seems to me that you have built quite a position in Leipzig. Respected former church organist, ex-chairman of the Bach festival. And your retirement is a peaceful one, I am guessing. You seem very settled in this community." Johnson indicated around the room with his hand. "It would be a shame if all that was to be shaken up and destroyed, especially at your age, because certain truths about your past were uncovered."

Helm exhaled and gazed at Johnson from beneath lowered white eyebrows. He had a look of resignation on his face, and when he spoke there was a defeatist tone in his voice. "Before we go any further, I just want to tell you that the Nazi Party and the SS were not organizations that I wanted to join. I didn't do so voluntarily. With my father being in the position he was in, I had no choice. I was only twenty years old. He would have had me killed if I had done otherwise. You can believe that or not, but it is the truth. I was relieved to get out when I did without having done too much damage to others. I never killed anyone—I can at least say that."

"Really? How can I believe that?"

Helm stared at the floor. "You can't know what it was like then. The leadership, the Nazi Party, were desperate to recruit and train more boys into the *Hitler-Jugend* and then the *Junkerschulen*. After the Sixth Army was defeated at Stalingrad, and the Germans were pushed out of North Africa and Italy was invaded by the Allies, there was a massive manpower shortage in the armed forces. The *Jugend* was the only way to fill the gap. We had no choice. There were fifteen- and sixteen-year-olds being sent to the Russian front. Thousands of them were being killed daily, but to have resisted joining would have been suicide. It seemed that either way lay death. I was fortunate that I was sent to *Junkerschule* instead of the front, and that was right at the very end of the war—that's why I survived."

Johnson nodded. He knew very well the background to events in Germany toward the end of the war as Hitler battled desperately to retain power. What Helm was telling him was probably correct.

"How did you manage to get into the Stasi with that SS background?" Johnson asked.

"I had to lie a little. I rewrote my history, my CV, to remove the *Junkerschule* period. That was the only way—we all did it, not just me."

"I thought so," Johnson said.

Eventually Helm looked up again. "Now, tell me how you found me. And what do you want, Mr. Johnson?"

Johnson scrutinized the old man. He had heard such mitigative claims many times before in his investigations into Nazi war criminals over the years, but what Helm was saying did tally with what was in his file. Johnson was inclined to give this one some credibility, although he assumed that, as a *Junker*, the old man must have done some things against the Jews or other minority groups that he wouldn't admit to.

He summarized for Helm the story of how he had come to visit Yezhov's apartment in St. Petersburg, the outcome of that, and details of his flight from Russia via the Saimaa Canal. The old man listened in silence, raising his eyebrows occasionally.

"Gennady Yezhov's daughter gave me a message," Johnson said. "She said her father had told her that if anything happened to him, and if anyone was investigating that, they should come and talk to you, as you were an old friend of his. Now, I happen to know that Gennady had information about La Belle that he was going to pass on but was unable to do so because the SVR gunned him down. And you were in the Stasi in Berlin at the time of the La Belle bombing. So what can you tell me?" He leaned back in his chair and fixed Helm with a level gaze.

Helm levered himself out of his armchair and got to his feet, wobbling a little as he did so. He made his way to a chest of drawers near the piano, his feet shuffling on the wooden floorboards. There he opened a drawer and took out a slim cardboard box. He brought it back to the armchair, removed the lid, and took out a sheaf of papers and photographs.

While Helm was focused on his drawer, Johnson took his phone from his pocket, opened his voice recorder app, and pressed the red start button. It would be useful to have a record of what the old man was going to say.

After shuffling through the papers, Helm handed Johnson a black-and-white photograph of a group of people sitting around a table that was covered in papers and boxes. A low-hanging ceiling light illuminated three of the five faces in the group, but the other two were in dark shadow. White plumes of smoke were curling up toward the light from cigarettes being smoked by several of the group.

Johnson studied the photograph. The three visible faces, despite being younger and slimmer, were recognizable.

"I know some of these people," Johnson said. "Your friend Gennady Yezhov?"

"Yes. He is there."

"And Reiner Schwartz, and that is you on the left, I think."

"Correct."

"But I can't see these other two in the shadows. The man on the right looks as though he has his arm around the shoulders of the other person, a woman, right?"

"The one on the right in the shadow is another KGB man, Yuri Severinov, and the woman—"

You have got to be kidding me, Johnson thought.

"*Yuri Severinov?*" Johnson could not help interrupting. It was difficult to see the face properly because he was sitting back, slightly out of the light. "Is it really?"

"Yes, it is him. Do you know him?"

Johnson pressed his lips into a thin smile. "You could say that. And the woman?"

"That is also a KGB officer. They were sleeping together. His girlfriend, I believe. Her name was Ana."

"Ana who?"

"I do know her last name. It has slipped my mind." He must have caught Johnson's impatient look because he gave a thin smile. "Don't worry. It will come back to me."

Johnson studied the photograph again. *So many questions to ask.*

"What is going on here—what is this meeting? Why the photograph?"

"You asked about La Belle. This meeting was about La Belle."

"I'm sorry. You need to explain."

It turned out that the meeting, in late March 1986, was one of a series of joint gatherings between KGB and Stasi officers to discuss the terrorist situation in West Germany. The Libyans in particular were very active in West Berlin at that time, but they were able to operate because they were based out of East Berlin, where the government gave them shelter and cover.

Helm reeled off a list of various terrorists who were given such refuge by the East German leader Erich Honecker and his Stasi henchmen.

They included Carlos the Jackal—Ilich Ramírez Sánchez —the Popular Front for the Liberation of Palestine mass killer who became an internationally wanted fugitive. "They gave him a car, a house, an office, secretaries, helpers. Everything," Helm said.

"There was the Red Army Faction as well as others like Abu Nidal and Yasser Arafat. And then there was Abu Daoud —he was the ringleader behind the massacre of the Israeli

Olympic team in Munich in 1972. We knew about them all—and because we talked all the time to the KGB, they knew about them all. And of course, the KGB passed on those details to the Soviet leaders, Brezhnev and his boys."

Johnson listened carefully. Having been a student in West Berlin in the early 1980s, he knew something about the backgrounds of all the terrorists whom Helm was listing. The Red Army Faction, also known as the Baader-Meinhof Group, had carried out bombings of West German targets, kidnappings of West Berlin businessmen, bank robberies, and assassinations.

"And La Belle?" Johnson asked. "What happened there?"

Helm paused. "We found out a few weeks beforehand that the Libyans were going to bomb La Belle. We told the Stasi boss, Erich Mielke, and he informed Honecker. And at this meeting, shown in the photo, we told the KGB—we gave Severinov and Ana all the details. The timings, the explosives that were going to be used."

He leaned forward and used a bony forefinger to stab at the photograph that Johnson was holding. "I had that photo taken because Mielke asked for it—he wanted to cover his ass. He wanted something to show who on the KGB side was attending those joint meetings."

Johnson nodded. That made sense.

"My feeling was that we should stop the attack—it was pointless," Helm continued. "It would not achieve anything. It wouldn't help East Germany, and it wouldn't help the Soviet Union. It wouldn't help Honecker. It wouldn't help Gorbachev."

"Did you have the power to stop it?" Johnson asked.

Helm gave a snort. "Of course. The Stasi had the power to do that—if the KGB would let us stop it. But they didn't. Severinov shrugged his shoulders and asked who normally used the disco. We told him it was mostly American troops.

And he smiled and said, 'That's just too bad. Sounds like it will be a good firework display.'"

Johnson felt his stomach tighten. "Did you challenge him?"

"You don't understand. They were the puppet masters; we were the puppets. He told us that the KGB and Moscow were content to let the attacks continue—he said he only liked dead Americans. Of course, his girlfriend Ana agreed with him, like she always did. She said they would go and watch the bombing—she said it would be interesting. The KGB had some safe house, an apartment, on the other side of the street from La Belle, but a bit farther along. They were going to watch it from there."

"And there was nothing you could do?" Johnson asked.

"Nothing. What the KGB said, we had to do. It would have been suicidal to do anything else."

From what Johnson knew of the relationship between the two organizations, he knew that Helm was most likely telling the truth.

There was silence for several seconds. Helm was breathing hard, as if he had just climbed a flight of stairs. The only sounds were those of a ticking clock in the room and the occasional faint growl of a car in the street outside. A dog barked in the distance.

"So tell me," Johnson said. "Why did Gennady Yezhov, a KGB officer, have this arrangement with you, a member of the Stasi, that you would be the guardian of all this information? I assume that what you have told me may be part of the information he was intending to hand over when he defected? Although, of course, he never quite made it."

Helm ran a hand through his white hair. "I am certain this is what he was intending to pass over, yes. He told me more than once that he planned to eventually make it public, at the right time. It was because we were like-minded on this issue.

We both did our jobs at the time, but we didn't like it, and we had conversations about that. We kept in touch over the years, and we both said we should do something." He shrugged. "But time went by, and neither of us had the guts to do so—until, that is, Gennady decided late in his life that it was the right time. I think his children had grown up by then, and he felt they could take care of themselves if needed, because what he was doing was high risk. As he unfortunately discovered."

"Yes, very high risk," Johnson said. He leaned forward. "Do you have any proof of this?" he asked. "You are telling me that the people in that room, in that photograph, effectively passed a death sentence on those in the La Belle nightclub. But how do I know that it's the truth?"

Helm nodded. "Actually, I do have proof. It has been sitting in a safe-deposit box in a bank vault in Vienna for the past twenty-five years or so."

"*What?*"

"Yes. There is a copy of that photograph you are holding, together with a few other photographs and the minutes I took of that meeting and others. I used to write a few notes during the meetings in my notebook, then turn them into longer notes afterward. I didn't tell the others, of course. The notebook, together with the papers containing the longer minutes, are all in the bank vault."

"Why in Vienna?"

"I took them there not long before the Berlin Wall came down, when I started getting suspicious that the KGB were putting me under surveillance, and I haven't moved them since. I wanted them out of the country."

"Can we get the notebook?"

Helm shrugged. "I guess so. I am not going to Vienna to fetch it, but you can if you want to. There is nothing else in the vault. I can give you the key and the password. I haven't been there for more than eight years. The last time I went, it was all there."

Johnson nodded. "Yes, please. That would be very helpful."

Helm reassured Johnson that provided he held the key and knew the password, he could get access to the box, no matter that he wasn't the person named as primary account holder.

Helm struggled to his feet and went to the drawer from which he had taken the photograph. He felt inside and came back holding a flat brass key and a business card, both of which he handed to Johnson. The key had a six-digit number imprinted on one side, and the business card, which was for a private bank in Vienna, had a handwritten number on the back.

"Take these," Helm said. "I would like you to return the key when you have what you need, of course. What will you do with the information, though?"

Johnson put the two items into his wallet, which he pocketed. "Thank you. That's very helpful. I am not sure what I will do yet. I would like to find a way to prosecute Severinov. It might be possible, especially if I can somehow arrange to have him arrested while outside Russia. I know that he travels frequently. We will see. Don't worry, you will not be under threat during the process."

Helm seemed to relax. "Good," he said.

There were so many more questions Johnson wanted to ask Helm, but one thing in particular had intrigued and puzzled him.

"How did you and your Stasi colleagues and the KGB get from East to West Berlin?" he asked. "And how did the Libyans and the other terrorists get through? It seemed so heavily guarded when I was a student in Berlin." He was wondering if there had been collusion on the West German side to facilitate that.

Helm said nothing for several seconds, then he wheezed. "You know Friedrichstrasse station?"

Johnson gave a faint smile. "Yes, you could say that. I knew it during the '80s when I was a student in Berlin. And I was reacquainted with it when I was expecting to debrief Gennady who arrived there. But before we could talk to him, he was shot dead."

Helm paused for several more seconds. "We got over the border through the station. There was a secret route through," he whispered. "The railway staff entrance on the East German side, the *Diensteingang*. It led through a control room and a few back passageways to a door on the West German side. The Stasi, the KGB, the PLO, the Red Army Faction and other terrorists, East German spies who had been blown . . . they all used that route."

Johnson nodded. "That's interesting. Thank you."

Helm nodded in acknowledgment.

"Now, have you remembered the name of the girlfriend, by chance? Ana?"

"No, I still can't recall it. I will do though. But it is in the notebooks in any case."

Johnson rose slowly to his feet. It seemed that over the past several days, via St. Petersburg, the Saimaa Canal, and Berlin, he had taken a very convoluted route to get the information that Helm had just handed to him, but it was more than worth it. It was real evidence. They had a case.

Helm also stood. "Before you go, would you like to see Thomaskirche? It is worth a quick visit, and it is only just across the street. It's a beautiful building—dates to the twelfth century."

"Why not? Yes, I can have a quick look."

Johnson scrutinized the old man.

The image he had conjured up in his mind when Katya had told him he needed to speak to the Nazi's son was somewhat different from the reality. It probably stemmed from years, decades, of chasing war criminals who had tortured and murdered large numbers of people.

The jury was out on what the old man had done during his short time in the SS, although it seemed highly unlikely to have been damaging. The role he had played in the Stasi was also somewhat shrouded in mist. Maybe his subsequent stint as organist at Thomaskirche had been somehow redemptive.

But Johnson knew one thing: the old man had provided the ammunition he needed in this investigation, and for that he was very grateful.

His mind went back to the lecture he had given at the University of Law in early March, when Vic had first approached him about this investigation. He had meant what he told the audience about the need to continue prosecuting elderly war criminals. However, his gut feeling was that Helm wasn't in that category.

Johnson followed Helm out the door, then waited patiently in the corridor as the elderly German struggled to lock it.

Finally Helm managed to turn the key in the lock, and the two men made their way to the elevators.

When the elevator stopped at the ground floor, the twin brass-plated doors opened, and Helm exited first.

An elderly woman was standing outside the elevator, a shopping bag in each hand, and Helm moved to one side to get around her.

Johnson had just stepped into the doorway when he caught a glimpse of a dark shadow emerging from an alcove farther along the corridor toward the main exit into the street. The figure stood, legs apart, and rapidly raised a hand

—it was holding a gun. In that second, Johnson instantly recognized the muscular, thickset outline of the man.

Vasily Balagula.

"Get down!" Johnson screamed at Helm, shoving down hard on his shoulder.

There was a flash and a deafening bang, and Helm staggered backward, his arms flailing, before falling against the wall behind him. The woman screamed and dropped her shopping bags.

Instinctively, Johnson dropped to the floor and rolled back into the elevator.

How the hell did that bastard know we were here?

He knew he had to act fast. Reaching up, he hit the elevator button for the third floor, where he had just come from, followed by the Door Close button, then threw himself to the floor again.

A split second later came another shot. The round crunched into the full-length mirror that covered one wall of the elevator car, smashing it and sending shards of glass flying.

Johnson threw up an arm to protect his face from the glass, but then felt something on his left wrist and looked down to see blood spurting from a cut.

He pulled the Beretta from his pocket and flicked off the safety, covering the door with his gun. Another round cannoned into the wreckage of the mirror, splattering more glass over him. Johnson could hear the thud of running footsteps—Balagula was coming for him.

Come on, close, Johnson willed the doors shut.

The twin doors slid across just as a third shot sliced between them and into the light fixture on the elevator wall at the top of the shattered mirror. It plunged the car into darkness just as the doors clanged shut.

CHAPTER FORTY-ONE

Friday, April 11, 2014
Leipzig

Johnson swore to himself in the darkness of the elevator car, his mind whirring at high speed. Balagula must have been sent by Severinov. Following the St. Petersburg encounter at the Yezhovs' apartment, he must have realized the reputational danger to himself if Katya sent Johnson to see Helm and if Helm started talking.

But who had tipped Severinov off about Johnson's progress? There was no way the timing of Balagula's visit was coincidental. It must have been the same mole who had leaked every other damn operation recently. And was Balagula operating alone? Severinov himself surely wouldn't dare head into Germany on an assassination operation. Or would he?

It also seemed unlikely that Balagula's work was done in shooting Helm dead. Johnson had to assume that he too was on the hit list.

The elevator doors opened at the third floor. At last, some light. Johnson gripped his Beretta and cautiously poked his head out of the car and checked carefully up and down the corridor before stepping out.

His wrist was dripping blood, but he ignored it. He grabbed a fire extinguisher from a hook on the wall in an alcove nearby and put it into the elevator doorway so it would not close, effectively disabling it.

Johnson looked up at the indicator lights above the elevator doors. The Russian would be able to see from the lights which floor Johnson's car was at. The other car was on the ground floor. That meant Balagula could be about to use it to head up to his level.

But there were also the stairs to consider. Johnson needed to check them too.

First, he decided to try and change his appearance as much as possible. It might just cause a few seconds of confusion when Balagula came looking for him again, possibly enough to save his life. He only had two props on him: a black woolen beanie hat and a pair of plain glass black-rimmed glasses, both of which he had brought from Berlin.

Johnson quickly put both items on and moved swiftly to his right toward the stairwell door, just a few yards away.

He stood to one side of the doorframe, then opened the door a fraction, poking his head around it just enough to see down into the stairwell. There was nobody visible. Johnson took a step onto the landing and edged closer to the railing that ran around the edge of the stairs so that he could see down to the levels below.

There was a loud clang as a door banged shut below. It sounded close, so Johnson assumed it was on the floor directly below, out of his line of vision.

But was it someone entering the stairwell or leaving it? He couldn't see.

Johnson swore silently.

He decided against descending the stairs—he could be walking right into Balagula's line of fire. Instead, Johnson retreated back into the corridor.

Now the elevator indicator lights were showing the other car was heading up. It was at level two, one floor below. But was Balagula in it? Johnson had no way of knowing.

He slid into the alcove that had housed the fire extinguisher and flattened himself against the wall, Beretta in his right hand.

The distinctive whirr of the elevator stopped. There was a pause, and the doors slid open. Johnson braced himself to move quickly. But there was silence. He poked his head forward, just enough to see the elevator doors, which remained open.

What the hell was Balagula doing?

Johnson decided in that second to go on the offensive—he held the initiative and had the possibility of surprising Balagula and opted to use it.

He emerged from the alcove and, holding himself flat to the wall, slid along until he was almost at the elevator doors. He raised the Beretta and stepped quickly forward toward the doors, ready to fire.

But the elevator was empty.

Shit. Where is he?

The Russian must have pressed the elevator button for the third floor and sent the car up but had not gone with it. Johnson looked around for something in the corridor that he could use to disable the doors of the second elevator, but there was nothing.

Then he spotted a picture hanging in a large frame on the wall. That would do. Johnson stepped over to remove it from its hook, but before he could do so, the elevator doors closed, and it began to descend.

If Balagula could play games with the elevators, Johnson could too. He pulled the fire extinguisher away from the doorway of the first elevator, pressed the button for the ground floor, and sent the wrecked car with its floor littered with broken mirror glass on its way down.

Then he ran down the corridor toward the fire escape. Maybe the elevator moving downward would distract Balagula sufficiently for Johnson to get to ground-floor level. Then, if Balagula decided to go up, Johnson could exit the building.

Johnson slowly opened the door to the emergency stairwell, gun at the ready. There was nobody there. He began to descend the concrete stairs, treading as silently as he could.

He made it to the landing for the second floor, and there was still no sign of the Russian. Johnson began to work his way down to the ground floor, his stomach now knotted, tension gripping his forehead like a vise.

God, I'm too old for this game, he thought. *Come on, concentrate.*

As he reached the ground-floor level and stepped off the bottom stair, Johnson's biggest concern was the lack of cover: there was very little of it in this building—the corridors were straight and unfurnished, and there were few alcoves. He also could not afford to get into a physical fight with the powerful Russian. There would be only one winner in that contest. He needed to outthink him.

On the wall, Johnson spotted a red fire alarm button next to the fire door that led to the main corridor. Maybe if there was no cover, Johnson could create some. Filling the corridors with people might be a good start. He brought the butt of his pistol down hard against the glass front of the alarm. Instantly, a piercing, whooping shriek began to echo through the building.

Johnson waited until he heard doors starting to bang and

open in the corridor behind the fire door. Immediately there came a chorus of screams and shouts. He knew what that was all about: they must have seen Helm's body lying near the elevators. And surely the old lady with the shopping bags must have called the police by now.

He slowly opened the fire door a little and glanced through the narrow gap. A group of people was gathered around someone on the floor farther up the corridor. That was obviously Helm.

The fire alarm, coupled with the sight of Helm lying in the corridor, was causing panic among the residents as they emerged from their apartment doors.

Women and girls were screaming and mothers were trying to steer their children around the body. Men were yelling into their phones, and doors were slamming. Now at least a score of people was in the corridor, all heading toward the main exit, jostling and pushing.

There was no sign of Balagula.

Johnson flicked the safety on and slipped his Beretta into his jacket pocket but kept his hand on it. He cautiously slipped out into the corridor and stood with his back to the wall, flattening his profile, just in case Balagula appeared. The layout of this corridor was similar to the one on the third floor. He slid along the wall and into the alcove near the elevators and then paused as a sea of people passed in front of him.

A few seconds later, out of his peripheral vision, Johnson caught a glimpse of a figure dressed in black emerging from the elevators.

Balagula.

Johnson shrank back into the alcove, out of Balagula's line of sight. He was certain the Russian hadn't seen him, but any second he was going to appear before Johnson if he kept moving toward the exit.

The problem Johnson had was that firing live rounds in this corridor would be asking for serious trouble, with so many adults and children all pushing toward the exit.

He pulled his Beretta from his pocket and, holding it by the barrel, twisted his body a little in order to get a better angle. He readied himself.

As Balagula suddenly appeared next to him, Johnson swung the butt of the gun hard, in as short an arc as he could, straight at the Russian's temple.

But Balagula must have seen it coming out of the corner of his eye because he raised his arm in self-defense, making some contact with Johnson's pistol as it descended.

Johnson's blow was slightly deflected but still managed to strike Balagula's skull hard. The Russian groaned and staggered backward, but as he did so, he pulled a pistol from his trouser pocket.

Johnson saw what was coming and threw himself to the floor, just as an off-balance Balagula pulled the trigger. The round cleared Johnson's head by no more than a few inches and smashed into the wall of the alcove, sending a cloud of plaster and dust over Johnson.

There were screams from the people standing in the immediate vicinity, who then scrambled in both directions to get away from the gunfire.

Immediately, Johnson, who was lying on his side, switched his pistol around in his hand and disengaged the safety while he rolled onto his front and loosed a round at Balagula, who had fallen off-balance and was on his backside no more than ten feet away.

The round hit Balagula somewhere near his right shoulder, spinning him sideways, and his pistol fell out of his hand. The Russian let out a low-pitched yelp but managed to haul himself up, lean over, and grab the gun with his left hand.

Johnson could see no alternative. He fired twice more.

One round hit Balagula somewhere in the stomach, the next higher up in the chest, and he fell backward, arms outstretched, dropping the gun once more.

Johnson scrambled to his feet, took a few steps, and dived past Balagula to grab the Russian's pistol in his left hand. He rolled sideways, out of Balagula's reach, and sprang to his feet.

Johnson pointed his Beretta at Balagula, who was now lying on his back, clutching his chest, his shirt drenched in blood, and barely moving. Further down the hallway lay the motionless figure of Ludwig Helm.

More screams came from a mother who was trying to shield her two toddlers from the fighting.

"This Russian has killed the old man over there," Johnson shouted in German. "Somebody call an ambulance. Call the police." He backed away toward the exit into the street.

When he reached the door, Johnson turned, pulled it open, and went into the street. He pulled his beanie farther down over his forehead and pushed his glasses up his nose. Then he started to run.

PART FOUR

CHAPTER FORTY-TWO

Saturday, April 12, 2014
Vienna

The glare from the sun reflecting on the snow-white lime-stone facades of the buildings that lined Bankgasse Street in Vienna caused Johnson to hold his hand to his eyes.

Without speaking, Johnson turned to Vic, who after being briefed following the shoot-out in Leipzig, had flown overnight directly to Vienna from Washington, DC. Veltman, who viewed tracing the mole as the CIA's number one priority, had insisted that Vic return to Europe.

Johnson pointed toward a ten-foot-high wooden door ahead of them. It looked as though it would have withstood a full-scale military assault, and judging by its battle wounds, it had probably been in service since the Second World War.

The business that lay within was only identified by a discreet six-inch-square brass plaque on the wall that read Österreichische ZPW Bank.

Johnson was about to push the wooden door open when

he realized that Vic, behind him, was standing still, staring down at the concrete sidewalk, seemingly lost in thought.

"Are you okay, buddy?" Johnson asked.

He had tried to put himself in Vic's shoes, given what had happened to his brother Nick, but found it hard. How could he know what his old friend was feeling?

Vic shook his head. "Give me a minute. I'll be all right."

After fleeing from Ludwig Helm's apartment in Leipzig, Johnson had decided to drive rather than fly to Vienna to obtain the crucial piece of evidence he needed: the notebook, papers, and photograph detailing the part Severinov and his colleagues had played in allowing the bombing of the La Belle discotheque by Libyan terrorists to go ahead.

It was a six-hour drive, but he figured that by the time he bought an air ticket and went through check-in and security processes at both airports, it was probably just as quick. More importantly, he was uncertain whether security forces and police might be on the lookout for him at the airport following the gunfight in Leipzig. Had anyone managed to get a good description of him? It was difficult to know, so traveling by car seemed a safer option.

Both Johnson and Vic agreed it was crucial that there were two witnesses present when they took possession of the written evidence from the bank vault. It might help avoid any future disputes about the origin and authenticity of the documents.

Johnson, his wrist bandaged after being cut during the shootout in Leipzig, had collected him from the airport and briefed him in the car on Helm's story. He had played the entire recording of the conversation with the old man, which Vic had listened to without speaking.

By the time the recording had finished, Vic's face had frozen.

"I'll kill them, Joe. I swear. Those KGB lot, I'll kill them," he said eventually, his voice sounding thick and hoarse.

Johnson nodded. "They could have stopped that bombing. There's no doubt. Moscow knew about it, and they ruled in East Berlin. It was their call."

Now, outside the bank, Vic seemed to be overcome. Maybe it was the prospect of seeing the evidence he had long been waiting for—that would change his entire perspective of the bombing that had indirectly ended his brother's life.

Eventually, Vic looked up again. "Let's go in. I'm fine."

Johnson nodded. He turned and pushed the aged wooden door open to find within a much more modern form of security entrance: an airlock system of double interlocking electronic doors made from bulletproof glass designed to control access and to effectively imprison any unauthorized visitor who might present a threat.

He strode to the bank's reception desk, explained that he wanted to access a deposit box, and waited until the assistant bank manager responsible for numbered accounts was summoned.

The manager took Johnson's and Vic's credentials and used a handheld device to input the security details that Johnson provided: Helm's name, the account number, and the password that he had given Johnson.

Johnson was then asked to show the key, from which the assistant inputted the six-digit number. He was then asked for his passport, given the ledger to sign, and told to take a seat.

After a twenty-minute wait, Johnson and Vic were taken down a corridor to another double-airlock security door, this time made from solid stainless steel.

The manager opened both security doors using an electronic fingerprint recognition pad, and Johnson and Vic found themselves in a room lined floor to ceiling with brass security boxes; four padded chairs were in the center next to a long, narrow table.

"Key, please," the manager said, holding out his hand.

Johnson handed it over, and the manager also produced a brass key from his pocket. He checked that the numbers on each were identical and used them to unlock a box halfway up the rack on the left. He did not open it.

"There you are. Give me a call using that phone when you have finished," the manager said, pointing toward a gray phone that hung from a wall bracket. "It rings my number automatically when you pick it up. No need to dial anything." He walked out.

Johnson opened the box. Inside was a fat brown paper envelope, which he removed and placed on the table. He sat on one side while Vic sat on the other and opened the envelope.

To Johnson's relief, the contents were exactly as Helm had described. There was a notebook with a wire spiral binding, together with a few photographs and some separate sheets of paper that were stapled together.

First Johnson focused on the stapled sheets. They were typewritten in German, and all had dates at the top from February, March, and April 1986. A short underlined heading on each read *SSD/KGB TREFFEN*. SSD/KGB Meeting.

The SSD was an abbreviation for *Staatssicherheitsdienst*, the old East German State Security Service, otherwise known as the Stasi.

Johnson flicked through the sheets, looking for the one that related to the meeting Helm had described.

The sheet, yellowed and creased, its staple rusted brown, was dated Tuesday, March 11, 1986. Johnson placed it on the table so they could both read the text.

"See that?" Johnson said, glancing up at Vic. "That's three and a half weeks before La Belle."

Vic pressed his lips together but said nothing. Johnson had to keep reminding himself that for his colleague, this wasn't just any old arm's-length investigation.

He read the text of the minutes. There was no preamble; it went straight to the business of the meeting, all written in summary form. The participants were identified by initials, not their full names.

RS and LH started by informing YS, GY and AS that information had been picked up from Eter (a Stasi asset working at Libyan embassy in East Berlin) about a planned bomb attack by the Libyans at La Belle discotheque in Hauptstrasse. Attack scheduled to be carried out 1.45am on Saturday April 5 and bomb to be planted just prior to that. RS outlined concerns that such bomb attacks would put GDR in a bad light and disrupt trade between East Germany and West Germany.

Johnson snorted and stabbed his finger on the sheet. "See that, Vic? Schwartz seems more concerned about a bomb disrupting trade with the West—not about killing Americans. Bastard." He continued to read.

LH recommended that YS take steps to alert KGB hierarchy and also recommended that SSD/KGB jointly work to prevent bomb attack. YS replied that his objective was to do all possible to destabilize and disrupt West Germany. American deaths would be incidental. AS agreed with him and said Moscow would be informed but she and YS would recommend that no action be taken to prevent bomb attack. YS said he expected the SSD to act only in line with KGB objectives.

"This is appalling," Vic said. "My brother and the people who were killed that night, were just victims of some KGB and Stasi effort to—what? *Disrupt West Germany?*" He spat the words out. "It was so pointless. It was never going to achieve anything."

He looked as close to despair as Johnson had ever seen

him. Johnson put his hand on his friend's shoulder for a few seconds, remaining silent: words were not enough.

Johnson scanned farther down the page. "Look at this. There's more. It gets worse," he said. He pointed to another paragraph.

YS asked whether Eter had indicated that the bomb attack was ordered by Libyan leader Muammar Gaddafi. RS said Eter had not been specific but had said the attack would be carried out jointly by Libyan and Palestine Liberation Organization people.

YS said that President Reagan was known to be looking for an excuse to bomb Gaddafi. He said he would be recommending to Moscow and to Honecker that if the La Belle bombing went ahead, a disinformation campaign should be launched to show it had been carried out by CIA agents to create an excuse for Reagan to launch an attack on Tripoli.

YS and AS would observe the operation from a KGB safe house on Hauptstrasse, which would give them useful intelligence regarding West German police response processes to such incidents.

Johnson remembered that those exact rumors about the US being behind the bombing had been circulating in the months after the La Belle attack. "Now we know where that filth all came from," he said. "Whichever way you look at this, Severinov was throwing shit in all directions."

"This must have been the material that Gennady Yezhov was going to bring over when he defected, then," Vic said. "It's interesting that Yezhov seems to have said very little at that meeting, according to the minutes. Maybe he opposed what they were doing?"

"Hmm. Maybe. He didn't actually say so. And it did then take him twenty-eight years to decide to do anything about it," Johnson said pointedly.

There were a few more paragraphs, but the meeting had moved on to discuss routine joint security operations along the Berlin Wall, and they contained nothing of significance.

Johnson stopped reading the minutes and picked up the photographs that were in the envelope. The first was an exact copy of the photo that Helm had showed to him in Leipzig. But the second was from a different angle, taken lower down at the same level as the heads of the people shown in it. This time, the other faces were clearly visible, not cast in shadow.

Johnson studied it carefully. There was Schwartz, Helm, and Yezhov. Now he could also see the man and the woman on the right quite clearly. Indeed, as Helm had said, the man was Severinov; there was no mistaking his face and outline, and his arm was drooped around the shoulder of the woman next to him.

But then, as he stared at the woman's face, Johnson again felt a little punch-drunk.

Helm's words at the apartment in Leipzig came back to him.

"That is also a KGB officer . . . His girlfriend . . . Her name was Ana . . ."

Her last name had not come back to Helm before the gunfight with Balagula. But despite the woman being more youthful, with smoother skin, and a little slimmer in the old photo than she was now, the face was easily recognizable to Johnson. He knew who it was.

Her name was Ana. But that was an abbreviation. Her full name was Anastasia Shevchenko—the current London *rezident* for the SVR. And apparently, the then girlfriend of Yuri Severinov.

CHAPTER FORTY-THREE

Saturday, April 12, 2014
London

The Defense Department report was classified as top secret and had gone to a restricted list of people in the defense, intelligence, and political communities: people who would be impacted by the inevitable tidal wave of media coverage and political spewing that would follow, both in Russia and the West.

ANTELOPE, who was sitting at a wood-paneled desk at home, scrolled down the report on the laptop. The computer screen and the desk lamp sitting on the surface next to it provided the only illumination in the room and cast a ghostly white layer across ANTELOPE's face and forehead, highlighting the lines of worry wrinkles.

The report, which extended to four pages of densely typewritten script outlining rationales and strategies and tactics, could have been summarized in a couple of lines, ANTELOPE thought.

At last, the timing of the USS *Donald Cook*'s arrival in the Black Sea: the guided missile warship would be there the day after tomorrow, Monday, April 14, early in the day. Furthermore, a frigate, the USS *Taylor*, was to join the *Donald Cook* later in the month.

But that wasn't the real dynamite contained in the report. No, the really explosive revelation, the golden nugget, was contained in the second paragraph: the US president was going to divert from a scheduled visit to the Romanian capital, Bucharest, to pay a secret visit to the *Donald Cook* as it sailed into the Black Sea on Monday.

ANTELOPE had to read the document twice, eyes narrowing as they scanned downward. A quick summary of this had to go to Shevchenko immediately, and the entire document would also need to be transmitted as quickly as possible: it was incendiary.

The precise timing of the arrival of a US destroyer and a frigate close to Russian territorial waters in itself was twenty-four-carat military intelligence, particularly when coupled with the information about three French warships heading for the Black Sea that had been passed on to Shevchenko three days earlier.

But the added detail that the president would be on board was something that would send shock waves through Moscow Center and the Kremlin.

This looked inflammatory: President Putin would want to prepare a military response to it instantly. ANTELOPE's first thought was that it would not be a surprise if Russian air force jets were scrambled in response. Would Putin want to fire warning shots across the bows of the oncoming ships? Might he even go one step further?

The SRAC equipment, which Shevchenko had handed over by Shevchenko when the two of them had met three days earlier, was safely concealed in ANTELOPE's apartment in Maida Vale and was easy enough to operate.

This seemed like the right opportunity to try out the kit. Certainly, there was no time to arrange a face-to-face meeting with Shevchenko in the next couple of days, and the Russian had made it very clear she wanted to wind down the face-to-face meetings anyway.

ANTELOPE walked to a concealed wall cupboard, opened it, and removed a burner phone from a safe attached to the wall inside. Then the agent tapped out a short message to a similar burner phone owned by Shevchenko, summarizing the top line in the report about the destroyer entering the Black Sea in two days, with the US president on board, and the frigate soon afterward. ANTELOPE followed it with another message.

Will transmit entire MoD document via SRAC and base station as soon as feasible. Good chance to test new kit.

A couple of minutes later, the phone pinged as a reply came back.

Thank you for information. Remarkable content. And agree regarding main document transmission. Please inform me when you have done it. I will also download it and so will our mutual assistant.

ANTELOPE used a microcamera from the safe to photograph the document on the laptop screen, then took the tiny memory card out of the camera and transferred the file onto the SRAC.

Now all that remained was to find an opportunity to get undetected and surveillance-free to the vicinity of the base station so the file could be uploaded for subsequent collection by Shevchenko's illegal.

That might prove to be a challenge, as the agenda was very full for the next couple of days. ANTELOPE was also doubtful about the wisdom of trying to upload data to the base station on foot. Going for walks and strolling in parks had never really been part of the daily routine, and it might seem odd to suddenly start doing something out of the ordinary.

ANTELOPE stood and walked to the window and stared at the street outside. It was busy with shoppers returning home, children playing games, and a couple of old ladies standing on the corner, talking.

What was the best way to do this? Using a car, as Shevchenko advised, was definitely one way. But the idea of having to slow down at a certain spot, even by just a few miles per hour, to ensure a proper connection had its disadvantages and might attract attention.

The more ANTELOPE thought it through, the more it seemed a better method was needed.

CHAPTER FORTY-FOUR

Sunday, April 13, 2014
London

There was silence around the briefing table in the safe house on Rossmore Road as Johnson outlined the story he had been told by Ludwig Helm and displayed copies of the papers and notebook he had retrieved from the safe-deposit box in Vienna. One of the MI6 staff had made them for him, using photographs he had taken on his phone.

When he had finished, Johnson looked at Jayne, Nicklin-Donovan, and Vic in turn.

Johnson and Vic had arrived in London on the first flight out of Vienna that morning and had gone directly to the safe house. It had been almost a week since he had seen Jayne, but it felt like longer given his narrow escape out of Russia via the Saimaa Canal, and then the encounter with Balagula in Leipzig.

Nicklin-Donovan was the first to speak. "What a bunch

of bastards. I'm glad I twisted your arm to do this investigation. Though obviously I get the credit now."

Johnson nodded but didn't smile.

"If that damned woman Shevchenko didn't have immunity, we could hit her with charges of conspiracy to murder, in my view," Nicklin-Donovan said as he flicked through Helm's meeting minutes. "We'll have her kicked out of the country at the very least. But—not yet."

"Indeed," Jayne nodded. "Not until we've used her to get to the mole. I agree."

"Speaking of which, what's the latest on that front?" Johnson asked.

Nicklin-Donovan called in Bennett to the meeting. The group then spent the next half hour discussing the progress made by the ongoing surveillance operation involving the B1 and B2 teams.

The B2 team had successfully tailed the Southern Europeean woman who had made a drop into the motorcycle pannier.

From the license plate of the aging green Nissan Micra that she drove and from her property details, she was identified as Natalia Espinosa, a single mother of two teenage children who was working legally in the UK as a language teacher.

Natalia lived in Wembley, only a stone's throw from England's glitzy national soccer stadium, in a house next to a run-down pub called the Green Man.

She held a Spanish passport and had a Spanish father, but a deep dive into her background by GCHQ showed that she had a Russian mother and had spent most of her formative years in Moscow. She also held a Russian passport, but that had never been used to enter the UK or the US, which she had visited on a number of occasions.

"Good work," Johnson said.

"Yes, good work by the team," Nicklin-Donovan agreed. "But so far, it's still not got us close to finding our mole. We still don't even have any actual evidence that Shevchenko is part of the chain, although to me it seems obvious."

Vic leaned back and surveyed the other four around the table. "Thank you, Mark," he said. "But I'm afraid there is something else to discuss. Gary, would you please excuse us?"

Bennett nodded and left the room.

Vic leaned forward, cupping his chin in his hands. "I only learned this yesterday, but there is a situation looming that if leaked to Moscow could potentially put the US president at risk. This is deeply restricted. The report I saw was for US eyes only, but the situation dictates that I have to tell you, and I have cleared it with my director."

"Okay, then, what is it?" Johnson asked.

"The president is currently on a visit to Romania, as you all know." The presidential visit to Bucharest had been well covered in the media, not least because of its proximity to the Crimean Peninsula. Romania bordered the eastern side of the Black Sea and was just 180 miles from Istanbul and only a little more from the Crimea.

"The president has made a last-minute decision to take a helicopter flight from Bucharest to join the USS *Donald Cook* in the Black Sea tomorrow," Vic continued. "Director Veltman tells me he has tried to persuade the president to drop the ship visit, but he is refusing. If this leaks to Moscow . . ." Vic let his voice trail away.

There was silence around the table.

"There's no sign that it has leaked so far," Nicklin-Donovan said eventually. "At least, not at this end."

He was correct about that, Johnson mused. After the Russian illegal Natalia Espinosa had loaded the dead drop site, the motorbike pannier had been emptied later the same day by a man who was tailed to Heathrow Airport and then

flew to Berlin. He was identified as Alexander Litvyak, traveling under a Russian passport, although it was assumed that
that was a false name and a false document. The team had
allowed him to go, not wanting to raise any suspicions before
the trail led them to the unidentified mole.

Johnson assumed that "Litvyak" was probably the same
courier whom Schwartz had described who ferried flash
drives to the mysterious handler code-named VIPER in
Berlin for onward transportation to Moscow. It obviously
wouldn't be Schwartz who was taking the flash drive to
Moscow this time. The SVR must have found another
courier, while the actual identity of VIPER remained
unknown.

Since then, however, Natalia had not appeared to take any
further suspicious actions, had not held any meetings, and
had not picked up any more material from anywhere. There
had been no more pickups from the motorbike.

Vic's phone rang, and he left the room to take the call.

"All we can do is continue to keep watching Shevchenko
and the illegal," Johnson said. "It's a waiting game. We'll get
them. Something will give. If we see a sign of action, we can
assume that the president's visit might have leaked."

"Yes," Vic said as he reentered the room, catching the last
of Johnson's words. "And if that happens, we can get Veltman
to try again to persuade the president to cancel. But that was
the Berlin station. They had some more news. This time
about Reiner Schwartz."

"What?" Johnson asked.

"He's dead. Shot inside his own house."

The Berlin station had learned from German police that
Schwartz had been killed by an unknown gunman, Vic said. A
neighbor had seen the man step out of a white Volkswagen
and was able to give police a description.

"It must have been Balagula," Johnson said. It was obvious. The Spetsnaz killer must have been under instructions, almost certainly from Severinov, to take out one valuable witness of events in Berlin in 1986 before traveling to Leipzig to try and take out the other.

Vic nodded. "Yes, it seems it was Balagula. The description certainly tallies with that."

When they had concluded the briefing session, Johnson took Jayne by the arm. There was a lot he needed to discuss about the operation with her, and apart from Vic, she was the only one he trusted completely. But there were more than just work issues to resolve: he also needed to try and sort out his feelings for her.

"Let's go for a walk and find somewhere to talk," he said. He picked up his jacket and stood there, giving her little option.

Jayne looked at him quizzically for a couple of seconds but then simply nodded, grabbing her jacket and walking out the door of the conference room.

They strolled out of the Rossmore Road safe house, which was on the ground floor of an eight-story redbrick building.

After checking carefully for surveillance, as usual, Jayne suggested they take a taxi to the Lancaster Hotel, a classy five-star place at the junction with Bayswater Road. There they found a corner table in the Island Grill next to full-length picture windows that overlooked Hyde Park on the other side of the street and ordered two lattes. There were only a few other occupants in the room.

"What's on your mind?" Jayne asked.

"There are a couple of things I want to discuss," Johnson said. "Business first."

"What kind of business do you have in mind?" She winked at him.

"That would be telling—although I will tell you later."

"I'll look forward to that." She smiled.

"But seriously, the first issue is the identity of the mole," Johnson said. "Everything is leaking right now—I mean, how the Russians knew I was at Helm's apartment in Leipzig is beyond me, given the tightness of our information flows. How did they know I was visiting Yezhov's widow in St. Petersburg?"

Jayne shrugged. "I don't know the answers, but it's definitely a lot messier than the two-week job we thought it would be."

"That's an understatement. But it's got to be coming from somewhere close to home. We have to assume this surveillance operation itself is compromised, don't we? And God knows what other secrets are being channeled to Moscow out of all the other classified documents that are circulating."

"Yes. The whole thing feels compromised."

"So, although I feel we've made huge strides in pinpointing what Severinov and Shevchenko did in Berlin, the big prize is still eluding us. I feel we owe it to Gennady Yezhov to complete the job given that he gave his life trying to hand us the identity of the mole and that his daughter damn near gave her life getting me out of Russia."

"Agreed. Maybe we should tighten our information flows even further, then," Jayne said.

"Yes, we should. And cut who out?"

Jayne lifted her hands, palms upward, in a gesture that said she didn't know.

"I'm thinking the support team," Johnson said. "The MI6 admin people. And the secretaries hear and see too much, in my view."

"All right, we'll do it. It will mean more paperwork and hassle for us to process everything, but maybe there's no option in this case."

"I think not. We must." Johnson leaned back in his chair and sipped his latte.

"Anything else you want to discuss?" Jayne asked.

"Yes, now that you mention it. There is something else."

Johnson glanced out the window at a group of schoolkids who were running into Hyde Park, near to a couple who were leaning against the iron railings at the entrance, busy kissing seemingly without bothering to breathe. He glanced at Jayne and then back outside again.

"Cat got your tongue?"

Johnson laughed. "Meow."

"Ooh. Playful."

"Speaking of cats, remember that one in Islamabad? It came in through the window."

Jayne giggled. "When I was naked. Yes. Good thing it couldn't talk to tell the tale."

"It's probably still dining out on the story," Johnson laughed. He placed his hands behind his head and gazed at Jayne. "Listen, I'm not very good at saying these things, but while I was on that boat up the Saimaa and after I'd extricated myself from Leipzig, I found myself sort of missing you, and—"

"For my handgun expertise?" Jayne asked, raising her eyebrows.

Johnson smiled. "Yes, that too. All kinds of expertise. And I'm serious."

It was true. He had suddenly found himself missing Jayne. In fact, during the months since their last investigation in Afghanistan had ended the previous year, he had thought about her many times.

There had been something about going back to the region where in 1988 they had conducted a furtive love affair while based in Islamabad. Johnson was working in Pakistan for the CIA and Jayne for MI6, both of them focused on secret

programs to help the Afghan mujahideen in their fight
against Russian troops who had invaded their country.

The affair was terminated after only a few months, when
Johnson was sent back to Langley by his then boss Robert
Watson and fired from the CIA. The catalyst for that had
been a cross-border operation into Afghanistan that went
wrong, but the final straw had been when Watson found out
about the affair. Having a relationship with an intelligence
officer from another country's service was seen as too much
of a risk.

After that, Johnson had married Kathy, while Jayne had
never married, despite a few relationships over the years, the
details of which Johnson had not delved into.

The two of them had remained vaguely in contact, but
apart from a brief dinner in 1996, when they both happened
to be in Buenos Aires on business, they didn't see each other
again until 2011. That was when Johnson headed to London
as part of an investigation into a former Nazi commander
who had disappeared after the Second World War and asked
her for help.

Their collaboration after the Nazi investigation deepened,
and Jayne left MI6 to go freelance the following year, when
she again worked with Johnson on a hunt for a Yugoslav war
criminal from Mostar who had vanished.

Since then they had flirted occasionally, and Johnson felt
there was still chemistry between them, but nothing had
happened. He had always had it at the back of his mind that
he needed to be based in Portland, where his two children
were rooted, and Jayne was based in London. He felt reluc-
tant to start a relationship that might not prove workable.

Yet, since last year's Afghanistan trip, he had started to
feel differently. They had a history and went back a long way
together.

Jayne was not only very smart, she had a steely, resilient

character and kept her head in a crisis. She had a good sense of humor and was resourceful—a damn good partner to have. He had almost lost count of the number of times she had saved his ass on various jobs.

Johnson admired all of that. But he had to admit to himself, the attraction also remained a physical one: Jayne had managed to keep her body almost in the same slim, lithe, sexy shape that had first attracted him to her in Islamabad. Yes, she had acquired a few wrinkles, her dark hair was graying in places, and she had put on a few pounds, but essentially she had stayed in remarkably good shape for someone who was now in her fifties.

Jayne's arm rested on the table, her hand next to her coffee cup. Johnson leaned over and placed his hand on hers. She looked down at his hand and back at him.

"That trip to Afghanistan last year," Johnson said.

"What about it?"

"It felt like the wheel had turned full circle. It was taking us back. I've thought about you differently since then." He felt his chest tighten as he said it.

Jayne's eyes met his, and for a moment, she didn't move, processing his words. Then she responded by turning her hand over and grasping his. Her face broke into a smile, her dark eyes twinkling at him.

Johnson smiled back.

Jayne looked out the window. "Look at those two," she said, pointing at the couple kissing by the park gate. She glanced back at Johnson, and ran her tongue over her lips.

"Shall we go for a walk in the park?" she asked in that low honey-and-whisky low tone that he had found so attractive in the first place.

Johnson nodded.

Ten minutes later, they were sitting on a black-painted wooden bench in the park beneath a giant oak tree that was just starting to sprout its first leaves of spring. Johnson had his arm around her shoulders, and she was pressing her thigh hard into his. They were kissing as if twenty-six years had never passed between them and the clock was being rewound.

Perhaps we should start again, Johnson wondered, as his tongue explored the inside of her mouth and she pressed closer. She tasted good. Maybe they *were* starting again.

CHAPTER FORTY-FIVE

Sunday, April 13, 2014
   London

When Johnson and Jayne arrived back at the Rossmore Road safe house, they walked in several yards apart. It was implicit between them that despite their relationship having just changed somewhat, in the work setting they were simply professional colleagues.

Johnson walked over to Bennett, who was hunched over his laptop. An analysis had just come back of Anastasia Shevchenko's movements over the previous couple of weeks, based on surveillance by the new and old teams, and the results had shown a pattern of sorts, Bennett said.

Johnson stared at the screen, which showed a satellite map of central and west London superimposed with a series of colored lines representing the routes that Shevchenko had taken around the city, at least up to the points where she had evaded coverage.

Many of the lines were in and around an axis between St.

John's Wood and Westminster on the Underground's Jubilee line and between Maida Vale and Embankment stations on the Bakerloo line. Even when she had taken taxis, the routes were broadly in that same arc. The stations she had used most often were Piccadilly Circus and Oxford Circus, both of them complex and busy.

"The main divergence from this directional bias is when she goes near to or into Regent's Park," Bennett said. "She's done that occasionally when we've managed to keep eyes on her."

"Interesting," Johnson said. He was pleased to see that Bennett's team was being so proactive, although he felt, as the analysis was only arriving now, that it probably had something to do with a push from Jayne.

"Now that we have the new team in place, can we play more of an anticipation game?" Johnson said.

Jayne was already nodding. "I'd like to have people on the ground in areas where we think she's heading to rather than having people behind her as she travels there. If we reduce the trailing coverage, it might persuade her she's black and to take more risks as well."

"The problem with that is if she does something unexpected and we lose her," Bennett said.

"Yes, but it's worth the risk of losing her if there's a chance of a big win," Jayne said. "She's more likely to be watching behind her ass, not in front."

"True," conceded Bennett. "We can give it a go, yes."

"Good," said Jayne. "Let's have people in Baker Street and Piccadilly Circus stations and in Regent's Park, as soon as she shows movement in those directions, starting tomorrow."

Bennett nodded. "Fine. We'll do that."

"What about the video analysis of her car journeys?" Johnson asked. "Anything showing up there?"

"That's what I wanted to show you," Bennett said. "It's

all from dashboard cameras, so it's a little limited since our surveillance cars are mostly hanging well back to avoid being spotted. However, there are a couple of instances where I think we should have a closer look. Check these out."

Bennett opened a video app on his laptop, selected a video file, and flicked the play button.

The footage showed Shevchenko's BMW heading along Outer Circle past the London Business School, just outside Regent's Park. A small monitor window at the bottom of the screen indicated the car's speed in real time.

"Just watch the speed indicator," Bennett said. "See what you think."

Johnson leaned over the screen and watched carefully as the BMW continued northward around Outer Circle, then turned left into Hanover Gate.

"Stop it there," Johnson said. "Can you replay that segment again?"

Bennett reran the video.

"There!" Johnson said as the car approached London Business School from the south. He pointed at the car speed indicator. "She's slowed from thirty miles per hour down to twenty-four, and there's no other cars in sight. Then after about fifty yards she's accelerated again. Why has she done that? Play it again."

Bennett again replayed the video. "That's what I hoped you would see."

"Has she done the same thing in that place before?" Jayne asked.

"That's the point. Just wait a second."

Bennett trawled through a few older video clips of Shevchenko driving in the same area until he found the one he wanted. It also showed the Russian slowing down, although to a less marked degree, when driving along Outer

Circle the previous week, also on a trip ostensibly to collect cigarettes.

"Interesting. Once is possibly just an anomaly. Twice might be deliberate. And it's more than just a slight speed variation," Jayne said. "And if you look carefully, in the second clip she's driving dead straight to start with, completely under control, but then the car wobbles a bit during that stretch when she's driving slower. Just a little, and it's hardly noticeable, and it may be nothing—but why?"

Johnson shrugged. "Sometimes we all do that. Maybe her phone rang and she looked down at the number calling and took her eyes off the street."

"Yes. Maybe she received a text message," Bennett said. "Maybe she was changing radio stations, changing music tracks. Or on the other hand . . ."

Bennett let his voice trail off, not speaking the obvious as they watched the video finish playing.

"You mean she might be activating a transmission device?" Johnson asked.

"Precisely." Bennett looked up. "And if she is depositing or collecting material there, then somebody else must also be doing likewise."

"Are there any CCTV cameras along that part of Outer Circle that we could get footage from?" Jayne asked.

Bennett went away to get his team to check and came back later on in the evening to report that that stretch of street was a CCTV blind spot. Although the London Business School had them outside its building and cameras were placed at the junction with Baker Street, there was nothing in-between.

"I suggest we get some temporary cameras of our own put in that spot as soon as possible, just in case she does it again or if someone else does," Jayne said. "Make sure the cameras are ultrahigh-definition ones so we can slow the footage right down, and make sure there's a few of them. On trees, lamp-posts, whatever, so we get a variety of angles and at different heights. And ensure we get license plate recognition software hooked up to the outputs."

"Good idea," Bennett said. "We'll get it fixed."

* * *

Sunday, April 13, 2014
Moscow

Putin's face remained motionless as he read the short report that Medvedev had handed to him.

Eventually he stood and walked slowly to the far end of his office and back again to his seat next to the chess table in front of his desk, where Medvedev was sitting.

"These damned Americans are being exceptionally fool-ish," Putin said. "Their president is an idiot if he really thinks he can do this. Taking a helicopter to visit a heavily armed warship when it is sailing right next to our territorial waters at a time like this is just a provocation."

"I agree," Medvedev said. "What the hell is he doing?"

"That is a good question. And I am going to put him through hell," Putin said, slapping the palm of his hand on the desk.

"What should we do?" Medvedev asked.

"I am going to put a few shots across the bows of this destroyer. I want to send a few Su-24s to carry out an extended exercise against the *Donald Cook* that will put so much shit up the asses of the crew and the White House that they will not come back in a hurry."

"Using armed aircraft?" Medvedev asked.

The Sukhoi Su-24 was a twin-engine attack aircraft that

could carry a variety of laser or satellite-guided bombs and was armed with various missiles and a 23 mm rotary cannon. But Putin knew that deploying them could swiftly escalate the conflict and turn the Black Sea into a battle zone.

Putin stroked his chin. "I don't know. Get Valery to have armed and unarmed aircraft ready for deployment, to give us options."

General Valery Vasilyevich Gerasimov was chief of the general staff of the Russian armed forces and first deputy defense minister.

"Yes, I will go and see him immediately," Medvedev said.

"And ensure the unarmed aircraft have the Khibiny on board. Even if we don't bomb and sink the damned ship, we will knock out their systems and give them a fright. If the president goes off the radar screen and can't phone home, that will send him the toughest of messages."

The Khibiny was an electronic warfare system that could be mounted beneath the fuselage of the Su-24 tactical bombers and was designed to disable enemy radar systems, communication networks, and certain electronic control systems.

Medvedev grimaced. "Indeed. I'll ensure that Valery gets it arranged."

CHAPTER FORTY-SIX

Monday, April 14, 2014
London

The array of cameras that had been installed overnight by MI6's technical team along the stretch of Outer Circle covered the street and the area of Regent's Park that bordered it. To Johnson's satisfaction, it was providing very comprehensive coverage of the area.

"Your boys have done a good job," he said to Bennett, who was about to run through the results of analysis on vehicle license plates that the cameras had captured from cars that had traveled along that stretch of the street.

A large video monitor screen on the wall was showing live footage from Outer Circle, taking its feed alternately at different angles from the cameras that were now operating. Johnson, Jayne, and Vic had been taking turns to watch the video, but nothing useful had shown up.

Bennett had also installed two unmarked cars at different points in the parking bays along Outer Circle, manned by members of the surveillance team, in case any anomalies or suspicious vehicles showed up that required an instant response.

At the same time as installing the cameras, the technical team had run metal detectors over an area of Regent's Park adjacent to the street. A number of large metal objects buried underground had shown up, including one in particular buried beneath some evergreen bushes next to the hedge that separated the park from the street. The techs were convinced it was an SRAC base unit. But they hadn't dug it up for fear it was somehow booby-trapped or that it might have an built-in shutdown facility or sensor that would turn it off if disturbed or, worse, alert the person using it.

Nevertheless, the fact that the suspected SRAC had shown up provided a lot of reassurance for Johnson and Vic. Both of them had until then remained slightly skeptical that two sightings of Shevchenko slowing down a little on a stretch of street equated to any certainty that she was operating a data transmission unit.

"Yes, the techs have done a good job, but it's not providing any results—so far," Bennett said. He explained that the analysis was showing no links between any of the thousands of license plates collected and anyone with any remote connection to the ongoing MI6, CIA, and military operations that were being leaked to Moscow Center.

The system was now delivering live analysis of all license plates passing along that stretch of the street and would automatically flag any vehicles that were registered to members of intelligence or security services or armed forces, or civil servants operating in the relevant sensitive areas, particularly the Ministry of Defense.

"Pedestrians?" Johnson asked. "Anyone in the park?"

"No. Our illegal hasn't been there since we started

surveillance on her. And there's no one else that has given us any grounds for concern."

Johnson strolled around the desk where Bennett was sitting with his laptop. He leaned against the windowsill and glanced at Jayne, who was sitting in an armchair opposite him.

"What do you think, Jayne?"

"What about motorbikes?" Jayne asked. "If they're using one for the dead drop, they might use one to load an SRAC."

"They've been covered as part of the license plate checks," Vic said. "Nothing."

Johnson folded his arms. "Buses. What if the person is just sitting on one of those red London double-deckers and activates their SRAC from there?"

Bennett shook his head. "Buses don't use that street. They all go along Park Road that runs parallel to it, the A41, behind London Business School."

"Taxis?"

"That's a possibility, yes. We are keeping a separate list of the plates of all those passing the site, but I admit they are difficult to monitor."

"What about cyclists?" Johnson asked.

"No, we haven't actually included them in the analysis. You can't trace them from just video. There's no way of easily identifying them."

"But do you have them all on video?"

"Yes, we've captured them all. We've got video clips of all of them—there's about four or five goddamn hundred of them. But we haven't been able to do any analysis."

Johnson remained silent for a few seconds. "Well, if the vehicle analysis is showing nothing, and the pedestrians are showing nothing, and we can't track the bus and taxi passengers, is it worth just looking through the cycle footage to see if we can spot anything there? I don't want to leave any stone unturned—that's how things slip through the cracks."

Bennett shrugged. "I guess we can. All the clips are running at about twenty seconds long, so it's going to take some time."

"Let's do it," Johnson said.

Bennett nodded reluctantly.

"In the meantime, Jayne and I will keep a watch on the live feed as soon as it's running again," Johnson said, nodding toward the monitor screen on the wall. A technician was fiddling with a cable connection, which was causing a problem.

While he was waiting, he needed to check on something. He took out his phone and began a web search.

It didn't take him very long to find a lengthy story on a Leipzig newspaper's website about a gunfight in an apartment building near Thomaskirche. The intro to the story said that one man had died and another was critically injured in the hospital after a shoot-out involving a Russian and a second unknown gunman.

Shit, Balagula's still alive, he thought.

But to Johnson's surprise, as he read down the story, it stated that the man who had died was the Russian gunman, Andrei Karazamov, who had been carrying a passport but no other identification. Karazamov was obviously Balagula's cover identity, Johnson surmised.

And the man fighting for his life in intensive care in Universitätsklinikum Leipzig—the university hospital—was Ludwig Helm, an eighty-nine-year-old former organist at Thomaskirche, who lived in the apartments.

Johnson hadn't expected that. He continued to scan down the story, looking for any mention of himself. Near the end, he found it.

The second gunman had not been identified and had

immediately fled the building, the report said. Descriptions of him were vague, other than that he was quite tall and was wearing a black beanie hat and black glasses.

Good.

Police were working on the assumption that the shootings might have been some kind of robbery attempt that had gone wrong, perhaps due to gang members fighting among themselves, but were unsure. It was thought the Russian mafia might have been involved. Investigations were continuing, the report said.

Johnson closed the app and stared up at the ceiling for a few seconds. He hated the idea of having killed someone— even a mindless murderer such as Balagula—but at the time he had no option but to defend himself. Otherwise there was no doubt *he* would have been in a Leipzig morgue, not Balagula.

He just hoped that Helm would pull through. It seemed highly unlikely that if he did he would turn Johnson in, not given the secrets Johnson now carried about Helm's history in the SS.

The technician finished fixing the cable as a member of the MI6 support team brought a tray of coffees into the room. Johnson and Jayne both took one and settled on a sofa in front of the monitor screen to watch.

They had been doing this off and on all morning. The mesmeric effect of watching traffic on the same stretch of street wasn't conducive to concentration, so the coffee was welcome. At least the picture quality from the feed was excellent—it was very high definition and made it easy to see even small details. It must have been using a huge amount of bandwidth on the local broadband networks, Johnson couldn't help thinking.

Johnson watched the screen as a line of cars meandered northward along Outer Circle toward London Business

School, with the park on their right. They were followed by a white van and a tourist coach. They were all driving at roughly the speed limit of thirty miles per hour, and the license plates were not triggering any alerts.

A couple of professional-looking female cyclists on light-weight machines and wearing branded Lycra were riding abreast of each other a hundred yards or so behind the coach. Their heads were down as they pedaled hard, clearly trying to have some sort of race with each other around Outer Circle.

Johnson and Jayne sat there for another ten minutes scrutinizing the screen carefully. Johnson checked his watch. There was little else to do for the next hour or so until they were due to have a team meeting to discuss progress and the next steps.

Out of the corner of his eye, he noticed Jayne occasionally glancing at him.

"Concentrate on the screen, not on me." He winked at her.

"Yes, I know," Jayne said. "Don't worry."

They scrutinized the monitor for another ten minutes. Then Johnson's eye was caught by a lone female cyclist on a drop-handle racing bike. Her hair was tied in a ponytail that hung down her back, and she was wearing tight black and pale blue Lycra. Unlike the two cyclists Johnson had seen earlier, she was riding at a sedate pace.

He watched as a green BMW overtook her. He couldn't help thinking that her orange bike helmet looked a little garish. Then she glanced to her right and put her right hand into what looked like a small black tool bag mounted on her handlebars, typical of the type that many cyclists use.

Immediately, a loud alert went off inside Johnson's brain.

He had seen another woman cyclist with a very similar orange helmet only quite recently and remembered thinking then that it also looked a little loud and obtrusive.

Wait. What the hell?

Johnson jumped to his feet, adrenaline now pumping, and approached the high-definition screen, watching intently.

The cyclist withdrew her hand from the tool bag. She was holding a snack bar, which she unwrapped with her teeth and proceeded to eat.

But Johnson wasn't looking at the snack bar now but rather at the cyclist's hair, the helmet, the athletic figure— and noting the fact that she had put her hand in the bag just at that spot. Those details all gave Johnson the same message.

Fucking hell.

"It's Bernice," he said in a low, unbelieving tone.

"Bernice? It can't be," Jayne said. She also rose to her feet.

"It damn well *is*," Johnson said, his voice rising.

The woman put her hand back on the handlebar, lowered her head, and pedaled a little harder, accelerating along the street.

Johnson turned around and yelled across the room to the group hunched over their laptops at the table on the far side. "Vic, Mark. I've just seen Bernice Franklin cycle past the drop zone. It's her, on some racing bike. Get one of those surveillance cars after her. Quick."

CHAPTER FORTY-SEVEN

Monday, April 14, 2014
London

Bernice Franklin was as certain as she could be that she had no coverage. After a surveillance detection run that lasted two and a half hours, involving a cycle ride into central London, followed by a lengthy walk in and around shops on Oxford Street and another ride back to Maida Vale by a circuitous route, she would have wagered a large amount of money that she was clean.

Thirty of her fifty-two years had been spent with the CIA, much of it in the field and on the street, and all of that experience told her she was correct. Pressure and occasion seemed if anything to heighten her senses rather than dull them.

She had a good feel for her environment, for the street, and had rarely been wrong across her career, especially when it mattered. Even on the toughest of days in places like

Moscow, St. Petersburg, Istanbul, and Berlin, she had performed faultlessly.

Indeed, Bernice's excellent track record, both in the field and at Langley in more senior management roles, was a major reason for her frustration in being passed over by Vic Walter for promotion to number three in the Directorate of Operations. Since then, her focus had switched from career building to retirement preparation. And to do that she required money.

Anastasia Shevchenko had somehow appeared at the right time—although Bernice suspected that the timing of Shevchenko's overtures had been no accident. She probably had a list of targets exactly like her: slightly disgruntled, their promotion hopes stymied for whatever reason, and more open to an approach than they might have been at an earlier, hungrier stage of their careers.

There was almost certainly a mole inside Langley who provided Moscow Center with a running list of such potential recruitment targets, although Bernice had no idea who that was.

Now, as she pedaled onward, her confidence in her black status meant she was quite relaxed about her decision to transmit the highly classified US Defense Department document detailing the president's visit to the *Donald Cook* and the subsequent arrival of the *Taylor*.

And doing so by bike seemed to be an excellent cover. She had been a regular rider for the past twenty years, having switched from running. It had been a great way to keep fit and also helped relieve the stresses and pressures of working in a demanding job in politically tough situations.

Bernice was slim, toned, and weighed only a few pounds more than she had in her early twenties. It meant that now she looked at least ten years younger than her actual age and attracted admiring glances from men much younger than she was.

She drew satisfaction from knowing that wearing skintight Lycra while out on the road wasn't something that many women in their fifties could get away with. Today she was wearing a black-and-pale-blue outfit and her usual orange helmet, which helped keep her visible to drivers.

Uploading her electronic files to the SRAC base station buried in Regent's Park hardly required a deviation from her usual routine. Her rides often took her that way; she knew the streets very well.

She did not need to install any special equipment onto her bike. She always had a small black bag attached to the center of her handlebars in which she kept her phone, a couple of snack bars, and a small purse with money and a credit card. There was just enough space in the bag to add the SRAC unit.

Even if she had been unsure of her status upon arrival back in the Maida Vale area, she could easily have aborted the drop. After all, the important message had already been dispatched to Moscow Center by Shevchenko. This was just the added detail that she was now sending.

But certain that her status continued to be black, she pressed ahead.

As she cycled at a steady, undemanding pace along Outer Circle, with the green expanse of Regent's Park on her right, she kept an eye out for the landmarks that Shevchenko had given her.

The first one as she rode northward was the right-hand bend at the junction with Baker Street, with the entrance to the park on the right.

Once she had rounded the bend, the next, on her left, was the elegant white stone colonnades of Clarence Terrace, a short row of houses and apartments with an in-and-out driveway for residents.

As she passed Clarence Terrace, the trigger point was the junction with Sussex Place on the left, just before she reached the white domes of the London Business School building.

That was where she had to press the button.

She looked to her right, where behind the hedge and beneath a clump of evergreen bushes the base unit was buried.

Bernice slipped a hand into the tool bag on her handlebars, felt for the button on the SRAC unit, and pressed it, holding for three seconds as Shevchenko had instructed her. Then she released the button. All being well, the upload had been completed. She would double-check when she got home. A green LED should be illuminated if the transfer had been successfully completed, but Shevchenko had reassured her the system was foolproof provided she wasn't going too fast. There was no chance of that happening on a bike.

While Bernice's hand was still in the bag, she grabbed one of the snack bars, withdrew her hand and, using her teeth and one hand, removed the wrapper from the snack, which she ate. That was her cover just in case anyone was watching, which she was certain was not the case.

She continued along Outer Circle past the northern end of the business school, now pedaling a little harder and accelerating but still going at an undemanding pace.

After about three hundred yards, as she approached the left turn she wanted to make onto Hanover Gate, she passed a row of parked cars on her right, next to the hedge. As she went by, a blue Volkswagen sedan pulled out and tucked in behind her. Since it hadn't overtaken her, she assumed it was also planning to turn left.

No other vehicles were nearby, and apart from the hiss of

her tires on the blacktop and the hum of the car behind, there was little noise.

Then Bernice heard the faint but unmistakable sound of a squelch break—a *click-pssht* sound from a communications radio. It was followed by another.

She jumped slightly as she pedaled.

Where the hell did that come from?

Bernice was all too familiar with how security services' radios operated. She had used them countless times on various operations. She looked to her right. Just before the Hanover Gate junction was a lone parked car, a gray sedan, in one of the parking spots next to the hedge, it's window partly open. Two men sat in the front seats.

There was no other possible source for the squelch breaks.

They must have come from the parked car or the car behind her.

There was no other possible source in sight.

She turned her head swiftly. The blue VW was still trailing behind her, some twenty yards back.

In that moment, her instincts flashed straight to red.

Only ten seconds before, all had looked good along that stretch of Outer Circle. Now her heart rate rocketed and a spike of alarm ran up her spine.

She cursed inwardly, still not completely sure if this was a threat or not. But there was no time to wait and find out.

If it *was* surveillance—and she had no way of knowing yet whether that was the case—it was time to test it. She had planned in some detail for the possibility that something like this might happen.

As she turned left onto Hanover Gate, Bernice pushed down hard on her pedals and simultaneously clicked up two gears. She accelerated hard, and the ultralightweight $7,500 Specialized carbon-fiber bike beneath her responded.

Bernice sprinted along Hanover Gate, a short street of no more than a hundred and thirty yards, then perfectly timed her right turn onto Park Road to slot between one red double-decker bus that was heading south and another that was going north.

That was neat. She glanced over her shoulder: the blue car that had followed her from Outer Circle was stuck at the junction, waiting for a line of cars and another bus to pass.

The tree-lined stretch of Park Road had two lanes in each direction.

Bernice cut straight to the left lane and continued pushing hard as she followed a black taxi.

She didn't go far, though.

After about a hundred yards, she braked hard to a standstill at the left side of the street, jumped off her bike, and picked up the lightweight frame, then ran with it through a black metal gate with a stone pillar and down some steps.

At the bottom of the steps lay the blue-black waters of the Regent's Canal, a waterway that ran eight and a half miles between the River Thames in east London and the Grand Union Canal that ran from London to Birmingham. En route it wound along the north side of Regent's Park and through to Little Venice.

Bernice sprinted down the first flight of stairs, holding the bike, then along a short landing and down another short flight of stairs to the concrete towpath that ran alongside the northern bank of the canal, built in the nineteenth century.

She turned and glanced upward. As she did so, the blue Volkswagen drew level with the gate that led to the street. It stopped, and a man looked out the window in her direction.

Shit.

The towpath was heavily used by pedestrians and cyclists —Bernice had often ridden along it. Now she jumped back on her bike and pedaled hard in a westerly direction beneath two ancient iron bridges that carried trains over the canal.

She had this escape route all worked out.

Bernice swerved around a couple who were walking hand in hand toward her and an old man on a rusty single-gear bike and went flat out, the murky canal waters to her left flanked by a high brick wall that ran along the far bank, with tall office buildings beyond. To her right, bordering the towpath, were bushes and trees, with industrial buildings and offices behind them.

Quickly, Bernice came to a broader section of the canal where a few dozen long residential canal barges were moored. Here the towpath was busier, with boat owners mingling with walkers. She ignored a sign instructing cyclists to dismount and pedaled onward but was forced every so often to dismount and jump over white concrete humps built on the path to stop speeding bikes. Potted plants at the side of the towpath also slowed her down.

As she reached the end of the stretch of moored boats, just before the canal and towpath passed through a tunnel beneath Lisson Grove, Bernice undid the Velcro fastening of the tool bag on her handlebars and removed the SRAC device and also the burner cell phone that she had ready to text Shevchenko once the upload to the base station was completed.

She steered sharply around a man placing plants in a large terra-cotta pot next to the last boat, continued a little farther until she thought she was out of his line of sight, and then with a discreet flick of her wrist threw both devices to her left into the canal, where they landed with a splash.

That was the best place for them. There was no way she was going to be caught with any evidence on her. And the SRAC unit and burner phone were the only items that could incriminate her. There was the camera in her apartment, but if necessary she could easily explain that she used that for CIA purposes, and there was no SD card left in it anyway.

Bernice did not enter the towpath tunnel that ran beneath Lisson Grove. Instead, she jumped off her bike and, turning right off the towpath, ran with it up a steep concrete alley lined with graffitied brick walls and iron railings, to street level, where she emerged through an archaic wrought-iron gate onto Lisson Grove.

That was the most direct route to her destination. From Lisson Grove, it was just about a third of a mile to the SVR's safe house overlooking Lord's Cricket Ground, on St. John's Wood Road. No more than a short sprint on her bike.

If she could just reach the apartment, it would give her a chance to regroup, to call Shevchenko, and to determine whether what she had fled from on Outer Circle really was surveillance. Nobody would find her there.

She jumped onto her bike and pushed off.

CHAPTER FORTY-EIGHT

Monday, April 14, 2014
London

"She's run," the now-cracked voice coming over the squawk box said, his intonation rising. "She's going like a frigging racing car into Park Road. Suddenly accelerated."

Johnson rushed over to the table where Nicklin-Donovan and Vic were sitting at their laptops, the conference speaker in the center of the desk linked to the radio network being used by the surveillance team. Jayne came after him.

"What the hell happened to freak her out like that?" Nicklin-Donovan asked, his voice staccato.

"Don't know," the officer's voice came back amid a cluster of crackles and hisses. "Must have seen us or sensed us. Somehow picked us up."

Vic thumped the table and tipped his head back, momentarily staring at the ceiling.

"Don't waste time discussing what freaked her. We've got

our mole," Johnson said, his words tumbling out. "Just get after her. We need to catch her with the SRAC on her."

"We *are* after her," the voice came again. "Wait. She's headed down to the canal. The towpath. Gone through a gate and down some steps. She's carrying her bike."

"Which direction?" Jayne snapped. "I know that towpath. I used to run along there."

"Don't know. Just pulling level with the gate now. The steps lead west. Must be west."

"Yes, must be west," Jayne said. "Been along there many times. The canal goes to Little Venice, but she'll have to come off it before then because there's a break in the towpath."

"Can we head her off?" Johnson asked.

"Yes. Think we could try." She looked at Nicklin-Donovan. "Mark, send one of the surveillance cars down to the A5 bridge over the canal, the Edgware Road. There's an exit off the canal there. Send the other one to the Lisson Grove bridge; there's also an exit there. Me and Joe will use one of the spare cars and drive to the Warwick Avenue exit—it's further out, but we'll go just in case she outruns the surveillance boys."

"Yes, makes sense," Nicklin-Donovan said. He turned to the squawk box, pressed a button, and rapped out a series of instructions to the surveillance team in line with what Jayne had recommended.

Two MI6 cars, both of them two-liter Volkswagen Golfs, were parked in bays outside the safe house on Rossmore Road, for use in case anyone on the team needed them in a hurry. The keys were in a ceramic bowl on the table.

Johnson grabbed one of the sets of keys from the bowl and tossed them to Jayne. "You drive. You know the area."

He strode to the door and was about to exit the building when Vic, who had followed them, tapped him on the shoulder. Now out of sight of Nicklin-Donovan, Vic removed a Walther from his jacket pocket and handed it to Johnson.

"Here, take this," Vic said. "Just in case. Go careful with it."

Johnson took the pistol, which he knew Vic must have spirited out of the weapons locker at the London CIA station. He quickly checked the safety and pushed it into his jacket pocket. "Thanks." He walked out the door.

"How long to get there?" Johnson asked as he stepped out of the entrance of the apartment block and onto the street.

"A few minutes to Warwick Avenue," Jayne said.

"Fine."

They jumped into a silver Golf, and Jayne gunned the accelerator and let out the clutch quickly, making the tires squeal a little. She raced in second gear the short distance to the end of Rossmore Road, cut left onto Park Road, then accelerated hard, overtaking three buses and a string of cars and delivery vans.

It felt strange to Johnson to be setting out on a chase in which the target was someone he had joined the CIA with thirty years earlier and who was now a senior officer heading the Agency's London station.

Could Bernice really have been giving away her country's secrets to Moscow? He still found it hard to believe. But all the situational evidence pointed to her, including her behavior on the bike, and she was in the inner circle that had access to a whole raft of top secret information and classified files.

The driver of a black Bentley gave a long blast on his horn as Jayne cut inside to the left lane, forcing him to brake. Then she went straight through a red light at a pedestrian crossing as she neared the traffic circle at the top of Park Road, triggering a stream of verbal abuse from a group of youths who were about to step off the sidewalk.

At the traffic circle, she turned left into St. John's Wood Road. The white-and-gray buildings of Lord's Cricket Ground now lay on their right as Jayne accelerated again, taking her speed to fifty miles an hour, well above the limit of thirty.

They approached a side street on their left, from where a truck pulled out in front of them, forcing Jayne to brake. As she accelerated again behind the truck, Johnson glanced out the left passenger-side window. His attention was caught by a Lycra-clad woman dismounting from her bike at the entrance to an apartment block.

She was wearing an orange helmet.

"It's Bernice," Johnson yelled. "Over there. Near the apartments."

He turned and looked over his shoulder as they went past.

It was definitely her.

Jayne hit the brakes and pulled onto the side of the street about forty yards past the apartment entrance.

Johnson opened the car door, jumped out onto the sidewalk, and began jogging toward the apartments, his eyes focused on Bernice, who was now standing at the front door removing something, presumably a key, from the black tool bag on her bike's handlebars.

Bernice closed the bag and lifted her head, then glanced to her left before swiveling right, checking the street. It was at that point that she saw Johnson running toward her, about thirty yards away.

Without hesitation, the CIA's London station chief immediately jumped on her bike and began pedaling across the forecourt in front of the apartments, onto the sidewalk, and toward the side street.

She had moved extremely quickly, and although Johnson continued running after her, he knew he wasn't going to catch her. He could hear Jayne's footsteps pounding after him.

Johnson had to do something. They couldn't just let her

disappear. He stopped and glanced swiftly around, just as Jayne caught up to him. There were no bystanders apart from a couple of teenage boys smoking cigarettes well behind them. He took the Walther from his belt and flicked off the safety, then dropped to one knee, taking careful aim.

He knew he couldn't shoot at Bernice.

"Hit the bike," Jayne said.

Johnson nodded. That was exactly what he was thinking —it was all he could do.

He pulled the trigger.

The round smashed into somewhere near the center of the bike's rear wheel, wrecking the hub, several spokes, and the derailleur gear mechanism. Bernice by that stage was pedaling furiously, but the impact caused the rear wheel to collapse, catapulting her off to her right and onto the concrete surface.

She threw out her arms and landed on her front, sliding across the sidewalk and coming to rest in front of a lamppost. Her wrecked bike skittered into a low brick wall.

CHAPTER FORTY-NINE

Monday, April 14, 2014
London

Shevchenko began to get anxious when one hour after the time that ANTELOPE had said she would be uploading data to the base station, she still hadn't sent a confirmatory text message.

After three hours, she knew that something had gone badly wrong.

ANTELOPE was too reliable an operator, too much of a professional, not to do what she had promised.

Had ANTELOPE done the drop by car, on foot, or by bike, as she had suggested she might? Shevchenko had no way of knowing.

The bike had seemed a sensible option. ANTELOPE was a regular and very fit cyclist, with a fast bike, and even if any observer did manage to stay with her, there should be nothing to arouse suspicions. It would almost certainly appear as if she were out for one of her regular training rides.

Despite Shevchenko's initial concerns, after she had thought it through, it did seem to be an almost perfect cover.

There had been no indication that the MI6 or CIA teams had any inkling there was a base station buried in Regent's Park and even less indication that ANTELOPE was under any kind of suspicion.

But such a long delay without any form of communication was definitely a major negative signal. And there was a huge amount at stake.

True, Shevchenko had sent the basic outline about the US president's planned visit to the USS *Donald Cook* to Moscow Center already. But the detail contained in the naval document procured by ANTELOPE would add a great deal of value to that. It was crucial that it was dispatched safely.

Shevchenko had been working at the Russian embassy since half past nine in the morning, trying to clear some of the backlog on her desk in advance of her scheduled departure back to Moscow from Heathrow Airport that evening. Most of the work was purely administrative and routine rather than urgent. Her bags were packed, and she simply needed to return home and collect them.

Shevchenko decided to head back to her apartment and try to make contact with ANTELOPE from there before heading to the airport. She closed her laptop, put it in her bag, and headed down the stairs to where her driver was waiting in the Mercedes to take her back to Dorset Square.

This was one of the journeys where she didn't have to worry about checking too hard for surveillance, unlike some of her other movements around London.

The traffic was light on the short trip home. Her driver pulled onto the side of the street outside the black double doors of her apartment building, and she got out.

It was only after she had removed her door key from her bag that she noticed the dark-blue station wagon that was parked at the end of the bay, beyond a builder's van. Its doors were opening.

Three men rapidly got out and began to walk toward her.

That was when her stomach flipped over inside her. The one on the left of the group was Joe Johnson, whom she recognized from the photo that ANTELOPE had showed her, and next to him was Vic Walter. She also thought she recognized the third man from the diplomatic circuit and from profiles kept in the *rezidentura*, although they had never spoken. Wasn't it Mark Nicklin-Donovan, from MI6? Yes, it was.

This didn't look good. Not when coupled with ANTE-LOPE's failure to make contact.

Nicklin-Donovan strode up to her. "Anastasia Shevchenko?"

She nodded. "Yes, that's me."

He introduced himself and the two others.

"We think you might want to come and talk to us," Nicklin-Donovan said.

"Why would I want to do that?"

"We have someone you know well in one of our offices. We have had a very interesting conversation with her this afternoon—quite enlightening."

"Really?"

"Yes. She tells us you have been helping her to pass classified British and American intelligence and military documents to Moscow."

Bljad. Son of a bitch.

"I don't know what you are talking about," Shevchenko said. "I am the declared *rezident* in London for the SVR. I wish I did have access to classified British documents, but sadly MI6 hasn't included me in their daily email distribution list. I can't think why. So I don't think I need to come and talk to you about anything. In any case, I have a flight this evening back to Moscow. So if you will excuse me, I need to go and get ready."

She knew that she had diplomatic immunity, so the damned British couldn't touch her on legal grounds. They weren't going to arrest her. However, her mind began whirring with images of her being escorted to Heathrow Airport, ejected from the UK, and sent back to Moscow Center under a cloud.

But that paled in comparison to the fact that it now seemed certain that her twenty-four-carat asset, Bernice Franklin, had been well and truly blown.

How the hell had that happened?

Bozhe. God.

What a mess.

Moscow Center would be incandescent with rage when they found out, as would the president. Only in the past couple of weeks, ANTELOPE had provided massively valuable military intelligence relating to the Black Sea. Now Shevchenko would likely take the blame for her demise, and with that the lost prospects of a decade or more of future priceless intelligence.

Shevchenko could feel her promotion aspirations evaporating into the gray skies above London.

Although Shevchenko was well practiced at maintaining an inscrutable, emotionless face at times like this, inside she felt as though she had been stabbed by a dagger.

"Yes, you will be going back to Moscow," Nicklin-Donovan said, glancing up and down the street. "But it probably won't be tonight."

"Get lost," Shevchenko said dismissively. She needed to sit down inside and think through what to do next. She turned her back on the trio and began to insert her key into the lock.

"There are other things we need to discuss too," Johnson said.

Now what's he going to throw at me?

"Like what?" she asked, turning her head back toward Johnson.

Johnson stared at her for several seconds before speaking. "Berlin, April 1986. I want to discuss your lover Yuri Severinov and the part you both played in the La Belle disco bombing."

This time, Shevchenko had to battle hard to keep her glacier expression intact. It was the last thing she had been expecting to hear. That had been twenty-eight years ago.

And worse, now she was dragging her old operational partner into it. Yuri, too, would be more than furious, especially since he had been alienated from the president and the prime minister recently.

Where had Johnson gotten this information from?

"We know what you did," Johnson said. "We know you ignored the warnings, even the warnings that came from the Stasi, and you let that bombing go ahead simply because it would kill Americans."

Shevchenko stared at Johnson, who was eyeballing her back, his gaze unblinking.

This was *enough*, especially out in the street. "All right. Let's go somewhere indoors and discuss this *dermo*, this shit that you are spreading around."

CHAPTER FIFTY

Monday, April 14, 2014
London

The television monitor hanging on the wall in the nonde-script brick office building that housed an MI6 remote office was showing news coverage from Istanbul when Johnson walked in with Vic, Nicklin-Donovan, and Shevchenko.

After the surveillance team had been through Bernice's belongings, Nicklin-Donovan had opted to take her to the satellite office building, just north of the Euston railway station and a ten-minute drive away from the Rossmore Road safe house, in an attempt to keep the situation low-profile. This made sense to Johnson, given that his inquiry wasn't offi-cially taking place.

Johnson also assumed that Nicklin-Donovan would not want Shevchenko to see the safe house for obvious security reasons, and taking her to Vauxhall Cross would have increased the likelihood of a leak, leading to uncontrolled and potentially damaging media coverage.

But it was the news coverage from Istanbul that was currently holding the room's attention. The three men paused to watch.

The footage showed the USS *Donald Cook*, apparently on patrol of the western Black Sea near to Russian territorial waters, being repeatedly buzzed by a Sukhoi Su-24 "Fencer" attack aircraft that was flying very low and very close to the destroyer.

Johnson was stunned to see a ticker beneath the picture that read, "Russians attack destroyer carrying US president."

The news anchor who was providing a somewhat excited commentary on the confrontation said the US president had decided to visit the *Donald Cook* as it entered the Black Sea. But no sooner had the president's helicopter landed on board than the warship had come under a series of sustained approaches by the Su-24.

Johnson turned to Vic. "It frigging leaked," he said, his voice rising. That had to have been Bernice's work.

Vic stood, rooted and speechless, watching the monitor screen.

The anchor, speaking in an excited machine-gun style delivery, reported that after initial concerns that there might be an exchange of fire between the two sides, it had become clear that the Su-24 was not carrying weapons.

However, the maneuvers were being interpreted as an obvious threat directly from President Putin's office to the US president as well as to US and NATO forces. Putin was clearly telling them to back off.

The report cut to a military expert who said that the Su-24 was probably carrying Khibiny electronic warfare technology that could disable the *Donald Cook*'s Aegis naval weapons control system that was designed to detect, track, and destroy targets.

Another expert said he thought that was unlikely, as he understood the Su-24s didn't carry the Khibiny technology.

Then a former intelligence officer was interviewed, arguing that Russia must have had some advance warning of the *Donald Cook*'s arrival and the president's visit to the Black Sea in order to respond so quickly. There must have been an intelligence breach, most likely in the US camp, he said.

The Su-24 had spent an hour and a half making close-range approaches to the *Donald Cook* before finally retreating. The anchor said the incident showed the sensitivity of military maneuvers by both sides in the Black Sea and highlighted the possibility of an all-out conflict in the area. He said that the stakes would be raised further if reports that a US frigate, the USS *Taylor*, was expected to arrive in the Black Sea in the coming days proved to be correct.

"So, it seems as though the Russians were well prepared," Johnson said. He turned to Shevchenko. "I wonder how the Kremlin could have obtained advance notice that a destroyer and a frigate and the US president were headed to the Black Sea?"

Shevchenko said nothing but made no effort to hide her smirk.

Nicklin-Donovan turned away from the television monitor. "I've called the head of counterterrorism command," he said to Johnson and Vic. "They'll be coming to fetch Bernice soon. In the meantime, we have a window to question her further."

He led the way to a sparsely furnished interview room where Bennett and Jayne were sitting at a table with Bernice, her right arm in a sling with a blood patch showing at the elbow and her left wrist bandaged. There was a large graze down her left cheek that was still oozing a little blood, and her left eye was purple and heavily swollen. She was still wearing her black-and-pale-blue Lycra cycling gear, the leggings of which had a large rip across the right knee, exposing the skin, which was also badly cut.

After Johnson had felled Bernice's bike, he had called Nicklin-Donovan and the two MI6 surveillance cars arrived within minutes. One of the officers was a trained first-aider, and after determining that Bernice had not broken any bones, he bandaged her up and took her to the Euston office.

Johnson stood for a few moments, eyeing Bernice. "You're a damn fool," he said. "I'm surprised, although maybe I shouldn't be. I don't know how you thought you would continue to get away with what you were doing."

She leaned back in her chair and scrutinized Johnson with a pair of laser-like gray eyes. "You're crazy," she said. "I haven't done anything. I was out for my usual cycle ride, and the next thing I know my bike is being shot from beneath me by you. Don't you know the British have laws against using firearms in public? You're the one breaking the law, not me."

Johnson wasn't going to waste his time arguing. It was true that nothing incriminating had been found on Bernice. The tool bag attached to her handlebars had been empty when he and the surveillance team had searched it.

But the video hadn't lied. He had seen her fiddling with something in the bag before her hand had emerged with the snack bar—he was certain of it. And it had all happened in exactly the same spot where Shevchenko had been seen slowing down while driving her car. This was no coincidence.

"We'll find the evidence," Johnson said. She had almost certainly off-loaded a transmitter device somewhere, probably by throwing it in some bushes or the canal while fleeing on her bike. Nicklin-Donovan would be able to get police search teams to find it.

The MI6 team would also now dig up the SRAC base station they believed was buried in Regent's Park.

"Is this a recent thing, spying for the Russians, because

you were passed over for promotion?" Johnson asked. "Was it because Vic gave Neal Scales the number three job? Or have you been doing this for years, decades?"

Bernice shook her head but didn't reply.

Johnson indicated with his thumb toward Shevchenko, who was standing next to Vic. "Did you know you were being handled by a war criminal here?" he asked Bernice. "A Cold War criminal, anyway—who together with her KGB boyfriend Yuri Severinov gave the green light to a Libyan attempt to murder a disco full of American servicemen and women and many Germans. They could have stopped it. They had control of all those terrorists who were holed up in East Berlin. But no. The attack killed three, injured more than two hundred, and indirectly caused the deaths of at least one of those injured."

Shevchenko snorted. "You have no proof of that. It's all lies. Now, I have had enough of this. You need to let me go—I have a flight to catch this evening, and you know very well you have no right to hold me here. It's unlawful."

"It's all true," Johnson said. He outlined the written proof he had collected from Helm's safe-deposit box in the Vienna bank vault.

"I wonder how many other death warrants you have effectively signed over the years?" he added.

"We think we have enough to put you behind bars in Germany, and we'll be going all out to get you extradited there," Vic said, his arms folded, his lips pressed tight together.

"No chance," Shevchenko said. "My president will never agree to an extradition. Anyway, that was twenty-eight years ago. A nice joke, but it's not funny."

"We'll see," Johnson said. "There's no statute of limitations for murder in Germany, so whether it's twenty-eight years or sixty-eight, it doesn't matter. How do you think Germany is still prosecuting Nazi war criminals?"

Shevchenko shrugged.

"And maybe your president won't be so amenable toward you once he discovers how you have screwed up this miserable attempt to run a spy in the CIA," Johnson said. "He might not like the idea that he's had an utter amateur running his British espionage operation and, what's more, recruiting agents in the CIA who are equally incompetent."

He pointed at Bernice. "Because she is utterly incompetent—and a traitor."

"Get lost, you piece of monkey shit," Shevchenko snapped.

Johnson was about to reply when there was a knock at the door. Nicklin-Donovan opened it to find three men standing there. One of them was uniformed, with neat gray hair showing beneath a peaked black police cap that had a trim of silver oak leaves. The other two were in slacks, open-neck shirts, and sweaters.

Nicklin-Donovan greeted the uniformed officer, then introduced him to the others as Commander Michael Marsh, head of Counter-Terrorism Command in the Metropolitan Police.

Johnson turned back to Shevchenko to find she had taken several steps across the room and was now standing near the table, about three feet to the right of Bernice, who was still seated.

Shevchenko was reaching into her small black handbag.

The next few seconds seemed to unfold in slow motion.

Shevchenko took her hand out of her handbag, clutching what appeared to be two silver lipstick holders.

Without pausing, she transferred one to her right hand and removed the cover before raising it, and it was then that Johnson realized what was going on.

He bellowed, "No!" Then he took a couple of steps and launched himself into a full-length dive toward Shevchenko, his arms outstretched, aiming for her midriff.

Just as Johnson made contact with Shevchenko, there was a bang, not that much louder than a champagne cork being released.

CHAPTER FIFTY-ONE

Monday, April 14, 2014
London

As Johnson made contact with Shevchenko, out of the corner of his eye he saw Bernice throw up her right arm reflexively to protect herself. She screamed and then tumbled backward off her chair.

Shevchenko crashed to the floor, with Johnson clasping her around the waist. As soon as she landed, he switched his grip to her wrists, grabbing one in each hand, and pinned her to the carpet.

Within a couple of seconds, the two plainclothes policemen also reacted and piled on top of the Russian.

Johnson pried the lipstick gun from Shevchenko's tightly clenched right fist, while one of the police officers did likewise with the other gun, which she was holding in her left palm.

Johnson hauled himself up, leaving the officers to hold Shevchenko. He looked at Bernice, who was flat on her back, yelping and holding her left arm. Blood was streaming from a circular red hole right in the center of her wrist.

Jayne immediately dropped to the floor and gently lifted Bernice's wrist, which had an exit wound on the other side. The round had gone straight through, but Johnson knew it could have been a lot worse: he wasn't sure if it was his dive or Bernice's reactive raising of her arm that had saved her, but either way, the now disgraced CIA London station chief was extremely fortunate to still be alive.

He swiftly examined the gun. He recognized it as a single-shot device of the type that had occasionally been deployed by the Russians during the Cold War period. Vic had once showed him a photograph of a similar weapon that had been handed to the CIA by a defector. He assumed it had to be used at very close range, hence why Shevchenko had stepped closer to Bernice.

Johnson looked down at the sprawl of bodies at his feet. Jayne removed a handkerchief from her pocket, wrapped it around Bernice's wrist, and pressed it tight to try and staunch the blood.

Vic, who was standing behind Johnson, let rip with a stream of curses and then slammed his fist down on the table. "Why the hell wasn't that damned woman searched?"

"She was," Johnson replied. "The surveillance team went through her bag and didn't see a gun or a knife. But they obviously didn't check her lipsticks. Let's save that discussion for later, Vic."

But Vic swore again, his face now a deep pink.

Commander Marsh's two police colleagues, who had been holding Shevchenko down on the floor, hauled her upright.

"Take her to the other room," Commander Marsh told them. "Then one of you radio for an ambulance, quickly."

The two men frog-marched Shevchenko out the door. They didn't handcuff her, but they might as well have—she had one officer immobilizing each arm. Johnson assumed that the protocols of diplomatic immunity did not allow cuffs to be used.

Over the next half hour came a rapid-fire round of emergency conference calls involving Nicklin-Donovan, his boss C at MI6, Marsh, the Foreign Office, and the Home Office, which was responsible for law and order.

They agreed that the civil servants and the politicians would now have to work out the process by which Shevchenko would be expelled in due course. This would almost certainly involve a statement by the British prime minister in the House of Commons. But for the time being, Shevchenko was to be returned to the Russian embassy. The Russian ambassador was being notified.

At the same time, it was agreed that a search for Bernice's missing SRAC device would begin immediately, with a focus on the area along the Regent's Canal bank and the streets leading to the apartment building where Johnson had shot her off her bike.

Despite loud squawks of protest from Shevchenko, Johnson accessed her phone by forcibly pushing her thumb onto the fingerprint recognition pad and then disabling its auto-lock facility. If that caused a diplomatic issue, it would have to be dealt with later.

Johnson handed the phone to an MI6 technical officer, who quietly downloaded the contents of the device onto a flash drive and sent a copy of the call register to GCHQ for analysis.

Meanwhile, four more officers from Marsh's team had arrived, as had an ambulance.

Two paramedics treated Bernice's bullet wound. The round had damaged ligaments in the wrist but had narrowly missed her bones. They stemmed the flow of blood and, after applying a swathe of bandages and giving her painkillers, placed her on a stretcher to take her to the ambulance, accompanied by three of Marsh's men.

As they prepared to carry Bernice away, Johnson stepped up to her stretcher. "I will be coming to talk to you later, once you've been patched up," he said. "But I just want to say that you have brought this on yourself. I suspect you have put American lives in danger, or worse, you've already caused deaths. All in return for a few bucks. Or if it's because you were passed over for the role at Langley, then there was a reason for that, and I'm guessing it was because you've got character flaws that have now been stripped bare for everyone to see."

Bernice looked up at him. "You've no proof of anything. You're wrong."

"We'll see about that."

Johnson stepped back and let the paramedics carry her away.

In the neighboring room, Vic was busy on a series of phone conversations with the director at Langley, Arthur Veltman, and the US ambassador at Grosvenor Square, Louise Bingham. Both were deeply shocked and angry but agreed that they would prime diplomats to begin the necessary processes to deal with Bernice once the medical experts had treated her.

It wasn't quite the sequence of events that Johnson had envisaged.

Clearly the prospect of Bernice revealing in minute detail in a United States federal court how she had been recruited and run by Shevchenko had been unthinkable for the Russian, Johnson assumed. There was a high probability that, under questioning, far too many secrets would be given away about technology, processes, methods, and perhaps even the identities of others in the SVR's espionage food chain.

Hence the assassination attempt.

But despite Bernice's injury, he expected the ultimate outcome to be similar. She would end up being dispatched back to Washington, DC, to face trial under the Espionage Act in a US federal court of law, followed by a very lengthy spell in prison.

Johnson inwardly shook his head.

Marsh told his two colleagues to take Shevchenko down to the unmarked police car waiting outside the MI6 offices. The two men hoisted Shevchenko out of her chair, holding her so tightly that her feet were hardly touching the ground.

Johnson took a step toward Shevchenko. He needed to have a last word before she disappeared. "You are just as inhuman as your boyfriend Severinov—and mark my words, I am going to nail both of you," Johnson said.

He hoped it didn't sound like an empty threat, because right then, he had no idea how he was going to make it reality. He also knew he should tone it down and keep the conversation professional, but now his emotions were getting the better of him.

"You can run back to Moscow," Johnson continued, "but you can't hide. Maybe your president won't like it when there is a wave of news coverage across the world about how his former KGB colleagues assisted in the bombing of La Belle."

All this seemed to strike a raw nerve. Shevchenko's face flushed red, then went a slight shade of purple. "*Ublyudok*," she hissed. "You bastard. The targets in Berlin were American —and they deserved it. You will now be my target, and you will be Yuri's target too."

"At least you admit what you did, then," Jayne said. "That's a step forward."

Shevchenko turned her head to look at Jayne, then back to Johnson. "Your girlfriend will also be my target."

CHAPTER FIFTY-TWO

Tuesday, April 15, 2014
London

Johnson woke to find Jayne's hand resting on his chest, rising and falling gently in time with his breathing. He turned his head. She was asleep, her dark hair tousled and her lips slightly parted.

He grinned to himself. This was strange yet not strange. He had very occasionally stayed at her apartment over the past three years when his work brought him to London, but always in her spare room, with its sunny yellow bedspread and modest furnishings.

Now, waking here, it felt like revisiting an old favorite place—knowing it and yet rediscovering new things about it at the same time.

Jayne's body hadn't changed all that much, as far as he remembered. She was still slim and still had that lithe, catlike way of moving that had attracted him in the first place. There was no doubt that, despite his attempts to run and keep fit, he had gained more pounds in the wrong places than she had.

After they had kissed in Hyde Park, it seemed inevitable that this would happen, that they would end up in bed together at some point. Johnson thought it probably would have happened sooner if they hadn't been working so late and so hard through the past few long, exhausting days.

But with Bernice now on her way to jail and Shevchenko being expelled from the UK, their task was largely complete. When they had arrived back at Jayne's apartment the previous evening, they had worked their way through a bottle and a half of red Châteauneuf-du-Pape and Chinese takeout. Afterward they had kissed again on the sofa.

After a while, Jayne got up, saying she needed a shower, and disappeared into her bathroom, while Johnson poured himself another glass and sent both his children a text message to let them know he would be home soon.

Twenty minutes later, he had heard the squeak of Jayne's bedroom door opening. He had looked up to see her leaning against the wall, arms folded, legs crossed, wearing a skimpy nightgown that left little to the imagination.

"I was wondering if you'd like to join me?" Jayne had asked.

And he had.

Now the morning sunlight was glinting in through a small gap in the wooden venetian blinds that covered her bedroom window as the distant, ever-present hum of London's traffic sounded in the background.

It seemed that everything had changed. Maybe it had.

At the back of his mind, he still had worries. He was unsure about the practicalities of working professionally with Jayne while also being intimate with her. There was also the distance: he had deep roots in Portland, three and a half thousand miles away from this apartment, where he had two teenage children to look after. What would his kids make of it? They were still his priority and would be until they were old enough to look after themselves.

Somehow, though, he had felt this was the right thing to do, just as he had felt it was right to expand his business from small-town investigations to international war crimes investigations. He had not looked back.

It remained to be seen whether this would be a similar positive change. Deep down inside, he hoped so.

Jayne's hand moved on his chest, and he felt her stir, edging closer to him, her knee grazing his thigh beneath the duvet. She leaned over and kissed him, then raised herself up and smiled.

The mixed feelings Johnson had about his current investigation, Shevchenko's attempt at a summary execution of Bernice, the deaths of Gennady and Varvara Yezhov, and the nagging anxiety that he should have done more to prevent them all melted away as Jayne's hand traced a path southward across his belly.

She swung a leg over his thighs.

"You did a great job, Joe," she said.

"You mean the last couple of weeks? Or . . .?" He waggled his eyebrows.

Jayne laughed. "Both."

"I could say the same about you. You've been great. There's no one else I'd rather be with—in every sense."

He grasped her shoulders, then wrapped his hands around the back of her neck as she once again bent forward to kiss him.

* * *

Tuesday, April 15, 2014
  London

. . .

They didn't have long to enjoy the moment. No sooner had Johnson stepped out of Jayne's shower than his phone rang. It was Vic, calling from his secure cell phone.

"I know you're with Jayne," Vic began, without preamble.

Was it really that obvious? Johnson thought.

"You both need to get yourselves back to Rossmore Road," Vic went on. "Nicklin-Donovan's team has found the SRAC base station in Regent's Park and arrested the illegal who was downloading from it. We've got some files that were on the base station, and Mark is getting GCHQ to decrypt them."

The unsuspecting illegal, Natalia Espinosa, had been arrested at her home in Wembley, where police had found an SRAC transmitter device and a few SD memory cards. One of the cards had two encrypted files on it, which were also being run through GCHQ, Vic said. The assumption was that she had been intending to place the card in the motorbike pannier dead drop site near St. Paul's Cathedral for dispatch to Moscow.

"Excellent," Johnson said. "But any luck with the transmitter that Bernice had in her bike tool bag? She must have off-loaded it somewhere. It's probably in the canal."

Vic explained that the route Bernice was believed to have taken on her bike along the Regent's Canal towpath and up through side streets to the apartment building in St. John's Wood had been sealed off, and an intensive search was continuing. The MI6 team had discovered one of the apartments in the building was an SVR safe house—that must have been Bernice's destination.

Bernice had remained unhelpful and had not confirmed the exact exit she had taken off the towpath, but an analysis of the time taken to arrive at the apartment opposite Lord's Cricket Ground dictated only two realistic possibilities.

"There's a police search crew gathering down at the canal, which Mark's team is directing. Other officers are interviewing boat owners and those who live in the canal boats moored down there in case they saw her cycle along there. It's a long shot, but they are going to give it a try."

Johnson ended the call, promising that he and Jayne would get to the safe house as quickly as possible.

As he ate the croissants and coffee that Jayne had fetched from the Starbucks on the ground floor of her apartment building, Johnson used his laptop to do a Google search for news articles about the La Belle bombing.

He was surprised to find that Dave Orton, a former Berlin correspondent whom Johnson knew, had written a recent feature article about it for *The Times* newspaper as part of a series on the Stasi.

Orton had also written a piece three years earlier about Johnson's hunt for a Nazi concentration camp commander, and Johnson had liked his style of work.

Johnson smiled as he scanned the article.

It seems as though I have another story for him.

CHAPTER FIFTY-THREE

Wednesday, April 16, 2014
London

It was at just before three o'clock on the third day of the
search for Bernice's SRAC device that the breakthrough
came. The chief inspector managing the canal search called
Nicklin-Donovan to say that a canal boat owner had reported
seeing a woman on a bike, wearing Lycra and an orange
helmet, throw something into the water near the short alley
that led from the canal path onto Lisson Grove.

The man, who had been potting plants next to his boat,
had then seen the woman jump off her bike and run with it
up the alley onto the street and out of sight.

The chief inspector had immediately sent a team of divers
into the canal at the spot identified by the boat owner, and
after a short search of the canal bed with underwater metal
detectors, they had found a circular steel electronic device
with a USB port, an SD memory card port, and LED lights.
Near to it they had also found a cell phone. Neither item had

been in the water for long, as there were no signs of rust or other degradation.

A police officer delivered both items, sealed in bags, to the MI6 satellite office at Euston shortly afterward. One glance at the steel device told Johnson all he needed to know: its design matched the base station from Regent's Park.

Nicklin-Donovan handed both items to a technical officer, who unsurprisingly failed to get any response from either device but did manage to extract files from the flash drive inside the SRAC device. GCHQ in turn decrypted the files, which were identical to those found on the base station.

Both sets of files included a four-page top secret US Defense Department report about strategy in the Black Sea and specifically the decision to send in the USS *Donald Cook* and the USS *Taylor*, together with details of the president's visit to the *Donald Cook*.

The report had been sent to a highly restricted list of people in the defense, intelligence, and political arenas—including Bernice Franklin.

Furthermore, although the waterlogged cell phone was not functional, GCHQ had managed to identify its number from the SIM card inside. It was a pay-as-you-go burner phone. A check of the call register showed that the phone had been used only a couple of times. One of the calls had gone to the same cell phone that had been found in Shevchenko's bag.

"Bernice is a goner," Johnson said.

"She was a goner anyway," Vic said. He smiled.

It was the first time in several days that Johnson had seen his old colleague show anything other than tension and anxiety, despite a reassuring note he had received from Director Veltman at Langley telling him not to worry.

Vic had been castigating himself for recommending to Veltman that Bernice be appointed London station chief and not anticipating how disgruntled she would be at being passed over for the number three role in the Directorate of Operations. But Veltman was blaming his counterintelligence team for failing to detect her contacts with Shevchenko.

Now Johnson could see the strain visibly draining from his friend's face, just he could feel his own stress levels beginning to fall.

True, it was extremely unlikely that legal action could be successfully taken against either Severinov or Shevchenko. There was no way Russia would agree to them being extradited to Germany to face trial, no matter how furious the president was.

But there's more than one way to skin a cat, Johnson thought to himself.

He was looking forward to seeing the chaos that would be stirred up by the *Times* article, which had broken that morning. Already it was being widely followed up by other news publications on both sides of the Atlantic. The coverage meant that justice would be handed down at least in some form—doubtless the version meted out by the Kremlin could potentially be more severe and more summary in nature than that by Germany's *Landgericht* judicial system.

Johnson would have given anything to be a fly on the wall at the meeting between Putin and Severinov. Maybe more detail would trickle out of Moscow in time.

Vic beckoned Johnson and Jayne into the room that Nicklin-Donovan was allowing him to use as a temporary office until the investigation was completed. He closed the door.

"I just want to thank you both," Vic said. "You've done an outstanding job under difficult and dangerous circumstances. I'm proud of you, and so is Veltman." He paused and brushed a hand across his right eye. "And what's more, my brother would have been proud of you."

He seemed close to tears as he spoke. Johnson put a hand on his old friend's shoulder.

"Listen, buddy," Johnson said. "I'm pleased we could help. We'll eventually get Severinov, and Shevchenko too. They're both going to be difficult to pin down. We all know that. They are both highly skilled operators. But I'm playing the long game here. I'm going to find a way."

There was a knock at the door. Nicklin-Donovan entered, stepped over to Johnson, and shook his hand, then Jayne's. "I'm glad you accepted my proposal to carry out this investigation, Joe. You delivered, just as I expected, as did Jayne."

Johnson nodded. "What investigation?" he said with a straight face. "I wasn't aware of one."

Nicklin-Donovan smiled. "Correct. There has been no investigation. But nonetheless, off the record we might need to leave one or two of our media friends with the impression that there has been. Then we can of course deny it again afterward."

Vic had now gathered himself. "All right, enough of that crap, Mark," he said.

He turned to Johnson and Jayne. "What are your plans? I mean both of you together."

Johnson did his best to spread an innocent expression across his face.

"Come on, Doc," Vic said. "I can read you two like a frigging book."

Johnson had to smile. Vic was right: he always had been able to read him like a book, as he put it. He could read most people and usually see right through them too, which was why he had carved out such a successful career in such a tough business.

"I don't know, Vic," Johnson said. He looked at Jayne, who was trying not to smile. "We haven't even discussed anything like that. But don't worry, you'll be the first to know."

"As long as you're still going to be available to work for me," Vic said.

Johnson gave a faint grin. "There's nothing quite like having someone who's both deniable and dispensable at your beck and call to do your dirty work for you, isn't that right, Jayne?"

He turned to Jayne, who was looking out the window. "It would seem so," she said without turning around.

"Are you seriously complaining?" Vic asked. "The daily amount you charge us seems to very clearly include a premium for being deniable and dispensable."

He flashed a grin at Johnson. "Look, I need to have a word privately with Mark about a few things, just to tie up the loose ends. If you don't mind leaving us alone for a few minutes."

Johnson and Jayne headed out the door, closing it behind them. They made their way to the kitchen, where Johnson turned on the coffee machine.

"So, I think Vic might be offering us more work now that he's in the top job. He's worried about Russia. But you seemed a little noncommittal when he hinted at it just then," Johnson said as he bent over the machine.

"Yes. I've been offered a job."

Johnson whirled around. "*What?*"

"Mark's offered me a role. He's worried about Russia too."

"Why didn't you tell me? What did you say?" Johnson asked the questions almost before she had finished speaking.

She shrugged. "I was waiting for the right time to tell you. But I've said no. For now. After all, I have a date to keep in Portland: meeting your kids."

Johnson leaned over and kissed her. "Ah, yes. An important appointment, that one. I've told the kids a lot about you. Don't worry, though—it's all good."

They both laughed.

EPILOGUE

Wednesday, April 16, 2014
Moscow

Despite the moderate temperature in the anteroom outside the president's office, Severinov could not stop beads of sweat from forming on his forehead and trickling slowly down into his eyebrows. It was infuriating. Just when he needed to appear cool, collected, and in control, he found it impossible to do so.

What he was feeling was something very primal, he knew —and it was because the man in charge literally had the power to take his wealth, his status, and indeed his life away, if he pleased.

There was a click of shoe leather on the parquet floor to his right, and an aide appeared. Severinov didn't know his name. It didn't really matter. They never lasted very long in the Kremlin.

"The president will see you now," the aide said. "Mr. Kruglov will also be there." He walked to the double doors that led to Putin's inner sanctum, pulled one of them open, and waited for a doorman to open the other, then nodded at Severinov.

Severinov closed his eyes momentarily. He knew very well why he had been summoned. It was always a double act—if it wasn't Prime Minister Medvedev, then it was old dog breath himself, SVR Director Kruglov. Two against one. They always liked to make one feel outnumbered and outflanked.

Events over the previous few days had already made Severinov feel under siege, in particular the death of his Spetsnaz sidekick Balagula. That had been a hard blow given the close working relationship the two men had had over many years. He was still puzzling over how the hell Johnson had gotten the better of him in a gunfight. It was strange. Would the president use that as a stick to give him another beating?

Severinov felt as though his legs were operating on autopilot as he made his way through the doors and into the lavishly decorated office.

Putin was sitting at one side of what his aides called his chess table, which stuck out in front of his main desk. The president was sipping a glass of water and did not look up as Severinov approached. On the other side sat Kruglov, an ape of a man, with a neck that had almost vanished beneath a mound of shoulder fat and muscle and the jowls that hung beneath his chin.

"Mr. President," Severinov said as he came to a halt two meters away. There was nowhere for him to sit.

Putin put the glass down on a coaster and turned his head to scrutinize Severinov with a pair of icy-blue laser eyes.

"When you screwed up last year in Afghanistan, I decided to give you a chance to put right your mistakes, your sewer pipe of bad decisions," Putin said. "What were your instructions?"

Severinov shifted from one foot to the other, his hands

clasped behind his back. "Sir, you wanted me to eliminate the American investigator Johnson. That was the message I received from Mr. Medvedev's assistant. And I—"

"No excuses."

"No, sir."

"You don't know how badly you have crapped all over yourself. Over the past few weeks and months, we have received a stream of golden intelligence from our asset in London. I will use the asset's code name, because I believe you are aware of it. ANTELOPE. It has put us at a material advantage against NATO in the Black Sea. It has been invaluable. There was the prospect of much more to come over many years. But that depended on you carrying out the simple instruction I gave you."

"Yes, sir."

Putin leaned back in his chair and placed his hands behind his head. His eyes bored into Severinov's.

"I have lost ANTELOPE. Her cover has been blown, and she is heading back to the States for trial," Putin said. "I have lost my *rezident* in London, possibly the best recruiter the SVR has ever had. She is being deported from the UK on Saturday. And with them, I have lost what was my key advantage in the battle against the West: accurate, precise, relevant political and military intelligence. And it has happened because you failed to deliver on a simple task. To make things even more incomprehensible, I understand that Johnson was served up to you on a plate, wrapped in a bow. He made his own way to St. Petersburg."

"Sir, if I could just explain something. There was—"

"Shut up. I'm talking," Putin said, his voice remaining perfectly level and emotionless. "Then Johnson tried to get out of Russia via the Saimaa Canal. A rattrap if ever I heard of one. Your target stuck on a boat—it should have been like shooting fish in a barrel for you. But no. You missed. You screwed up yet again, and he got over the border into Finland."

Putin paused and took another sip of water, then reached over to his main desk and picked up a large sheet of paper that was facedown. He turned it over and placed it on the chess table.

"Then to cap it all off, there is this toilet piss," Putin said, tapping his fingers on the sheet of paper.

Severinov leaned over to look. It was a scanned copy of page one of *The Times*. The lead headline stretched across the top of the page.

KGB complicit in Berlin La Belle nightclub bombing.

The story, written by a journalist called Dave Orton, ran across five columns. Below it was a large black-and-white photograph showing the damage to the nightclub building the morning after the bomb blast, with large piles of wreckage in the street outside.

"Read it," Putin ordered.

Severinov tried to focus on the story.

New evidence has emerged of KGB involvement in the 1986 bombing by Libyan terrorists of the La Belle nightclub in Berlin, which killed three US servicemen and injured 249 more people.

The bombing was effectively given the green light by the KGB, Russia's main intelligence agency, as well as the East German counterpart it controlled, the Stasi, it has emerged.

Both agencies were aware of the planned attacks several weeks in advance, according to new evidence from a former Stasi officer who secretly recorded minutes of meetings between KGB and Stasi officers at which the bombings were discussed.

The Times has seen the minutes, which were provided by a source who has recently been in touch with the Stasi officer.

The KGB officers implicated include billionaire oil and gas oligarch Yuri Severinov and Anastasia Shevchenko, currently in charge of the London office of the KGB's successor organization, the

SVR. Both of them were members of the KGB in 1986 and present at the meetings.

Other KGB officers who operated in East Berlin at that time included the current Russian president, Vladimir Putin.

It is clear that the Soviet government in the Kremlin agreed with the KGB and decided to take no action to stop the Libyan terrorists. Along with many other terrorist groups that were aiming to strike at the West, the Libyans were given refuge and accommodation in East Berlin during that period, again with Moscow's blessing.

The report went on for several more paragraphs on page one, and a line in italics at the bottom said it was continued on page three.

Putin stabbed a finger at the text. "Look at this *dermo*, this shit. It is even implicating me in this rubbish. I had nothing to do with it. My reputation is being shredded, and so is the reputation of the *Rodina*, the Motherland."

Putin picked up the sheet of paper, screwed it into a large ball, and threw it at Severinov; it hit him squarely in the chest before falling to the floor.

"As punishment for your incompetence, I have decided to remove another portion of the equity you hold in those three Siberian oil and gas fields," Putin said. "Your stake will come down by another third. It will be transferred from Besoi Energy to either Rosneft or Gazprom. I don't know which yet. We will decide."

Severinov felt his stomach sink to the floor and he felt suddenly dizzy. Surely this wasn't happening? Rosneft and Gazprom were the two largest state-owned oil and gas companies. Losing another third of his revenues to them would put his business under so much financial pressure that it would be at high risk of collapsing. He could not see how he could possibly meet his banking covenants and his monthly repayments if that cash flow disappeared.

And Putin didn't seem to have been informed about

Balagula's death in Leipzig. He certainly hadn't mentioned it. Given that Balagula had carried out various special freelance operations for the president's office, it was likely to result in another backlash once Putin learned of it.

"Finally," Putin said, "there are a couple of other orders I want you to carry out in the near future in which I do not want the Motherland implicated. They will need to be done at arm's length and not involve Moscow Center." He fixed his gaze on Severinov from beneath lowered eyebrows.

Severinov nodded. "I understand. What are those?" he asked, his voice cracking.

The president briefly detailed the first item that he had in mind, then paused, his eyes still focused unblinkingly on Severinov.

"I think that is doable," Severinov said. "Yes, I am certain I can deliver that."

"Good. You will receive further instructions in due course," Putin said. "And second, if you want to keep the final third of your equity, you still need to deliver on my instructions regarding Johnson. I want that to be done."

Putin slammed his fist down on the table, his first sign of temper, and turned his gaze back to Severinov, then pointed at the door. "Now. *Poshël ty*." Piss off.

Severinov was too stunned to reply. He simply turned and walked out of the room.

* * *

BOOK 6 IN THE JOE JOHNSON SERIES: THE BLACK SEA

If you enjoyed **The Nazi's Son** you'll probably like the sixth book in the Joe Johnson series, **The Black Sea**.

If you liked it so much you want several other books from the series, you can buy various bundles of my paperbacks from my website shop at a significant discount to Amazon. I can only currently ship to the US and UK though. Support the author—buy direct! Go and visit:

https://www.andrewturpin.com/shop/

If you live outside the US or UK, it is best to use Amazon —just type "Andrew Turpin The Black Sea" into the search box at the top of the Amazon sales web page.

To give you a flavor of **The Black Sea**, here's the blurb:

A Russian conspiracy in Washington, DC . . . A passenger jet is shot down, killing hundreds. A mole wreaks havoc in the White House. And an oligarch bent on the most malicious kind of revenge targets Joe Johnson.

War crimes investigator Johnson is sent undercover by his former employer, the CIA, to untangle a web of deceit and online blame games in Russia's Black Sea region after the destruction of a Malaysian airliner in Ukraine.

But he quickly finds he has bitten off more than he can chew—and that the key to the conspiracy lies not in Moscow, but on Capitol Hill in Washington.

Johnson, his partner Jayne Robinson, and his friends in the CIA eventually have to come to terms with the fact that Russian methods of infiltrating the US are evolving faster than American counterintelligence realizes in the post-Cold War era, and they are struggling to catch up.

The drama reaches a climax in the US capital and on the Black Sea coast, where Johnson's long-term nemesis Yuri Severinov has a stronghold.

The Black Sea, book number six in the Joe Johnson

series, is a compelling spy thriller with multiple twists
that you won't want to put down.

* * *

ANDREW'S READERS GROUP AND OTHER BOOKS IN THE SERIES

If you enjoyed this book, I would like to keep in touch. This
is not always easy, as I usually only publish a couple of books a
year and there are many authors and books out there. So the
best way is for you to be on my Readers Group email list. I
can then send you updates on the next book, plus occasional
special offers. There's no spam and you can unsubscribe at
any time.

If you would like to join my Readers Group and receive
the email updates, I will send you, **FREE** of charge, the
ebook version of another Joe Johnson thriller, *The Afghan*,
which is a prequel to the series and normally sells at
$2.99/£2.99 (paperback $9.99/£9.99).

The Afghan is a thriller set in 1988 when Johnson was still
in the CIA. Most of the action takes place in Afghanistan,
then occupied by the Soviet Union, and in Washington, DC.
Some of the characters and story lines that emerge in the
other books have their roots in this period. I think you will
enjoy it!

The Afghan can be downloaded **FREE** from the
following link:

https://bookhip.com/RJGFPAW

If you only like reading paperbacks you can still sign up
for the email list at that link to get news of my books and
forthcoming releases. Just ignore the email that arrives with
the ebook attached. A paperback version of *The Afghan* and

all my books is for sale at my website, where you will find large discounts on bundles of my books. I can currently ship to the US and UK:

https://www.andrewturpin.com/shop/

Have you read the other thrillers in the Joe Johnson series?

Prologue: *The Afghan*
1. *The Last Nazi*
2. *The Old Bridge*
3. *Bandit Country*
4. *Stalin's Final Sting*
5. *The Nazi's Son*
6. *The Black Sea*

I have also begun writing a separate spy conspiracy thriller series, albeit with strong connections to the Johnson series—the **Jayne Robinson** thrillers. So far the books in this series are:

1. *The Kremlin's Vote*
2. *The Dark Shah (due to be published late in 2021)*

To find the books, go to my website or just type "Andrew Turpin Joe Johnson thriller series" in the search box at the top of the Amazon website sales page — you can't miss them!

IF YOU ENJOYED THIS BOOK PLEASE WRITE A REVIEW

As an independently published author, through my own imprint The Write Direction Publishing, I find that honest reviews of my books are the most powerful way for me to bring them to the attention of other potential readers.

As you'll appreciate, unlike the big international publishers, I can't take out full-page advertisements in the newspapers or place posters on the subway.

So I am committed to producing books of the best quality I can in order to attract a loyal group of readers who are happy to recommend my books to others.

Therefore, if you enjoyed reading this novel, then I would very much appreciate it if you would spend five minutes and leave a review—which can be as short as you like—preferably on the page or website where you bought it.

You can find the book on the Amazon website by typing "Andrew Turpin The Nazi's Son" in the search box at the top of the Amazon website.

Once you have clicked on the page, scroll down to "Customer Reviews," then click on "Leave a Review."

Reviews are also a great encouragement to me to write more!

Many thanks.

THANKS AND ACKNOWLEDGEMENTS

Thank you to everyone who reads my books. You are the reason I began to write in the first place, and I hope I can provide you with entertainment and interest for a long time into the future.

Every time I get an encouraging email from a reader, or a positive comment on my Facebook page, or a nice review on Amazon, it spurs me on to press ahead with my research and writing for the next book. So keep them coming!

Specifically with regard to *The Nazi's Son*, there are several people who have helped me during the long process of research, writing, and editing.

I have two editors who consistently provide helpful advice, food for thought, great ideas, and constructive criticism, and between them have enabled me to considerably improve the initial draft. Katrina Diaz Arnold, owner of Refine Editing, again gave me a lot of valuable feedback at the structural and line levels, and Jon Ford, as ever, helped me to maintain the authenticity of the story in many areas through his great eye for detail. I would like to thank both of them—the responsibility for any remaining mistakes lies solely with me.

As always, my brother, Adrian Turpin, was a very helpful reader of my early drafts and highlighted areas where I need to improve. Others, such as Martin Scales, Valeriya Salt, and Warren Smith, have done likewise. The small but dedicated team in my Advance Readers group went through the final version prior to proofreading and also highlighted a number of issues that required changes and improvements—a big thank-you to them all.

I would also like to thank the team at Damonza for what I think is a great cover design.

AUTHOR'S NOTE

In 1989, I was right at the start of my career in journalism and was fascinated by the newspaper and TV coverage of events in Eastern Europe as, one by one, the communist regimes across that region were toppled in a series of revolutions, each feeding off the others—Poland, Hungary, East Germany, Bulgaria, Czechoslovakia, Romania.

The Soviet leader Mikhail Gorbachev accepted during 1989 that the USSR could not continue to control its satellite states, and the Berlin Wall finally fell in November of that year following demonstrations in Leipzig and Berlin.

These revolutions mainly came about as the result of widespread and persistent demonstrations, but they were almost all peaceful in nature. Despite the presence of military and riot police, the rumors of planned massacres never turned into reality. There was little violence, apart from in Romania. Indeed, the move to overthrow the communist regime in Czechoslovakia was dubbed the Velvet Revolution for that reason.

A few months later, in 1990, I visited Berlin and Prague. The inhabitants of both cities were still partying like there was no tomorrow. Beer cost the equivalent of ten pence (or eight US cents) a pint, the bars and clubs were full, and everyone seemed to be permanently drunk or high on euphoria.

The capitalists had moved in, and along Unter den Linden and Pariser Platz in Berlin, hawkers were selling pieces of concrete from the wall to souvenir hunters. Not that you needed to buy a piece—large chunks of the wall were still standing, and it was possible to simply go and remove a piece of concrete to take home, complete with a colored piece of graffiti visible, as I did.

I have been back to Berlin a few times since then, but the atmosphere has never been as vibrant and joyful as it was in 1990.

It was hard to believe then that a short period earlier, the street scenes in both Berlin and Prague were so very different. Berlin was divided, with a hard-line Soviet-controlled regime still in place in the eastern half of the city, and security was enforced with an iron fist. Protesters and defectors were dealt with summarily.

Berlin found itself at the center of a perfect storm in the 1980s. A raft of terrorist organizations, including the Palestine Liberation Organization and the Red Army Faction, were highly active across Europe at that time, striking at any number of American, Israeli, and other Western targets.

Many of them found a natural home in Berlin, partly because there were plenty of American targets available in the western part of the city, but also because the East German communist regime—the German Democratic Republic—often facilitated or provided them with the shelter, assistance, training, weapons, and equipment they needed.

The GDR leader, Erich Honecker, allowed many of the terrorist groups to use East Berlin as a base. Several of the Arab embassies there were in effect permitted to act as weapons and explosives storage centers for the terrorists.

Most of this facilitating work was coordinated by the Stasi, the East German security service.

Notorious terrorists such as Venezuelan Ilich Ramírez Sánchez, better known as Carlos the Jackal, operated from East Berlin and orchestrated many deadly bombings across Western Europe. They included, in August 1983, an attack on the French consulate in West Berlin, which killed one person and injured twenty-three.

The Red Army Faction—also known as the Baader-

Meinhof Gang after two of their key operators, Andreas Baader and Ulrike Meinhof—was a terrorist group with a far-left political agenda that carried out a long series of bombings, shootings, and kidnappings in West Germany from their base in East Berlin. Most of the attacks were during the 1970s and 1980s but continued into the '90s.

In 1986, it was the turn of the Libyans. The bombing of the La Belle disco, described in *The Nazi's Son*, was carried out by a gang that operated from East Berlin. Five people were later convicted for the attack. Of these, Yasser Mohammed Chreidi held a job for the Libyan People's Bureau in East Berlin, and Musbah Abdulghasem Eter was an employee at the Libyan embassy in East Berlin.

Of course, given the control that the USSR had during that period over its satellite states in Eastern Europe, the KGB and the Kremlin would have been fully aware of what was going on. Indeed, it went a lot further than that—they effectively sponsored the wave of terrorism that flowed across the continent at that time. The Soviets were the puppet masters. In the sense that the various terrorist groups all had an anti-American, pro-Palestinian, far-left agenda, their interests were aligned with Moscow, which maximized the value it got from that situation. The terrorists were an invaluable weapon for the Kremlin as the Cold War unfolded.

However, no Stasi or KGB officers were ever prosecuted over the La Belle bombing—although many Stasi employees were prosecuted for other crimes after German reunification in 1990.

Given all this, it is hardly surprising that the Cold War period in Berlin has yielded a rich vein of material and ideas for fiction writers and filmmakers over the years. It was not just about Russia and the United States—many other players became involved, adding multiple layers of complexity to the political and military drama that played out between the West and the communist East.

So this is the historical backdrop against which **The Nazi's Son** is set. For those of you who are interested enough in the history to read more, I have listed a good selection of the sources I drew on in the Research and Bibliography section that follows this one.

Also, a point that I include in all my author's notes—just in case readers want to know! As with all the books in this series, because my protagonist, Joe Johnson, is from the United States, and most scenes are from his point of view, it seemed to make sense to try to use American spellings and terminology wherever possible, rather than my native British. If I have missed some or could have done this better, please email and let me know. I will aim to correct them.

Finally, on a lighter note, I should mention that the one thing that keeps me going through all the long months of research, writing, and editing before I can publish each book is coffee. I do enjoy a good latte—it is essential brain fuel!

So when I was invited to join **Buy Me A Coffee**—a website you might have heard of that allows supporters to give the providers of their favorite goods and services a cup or two—I thought it sounded like a good idea.

Therefore, if you enjoy my books and would like to buy me a latte, I would be extremely grateful. You will definitely be playing an essential part in the production of the next book!

You will find my online coffee shop at:

https://www.buymeacoffee.com/andrewturpin

Many thanks.
Andrew

RESEARCH AND BIBLIOGRAPHY

The research process for **The Nazi's Son** was a fairly lengthy one and proved fascinating. I know that many of my readers like to check out some of the sources I have drawn on and do their own background reading into the factual backdrops I use for my fictional stories, so here is just a flavor of some of the main websites, books, and articles that proved useful to me.

To get an overview of the fall of the Soviet empire and the domino-style collapse of the communist regimes in Eastern Europe, there is no better starting point than a Pulitzer Prize–winning book by David Remnick entitled Lenin's Tomb: The Last Days of the Soviet Empire. It is a combination of history and modern journalism by a writer who was a Moscow correspondent for *The Washington Post*. You can find it on Amazon at https://www.amazon.co.uk/dp/0679751254.

Another good overview can be found in *The Fall of the GDR: Germany's Road to Unity*, by David Childs, available on Amazon at https://www.amazon.co.uk/dp/B00M9AR1I8.

A thorough and interesting review of Childs's book can be found here: https://archives.history.ac.uk/history-in-focus/cold/reviews/palmowski.html

At the time of the 1989 revolutions, Vladimir Putin was a KGB officer in East Germany, based in Dresden. There has been speculation that the spectacle of the USSR's empire crumbling has been one factor that has driven his current hard-line stance toward former Soviet countries. This includes the Ukraine, where during 2014 Russia took military action to annex the Crimea. The Crimea crisis features in **The Nazi's Son** and the Putin theory is featured in *The Guardian* newspaper here: https://www.theguardian.com/

commentisfree/2014/oct/01/putin-power-east-germany-russia-kgb-dresden

The strong links between the Stasi, the KGB, and various terrorist groups operating out of East Berlin during the 1970s and 1980s is a theme that is closely examined in a number of articles that are easily found online.

One of these is in *The Washington Post*, headlined "East Germany's Dirty Secret." The article includes an interview with an unnamed former Stasi agent who describes the way in which the Stasi and the KGB protected and assisted a variety of international terrorist organizations. You can find it at: https://www.washingtonpost.com/archive/opinions/1990/10/14/east-germanys-dirty-secret/09375b6f-2ae1-4173-a0dc-77a9c276aa4b/?noredirect=on&utm_term=.4b3fb186aaf1

This feature tells how the head of the Stasi until 1986, Markus Wolf, had responsibility for the department that was most closely connected with Arab terrorism. The unnamed agent confirms how the Stasi and the KGB both knew that La Belle discotheque was to be bombed by the Libyan terrorists and did nothing to prevent it happening.

A book that also describes this scenario is *Stasi: The Untold Story of the East German Secret Police*, by John O. Koehler, which can be found at: https://www.amazon.co.uk/dp/0813337445.

A good review of Koehler's book by Frank Bourgholtzer, entitled "The Agony and the Ex-Stasi," can be found in the *Bulletin of the Atomic Scientists* here: https://journals.sagepub.com/doi/pdf/10.2968/055004017

An insight into how the Soviet Union effectively acted as a state sponsor of terrorism during that period can be found in *The Atlantic* here: https://www.theatlantic.com/international/archive/2011/12/how-the-soviet-union-transformed-terrorism/250433/

And *The Times* has reported how the Stasi acted as a proxy

consultant, facilitator, and provider of weapons and training for the KGB, delivering on the anti-American and anti-Western projects that the Kremlin wanted to implement during the Cold War period. These may have included the bombing of Pan Am Flight 103 over Scotland in 1988. See: https://www.thetimes.co.uk/article/lockerbie-reveals-stasi-s-history-of-exporting-terror-6rwvmq5fh

The bombing of La Belle itself is detailed in many news articles available online. For example, the *New York Times* coverage can be found here: https://www.nytimes.com/1986/04/06/world/2-killed-155-hurt-in-bomb-explosion-at-club-in-berlin.html

There is a YouTube video that shows footage from the time, including all the damage outside the nightclub. Ignore the propaganda text below the video: https://www.youtube.com/watch?v=mpNcZVepLKw

And the BBC's website carried a flashback in 2001: http://news.bbc.co.uk/1/hi/world/europe/1653848.stm

There is a short summary of the La Belle bombing and its aftermath on the Wikipedia website: https://en.wikipedia.org/wiki/1986_West_Berlin_discotheque_bombing

One issue that is not in doubt is that the attack on La Belle led directly to President Ronald Reagan ordering the US bombing of Libya on April 15, 1986. This strike, involving F-111 strike aircraft based in the United Kingdom, hit a Tripoli airfield, an army barracks in Tripoli, and a frogman training center. Colonel Muammar Gaddafi had a residence at the barracks, but managed to escape after receiving advance warning.

Moving on to other issues, it came as a surprise to me to find that large numbers of former Stasi employees had been able to obtain jobs in the German civil service—and we are talking about thousands of people. So it should not come as a surprise to you that a key character in *The Nazi's Son*,

Reiner Schwartz, is working in a senior role for the German Ministry of Defense. More detail on this topic can be found in this article in the German news magazine *Der Spiegel*: http://www.spiegel.de/international/germany/desk-jobs-for-secret-police-thousands-of-ex-stasi-still-work-for-german-civil-service-a-635230.html

Another article, about ex-Stasi staff working at the archives department of the former East German secret police, appeared in *The Guardian*: https://www.theguardian.com/world/2013/dec/27/stasi-officers-still-employed-east-german-secret-police-archives

Those who enjoyed my account of Joe Johnson's desperate escape from Russia into Finland via the Saimaa Canal and decide that a similar boat trip sounds appealing will find that it is actually quite feasible to achieve. A lot of leisure boats traverse the canal alongside the commercial traffic. Try these two videos to get a feel for how the waterway operates and the surrounding terrain.

The first is at: https://secure.action.news/watch?v=AMJ99WajV-A

The second, on YouTube, can be found at: https://www.youtube.com/watch?v=wWHTetb2Ugw

There actually is an issue regarding the smuggling of illegal migrants through the canal from Russia into Finland, with the Finnish Border Guard taking action against the owners of boats used for this purpose. See this news story: http://www.helsinkitimes.fi/finland/finland-news/domestic/15165-hs-family-of-three-suspected-of-smuggling-over-70-people-to-finland.html

The Nazi's Son is largely set during the weeks following the annexation of the Crimea by Russia in 2014, and most of the steps taken by NATO countries to send naval vessels into the Black Sea happened as described in the book. Perhaps the most dramatic incident during that period was when a destroyer, the USS *Donald Cook*, was repeatedly buzzed over a ninety-minute period by a Russian Sukhoi SU-24 fighter aircraft. This episode features in the book. However, in real life, the US president did not visit the ship and was not on board at the time—I invented that aspect for dramatic effect.

For an account by Reuters of that incident, see: https://www.reuters.com/article/usa-russia-blacksea/update-1-russian-jets-passes-near-u-s-ship-in-black-sea-provocative-pentagon-idUSL2N0N60V520140414

A number of other NATO ships were also sent to the region, including French and US vessels, as described in the book.

Yuri Severinov is described in the book as owning the fictional Krasnodar oil refinery near Tuapse, on Russia's Black Sea coast. There actually is a real oil refinery in that area, the Tuapse refinery, owned by Russian oil and gas giant Rosneft. See: https://www.rosneft.com/business/Downstream/Neftepererabotka/OilRefineries/TuapseRefinery/

There were, of course, many other sources that I drew on while compiling *The Nazi's Son*. I could not possibly list them all, but the ones I have listed above represent a reasonable selection and might form a starting point for any readers who want to investigate the details in this book further.

ABOUT THE AUTHOR AND CONTACT DETAILS

I have always had a love of writing and a passion for reading good thrillers. But despite having a long-standing dream of writing my own novels, it took me more than five decades to finally get around to completing the first.

The Nazi's Son is the fifth in the **Joe Johnson** series of thrillers, which pulls together some of my other interests, particularly history, world news, and travel.

I studied history at Loughborough University and worked for many years as a business and financial journalist before becoming a corporate and financial communications adviser with several large energy companies, specializing in media relations.

Originally I came from Grantham, Lincolnshire, and I now live with my family in St. Albans, Hertfordshire, UK.

You can connect with me via these routes:

E-mail: andrew@andrewturpin.com

Website: www.andrewturpin.com.

Facebook: @AndrewTurpinAuthor

Twitter: @AndrewTurpin

Instagram: @andrewturpin.author

Please also follow me on Bookbub and Amazon!

https://www.bookbub.com/authors/andrew-turpin

https://www.amazon.com/Andrew-Turpin/e/B074V87WWL/

Do get in touch with your comments and views on the books, or anything else for that matter. I enjoy hearing from readers and promise to reply.

<<<<>>>>

Made in United States
North Haven, CT
29 June 2022

20789763R00264